Safekeeping

Safekeeping

a novel

Jessamyn Hope

FIG TREE
BOOKS

BEDFORD, NEW YORK

My deepest appreciation goes to Michelle Caplan, who was everything I could want in an editor: tireless, passionate, insightful. Without her, *Safekeeping* would have been a lesser novel. The book owes much to Fred Price and the whole team at Fig Tree Books, including the support of Erika Dreifus. I am also indebted to the unflagging championship of my agent, Mitchell Waters. Over the eight years it took to write *Safekeeping*, many writers read earlier drafts, and I am grateful for all their critiques. Special thank-yous go to Douglas Silver, both for his friendship and his invaluable feedback on a last draft, and to Jonathan Papernick, who helped the book find a home. The road to my first published novel has been a long one, and a few people walked the whole way with me: my best friend, Mat Dry; my sister, Ashley; my dad, the consummate storyteller, who never once encouraged me to go into a more secure profession; and my mom, who has been dead for twenty-five years, but I could imagine her rooting for me. And then there's my husband, Yoav Bergner. My patron, my biggest fan, my most demanding critic. My love. He is behind this book and so much of my happiness.

Excerpts previously appeared in *Green Mountain Review* and *Descant Magazine.*

Published in the United States by Fig Tree Books LLC, Bedford, New York

www.FigTreeBooks.net

Jacket design by Strick&Williams
Interior design by Neuwirth & Associates

Library of Congress Cataloging-in-Publication Data Available Upon Request

ISBN number 978-1-941493-06-9

Printed in the United States
Distributed by Publishers Group West

First edition

10 9 8 7 6 5 4 3 2

To Yoav

Contents

Part One

*A*dam trudged up the darkening country road with a giant centipede stuck to his back, wiggling its army of legs. He could see to the top of the hill, where the road ended with the gate to the kibbutz. A rusted wrought-iron sign arched over the entrance, stamping the yellow sky in both Hebrew and Latin letters: SADOT HADAR. Fields of Splendor, his grandfather had taught him. The eucalyptuses towering along the left side of the road refreshed the air with their sweet, medicinal scent. To the right, horses grazed in a willowy meadow, and beyond them, a sliver of moon floated over the shadowed face of Mount Carmel. Was this what his grandfather saw when he first approached the kibbutz? Adam wiped his brow. He was sweat-soaked. His jaw ached from clamping his teeth, and his swollen feet felt fused to the insides of his sneakers. But it could've been worse. Last time he went cold turkey, the centipedes were crawling out of his mouth.

He reached the kibbutz's guardhouse without the young soldier inside noticing him. Hunched over his desk, the soldier pored over handwritten sheet music.

Adam knocked next to the window. "Hey, hi. I'm here to volunteer."

The soldier startled. "What?"

"Hi. Me. Volunteer."

"I wasn't told to expect a volunteer."

Adam had heard anyone could volunteer. This soldier, this kid, better not turn him away. "I didn't register ahead of time. I hope that's okay. My grandfather—"

"Are you cold?"

"Excuse me?"

The soldier looked him up and down. "It's the end of April. Twenty-eight degrees. Why the jacket?"

"'Cause it's not twenty-eight degrees or whatever that is in Fahrenheit in New York. I just got here."

The lips at the end of the soldier's long pimpled face pressed together. He sighed, put down his pencil. "Take it off."

Adam did not appreciate being ordered about, especially from someone who didn't look eighteen years old. The jacket had to stay on. He was clammy and shivering and taking it off might freak out the centipede hiding underneath. He wiped the sweat dripping into his eyes. "Seriously?"

The soldier pushed away from his desk and picked up his M-16, making Adam regret not doing whatever the hell the kid asked. The last thing he needed was to make a scene. He dropped his backpack and tore off his jacket while the soldier, rifle slung on his shoulder, stepped out of the booth, surprising Adam with his gangly height. Even with his poor posture, the kid was half a head taller than him, and almost as skinny, the green army uniform hanging off his bony shoulders and hips. Adam resisted the urge to hug himself, but he couldn't stop his teeth from rattling. His cold, damp T-shirt clung to his skin, and the pungency of his own BO revolted him. He hadn't showered in a week. At least.

The soldier pointed at his backpack on the ground. "Open it."

Adam grabbed the backpack, unzipped it, and tried to hand it over.

"Just hold it open."

The soldier dipped his lanky arm inside the bag and shuffled around the two balls of socks and one pair of boxer shorts. "You're here to volunteer, and that's all you've packed? Two socks? Where's your toothbrush?"

The El Al security girl had confronted him with the same questions at JFK, moments before two other security personnel wearing radio earpieces appeared. As those guys silently led him from the spacious terminal through an unmarked door and into a small windowless side room, his heart thumped so hard he feared he was going to black out. To his relief they didn't search his pockets or body cavities, only grilled him with a hundred questions about his lack of luggage and where he went to school and why was he was jackhammering his leg; they even asked if he believed in God and then why not. After surviving that interrogation, once he was

4

up in the sky, out of the five boroughs for the first time, gazing out the oval window at the tiny glinting ocean waves far below, he figured he was safe, at least when it came to the police. But maybe that was wishful thinking. This was 1994, after all. Everything was so high-tech. What if the NYPD somehow identified him and transmitted a worldwide warrant for his arrest? He pictured his name and face streaming out of a million fax machines, and the centipede crept up the nape of his neck. The effort it took not to swat at it made him shudder.

"I travel light."

"Did you come here straight from the airport?"

"Yeah, on the bus. Got off at the stop down the hill."

"Give me your plane ticket. And passport."

Adam pulled his documents out of his back pocket, thinking he had to keep cool. Not lose his head. This pimply Israeli soldier couldn't know anything about Weisberg's Gold and Diamonds on Forty-Seventh Street. If Mr. Weisberg was well enough to talk—and Adam hoped with all his heart that he was—he still didn't know Adam's real name. The no-frills family-run store didn't seem to have a security camera, and even if it did, the picture on those black-and-white videos was too fuzzy to make out facial features, not to mention that everything happened in the back room; at most they had a tape of a blurry figure moseying in and out of the front shop, even saying, "Goodbye, Mrs. Weisberg!" All this soldier wanted to do, like the El Al guys at the airport, was make sure his lack of a tooth-brush had nothing to do with "Allahu Akbar."

After the soldier compared the ticket to the visa stamp, he turned to the passport's picture, peering at the photo and up at Adam and back at the photo. Adam wished he still resembled the handsome guy in that picture, the guy girls likened to Johnny Depp when he was on *21 Jump Street*. He still had the thick inky hair, but it was overgrown, shaggy, not art-fully crafted into a messy pompadour. Dark circles surrounded the black eyes he inherited from his grandfather. His sharp cheekbones, straight nose, and thin lips were now too sharp, too thin, and his olive skin had a greenish cast. Most disgustingly, a few cavities had turned black. What he wouldn't do to be washed and put together, like in that photo, taken only two years ago, when he was sixteen months clean and still a person somebody could love.

The soldier asked if he was Jewish.

"Yeah."

"Socco. . ." The soldier struggled to read the last name. "That doesn't sound Jewish."

"Soccorso. You never heard of a pizza bagel? My mom was Jewish."

"Was? She isn't Jewish anymore?"

"I don't know. Are you still Jewish when you're dead?" It came out more aggressively than he intended. He had to sound nicer.

Instead of getting riled up, however, the soldier softened his voice. "Did your father convert?"

"Honestly, I never met him. I was brought up by my grandfather, my zayde. He was Jewish. He used to live on this kibbutz. After the war."

"Really? Do you speak Hebrew?"

"Only the usual: schlep, putz, schmuck."

This got no smile. The soldier said those words were Yiddish and took the passport back with him into the guardhouse, where he flipped on its ceiling lamp. Twilight smudged the world beyond the glow of the guardhouse, hiding the horses in the dusky fields, flattening the mountain to a black silhouette sprinkled with village lights. A blue and white banner tied to the kibbutz's chain-wire fence fluttered in the breeze: A STRONG PEOPLE MAKES PEACE.

The soldier opened an oversized logbook and skimmed through the pencilings on the last page. The logbook, with its battered leather cover, looked like it could have been here fifty years ago. They hadn't gotten any fax about him. Adam wasn't even sure the kibbutz had a fax machine.

The soldier paused before writing. "Did your grandfather really live on Sadot Hadar?"

"He did. For three years. He was a Holocaust refugee."

The soldier proceeded to copy the information from Adam's passport into the logbook. "I'm going to let you stay here tonight, but you should've signed up through the Kibbutz Volunteer Desk."

Adam exhaled. "Thanks, man. Thanks so much."

The soldier handed back his passport. "You can have room eighteen. I don't have a key to give you, but nobody uses keys around here. To get to the foreign volunteers' section, walk straight and make a right after the jasmine bushes. Tomorrow, see the kibbutz secretary, Eyal, about being a volunteer. If you don't see Eyal first thing in the morning, you're going to get kicked off the kibbutz, and I'm going to get in serious trouble."

"First thing in the morning, I promise." Adam hardly got the words out before the soldier was back to his music sheets, rubbing out a bar of notes as if he'd never been interrupted.

Adam zipped on his leather jacket and walked into the kibbutz. He followed the road, feeling uneasy in the quiet. This was unlike anywhere he'd ever been before. Dark feathery cedars loomed against a violet-blue sky. Fireflies flashed over a tenebrous sweep of lawn. Crickets chirred. As he passed the small, boxy white bungalows, he heard the modest lives inside: a running faucet, a woman's raspy laugh, a TV chattering in Hebrew. His grandfather must have felt out of place his first night. Homesick. Homesick for Germany? That seemed impossible, and yet, as long as Adam could remember, a pencil drawing of a gaslit street in Dresden had hung in their apartment in New York. Their apartment. The thought of it stoked his nausea, and he cupped his stomach as if that could keep down the horror. Fearing he might throw up, he staggered alongside a high hedge dappled with small white flowers. Were these jasmine? Their cloying perfume didn't help his nausea. When the hedge ended, he saw a wooden sign marked VOLUNTEERS.

He descended some steppingstones into a sunken quad flanked by two long, single-story buildings. Lined with doors and covered in cracking white stucco, the buildings resembled the run-down highway motels in action movies where criminals and vigilantes always took refuge. Adam had holed up in a number of shabby hotels, but they'd all been in the city and had at least four shabby floors. In the center of the quad bloomed a solitary tree, its flowers still red in the dimming light. On a picnic table beside the tree, a half-full bottle of gin or vodka stood amid crushed beer cans, its clear liquid catching the moonlight.

A glance at the nearest doors—1 and 9—told him 18 was at the far end of the quad, meaning he would have to pass that bottle. He could do it. He'd made it through an eleven-hour flight without accepting one of those cute thimbles of free booze. But then the withdrawal hadn't kicked in yet. Not like now, clawing at the back of his ribs, making him shudder like an old air conditioner. To be safe he would avoid the bottle by circling behind one of the buildings.

He walked around the right-hand building, down the narrow gravel alleyway between its back wall and a three-foot bank. The rear windows looked into spartan dorm rooms meant for two, similar to the ones at

Lodmoor Rehab: a bed and dresser against each sidewall, gray wool blankets, a few makeshift decorations pasted to the walls, mostly pages ripped out of magazines.

He stopped. In the next window, a young woman stood naked before a full-length mirror. The window had no pane, no bug screen, only the open white blinds striping the scene. Her back was to him: a dark line dividing her round ass cheeks; two dimples at the base of her back; a lovely waist; shoulder-length hair dyed an unnatural Raggedy Ann red. The mirror revealed her front, the V-shaped thatch of brown hair nestled beneath a flat stomach, and her beautiful breasts. Sweetly buoyant, but with womanly heft. Nipples like the flushed cherry blossoms his zayde took him to see every spring at the Brooklyn Botanic Garden.

It was surprisingly hard to look away from a naked woman, even when he felt no arousal. And it wasn't only her nakedness that arrested him, but the intensity with which she studied her reflection, her face stern, eyes exacting, like a general evaluating a battle plan. She turned to scrutinize her profile, and her lips pursed in disappointment, anger. She did have something of a schnoz, but that would've only made her more desirable to Adam if he were able to feel desire; he didn't like perfect, always had a soft spot for nearly perfect. But it had been two months since he'd had a hard-on. Even longer since he last managed to get himself off in a porno booth on Eighth Avenue.

When the girl leaned close to the mirror to draw on eyeliner, he managed to tear his eyes away, but as he did, he caught sight of another woman in the room, curled on the bed beside the mirror, a mop of chestnut hair covering her eyes, a brown skirt tucked over her knees. Her mouth moved as if she were endlessly whispering while her hands fidgeted with . . . what? A silver crucifix hung off the side of the bed. It was a rosary. She was saying Hail Marys. What a strange picture these two women made together.

The naked girl's head jerked toward the window. His heart leaped. Had he made a sound? Could she see him in the darkness beyond the blinds? If he walked, would the gravel's crunch give him away? He couldn't think, his head too foggy. He failed to move; only his mouth fell as the girl's deep blue eyes, bordered in thick black kohl, landed on his. She turned her body to face him, standing tall, not covering herself up. Her stare was inscrutable. Was it anger? Playfulness? Power? All of the above? He wanted to

8

tell her that he felt nothing, nothing lewd, that it was like viewing an old painting in the Met. While the other woman, seemingly unaware, continued working through her Rosary, the naked girl grabbed a hairbrush from her dresser and hurled it at the window.

Adam bolted. He beat it down the length of the building, listening for an outcry. All he heard was his panting and the crunching gravel as he threw one foot in front of the other. He ducked around the corner of the building and collapsed against the wall, panting for air. The veins at his temples thrummed, feeling like they might pop. He unzipped his jacket and clutched the T-shirt and skin over his heart, over the stabbing that he might have mistaken for a heart attack if he hadn't been through withdrawal too many times. It was brutal, making a break for it while detoxing. And for the second time in twenty-four hours. Could that rush through the Diamond District really have been this morning? Traveling such a far distance warped his sense of time.

His breath returning to him, he leaned his head back on the wall. Above was an unfamiliar sky—black, star-ridden, bottomless. So that was the Milky Way: a band of stars streaked across the universe like a ghostly line of coke. It was frightening, this sky. He preferred the one back home: polluted and starless, all the twinkling on the ground. This sky made him feel like he had to be kidding, thinking anything people did mattered. Anything he did to anyone. But that wasn't true. He must have looked like a Peeping Tom, there at her back window. Imagine coming all this way and getting kicked off after five minutes because of something so stupid. He had to be more careful. He couldn't fuck this up. This was his last chance.

He peeked into the quad, praying the girl wasn't standing there with the soldier or a boyfriend out to prove his worth. She wasn't. Some young guys now sat around the picnic table, laughing and talking in what sounded like Russian. They didn't seem to be on the lookout for anyone as they passed around that bottle.

Adam walked fast for room eighteen and knocked on the door. Afraid the girl might come out, he didn't wait for an answer before turning the knob and slipping inside. Luckily, he didn't appear to have a roommate. The beds were made. No personal belongings anywhere.

Leaving the lights off, he hung up his leather jacket and sat on a bed. He didn't immediately lie down. He felt too guilty, like he didn't deserve to lie down. Like he might never deserve to lie down for the rest of his life. Untying his blue high-tops for the first time in days, he gently freed his throbbing feet and lifted his legs onto the mattress. He slowly lay back onto the scratchy wool blanket. As his head lowered onto the pillow, it exhaled a detergenty smell. He stared at the closet door, where a Mikey Katz had scratched into the wood that he was here in '82. Where was the centipede? It had crawled away, but his teeth still chattered if he didn't clench them. Was it only the withdrawal making him shake, or also his conscience? He would know soon enough. Through the back window came an owl's low-pitched hoot, repetitive like a car alarm, yet soothing.

If only it were two years ago, and he were lying in his bed on Essex, the city lights pouring through his second-floor window, blanching the Nirvana poster. The cast of old Star Wars figurines on his bookcase. The college textbooks neatly piled on his desk, the wooden desk that had belonged to his mother when she was young. Closing his eyes, he would be surrounded by all that comforting sound, people shouting on the sidewalk, the hum of the idling delivery trucks, the occasional *ch-ch-cha* of maracas when the door opened to the Mexican restaurant on the ground floor, and Zayde's scratchy swing records playing in the next room: *After you've gone and left me crying, after you've gone there's no denying*. Might Zayde, when he was only five years older than Adam was now, have slept in this very room? No, this building wasn't old enough. And hadn't he mentioned a tent?

Adam turned on his side, reached into his jean pocket, and pulled out the brooch. He'd had a glimpse at it in the airplane bathroom, but this was his first chance to take a good look since stealing it back. He tried to blur out his hands—the fingertips blackened on crack pipes, the nails packed with grime—and see only what they were holding, that one-and-a-half-inch square. Just a one-and-a-half-inch square. And yet.

The first time Adam saw the brooch he was eight years old. He'd awoken from a nightmare and was on his way to sleep with his grandfather, as he often did that first year he lived with him, when he was stopped in the doorway. He had expected to find the old man sleeping, but he lay awake in his green pajama set, canted on his side, as Adam was right now, studying something small in his hands, his eyes glistening in the lamplight. Adam tiptoed into the tidy bedroom, so different than his mother's, where he'd had to navigate around dirty clothes and empty wine bottles to reach her passed-out body, half covered by a stained T-shirt.

His grandfather only noticed him when he climbed onto the foot of the mattress. "Another nightmare, Adam?"

Adam nestled behind his grandfather's back and peered over him at the radiant square, like something from a fairy tale. "What's that?"

"This?" His grandfather returned his gaze to the brooch. "This is . . . a very special thing."

"What's so special about it?"

His grandfather sat up, slipped on his plaid slippers.

"I'm afraid it's not a story for little boys. But I promise to tell you one day." He looked back at Adam, laid a hand on his shin. "Maybe when it becomes your brooch."

In the dark dorm room, the brooch seemed to stare at Adam as much as he stared at it. An uncut sapphire, the size and shape of a Milk Dud, glowed in its center, so blue. Pearls and smaller gems, also in their natural shapes, hemmed the edges of the brooch—red rubies in the corners, and, halfway between, either a purple amethyst or green garnet. It was the rich gold filigree that stirred Adam, though, far more than the precious stones; in it, he sensed the long-dead goldsmith who had painstakingly fashioned the tangle of thin vines and little flowers that covered two of the brooch's quarters, as well as the small pomegranates and leaves in the other two. Adam, having never seen a pomegranate and not entirely sure what they were, thought they looked like small round heads wearing those funny three-pronged jester hats, but the jeweler, Mr. Weisberg, had explained they were stylized pomegranates. He couldn't bear to think of the jeweler, but didn't he say one of the flowers was missing a petal? Adam brought the brooch closer to his eyes and searched for the one with only five. It took a moment, but there it was, in the bottom left. A little malformed flower. It was such a heartbreaking mistake. So tiny most people would never notice. But Mr. Weisberg had.

There was that ache again, that pressure against the back of his breastbone, so familiar, but more painful than ever before. He cupped his hands around the brooch and curled into a shivering ball.

He had no illusion that his zayde was up in heaven right now, watching him. The old man would never know that his grandson had come halfway around the world to set things right with his brooch.

But he had. He was here.

*A*dam shifted in his chair while Eyal, the kibbutz secretary, struggled to read his chicken-scratched application. He'd still had the shakes, couldn't steady his hand, while rushing to fill in all those upsetting questions: *What year did you graduate from college?* Somehow he had to make it through this interview. It was almost midnight in New York, and he barely slept last night. He was eye-burning tired and, though he had no appetite, his body was revolting against not being fed in three days. His gut seethed, threatening to send him bolting for the toilet. He ran a hand along his bristly jawline, wishing he'd at least been able to shave. Being interviewed was easier when you were good-looking, but he only ever seemed to be in front of someone's desk—social worker, principal, cop—when he was low.

The balding secretary rubbed his bloodshot eyes with his thick fingers and flipped the page. Weren't kibbutzim supposed to be tranquil oases? The secretary's desk, covered with coffee-stained spreadsheets, invoices, and unopened mail, appeared as overwhelmed as its middle-aged owner. Adam glanced over at the other applicant seated beside him. The rosary woman. She sat straight-backed, legs pressed together, staring into space, as if she were riding the subway and Adam and the secretary were merely other passengers in the car. Stranger still was the way she held her hands above her lap and tapped her spread fingers together, like a cymbal-banging-monkey toy. Thankfully she either didn't know or care about him being at her window last night.

"You're on the kibbutz at a very tense time." Eyal laid their applications in front of him. "This is why, Claudette, I apologize, I didn't get to you for a couple of days. Let me start by telling you both what we expect from our volunteers and what you can expect from us."

Between chugs of coffee the secretary explained that over the years the kibbutz had hosted over three hundred young people from over thirty countries who wanted to experience living on a commune. Volunteers were treated like members, meaning they were expected to live by the kibbutz motto, to give according to their ability and take according to their need. The volunteers worked like members, and in return they ate in the dining hall, received a room with a bed, and were welcome to use all the facilities—the pool, laundry services, medical center. In the sixties and seventies, they had more North American volunteers, but now most of the foreigners on the kibbutz were from the former Soviet Union.

"You have to take your job seriously, show up on time, work hard. Some volunteers come here to party." The secretary's eyes rested on Adam. "We like young people to have fun. But why should you be allowed to come here and live for free? We have Americans and Europeans who get angry when we insist that they do their jobs, as if they would let me, a stranger from Israel, come and do nothing but party in their house for the summer."

Adam gritted his teeth, nodded. He had to play nice, get the green light to stay here. The application required a two-month commitment, but really he'd be gone in two or three days. It was one of a slew of lies he'd put down. If he'd had more than two hundred dollars to his name, he'd have checked into a nearby hotel.

Eyal promised to do his best to find them both satisfying jobs and turned his attention to Claudette. After gulping down the last of his coffee, he asked her if she knew anything about computers. Claudette stopped tapping her fingers and shook her head.

"That's too bad. We got two new IBM compatibles and I can't figure them out. Would you like to work with children? In the school?"

She shook her head again. "No."

"Why not? That's the most coveted job among the volunteers."

"I don't . . . read or write very well."

Her candid admission surprised Adam. He couldn't place her accent. Where was she from? Her round freckled face was makeup-free, eyes the same burnt umber as her wavy mop, which looked as if someone had taken scissors to it with the sole aim of making every strand three inches long. Against her creased white button-down rested a cheap-looking saint pendant that reminded him of a military dog tag.

Eyal turned a pen over his hands. "I meant English, Claudette, not Hebrew."

"I don't read English." She bowed her head. "In French I read a little."

Frowning, Eyal revisited her papers. "But you're from Canada . . ."

"I didn't go to school," she said, quietly. "I grew up in an orphanage."

That's it: she had the accent of the French Canadian fir tree sellers who set up on street corners in the weeks before Christmas. For some reason his grandfather couldn't stand the piney smell of the trees and used to cross the street to avoid them.

"The orphanage didn't school you? What did you do all day?"

Her eyes seemed to be focused not on Eyal's face, but a few inches above. "Kept care of the younger or sicker orphans. Cleaned. For the last fifteen years, I did laundry. I was told I could do laundry here."

"You were born July 30th, 1962, so that makes you, let me see, almost thirty-two, correct? That's quite a few years older than most volunteers. We could benefit from your experience. So why don't you tell me what you've been up to since the orphanage and I can try to make use of your skills. Does that sound good?"

"I only left the orphanage seven months ago."

Adam widened his eyes while Eyal, visibly flummoxed by this information, ran a hand over his balding pate. How could a thirty-year-old still be in an orphanage? Was she also lying on her application? Why would anyone make up such an absurd lie? And she didn't strike him as a liar. She had to have the wrong word. She meant some other kind of home.

Eyal set her application to the side as if it were no use. "Claudette, if you don't mind me asking, what brings you to the kibbutz?"

Claudette described how she ended up on the kibbutz in a hushed voice, free from emotion, except perhaps discomfort. For the last seven months she had lived with her half sister Louise while continuing to work in the orphanage's laundry. When Louise got married last week, her brother-in-law, who had once volunteered on a kibbutz, insisted she should do it. He promised she could do laundry here in exchange for room and board. Just like in the orphanage. Adam imagined the starry-eyed newlyweds who didn't want this weirdo hanging around their honeymoon nest. They must have been giddy with relief when they realized they could pawn her off on the kibbutz for a while. Claudette finished: "And I supposed it couldn't hurt to be where Jesus had His ministry."

Eyal said he was very sorry, but they didn't need anyone full-time in the laundry, that they would have to think of something else for her to do, and picked up Adam's application. Adam straightened, clasped his hands.

"Honestly, I can't read a word of this. I can't even make out your name. Alan?"

"Sorry. My penmanship needs work. My name's Adam."

"Adam. It looks like you went to college for . . . what was it?"

"History. I majored in New York City history at Baruch College, which is one of the best schools in the City University. That high school I went to, Stuyvesant, it's the best public high school in the city, maybe the country. Three Nobel Prize winners went there."

These weren't entirely lies. He had gone to Stuy, but they wouldn't readmit him after he got back from rehab. As for Baruch, he was about to declare himself a history major when he was suspended that last time. He did love those history classes, and actually got an A- in "NYC: The People Who Shaped the City." The only reason he hadn't yet declared his major—how stupid it seemed now—was because he had worried that it was kind of pathetic to be a historian, that people who wanted to be great became great, and people who couldn't become great became historians and studied great people.

"Not much I can do with history. What about jobs?"

He'd been fired from many shitty jobs—painting apartments, moving furniture, scooping ice cream—usually within a month.

"Well, I've had a lot of internships and other jobs, but—" What had his grandfather done on the kibbutz? He thought hard. "Cotton! What about picking cotton? My grandfather was on this kibbutz for a couple of years after the war, and that's something he did."

"Your grandfather was on Sadot Hadar?" Eyal raised his eyebrows, impressed. "Sadly the cotton fields are long gone. Even with the machines we couldn't compete with India, where people pick for seventy cents a day. Seventy cents a day—wrap your head around that. There's a plastics factory now where the cotton used to be, which means we now have to compete with China."

Eyal massaged his forehead. Behind him a moth fluttered along the wall, past an oversized calendar scrawled with notes and scratched-out notes. Not a single day blank. Again, not the kind of calendar Adam would have expected on a kibbutz.

"I have an idea." Eyal waved his pen at Claudette. "You worked with sick people, yes? We have an old woman on the kibbutz who's very sick, but she won't stop working. The problem is—and it breaks my heart to say this—wherever she goes, she's more a nuisance than help. I try to send her somewhere different every day, spread the burden. Your job will be to accompany her, to help her get around. And to do some of the work she isn't."

Adam buried his hand in his pocket, clutched the brooch. Could this be the old woman he was looking for?

Claudette shook her head. "I would be better in the laundry."

"But we don't need anyone in the laundry." Eyal picked up the phone. "Trust me, this is better. You'll experience the whole kibbutz working with Ziva—picking mandarins, working in the dining hall. But whatever we do, we can't let on that it's *you* looking after *her*." He raised his finger to suggest everything would be clear in a moment.

Adam released the brooch. He wasn't looking for a Ziva.

"Hello, Ima," Eyal said into the receiver. "We have a young Canadian woman for you to take charge of. She will follow you to your assignments, and you will make sure she understands the tasks and gets them done. *Beseder?*"

A squawk burst out of the handset, and Eyal jerked it away from his ear. He switched to Hebrew, but Adam understood by the jut of the secretary's jaw that he was frustrated. He banged down the phone and lifted his hands in a what-can-you-do.

"I should warn you, Claudette, Ziva can be very . . . what's a nice word for it? Forthright? Even Israelis find her rude. Don't take anything she says personally. Believe me, I should know. She's my mother." He turned to Adam. "And you we can put in the plastics factory or the dishwashing room. It's your choice."

Neither sounded very Fields of Splendor, but Adam was relieved he could stay. "Dishwashing, thanks."

Eyal pulled Monopoly money out of a drawer, two wads of colored copy paper stamped with numbers. "You can use these at the general store, the *kolbo*, to buy toiletries or other things you might need. In addition, we'll give you a small stipend, a hundred and twenty shekels a month. You can pick up your work clothes and boots at the laundry." Eyal stood, and Adam and Claudette followed suit. "Enjoy your time here at Sadot Hadar."

Claudette departed without saying goodbye, while Adam hung back. He steadied himself on the back of his chair. "Hey, Eyal, one more thing. Can you tell me where I can find Dagmar?"

"Who?" Eyal carried his JNF mug to the kitchenette and scooped in a heap of Nescafé.

"I'm looking for an older woman named Dagmar. She lives on the kibbutz."

"Not this kibbutz." Eyal poured steaming water from an electric kettle. "There's no one named Dagmar here. Never has been."

Adam took a second to absorb the news that Dagmar might not live here anymore. Why hadn't he prepared for that? He had assumed she'd either be here or dead. She wrote his grandfather that she would be on the kibbutz "for the rest of her life."

The secretary carried the brimming mug back to his desk and settled into his chair behind the mounds of papers. He gazed up at Adam, clearly itching for him to leave.

Adam said, "Maybe she doesn't live here right now, but I know she did in 1947."

"Forty-seven?" Eyal shook his head. "Maybe in the DP section. Temporarily. But she couldn't have been a kibbutznik."

"She was a kibbutznik. I'm sure of it."

Eyal spread his fingers out on his desk. "Listen, Adam. I was born here in forty-eight and have lived here my whole life. My mother is a founding member of the kibbutz, the only founder still alive. I'm the longest-running secretary we've ever had, and I know the name of every single person who's ever been a member. I've been through their papers so many times I could draw their family trees. There was never any Dagmar on this kibbutz."

Adam shrugged. "You're wrong. My grandfather was here in forty-seven, and he knew her."

"I'm not wrong."

"Was your mom here then?"

"Yes."

"Then I'll ask her."

"Fine, ask her. But she's not going to give you a different answer. And please, please, leave her alone until after tomorrow night. We're having a meeting, and . . . actually, leave her alone the next day too. This meeting—" He briefly closed his eyes. "It's just not a good time."

Adam didn't want to wait two days, but what could he do? He promised not to bother this woman before Wednesday and turned to leave. As he was passing through the door, Eyal called him back.

"I want you to know, Adam, for your sake and ours, that we don't give second chances."

Adam leaned in the doorway. "What? I didn't know it was a crime to ask about an old lady."

"It's not that. It's just that I've had this job a long time, and I've met a lot of volunteers. All I'm saying is do your job, keep out of trouble, and everything will be fine."

Adam descended the stairs of the small office building, shaking his head. Why did some people think they knew everything? Outside, the kibbutz's poky main square was deserted except for Claudette, who stood in its center, head down, slowly rotating as if scanning the beige bricks for a lost earring.

Which way was the volunteers' section? It wasn't far, but he'd been such a wreck walking over here, nothing looked familiar. Across the square was the dining hall, a single-story concrete building with glass doors. On the left was presumably the general store, its corrugated steel awning shading an ice-cream freezer and fruit stands. A few yards over from the store stood a door. Just a door. Nothing on either side or above it but a hem of concrete, making it look as if the door led to an invisible world. To the right of the square was the main lawn. Too embarrassed to ask for directions, he'd see if Claudette were heading back soon.

He sidled up to her. "What did you lose?"

She turned with a start. "Nothing."

Glancing down at the plaza's interlocking bricks, he had no idea what she could be doing. "You heading back to the volunteers' section?"

Claudette circled one more time, eyeing the bricks, before nodding.

Together they walked across the square, Adam's hands in his jean pockets, one clasping the brooch, Claudette's arms folded, fingers clutching the flesh over her elbows. A row of unchained bicycles waited outside the dining hall, handlebars gleaming with sunlight. Adam waited for Claudette to start a conversation, but she didn't, and he was grateful to avoid chitchat. They followed a path around the side of the dining hall and walked along its wall of windows, upon which their mirror images followed them, surrounded by the blurry green reflection of the main lawn. No wonder Eyal had given him a hard time. He was the image of a junkie: twiggy arms coming out of a black T-shirt and disappearing into the pockets of jeans so big they barely hung on.

This must have been how he looked that last time Zayde walked him from Lodmoor to the train station. If he'd kept the promise he made on that walk, he wouldn't have had to lie on the application. When he came down to the foyer that morning, where Zayde waited for him, the receptionist had asked if she should call them a cab, but Zayde said, No, no, they would walk to the train station. Adam's backpack was heavy, but he wasn't about to complain; this was the third time they were doing this trip.

At first they had walked in silence through the Queens neighborhood, past the houses covered in pastel aluminum siding, the small yards closed in by chain-link fences; hardly the picket-fence suburbs seen in sitcoms, but it always surprised Adam that New York City had houses at all. Zayde's eyes, shaded by the brim of his straw fedora, squinted at a house with a plastic kiddie pool on its mowed lawn and a red BMX chained to its porch.

"Maybe I should have moved us out here, where you could have had a nice bicycle."

Adam shook his head. "No. No way. I love where I grew up. Zayde, this . . . this has nothing to do with you."

Zayde sucked in his lips, lowered his gaze to his brown oxfords. "Just when I was supposed to start university, they stopped letting in Jews. To this day I have no idea what I would've studied, what I would have become. A musicologist? Maybe a dance critic. Probably not a furniture salesman."

Adam tasted blood. He'd been chewing on his cheek. His grandfather almost never spoke about those times. Should he say something? What?

"Finish college, Adam. I worked hard to save that money so you could go. I don't want to make you feel bad, but it's true."

Adam forced himself to look at his grandfather, to make a promise he wasn't entirely sure he could keep. "I promise, Zayde, I'm done. Seriously. You'll see. I'm going to be somebody you can be proud of."

His grandfather looked at him out of the corner of his eye. "I don't want it for me, Adam."

Adam was shaken out of his thoughts when Claudette about-faced and started marching back. He turned. "Hey, where you going?"

After three or four steps, she pivoted again and came back. They continued walking.

"What just happened?" asked Adam.

Eyes fixed on the path in front of her feet, she said, "Sorry. I . . . had to do that."

"Why?"

"Because I did."

Adam noticed now that Claudette's eyes never left the ground. And once in a while she did that thing with her hands, clapping like the Musical Jolly Chimp. He was getting a better idea of what kind of institution she might have been in.

"Claudette, can I ask you a question? Did you really live in an orphanage until a few months ago?"

She nodded.

"But orphanages are homes for children. Are you sure you don't mean some other kind of, you know, institution? It's safe to tell me. I'm a four-time, not-so-proud resident of Lodmoor Rehab."

She made no response, only pulled her crossed arms into her chest, and Adam let it go.

They passed another one of those strange doors, which he now saw had a slope of concrete behind it, and made a turn before the jasmine bushes. He trailed Claudette down the steppingstones, which she took like a bride going down the aisle, bringing her feet together on each stone. When they reached the bottom, a sandy-haired chihuahua rose from the grass around the flowering tree and trotted alongside them, surprising Adam. He associated chihuahuas with uptown wives who lunched after Bergdorf's, not the Middle East. As they neared the room where Adam had seen the naked girl, Claudette pulled a key out of her pocket.

He said, "I thought nobody used keys around here."

"My roommate wants the door locked at all times. Every night she goes out and locks me in the room."

The partying roommate, putting on all that eyeliner. Where could she be going on a kibbutz? What nightlife could they possibly have? Did kibbutzim have bars? Forget it. He shouldn't even wonder. He took a gander at the picnic table: the bottle was gone.

To ask anything other than whether the kibbutz had a bar, he pointed to Claudette's pendant. "So who is that anyway? Guessing it's a saint."

She pressed the medallion against her chest, seeming at once proud and shy to talk about it. "Yes, it's Sainte Christine de Liège. In English, she is called Christina the Astonishing."

The chihuahua reared onto its hind legs and pawed at Adam's calf, forcing him to scratch its tiny head. The dog closed its eyes to bask in the affection.

"Yeah? What was so astonishing about her?"

"So much."

"Such as?"

"At Christine's funeral—she was only twenty-two when she died—she floated out of her coffin, and God spoke to her. He gave her a choice: she could either go to Heaven or she could come back to life and save people in Purgatory by suffering on their behalf. Every time she suffered, a soul would be released. She chose to come back, and for the next fifty years, she tortured herself. Jumped into fires. Swam in frozen rivers. She starved herself, never ate any food, except the milk from her breasts. She had milk even though she was a virgin."

Adam struggled not to smile. "That is pretty astonishing." After a second's thought, he added, "I guess it would be nice to believe someone was out there, atoning on my behalf. Poof! I'm sin free."

Claudette wrapped her hand around the saint. "All you have to do to believe is believe."

"Right."

Adam continued to his room. He didn't want to lie down, but he had no choice. His eyes were closing against his will. And he needed to keep close to the toilet. The cramps were only warming up, and he didn't want to risk a repeat of what happened last time he was detoxing: while standing on line at Duane Reade, trying to ignore the cramps, before he understood what was happening, he felt a warm liquid flowing down his leg. He lowered his eyes, thinking, God no, but there it was, diarrhea oozing out of his jean leg and pooling around his Converse.

"Hey, buddy," he said to the chihuahua trotting next to his ankles. "Where do you think you're going?"

The chihuahua whipped its tail. Adam stopped, looked around for its owner. Claudette still stood at her door, wiping its knob with her shirttail.

"Yo, Claudette. Do you know who this little guy belongs to?"

Claudette clutched the shirttail in front of her. "It lives in the volunteers' section. People leave food and water for it by the tree."

"It got a name?"

"Golda, I think."

The tiny dog gaped up at him, its big black eyes wide, giant ears on end. A dog had always been something other people had, normal people.

When he started walking and the dog followed again, he asked, "Are you going to insist on coming with me?"

The chihuahua's tail wagged faster, and Adam felt his eyes closing on him again.

"All right. Let's nap."

*A*dam sat cross-legged on the grass, wearing the kibbutz work clothes, scanning their phone directory for a Dagmar, while Golda slept in a warm coil beside him. He'd just returned from his first shift in the dishroom and felt better, at least physically. Yesterday, after saying goodbye to Claudette, he had spent the rest of the day running between the bed and the toilet, only leaving his room to pick up toiletries around dinnertime. After managing to swallow a couple of boiled potatoes in the dining hall, he returned to his room and lay facedown on the bed, intending to rise in a few minutes to shower, but it was four o'clock in the morning when he awoke, having no idea where he was or what he'd done, and then it all came back. With the windows full of darkness, he showered, shaved, and showed up for his shift an hour early. When eight hours of wiping ketchup and hummus off plates were over, his boss, Yossi, a stubby guy with a salt-and-pepper buzz cut, thanked him for doing a great job. He also informed him that he'd never met anyone named Dagmar, but that he should check the archives when its manager, Barry, got back from reserve duty next week. After circling Barry's name, he handed him the kibbutz directory.

A stapled packet no thicker than a term paper, the kibbutz directory couldn't have been more different from the five-inch-thick Manhattan phone book, but Adam was still brought back to those afternoons he spent in a phone booth on the corner of Essex and Delancey, scanning the names for his father. When he was twelve years old, his grandfather finally told him that, honestly, he couldn't be sure who his dad was, that his mom had named him Soccorso because her boyfriend at the time was Tony Soccorso, and she had hoped that using his name would keep him in the picture; but Tony insisted the dad was Jerry Cohen, a boy who did come around a lot. Adam didn't want to hurt Zayde, didn't want him to feel like he wasn't enough, so he used the pay phone to call the eight Tony and Anthony Soccorsos in the white pages and the ninety-four Gerry, Jerry, Gerald, and Jerald Cohens. Four separate afternoons he spent in that glass booth scratched with slurs and sprayed with tags, his pockets bulging with quarters. Had one of those voices he'd heard been his dad's? None of them even admitted to knowing a Sharon Rosenberg.

"Pervert."

Adam raised his head. The girl towered over him, wearing the same navy work shirt and beige work pants as him, and plenty of eyeliner, though not as much as that night. The late afternoon sunlight inflamed her absurdly red hair.

He brought his hands together. "I'm so so so sorry about that. I swear it wasn't what it looked like. You know, you really should shut your blinds when you're getting dressed."

"And you really should not be having your eyes in people's windows." Her flinty Russian accent made it hard to tell if she was angry or simply giving an idiot some advice.

"Listen, I was walking around the back of the building for totally other reasons and . . . well, there you were. But I swear on my life I wasn't getting my rocks off. Honest to God. Did you report me?"

"No."

"Are you going to?"

"No."

Adam blew through his lips. "Okay. That's good. Thank you."

"I do not report people."

She shot him a pitying look before leaving to join the other Russians playing cards around the picnic table.

Adam went back to the directory. He was nearing the end without any luck. If only he had a last name. Many of the listings were simply the "Horesh Family" or "Kaplan Family." He reached the last page. No Dagmar. A red petal fell on the list of names. The tree was shedding its flowers, dappling the lawn. Adam lay back on the grass and gazed into its branches. Golden sunbursts came through the leaves and flowers. One more day, and he could talk to Eyal's mother. He had seen her name in the directory.

He closed his eyes. The exotic smell of the freshly mowed lawn put him on edge, but the sound of the Russians bantering around the picnic table was homey. Adam had been lullabied to sleep on many a summer night by people chitchatting in a foreign tongue, ever since that first sweltering July night he moved in with his grandfather, almost twenty years ago. Several old people, seeking relief from their lonely, muggy apartments, had dragged kitchen chairs onto the sidewalk, and for hours they sat beneath his second-floor window, kibitzing in German and Yiddish. He lay listening to them for a long time after Zayde explained what had happened to his mom.

When his mother first failed to pick him up that afternoon, nobody had been surprised. Certainly not Mrs. Wadhwa, the Indian woman who babysat several kids in their apartment building in Gowanus. It was normal for Adam to still be sitting in front of the TV long after the other children had been picked up, while Mrs. Wadhwa collected the toys off her floor, mumbling, "I should charge your mother more, I really should." Things only started to seem different when he was still on the couch as Mr. Wadhwa came through the door in his bus driver's uniform. After saying hello to Adam, Mr. Wadhwa pulled his wife into the kitchen, where Adam could hear them whispering between muffled phone calls.

Hours passed. Night fell. A knock came at the door, and Adam went running at the sight of his tall grandfather standing with his straw fedora in his hands. "Zayde!" He threw his arms around his legs. His grandfather, cradling his head against his waist, said, "You're coming home with me." Didn't it seem strange to the old man that he took his hand and followed him down four flights of stairs and across the foyer's black-and-white checkered floor and out the building and down the street without ever asking, "Where's my mom?"

They took a cab to Manhattan, not the train—another sign this was not a regular day. Adam had never traversed the bridge in a car and was hypnotized by the ever-changing rhombuses made by the Brooklyn Bridge's crisscrossing silvery cables. The city lay in wait for him, an enormous Lite-Brite, the two new towers soaring into the sky. When they got to the apartment on Essex, Zayde ordered pepperoni pizza, which they ate at the small wooden table pushed against the kitchen wall. Actually, only Adam ate; Zayde sawed off a bite with his knife and fork, but never brought it to his mouth. When Adam had eaten as many slices as he could, Zayde said, "Adam . . ." Adam fell quiet, braced for the bad news about his mother, whatever it was this time. But then Zayde stacked the unused napkins. "Let's clean up first."

They did the dishes right away instead of leaving them on the table, as Adam was used to. Zayde washed, Adam dried: they were a team. While Adam brushed his teeth, Zayde sat on the toilet. "Always brush for a count of a hundred," he said. "Your teeth will sparkle." Adam hoped Zayde would never get to whatever it was he had to tell him. Why couldn't they just do this? Just carry on? Adam was led to his mother's old bedroom. His very own room. No sleeping on the couch. Zayde tucked him in so tight he couldn't move. Then the old man sat on the edge of the bed and took his hand.

Other grandfathers might have lied, made up a more comforting story, planning to tell the truth some day, but Zayde simply told him his mom had fallen on the subway tracks and the train just couldn't stop in time. "It didn't hurt her. It happened so fast, Adam, your mom couldn't have felt any pain."

Fallen? The wondering would come years later. Drunkenly? Jumped? Sober?

The Russians around the table burst into laughter. Adam opened his eyes. Beyond the tree and its raining red petals was a cloudless sky. The Russian girl's face appeared before the perfect blue.

"You're awake."

"I wasn't asleep."

"What's your name?"

Adam sat up. "Why? Have you changed your mind about reporting me?"

She shook her head.

"Adam."

She withdrew a pack of cigarettes from her shirt pocket, the nails on her pale fingers painted pylon orange. "Someone just told me you are from Manhattan. Is that true?"

"Is that what they actually said? Manhattan?" He eyed the people around the picnic table. He'd never spoken to any of them. "That's surprisingly specific."

"They know I am obsessed with Manhattan. So they are probably just teasing me. But are you?"

"I am, in fact."

She paused before lighting her cigarette. "The one in New York?"

"Is there another?"

She dropped the lighter in her pocket and, exhaling smoke, looked at him as if she were trying to decide whether to believe him. "Yes. There are fake Manhattans all over America. There is Manhattan, Kansas. Manhattan, Montana. Manhattan, Indiana. I know everything about Manhattan. If you were from the real Manhattan, you would be more stylish."

Adam patted his overgrown hair. "Yeah, I don't look my best. Thanks for pointing that out."

Golda climbed into the pocket of Adam's crossed legs and peered up at the girl as if making clear whose side she was on.

"Oh, thank you for asking about me," said the girl, resting a hand on one hip. "I am Ulyana from Belarus, but I will let you call me Ulya. You know where this is, Belarus? No, of course not."

"I know where Belarus is," he lied.

"Can I show you something, Adam of Manhattan?"

"I'm busy." He held up the directory he wanted to go through one more time, just in case. "Maybe later."

"This is a kibbutz. Nobody is busy on a kibbutz."

"I am."

She cocked her head, smirked. "Maybe you have to be nice to me, or I will report you."

Adam cocked his head too. "Are you fucking kidding me?"

"Of course I am kidding!" She grabbed his hand and pulled. "But you have to come! Please. Come to thank me for not reporting you."

Adam sighed and allowed her to help him up. He tapped his jean pocket, checking for the brooch, and followed the girl to her room. As they approached her door, his eyes fell to her butt. She must have requested workpants a size too small. As she walked, a crease switched from beneath one round cheek to the other, but the sight didn't rouse him. Even when he remembered seeing the white swells inside the pants, he felt nothing. And that was a good thing. He didn't need that kind of distraction.

Ulya unlocked the door, and Claudette, on her hands and knees in the dark, looked up with wide eyes.

"Oh, you." Ulya dropped her keys on her dresser and walked toward the back window. "I keep forgetting I have a roommate now."

Adam saluted Claudette as she rose from the linoleum floor, brushing off her knees. "Hey, Claudette the Astonishing."

Ulya opened the blinds, and the low, golden sun streamed in. She smiled at Adam. "I promise to close them again when I change."

"Very funny," he said. "What did you want to show me?"

She pulled from under her bed a powder-blue leatherette suitcase, similar to the one Zayde stored on the top shelf of his tidy closet. He had an awful flash of his burned and shaky hands rifling as fast as possible through the junk on the shelf beneath the suitcase, shoving aside the ancient *Life* magazines, the jam jars filled with buttons, the old Polaroid camera, to get to the hidden shoebox.

"My grandfather had a suitcase just like that one."

Ulya pinched the rusty steel snaps. "It's an old, ugly thing."

As she lifted its top, hope shot through him—hope that she was about to disclose something illicit, drugs or a flask of some strange Eastern European absinthe-like drink. He rubbed his hand over his mouth. No, no, no. He didn't want that.

The only thing resting in the faded lilac lining was a magazine, an old *Vogue* with Kelly LeBrock on the cover, giant plastic pink hoops hanging from her ears and over-the-top eighties makeup. Ulya picked up the well-thumbed magazine, and it fell open to the right page. Cradling the magazine on her arm, she showed Adam a two-page spread of Manhattan at night.

An aerial shot, it was taken somewhere in the East Seventies, looking south down Park Avenue toward Grand Central and the Pan Am Building. Didn't they just change that building to something else? Even though this wasn't exactly his New York City, the picture still filled him with longing: the exciting red streaks left by the taillights, the many windows hinting at the many lives, the majestic green and gilded cap of the Helmsley Building against the gray practical lines of the Pan Am. In the top right corner, a woman stood on a rooftop, the chiffony train of her yellow dress and her long red hair blowing in the wind like bright water reeds.

Ulya looked up at him. "Does it really look like this?"

"How old's this magazine?"

"1986."

"Eighty-six? Why do you have an eight-year-old fashion magazine?"

"It doesn't look like this anymore?"

"I guess if you're in a helicopter or something. Or maybe if you can afford to live in a penthouse. But I think it looks a lot better from below, anyway, you know, like when you're in the thick of it."

"The thick of it? What is the thick of it?"

"Like when you're in it. When you're a part of it."

Ulya turned back to the picture. "I'm going to be a part of it. One day I'm going to be that woman on the roof. Far, far away from this shit kibbutz."

As she laid the magazine down on the lilac lining, Adam said, "If you hate the kibbutz so much, why'd you volunteer?"

"Volunteer?" She snorted and pushed the suitcase back under her bed. "Ha! I wish I was just a volunteer, like you."

"You're not?"

"Are you crazy? None of the Russians are volunteers. We're *olim chadashim*. New immigrants. The government puts us in places where we can live for cheap, learn Hebrew. I got put on a kibbutz, of course. Not a *merkaz klita* in Tel Aviv. I am never lucky. I don't even want to be in this country, but I'm here because this was the only way to get out of the Soviet Union, to be a Jew moving to Israel. But the truth is I'm hardly a Jew. My grandmother, she was . . . a Jew."

Adam leaned against the wall. "You know why Israel gives automatic citizenship to anyone with one Jewish grandparent, right?"

"Actually," Ulya said, pulling a hot pink T-shirt out of her closet, "my grandmother was only half Jewish, so I am only one-eighth. But I stay in this shit country, because it is easier to go from here to the U.S.A. To the real Manhattan."

"Because one Jewish grandparent was all you needed to be sent to a concentration camp. That's what my grandfather told me."

Ulya turned from her closet. "My grandfather had this suitcase. My grandfather told me. My grandfather, my grandfather. It's like you're twelve years old."

Adam gripped the back of his neck. "Sorry. I didn't realize I was talking about him so much. He died last month."

Ulya stomped for the bathroom with a bundle of clothes in her hands. "This is no tragedy, Adam of Manhattan. Everybody has a dead grandfather. I cannot wait to take off this ugly uniform. Wait here! I will be out in two minutes."

Adam pushed off the wall. "You showed me what you had to show me, and now I got to go."

"No! Stay one minute, Adam of Manhattan! I have another thing to ask you."

She shut the bathroom door, and Adam pushed aside the newer magazines Ulya had on her bed to sit down. He sat face-to-face with Claudette, who was perched on the edge of her bed. He had almost forgotten she was there.

"So what were you doing on the floor, in the dark? Praying?"

The odd woman shook her head.

"What were you doing then?"

She looked off to the side, shook her head again.

He hadn't pushed when he asked her what she was looking for in the square or what the deal was with her "orphanage." This time he would press a little more. "Come on, what were you doing?"

She dropped her head, whispered. "Counting the tiles."

Golda jumped, clawing at the side of Ulya's mattress. Adam picked her up, and the dog stationed herself on his lap like the Sphinx. Stroking her back, he said, "Why were you counting the tiles?"

Claudette rubbed her knees a good ten seconds before responding. "To make sure there were . . . an even number . . . between our beds."

"Why does there have to be an even number?"

The sun was setting quickly now, the room dimming. When Claudette didn't answer, he said, "I don't get it. Why does there need to be an even number of tiles between your beds?"

"To . . . to protect Ulya."

"Protect Ulya? From what?"

Ulya emerged from the bathroom, eyes lined as vixenish as the other night, only in purple instead of black. She had changed from the work clothes into a pink crop top and jean miniskirt. Her shapely legs balanced on strappy green heels. She flipped on the ceiling light. "Ta-da! How do I look?"

Adam got to his feet. "Is this what you wanted to ask me?"

"Do I look like I could be going out in Manhattan?"

Adam didn't think so. Maybe Brighton Beach.

"Totally. You look like you're headed off to the Tunnel. Where are you going every night anyway?"

Fuck. He asked. He shouldn't have asked. He just had to hear "bar."

Ulya's eyebrows came together. "Why do you say I go out every night?"

He sensed she was hiding something. When you're using, you end up in your fair share of strip clubs, and a lot of those girls were Russian. Was that true in Israel? Was this girl stripping in a nearby town? He glanced at Claudette.

Ulya caught the glance. "Her? She told you? I didn't even know she could talk."

"She didn't tell me," Adam hurried to say. "Maybe it was the same person who told you I was from Manhattan."

Ulya's lips pursed. Then she shrugged, went to the mirror, and brushed her hair as if she couldn't care less who knew what, but she brushed too violently. "You can go now," she said.

"Oh, can I? Thank you, Your Highness." Adam headed for the door, Golda at his heels. "And don't worry. I don't give a shit where you go at night."

Adam walked out of the room into the half-light. That meeting would be starting soon, the one that had Eyal all worried. If he went, maybe he could question one or two people about Dagmar. As he climbed the stepping-stones onto the main road, the streetlamps lit up. Fat, frosted globes on short posts, the lamps looked like giant electric lollipops, making the kibbutz feel even more like an elf village. He paused in front of one of those strange doors, the number 4 stenciled onto the concrete slope behind it. They all had a different number. He pulled on the door, and to his surprise it opened. He peered down a dark concrete stairwell tunneling into the ground. At the bottom of the stairs loomed another steel door. Bomb shelters. He felt stupid for not realizing it sooner.

He crossed the kibbutz's only road for cars, already hearing the commotion in the dining hall. He walked up to the back entrance, where a tall boy in a striped sweatshirt smoked under the awning. He bypassed the puffing teenager and leaned in the doorway. All the tables were stacked on the sides, and everyone sat in rows facing a platform. Latecomers shouted to their friends. Chairs screeched against the terrazzo floor. The speakers boomed as a young man tapped the microphone.

"Excuse me," Adam heard from behind.

31

He turned to see a very old woman: sun-worn face cracked like a dried riverbed, the sclera around her muddy green eyes a light yellow, her hair a wispy white tempest. Thin and hunched, everything about the old woman was shrunken, except her belly, which stuck out as if she were ten months pregnant. Adam's heart pounded. What if Eyal had been wrong? What if this was Dagmar?

"Young man! Are you going to get out of the way? I'm needed onstage."

"Sorry." He jumped to the side, and she glared at him as she passed through the doorway.

Adam watched as the audience turned in their chairs to behold the old woman. A wave of whispers followed her as she walked toward the stage. How different this old woman was from the geriatrics who sat blinking into space on the benches in Seward Park all day, like breadcrumbs on the table the morning after a big dinner party, just waiting to be swept up and thrown away. This was the kind of woman Adam could picture his grandfather falling for.

Adam turned to the teenage smoker to inquire about the old woman and realized it was the soldier from the gate. "Wow, I didn't recognize you without your uniform."

The boy shrugged and sucked at his cigarette. The binder tucked under his arm brimmed with papers.

"I'm the guy from New York. You know, the guy you gave the third degree to."

"I know. Adam. I had no choice. You were sweating like a nervous wreck."

"Yeah, I had . . . jet lag. Sorry, I don't remember your name."

"Never gave it to you. Ofir."

"Ofir, tell me . . ." Adam pointed at the old woman stepping onto the stage. "Do you know who that is? That old lady?"

"Of course. That's Ziva."

Adam's heart sank. It would have been so satisfying to give that woman the brooch. So easy.

"What about an old woman named Dagmar? Is there anyone named Dagmar on the kibbutz?"

Ofir shook his head.

"You sure?"

"Of course I'm sure. Everybody knows everybody on a kibbutz. And everything they do."

"How many people live here?"

"Five hundred adults, and two or three hundred people under twenty-six."

Adam couldn't imagine living in a town with seven hundred people, not to mention one where everyone ate all their meals together. What hell.

"Eyal said there's never been anyone named Dagmar on the kibbutz."

"He would know." Ofir exhaled the last of his cigarette. After smashing it into the standing ashtray, he lit another.

"Chain-smoke much?" said Adam.

Ofir half smiled and peered into the dining hall with restless gray eyes.

"This meeting, it seems to be making everyone real jumpy."

"Yeah, this meeting's a big deal. But me . . ." Ofir aimed his cigarette at a standing piano to the left of the dais. "I'm just waiting to get on that piano. That poor excuse for a piano is the only one on the kibbutz, and I only get to use it when I'm on leave. Three days a month, that's all I get to play."

The microphone squealed as Eyal adjusted it toward his mouth. Even from the back door, Adam could see the secretary's fear as he waited for the congregation to quiet down. His face was slick with sweat, and dark circles spread from the pits of his light blue T-shirt.

Also on the stage sat a middle-aged woman studying her notes through reading glasses. Her long curly hair draped over her loose purple frock. In the chair beside her sat Eyal's mother, Ziva, dressed in the same canvas work clothes Adam wore and Ulya couldn't wait to take off. Sitting erect, chin extended, eyes surveying the audience, Ziva gave the impression that whatever she had to say didn't need notes.

Eyal tapped the microphone and got a nod to proceed from the young guy working the amplifier.

"I know everyone is scared," he began, his magnified voice reverberating in the hushed dining hall. "I'm scared too."

*M*other shit *pizdets* fucking *ebanniy* kibbutz, thought Ulya as her green stilettos kept lodging in the soil of the cabbage field. But what was she supposed to do? Meet her lover in work boots? A gust of wind blew a strand of red hair into her gluey lip gloss. As she tried to pick the hair off her lip, her shoe jammed again, and a bare foot with freshly painted fuchsia toenails slipped out and plunged into the mud.

She slipped her mucky foot back into her shoe and scanned the world around her: the rows and rows of cabbages, the modest white houses of the kibbutz on the plateau, the smattering of village lights along the black mountaintops. How long was she going to have to live in this dusty corner of the world surrounded by Jews and Arabs? Until fifty years ago, half the people in her hometown of Mazyr had been Jews, but it was difficult to imagine when the only evidence was the eighteenth-century cemetery overlooking the Pripyat River where cows and goats grazed among sunken stones. It was off one of these stones that she stole the name for her fake Jewish grandmother.

At last she reached the fragrant grove where the trees were swollen with ripe mandarins and the leaves appeared gray in the moonlight. The hard orchard dirt allowed for easier walking and a more optimistic train of thought. When the USSR announced they were letting Jews leave for Israel, she had jumped at the rare chance to get an exit visa, and what was the use of blubbering about it now? So what if by the time she got the visa the Union had crumbled? Life in Belarus still wasn't a bowl of raspberry jam. In her last letter, her mother wrote that she now wrapped her feet in plastic bags before slipping on her shoes because the spring puddles seeped through her worn-out soles. Ulya was lucky to have found a way out, and soon she was going to be in New York City. Of this she had no doubt. She doubted almost everything—politicians, religions, isms in general, science, declarations of love, even her family—but one thing she knew she could depend on no matter what: Ulya. With her dyed scarlet hair, she likened herself to molten lava, a smoldering force that coursed through the world dissolving anything and anyone in her way. She shook her head, amused by her own melodrama.

A match flared in the trees up ahead, making her stomach turn. Why did she keep coming to see this man? She watched the orange cigarette tip rise and fall in the darkness. This was very un-molten lava of her. Stupid. He wouldn't help her get to New York. That new boy, Adam of Manhattan, perhaps he could help her. But how? She couldn't imagine falling in love with him: he was so skinny, with purplish bags under his eyes, and all he talked about was his grandfather. She might be able to pay him to marry her, to be her green-card husband—he smacked of someone who might go for that sort of thing—but how much would she have to pay? If it was anything more than nothing, she didn't have it. What if he fell in love with her? Maybe he would marry her for free, without her having to pretend she loved him, in the hopes of winning her over? This didn't seem likely though. He showed surprisingly little interest in her, even after seeing her naked. Was it because she was nothing compared to the women in New York?

Ulya's heart had been set on living in that city of cities for eight years now, ever since that day she was working beside her mother selling dried fish on the platform of the Mazyr train station, and a stunning woman stepped off the Minsk-Kiev express wrapped in a sable fur coat with the most lavish cape collar. November 1986, only a few months after the radioactive rains, and her twelve-year-old self couldn't take her eyes off the woman as she sashayed toward their small stand with her high sleek ponytail and ballerina posture.

The woman bestowed a smile on her, white teeth glistening between painted red lips, and turned to her mother and ordered fifty kopeks of *vobla* in a Moskva accent. As her mother selected the best fish from her offerings, the woman explained that she would never eat food from so close to Chernobyl, but it was good enough for her cat. The woman's luminous skin and rosy cheeks made Ulya embarrassed by her mother's faint mustache and the large chin mole that echoed the black eyes of their dried perch.

A man in sunglasses and a shiny mink *ushanka* strode toward their stall with open arms. "Hey, *privyet*! Look who's here!" The woman put down her red leather bag, and they stood, clasping each other's arms, gushing over what a delight this chance encounter was and how splendid the other looked. Seeing her mother was too transfixed by the beautiful people to notice anything else in the station, Ulya dropped to her knees and crawled around the fish cart until her extended hand could snatch something, anything, out of the woman's bag. Before she had acknowledged what she was doing, she had done it and was back on the other side of the fish cart fumbling to hide a manila envelope in her coat. She had never stolen before, not even a fruit dumpling from her mother's kitchen.

Fortunately the train started at once, and the woman grabbed her red handbag and paper-wrapped fish and ran laughing with her male companion toward her car. Ulya's luck continued when, as soon as the dark green caboose chuffed out of the station, her mother mumbled that she was going to the toilet. Ulya knew she was also going to pay the station guard his bribe before he had the chance to mosey over and insinuate how much trouble he could get in for letting them sell their fish. Impatient to see what was in her secret envelope, Ulya watched her mother trudge across the railroad tracks and climb onto the opposite platform, her charcoal coat and brown headscarf matching the rusty tracks and cement station building. The giant red digital clock above the station's doors seemed the only color for miles. The second her mother disappeared through the doors, followed by the guard, eager for his ten kopeks, Ulya whisked the envelope out of her coat.

Fingers raw and stiff from having lost her gloves earlier that winter, she struggled with the fastener, the red string seemingly wrapped around the buttons a hundred times, but at last she got the envelope open and pulled out—a fashion magazine! In English! Between glances to see if her mother was returning, Ulya riffled through the vivid pages, glimpsing legs in bold purple stockings, unnaturally red or platinum blond hair, shiny high heels, gold purses, and outrageously padded shoulders. A two-page spread featured a dizzying nighttime wonderland where yellow cars streaked down streets and glittering towers pierced the black sky with silver and gold pinnacles; it would be a year before she dared to show the magazine to a classmate's father, a playwright rumored to be lax about contraband, and learn that this place was real and called *Manhattan*.

While she and her mother waited for the next train, her mother turned to her. "Why do you stare at me? I disgust you, selling *vobla*?"

Ulya had been busy daydreaming about later that night, when she would study the magazine behind the locked bathroom door, and had forgotten that her mother was even there. "No, Mamochka."

Her mother shrugged and absently rearranged the fish. "You will grow up and you will see. Learn for yourself. That in life you don't have a choice. It is what it is."

Ulya peered sideways at her mother, wiping her stinky fish hands on a tattered cloth, and considered for the first time whether one of her parents might be wrong. It felt like betrayal to think such a thing, but she couldn't believe she had no choice, no say in who she could be or what she could have. Look! She had chosen to snatch the magazine, and now its magic was tucked inside her coat.

Ulya straightened her jean skirt, reaffirmed that the cropped pink T-shirt showed off her flat stomach, and faced the shadows of the mandarin grove where the useless man awaited her. This fling was for the time being. While she was stuck in this boring collective-farm hell, spending her days in a windowless milk house, straining yogurt. She was young, and flings were a part of being young. If he got all caught up in it and had his heart broken, that was his fault. It wasn't her responsibility to look after other people's hearts. She had never had her heart broken. Why? Because she was so beautiful nobody would leave her? No. Because she took care of hers and didn't stupidly hand it over to someone else to safeguard.

When Ulya reached the barbed wire that ran along the perimeter of the kibbutz, she called, "Farid!"

Her Arab lover rose from where he'd been sitting on a boulder. He approached the cattle fence, his wide smile betraying how thrilled he was to spend another night lying with her among the hill's wildflowers and silvery olive trees. Ulya's stomach stirred again, but in excitement. Though they had been meeting like this for half a year, it still surprised her how coppery-gold his eyes were, even in the shadows. She had to grant him that much: he had extraordinary eyes.

Farid chucked his cigarette, leaned over the moonlit barbs, and kissed her, not only with his lips, but with the smell of tobacco and coffee and musk and a grassy whiff of the kibbutz's avocado orchard, where he had worked all day.

"What's this?"

She felt him tugging on the back of her T-shirt and realized she had forgotten to remove the price tag.

"Oh, it's new." She hurried to rip off the tag before he saw the price. It wasn't even that expensive, not even a hundred shekels, but still, if he saw the price he'd know she couldn't possibly have bought it. And he wouldn't like that most of her clothes were shoplifted.

He brushed her exposed belly. "It's a nice shirt."

She gave him an aren't-you-lucky look.

He pulled on the top barbed wire and stepped on the lower ones, creating a hole for her to climb through. Ulya shook her head at the way he parted the barbed wires, as if he were holding open a shiny car door for her.

"I don't know why I come here," she said.

Farid grinned. "I do."

"**W**e have no choice." Eyal spoke into the microphone, relieved his voice wasn't quivering as much as the notes in his hands. He couldn't remember the last time a meeting garnered such a crowd. Even the emergency assembly on the eve of the Gulf War, when they doled out gas masks, hadn't drawn this many people; never mind the usual meetings, when at most eight or nine people came to discuss the broken irrigation system or the output at the plastics factory, everyone else preferring to stay home and watch *The Simpsons*. In the corner of Eyal's vision sat the one person who hadn't missed a communal meeting in sixty-one years, and she was watching him with livid eyes.

"The ending of equal pay. I know it flies in the face of everything the kibbutz has stood for. It's difficult to accept that some of us will get more money for our work than others. The street sweeper will no longer earn as much as the doctor."

"Why?" A scraggy man jumped to his feet, propped his hands on his narrow hips. "I only see a doctor once a year, but I walk on the streets every day."

Eyal turned to the man whose job for the last two years happened to be sweeping and weeding the kibbutz's paths, but before he had a chance to say anything, a woman standing along the wall shouted: "So what? You have to be smart to be a doctor. Any moron can sweep."

This got titters from the crowd, and the street sweeper reddened.

A bellow came from the back: "Maybe you're the moron! If the streets are dirty, more people get sick!"

"Friends." Eyal clutched the microphone stand. He'd barely started his speech and had already lost control of his audience. His mother was visibly pleased. Her eyes now observed him with a victorious gleam, her lips fighting back a smirk. Couldn't she see the only members defending equal pay were the freeloaders and the unfortunate few who were going to find themselves at the bottom of the salary scale? "Friends, please!"

A fiftyish woman with a thick American accent rose from her seat. "Soon people with bigger incomes will have bigger houses. Nicer clothes. A car! How will it feel when your next-door neighbor has a nice car and you don't? I might as well have stayed on Long Island!"

Next stood a woman with bleached hair and a leathery face. "If we have different pay scales, then we're no longer a kibbutz! That's it!" Bolstered by a chorus of approval—*So true! Amen!*—she continued, turning as she spoke to take in the whole crowd. "We could keep calling ourselves a kibbutz, but so what? We could call ourselves France, that wouldn't make us France."

A grizzled man from the accounting office shot up, sending his chair crashing behind him. He pointed a shaking finger at the woman. "You make me sick! You don't deserve to get paid anything! You're a lazy *bat zona*! A parasite!"

"A parasite?" The woman's husband charged at the accountant, sending onlookers scrambling.

Eyal brought his mouth closer to the microphone. "Please!"

"When was the last time you worked outdoors?" Spittle rained off the husband's mouth as he held his right fist low and back, as if struggling not to throw a punch. "I would like to see how well you pick bananas! My wife has skin cancer from picking goddamn bananas!"

Eyal's lips brushed the microphone as he shouted: "ENOUGH!"

The speakers shrieked, drawing the hall's attention back to the stage, where Eyal stood, his notes crunched in his hands. The sound guy, a twenty-something who DJed the kibbutz's weddings and bar mitzvahs, leaped to the controls. Eyal uncrumpled his papers while everyone settled back into their seats. He glimpsed his mother shifting all her weight onto one hip and realized he should have made certain for her sake that the seats onstage had cushions.

He took a deep breath and faced the crowd. "Before we go into specifics, I want to make it clear right now that as kibbutzniks we will never consider one job more valuable than another. We understand everyone contributes to a society. We are only talking about market value, not any other kind of value. How much money a person makes says nothing about how much a person is worth."

"Yeah, right!" came from the last row, but the house resisted further eruption. Eyal hoped his mother, craning to glimpse the heckler, would see it was Chaim, a man who had called in sick twice a week for the last three decades and spent whatever days he did go to work on endless cigarette breaks.

Eyal searched through his notes. He was lost. He had let the crowd and concern for his mother veer him off course, and now he had no idea where to resume his speech. Rows of expectant faces watched him. He would have to ad lib. He patted his brow. All he had to do was tell it like it was, and there would be no room for argument. He wished the situation weren't so dire. He wished he didn't have to be the one to ring the death knell. But such was his duty.

"If half of you had shown as much interest in our books over the last twenty years as you're showing tonight, maybe we wouldn't have to do this. But now it's this simple: the banks won't lend us any more money. We don't earn half as much as we spend. The country doesn't hold up the kibbutz as a national icon anymore, which means no more government subsidies. Kibbutzim are privatizing all over the country. Like it or not, if we keep doing things the way we are, we're going to go bankrupt before the end of the year. Before the end of the year! Imagine it for a second." He pointed beyond the dining hall windows, to the black night. "We will all have to go out into that world alone. A world none of us knows anything about. A world of job interviews and mortgages and layoffs and retirement plans ..."

Eyal caught sight of Dana, the frizzy-haired gossipmonger, covering her mouth and whispering to her neighbor. The woman was a menace. Last week, as he and his mother passed her table at lunch, she had babbled in a raised voice: *My mom said Ziva was a slut. Eyal's dad could be anybody.* Over their plates of spaghetti, his mother had sighed and said she'd long ago accepted that kibbutzniks, like the residents of any small town, like their forefathers in the shtetlach, were bound to gossip, but an old woman's love life? Eyal shrugged too, as if the rumor were new to him, though he had been hearing it since he was a little boy, since that autumn morning in 1959 when in the middle of the teacher's story about the great Dov

Margolin, who had founded their kibbutz, smuggled Jews out of Europe, and died fighting in the War of Independence, another boy had leaned over and whispered through his buckteeth, "Don't get all stuck-up, Eyal. He wasn't your real dad."

"We don't have to think of it as pragmatism versus idealism." He had found his place in his notes. "Is freedom not an ideal? Is personal expression not an ideal? Of course they are! You should be able to spend your earnings on what is important to you, not what a committee has decided it was your turn to have."

The room erupted with applause. Everyone had a stereo or airplane ticket they had applied for and been denied. Eyal waited through the clapping, not daring to look at his mother. For someone who did everything for "the people," she hated people. They had argued for so many years that he could hear her thoughts: *Look at them, clapping for freedom—the freedom to buy, buy, buy! By "personal expression," these good-for-nothings meant owning a certain car or walking around like billboards in oversized sweatshirts emblazoned with brand names.* As far as his mother was concerned, no better place existed for the "self-expressive type" than the kibbutz—not that she held much esteem for these types, but she acknowledged that they existed, and claimed that the kibbutz gave them everything they needed: paints, a printing press, dance classes, musical instruments, and, most importantly, an abundance of free time. She believed they had no idea how unusual their amount of free time was, having never had to come home after a long day at work and pay their bills or cut the lawn or do the dishes. She liked to shout statistics: the average American spends two hundred hours a year in commute.

Eyal wrapped up his speech, feeling it had gone well despite the rocky beginning, and introduced the woman in the purple frock, a representative from a kibbutz that had privatized a year ago. The guest speaker smiled at Eyal as she passed him. While she adjusted her glasses and lowered the mic, Eyal sat in the chair she had vacated, next to his mother.

Rubbing his sweaty palms on his jeans, he whispered, "Is your speech ready, Ima?"

Ziva sat up straighter. "Did that woman just say *privatized commune* with a straight face?"

While the visiting speaker relayed how her kibbutz had earned twice as much money since privatizing than it had made in the previous five years combined, Eyal looked sidelong at his mother. Her cirrhosis was worsening. Her fingers, gripping the thighs of her faded blue work pants, were thicker than ever, and beginning to curl back. Her gut, drained only two months ago, already bulged out of her rickety frame. Her old skin grew ever more yellow, and she constantly shifted in her seat, obviously in pain. And yet every morning the old woman consulted the task sheet, reported to her work assignment, and labored all day, often without a rest. She was tough, his mother. Such a tough, dedicated idealist that part of him couldn't help but wish that he would lose tonight, and she would triumph.

The visiting speaker's voice faded into the background as Eyal's eyes floated over the audience. He knew everything she was going to say anyway. In the front row a young redheaded mother kissed the pudgy cheeks of the redheaded boy wriggling on her lap. The image brought home how absurd it was for even the smallest part of him to wish that his mother would come out on top tonight. His mother had taught him nothing if not that the community should come before the individual— before his mother. When he was that redheaded boy's age, it was normal for kibbutzniks to sneer at the bourgeois idea of the nuclear family and be all gung ho about the communal upbringing of children, saying yes, yes, of course, children should be brought up separately from their parents in a large children's house—until a woman had her own child. Then the new mother would sneak into the children's house and leave chocolates on her *bubeleh*'s bed or make up reasons why she had to steal him away for an afternoon. Every mother, that is, but Ziva. She took the tenet that each child belonged to the whole community and the whole community was responsible for each child as seriously as she took everything about Socialist Zionism; if anything, when she was on duty in the children's house, she went out of her way to make sure Eyal was the last to get a lemon popsicle or a turn at the toilet. She preferred to ignore him rather than risk anyone thinking she played favorites. If he awoke in the middle of the night screaming from a nightmare, Ziva would sit back, waiting for the other woman on night duty to attend to him. Eyal shook his head. It was pathetic how long a child could keep resenting his mother, keep yearning for her approval, keep hoping their relationship would change. He was a fat, balding, forty-six-year-old man, for God's sake.

He noticed his mother kept looking toward the back of the dining hall. He followed her eyes and spotted the new volunteer, the troubled kid from

New York, lolling in the side entrance. His mother shifted her weight yet again and brushed the front of her shirt. He knew it wasn't only her distended belly and aching back behind her restlessness. She was eager to take the microphone. The truth was his mother could win tonight regardless of what he wished or what was good in the long run for everybody. She had always been the kibbutz's best orator. She had been rallying people for sixty years. When she was only seventeen years old, she had inspired other adolescents, including his father, Dov, to abandon their families and the parlor rooms and universities of Europe for the desert and swamps of the Promised Land. Soon after, she roused men and women to meet Syrian and Lebanese and Transjordanian armies with nineteenth-century rifles stolen from a museum in Haifa. Alone she had ventured into nearby Arab villages to persuade their elders to share the river with the new Jewish settlement. And now, she had told him this morning, she had to be as persuasive as ever, because here at the end of her life was the most important fight of all, the most important because if she failed tonight, she might as well have failed all along.

Eyal heard clapping. The speaker had finished, and he hadn't registered a word. He rose, shook the visitor's hand, and approached the microphone again.

"At last, we will hear from Ziva, who will present the arguments for sticking to our socialist principles." He had saved his mother for the finale. Why? Because whether she deserved it or not, he loved her. He also loved her socialist principles; it wasn't his fault they didn't work. Besides, his speech wouldn't have sounded as good following hers.

His mother stood, smiling as if she had already won. She had ignored him when he asked if her speech was ready because she knew he was well aware that it was beyond ready. She had been perfecting it for two months and had committed it to memory over the last few days, practicing until she could say it with a driving rhythm that soared in all the right places.

Strangely, his mother didn't move for the microphone. She stood in place, staring at the crowd. Was this an oratory trick, a way to commandeer the audience's attention before she started? He thought he knew all her techniques. Ziva groped behind her, but her deformed hands couldn't seem to find what she wanted. The back of her chair? Her eyelids fluttered.

Eyal took a step toward her. "Ima?"

She lurched, the crowd gasped, and Eyal dropped his notes and ran. He grabbed his mother by the upper arms; so frail, all he could feel in his hands were the canvas sleeves and bones. The fat on his own arms shook as he held her up while her legs buckled beneath her. Ziva's head dropped back, offering her yellow face to the ceiling lights. Had she stood too quickly? Had her heart been pounding too violently while she waited for her turn to speak? Her hazel eyes blinked at the overhead lights.

"Ima, can you hear me?"

She let out a groan.

"Ima?"

She stopped blinking. The consciousness rushed back into her eyes. She closed her mouth. Lifting her head, she tried to jerk out of Eyal's grip, but he wouldn't let go, not until she was securely on her feet. Then he hovered while she brushed her sleeves.

Ziva cleared her throat, turned to the audience. The whole dining hall had risen. Eyal knew this wasn't the standing ovation his mother had imagined for tonight. Her eyes darted as if she were searching the back of her mind.

"Ima," he whispered. "Do you want me to help you to the microphone?"

She didn't respond. Wordlessly, she sat back down in the plastic chair.

Eyal didn't want to believe it. His mother wasn't going to give her speech. Couldn't.

He walked back to the microphone and spoke over the crowd that was already gathering its stuff and heading for the doors.

"At the end of September, we will vote on whether to institute different wages. This gives you the whole summer to consider it. No one will be able to say they weren't given enough time to think about this very carefully. If anyone wants to come by my office and ask questions, please do. And—"

He gestured toward his mother, sitting straighter than ever, but looking terribly small. Reduced. She glared into the emptiness above the crowd. He raised his voice.

"And, please, please, if anyone would like to hear the arguments of the opposing side, I encourage you to go to Ziva. I know she would be happy to speak to you. Please, please do not hesitate to talk to her."

*A*dam checked his wristwatch again. 2:17 a.m. Was that soldier ever going to stop playing the piano? In four hours he had to get up and wash seven hundred people's dishes. The kid would never be allowed to play all night if the only people within earshot of the dining hall weren't the foreign volunteers and senior citizens. Before going to bed, Adam had scoped out Ziva's apartment in the old people's building, her window the only one still filled with light.

When Adam first climbed into bed, he had been grateful for the piano. As he drifted in and out of a light sleep, he heard Ofir trying a bar one way, then another, tripping up and trying again, and it was much better than the inescapable quiet of the last two nights. But now the soldier had hit his stride. Every time Adam closed his eyes, the wistful melody sent him up the stairs of their five-story walkup, two steps at a time, carrying grocery bags filled with Oreos, Pop-Tarts, Mountain Dew, and a large container of kasha varnishkes, that tasteless mix of buckwheat groats and bow-tie pasta his grandfather loved so much. Every time he reached their door—2C—he managed to pop open his eyes.

Golda slept beside him, her chest pressing into his thigh with every inhale. Why did this little creature attach herself to him? He rested his hand on her warm furry body and immediately removed it. He couldn't bear the fragility of her tiny ribs under his palm.

2C. Would he ever be able to stomach being in that apartment again? Just two bedrooms, a family room, a bathroom, and a kitchen, all of them just big enough. Anyone else would find the place nothing special, no different than a billion other small apartments in the city, in the world, but that's where he had spent a happy childhood and had planned on living out the rest of his life—loving a wife, maybe raising a child, and at the end of it all being just like Zayde, an old man setting the potted plants out on the fire escape in the spring, then bringing them back in before the first snowfall. If a person wanted to have a real home, he couldn't keep moving around; he had to stay put.

He closed his eyes and there he was going up the stairs again, carrying the bags of goodies. When he arrived at their door, he allowed himself to unlock it, turn the knob. Inside, he found the apartment unusually quiet. He wiped his Converses on the coir doormat and hung his parka. He supposed the old man was napping; otherwise he'd be in the family room, reading a mystery novel or listening to a favorite swing tune. Mostly he listened to the old records sitting on the couch with a faraway look, but once in a while he danced with an imaginary partner, especially to Bing Crosby's "After You've Gone." Swaying, eyes half closed, an invisible woman in his arms, he'd mouth, *You'll feel blue, you'll feel sad, you'll miss the bestest pal you've ever had.*

Adam dumped the kasha varnishkes into a bowl and popped it in the microwave. While the timer counted down, he assured himself that objects were just objects. Even that brooch, when all was said and done, was just an object. And he had no choice. When Bones's thugs trailed him home from the East Broadway station, smashed his head into a mailbox in broad daylight, and warned him that next time they would kill him and force the money out of his old man, he knew he had to come up with the fifteen thousand dollars fast. And the brooch—eventually it was going to be his anyway, right? Since he was the only person around to inherit it. Zayde had only Adam and Adam only Zayde; so maybe his grandfather wouldn't have done it with pleasure, but he would have let him sell the brooch to save his life. This way the old man got to make that sacrifice without the hurt of knowing it.

"Zayde!" Adam headed for his grandfather's bedroom. "Wake up! I got your favorite, kasha varnishkes from Moishe's."

He carried the warm bowl through the family room, where snow dusted the fire escape beyond the window. A cold March. Usually at this hour in the afternoon, a golden square of dusty sunlight glowed on the wooden floor in front of the television, but today the wintry light was pale and diffused. The radiators rattled. The apartment, barely renovated since Zayde and Bobbe moved into it in 1950, was anchored with anachronisms: a wooden breadbox sat next to the microwave; a midcentury credenza housed the VCR; an old-world cuckoo clock hung beside the wireless phone. All the furniture came from Leo's! on Delancey, where Zayde had worked the floor for forty-six years before his retirement two months earlier.

"Zayde?" Adam stood outside his door. "Don't you want some kasha varnishkes? I warmed them up for you."

Not a rustle. If the old man were sleeping, where was his snore? Maybe he wasn't home? Where could he have gone? He'd already taken his daily walk to Duane Reade. Adam slowly turned the knob. "Zayde?"

The old man's bedroom hadn't changed since the days when Adam would crawl into his bed after a nightmare: the framed drawing of a gaslit street in Dresden, the blue acrylic blanket, the window onto the brick air-shaft that echoed with cooing pigeons. As Adam turned to leave, he spied the slippered foot sticking out from behind the bed.

He dropped the bowl of kasha and ran to where his grandfather lay on the hardwood floor, body facing one way, head the other, the old Flor-sheim shoebox open beside him, the shoebox that earlier that morning, while his grandfather was on his walk to Duane Reade, Adam had pulled from the shelf in the closet, pulled out from behind all that junk, the mag-azines and jars of spare buttons and pens. He'd been careful to replace it all just so, was certain nobody could have detected anything.

He took the old man's face in his hands, the cheeks smooth, cold. He searched the eyes, the black eyes like his own. Their light was out—that loving, amused, nostalgic shine gone. He brought his face to the slack mouth, checked for breath. Nothing. Only the familiar, safe smell of his grandfather, a warm human smell, slightly peppery, overlaid by a rum-based aftershave, laundry starch, scotch mints. Brylcreem.

It was the Brylcreem Zayde had gone to buy at Duane Reade when Adam hunted for the brooch and found it in a blue felt bag in the shoebox.

Adam sat back, hands pressed against his mouth. If only he too would stop breathing. In his grandfather's fist was the yellowed note, the one that had been in the felt bag with the brooch, the one he had been in too big a hurry to read.

Adam opened his eyes, back again in the kibbutz dorm room. The music had only grown more haunting, more insistent. He got out of bed, padded over to his bureau, and retrieved the old note from inside his passport. He unfolded the brittle paper, revealing the slanted black cursive.

It had taken three people to translate the note for Adam—Mrs. Silver in 4C did the German, Moishe of Moishe's deli the Yiddish, and the Israeli punk from the head shop on Avenue A explained the Hebrew—but since then Adam had read the note so many times with the translations in his head that as his eyes skimmed over the words, the languages felt familiar. As if he were his grandfather. And now he was reading it where his grandfather had read it that first time all those years ago.

November 30, 1947
Kibbutz Sadot Hadar

Mein liebster Liebling Franz,

It's so painful for me to write this letter that I'm having trouble moving the pen. Please forgive me for returning your brooch like this. What I did last night, what I'm doing right now, I hate myself for it, but please don't hate me. You must know how much I've loved you these last two years. If only I believed in something beyond the here and now, I could take comfort in the idea that we might be together again one day in the *olam ha-ba*. But, of course, I don't believe in such things. This is our one life, and we will not spend it together. We will probably never see each other again. It's unbearable to think. Or at least it seems so now, but the truth is we are still quite young with a fair amount of time ahead of us. A day will come when it won't seem so unbearable. Your mother said the brooch should only go to someone special. I hope you find her, I really do (though, selfishly, the thought also kills me. Isn't that horrible?). I'm afraid your heart will heal faster than mine. I'm sure of it. Wherever I go on the kibbutz, for the rest of my life, I will be greeted with memories of you, whereas you are sure to forget this plain little kibbutznik amid the glamour of your *goldene medina*.

I hope the second half of your life will be much, much easier than the first.

Love always,
Dagmar

Adam looked up from the note. In twenty years, he'd only seen his grandfather with the brooch twice. How was he supposed to know that he went into that shoebox so often? If he'd known that within a day the old man would've noticed it missing, he might have done things differently. Might have. It was hard to say when a person was using. He still might have been too fucked up, too desperate, too selfish to care. This is what he'd hoped: that his grandfather would only notice the brooch missing after a few years, after he had been a good grandson, a good person, so long his grandfather would be forced to forgive him. He also figured chances were good the old man might die without ever finding out. But it had never occurred to him that finding the brooch missing would give the old man a full-on heart attack. That it would kill him.

The music stopped. Adam waited with the note in his hand for the boy to start up again, but he didn't. 3:32 now. The music may have sent him up the stairs, but at least it had sympathy. How did people live with such coldhearted silence? He refolded the note along its worn creases and returned it with his passport to the top drawer. He couldn't get in the bed though, not yet, not with his heart racing like this. He paced with Golda watching him.

Someone special. The wrong hands. Only after the ambulance—no strobes necessary—carried Zayde away, and he was left standing alone in the middle of their family room, did he remember his grandfather telling him about "the wrong hands." *Remembered* wasn't the honest word, more like *couldn't forget*. He did remember before stealing the brooch, but he could forget, could push it out of his mind. Now it was all he could think about: his grandfather sitting on a bench in Seward Park, repeating with cross-eyed intensity that the brooch couldn't end up in "the wrong hands."

What else could he remember from that story? Almost nothing. Fourteen, finally old enough to hear about the brooch, and what did he do while his grandfather was talking? Daydream about his new girlfriend Monica, who told him on the phone that afternoon that she wanted to wait until they'd been together a year before losing their virginity. He kept imagining pulling off her pink velour pants while his grandfather told him a story that may have involved Buchenwald. Had it? God, he hoped not. Sometimes when he tried to remember the story, he got a flash of rubble. Rubble as far as the eye could see—but that could just be a weird connection his mind was making because maybe there had been construction that day in Seward Park. He never got up the nerve to ask his grandfather to tell the story again. The only thing he could remember for certain was the part about "the wrong hands," how he had to make sure the brooch didn't end up in them, and he only remembered that part because the old man said it four or five times.

Adam climbed into the bed, where Golda hurried to burrow under the blanket and snuggle against him. What Dagmar had begrudgingly wished for his grandfather, that he would find another special person for the brooch, never happened. For the rest of his life, decade after decade, it remained in the felt bag with that goodbye letter. What did Bobbe, his wife of twenty-some years, think of him never giving her the brooch? Did she even know about it? As for their daughter, Adam's mother, it was no mystery why it never went to her: she would have sold it before Adam had the chance to. Adam's hands had turned out to be the wrong hands.

The only way to make sure the brooch ended up in the right hands was to leave it with the one person his grandfather had ever wanted to have it, the one person he had ever found worthy. It wouldn't undo the past, Adam understood that, but it was both the least and the most he could do. There was only Dagmar. He had to find her.

Ziva watched her new charge roll a lychee around in her palm. The two women were sorting the little red fruits, seated on upturned plastic crates on the edge of the orchard. Ziva found the girl beyond irritating. Not only did she inspect every lychee for a full minute before tossing it into either the good crate or the bad crate; more often than not, she would retrieve the lychee and reexamine it. The same little drupe! One time she caught her inspecting the same lychee three times. And always with a distracted look in her eyes.

Ziva tossed a cracked lychee into the reject pile. "Claudette, I hope you don't think you're above sorting fruit."

Claudette shook her head. "No. Of course not."

"Working the land is good for you. *Build the land, and it will build you.*"

Claudette held a lychee closer to her eyes. "It is important to keep busy. The devil finds work for idle hands."

Ziva squinted at the girl. Was she being sarcastic? The girl wouldn't be the first in her generation to mock Ziva's idealism. Ziva sorted the fruit in her lap as quickly as she could with her misshapen fingers and tossed an emptied crate to the side. She would lead by example. The young foreigner would be forced to pick up her pace when she saw an old lady with hideous hands was on a third crate while she was only halfway through her first.

Instead the younger woman withdrew more and more into her own world. By the time Ziva had finished a fourth crate, the girl was staring into her crate of lychees, motionless. What was the feckless foreigner daydreaming about? The latest fashion? Some boy?

"You know you can't sort fruit telepathically, Claudette!"

Startled, the young woman looked up at Ziva and nodded, but Ziva could tell she was nodding at her without seeing her. She wasn't present. Claudette reached for a lychee.

"Grab a handful, Claudette! Enough with this one lychee at a time."

Ziva dragged a fifth crate toward her. She wasn't going to let this young woman or what happened at last night's meeting slow her down. What had happened? She had felt fine walking over. Angry, yes, horrified, but not sick, not weak. Well, of course, she'd felt a little sick: she was old, had cirrhosis. She always felt a little sick. But she felt capable. Prepared. She approached the dining hall, said "Excuse me" to the boy blocking the doorway, and then when the boy turned . . .

She didn't know him. She was sure she had never seen him before, and yet his face felt familiar. Terribly. The familiarity was so disorienting that for a second she thought: here he is, the Angel of Death, come for me. That's how much this boy's face threw her off her bearings. She proceeded into the dining hall, climbed onto the stage, but the confusion followed her.

The whole time her son blathered about freedom and that other idiot prattled on about privatized communes, the boy leaned in the doorway, like a ghost, like . . . Of course. He resembled him so much: Franz. After he had been on the kibbutz for a couple of months, put on some weight, but wasn't entirely healthy yet. She had told herself that it was absurd to be so unnerved about it; at her age everyone looked like someone else, someone from the past. So maybe it was the stress of the meeting, or all that medication, or the cirrhosis itself, but when she stood up—

"Should we take these?" A young man pointed at the good crates. It was Yossi's son, not a bad boy, but how did Yossi have a grown-up son? She still thought of Yossi as a boy. Did this young man see her faint last night? He wouldn't remember when she was the secretary and ran the show. Probably wasn't even alive yet.

"Yes, yes. These are done. No thanks to this young woman. Two hours and she hasn't sorted a single crate."

"I'm sorry." Claudette hastened to get another lychee. "I told the secretary I would be better in the—"

"What good is sorry?"

The young man carried the crates away, and Ziva went back to sorting the fruit. Had she ever seen gnarlier hands? Bony, dry, spotted, yellow. She had never seen her mother or grandmother with such old hands. The last time she laid eyes on them, when their families had come to the Lehrte train station to see her and Dov off, her mother had been only thirty-nine years old, and her grandmother—how strange to think it—must have been twenty years younger than Ziva was today. Excited, nervous, she and Dov had held hands throughout that train ride to the port in Venice—fat, smooth, childish hands that didn't even appear to have veins in them.

Her mother had been painting a blue bird the night she came home with the ocean liner tickets. Their parlor, once reserved for special occasions, had been transformed into her mother's makeshift studio: bedsheets covering the Persian rug, the settee, and piano. Her mother's back faced the foyer, the studio lamp highlighting the grays in her brown hair and the hand applying feathery, blue brushstrokes to a bird's extravagant wing.

"Dagmar." Her mother didn't turn from the canvas. "Why so late?"

Dagmar hung up the wool coat, tickets tucked inside the inner pocket. "We had trouble drafting this month's newsletter, Mutti."

It was true the Maccabi Hatzair meeting went longer than usual, but it was also true that she and her best friend, Dov, had taken the long way home so they could plot, as they had for years, their departure to the Land of Israel, only this time they had the tickets, bought that afternoon, for a ship leaving in three weeks. They were seventeen years old: if Hitler hadn't come to power, their parents never would have approved of them setting off on their own for the dusty edge of Arabia, but now she and Dov believed they would let them go without too much of a fight.

Dagmar hurried to the kitchen, grabbed a chocolate-ginger cookie from the counter, and sat at the breakfast table with a marked-up copy of the newsletter. The chocolate-ginger cookies were the only thing her mother baked that she could still swallow. Ever since her mother had been barred from the art school, she filled the hours she would have spent teaching with baking. Since the family of three could only eat so many pastries, Dagmar and her mother had walked plate after tinfoiled plate over to the neighbors, until they stopped answering their doors. Dagmar read through the statement, circling the Hebrew words she didn't know. Having the best Modern Hebrew in the chapter, she had been voted translator, and even if she had to work through the night, she would have the translation perfected for tomorrow's printing.

"Dagmar, sweetie, come paint with me," called her mother.

"I'm busy!"

Her mother came and leaned in the kitchen doorway. She wore lipstick and a wool skirt even though she hadn't left the house that day. Dagmar admired the strength her mother showed in keeping up appearances, but lipstick was degrading, and the woman who put it on while fellow Jews were having their beards cut in the streets ridiculous. Worse than ridiculous.

Her mother said, "I don't like these meetings. They're dangerous."

Dangerous! In other words: courageous, admirable. Imagine her reaction when she finds out about the tickets for the *Kampala*. Without looking up from her notes, Dagmar answered, "It's better to die on your feet, Mutti, than live on your knees."

Her mother walked over and kissed her on the head. "Oh, my Dagmar. My little Dagmar and her big plans."

Ziva tossed a bruised lychee at the rotten basket, wondering if she could have painted with her mother that night and still have completed her translation. She picked another lychee from her lap. It too was bruised. Tossing it, she realized she was moving as slowly as her empty-headed young charge.

Enough. She sat up straighter. She had to focus. Keep working, fighting. She might have lost an important battle at last night's meeting, but she hadn't lost the war. Articles needed to be written for the kibbutz newsletter, question-and-answer sessions had to be organized, posters needed to be printed and tacked everywhere. There was no time for woolgathering. The answer was no. No, she could not have painted with her mother that night. It was as true then as it was now: the only way to accomplish something extraordinary was with extraordinary commitment.

"We're not leaving until we sort through every one of these crates," Ziva told Claudette. "Don't sit back every time you pick up a lychee. It's a small waste of time, and small wastes of time add up to a big waste of time. You don't want to be a big waste of time, do you?"

Claudette shook her head, hunched forward.

"Oh!" Ziva gasped. She'd forgotten to take her arthritis pill.

She reached over her distended belly for her bag. How could she be expected to remember to take all these pills at their various prescribed times? With food, without food, before bedtime, in the morning, these together, these at least four hours apart? She opened the pill organizer, a big, ugly plastic thing with as many pockets of color as her mother's palette, and struggled to identify the steroids. The green capsules curbed nausea, the white tablets numbed her throbbing bones, the yellow ones prevented dizziness, the red and blue gelcaps supposedly stemmed the accumulation of fluid in her abdomen, the tiny orange pills thinned her blood so it didn't pool in painful blue bulges around her ankles, and the pink antihistamines soothed the incessant itchiness caused by all this medication.

As she picked out two chalky tablets, she noticed the younger woman gawking at her and her stockpile of pills. "What are you looking at?"

"Sorry." Claudette averted her eyes.

"Sorry again."

Ziva washed down the pills with a chug from her tin canteen. In the distance, beyond the peanut fields and cabbage fields, tall eucalyptuses marked the kibbutz graveyard. Under the shade of those trees lay Dov and the other pioneers and a slab of earth waiting for her. Tonight she would remind Eyal that the cemetery hadn't been tended to since last autumn.

When the truck came at the end of the day to fetch the women, Ziva insisted they sit in the back on the metal benches with the other field workers, mostly Arab men. Once again she had to tell the driver that she didn't see why she should sit in the front on cushy seats. Because she was a woman? A Jew? An employer? She left out "old." As the truck bumped over the dirt path, the setting sun made a golden wonder of the wheat fields. Ziva breathed in the early evening air, so cool and loamy, sweetened by the overripe lemon trees. In the distance, the lights of the villages twinkled on the darkening hilltops, little man-made constellations.

The truck parked behind the dairy house, and the tired workers clambered out. A young Arab with the most striking eyes—irises as gold as honey and long black lashes—held out his hand to help her down, but she waved him off, saying, "Go away!" Everyone tried to help her now. You reach a given age, and people think you can't do the simplest things on your own. Shaking his head, the fieldhand ran to catch up with the other men heading back to the nearby Arab village of Kfar Al-Musa. Sitting on the floor of the truck, Ziva eased herself over its edge. When her feet were secure on the asphalt, she stood and brushed off her backside.

"Your Eyal's a busy man, eh?"

Ziva turned to find Hanoch, still bitter over her insistence, back in 1978, that the television his brother had sent him from America should be installed in the clubhouse. His decrepit gray mutt sat beside him.

"And how's Noam?" said Ziva, knowing his grandson was rumored to be a drug dealer in Miami. "Busy, too, I hear."

Hanoch would not be deterred. He smiled and clapped his hands as if someone had finished a grand joke. "Remember when we replaced the benches in the dining hall with chairs? And oy, what a hullabaloo you made! Individual chairs, you claimed, would undermine our sense of comradeship. Ha! And now look at what we're talking about and who's the mastermind behind it. The son of the great Ziva Peled."

Watching Hanoch and his tired dog tottering away, Ziva found it hard to accept that the bitter old man was ten years her junior. Turning for the seniors' quarters, she said, "Hopefully you'll do a better job tomorrow, Claudette."

Claudette followed. "Eyal wants me to see you home."

Ziva gave her a sidelong scowl. "I don't need anyone to walk me home."

Claudette walked alongside her anyway, gaze fixed on the pavement.

Ziva clenched her fists and looked ahead. "I'll let you walk me home—for your sake, not mine."

In silence the women passed the water tower, the tallest structure on the kibbutz by far, and a row of houses belonging to younger families, their porches strewn with soccer balls, scooters, small shoes. How long had it been since they closed the children's house? Allowed children to live with their parents? It wasn't that long ago, was it? 1989. Only five years ago. Five years! And look what people dared talk about now. Unequal pay. How could things unravel so quickly?

Dizziness, like a squall of wind, rushed up the white path at Ziva, threatening to knock her over. She forced one foot in front of the other as if the ground weren't seesawing. She'd rather fall and break a hip than lean on the self-absorbed foreigner who never lifted her eyes from the sidewalk.

"There." Sweating, Ziva leaned on her door handle, struggling to hide her shortness of breath. "You've walked me home, Claudette. Now you can be under the ridiculous illusion that you've done something useful today."

Ziva waited for the young woman to say something, apologize or defend herself, but the girl merely turned and started back down the path, staring at her feet.

Alone at last in her apartment, Ziva wiped her forehead on her shirtsleeve and let her shoulders drop. She stumbled over to her faded green sofa and only realized after she had collapsed into it how viciously thirsty she was. After fourteen years, this apartment still felt new to her. Aside from the wider doorways and the red emergency buttons embedded into the walls, it didn't look like an old age home, but the smell of decay and disinfectant was a giveaway. She smelled it every time she opened the door. Was it her or did the odor seep through the walls from other people's apartments? At least on a kibbutz senior citizens weren't packed up and sent to live in sad isolation. The old age home was still home, situated smack-dab in the middle of the commune, right off the main square. Why couldn't these stupid ingrates see how special that was? Did they think they weren't going to grow old? Her eyes ran over the black-and-white portraits propped on the sideboard—young her, young Dov—and up to the yellowing WORKERS OF THE WORLD UNITE! banner nailed to the wall.

It had been one of the worst moments of her life, last night, when it all rushed back—her balance, her whereabouts, her fat middle-aged son, the reason for the crowded dining hall, the boy leaning in the doorway—it all rushed back, except the speech. It hid from her. Gazing out at the audience, she had ransacked her mind for it, but couldn't find a single word.

She closed her eyes on her lonely apartment and imagined being back on that stage. How easy it would be to deliver the speech now.

"Time and time again, my friends, people have tried to establish ethical societies. Classless societies. The ancient Sun State of Spartacus, the medieval Hutterites, the Soviet Union, the hippy communes of Nevada. People have tried, and people have failed. Greed, egotism, corruption have always won out in the end, always, except here. The kibbutz. The kibbutz is the only long-lasting, completely voluntary, socialist utopia in the world. If you want to own a private home or an SUV or climb a corporate ladder— fine, by all means, go ahead. Move to Tel Aviv. Or New York. London, Tokyo, Bombay. Anywhere in the world. But, please, leave this one small corner of the map alone."

Just please don't make her whole life a pointless endeavor.

She would have to turn the speech into an article for the monthly newsletter. Despite her exhaustion, her sore back, her throbbing hands, she grabbed the pencil and notepad from the coffee table. She had to think of a grand title. Something that couldn't be ignored.

Something that would ignite that noble fire, that will to rise above the measly self.

*O*fir sweltered in the back of an army truck zigzagging down a hill. Only hours ago he had been at the piano. In American movies, GIs took ocean liners and stopped at foreign cities on the way to the front, but he had only an hour on a public bus and a short hitchhike between kissing his mom goodbye and heading down to stifle a West Bank riot.

Everyone in the truck was mum. Postings were supposed to last four months in the territories, but their unit had been in Nablus half a year already. Ofir leaned over to see what his friend Gadi viewed through a hole in the truck's dark green canvas. Mostly half-finished houses with flat roofs and burs of black antennas. A young woman stood in front of a gate, blocking the sunlight from her eyes, her blue skirt whipping in the wind. Gadi joked: "I did her."

Ofir sat back again and reached for his cigarettes. He held the pack out to the others, and the truck filled with smoke. Taking a drag, Ofir considered his composition. He was so damn close. But something, some quality, was missing, like a word on the tip of the tongue. The melody was about taking flight; no, it was about the feeling of taking flight, but . . . If only he were at home right now, figuring it out. Why did he have to be in this fucking truck?

He noticed Gadi's leg shaking, and glanced sideways at his diminutive face. Poor Gadi. Never mind the Palestinian girl, he'd never done any girl. After every weekend leave, he came back with some story about a beach bonfire or a desert trance party where he almost, always *almost*, did it with some hot girl. Ofir never gave him a hard time because Gadi was the only one who didn't tease him about the cassette in his Walkman—Bach instead of Paul van Dyk. Gadi, drawing on his cigarette, gave Ofir a shrug that said, *This sucks, but what can you do?*

"All right, listen up." Their commander, Dan, looked at them from the front passenger seat. "No escalation. Just containment. No shouting, no threatening, no rubber bullets. Just keep things contained. *Beseder?*"

The soldier across from Ofir, Shai, rolled his eyes and clucked his tongue. Last night at dinner Shai had demanded, as he demanded every dinner, why didn't we just bomb the place until all the terrorists were dead? Why did we have to risk our lives? It wasn't our fault the assholes built their bombs right in the middle of their towns, surrounded by women and children. Hell, he said, their women loved them for it. Cheered them on. What would Paris do if bombs were going off in her subways? Just deal? For the first time in thousands of years, Jews didn't have to be victims; we could fight back, so why the hell weren't we fighting back with everything we've got? Because of world opinion? Fuck the world. The last thing a Jew should take into consideration is the world's opinion. The world would sit back and watch us all die. Again.

Dan pointed at Shai. "I mean it. Keep cool. I'm going to watch you."

Dan was only four years older than the rest of them, and Ofir often amused himself with the idea that this whole show was being carried out by kids barely old enough for *The Real World*. Ofir regularly compared his life to an alternative version of himself living in the United States, a doppelgänger based partly on TV and movies, but mostly on the photos in the booklets he ordered from Julliard and the Yale School of Music. Ofir nagged his mother until she signed the forms allowing him to start his army service a year early. Her tears left wrinkled spots on the papers. But he didn't want to be so much older than his doppelgänger when he started music school. Still, it was hard to do it to his mom. When he was still a lump in her belly, his father was shot and killed on a hill in the Golan.

As the truck neared the town square, the dissonance of the riot grew louder, like an orchestra warming up. Remaining cigarettes were crushed in the sand-bucket ashtray. It's okay, Ofir told himself as he rolled up his sleeves. Today his American alter ego was at the piano while he was at a riot, but he could still end up being the better artist, for whatever he lost in technical proficiency during these long days and nights when his fingers busied with binoculars and firearms instead of ivory and ebony keys, he gained in poetic urgency. That was the salvation of being an artist. The worst experiences could be transformed into meaning and beauty.

The truck stopped. The soldiers scrambled out the back. Smoldering tires poisoned the air. Chanting supporters brandished portraits of the suicide bomber who blew up a bus last week in Jerusalem. Glass crashed. Car alarms whined. Men swarmed, shouted, climbed on top of cars and shook their fists. Dan led his unit along the chain of soldiers bordering the square until he found a weak link. "Here!"

Ofir took his place, legs shoulder-width apart, M-16 in front of his abdomen, ready to swing it into position, even though it was only loaded with rubber bullets that he wasn't allowed to shoot. There were a hundred Palestinians to every soldier. More. What if, despite their guns, they all charged at once? It wasn't clear who was more afraid of whom. What was the sound of fear? Its pitch? Did it have breaks, like a pounding heart, or was it more like the whistle of an approaching Katyusha rocket, getting louder and higher and louder and higher? No, that was too easy. He had to think of something else.

A boy ran up to the soldiers and shouted, "Jewish whores take it up the ass." Shai snorted: "I wish." That was the extent of their Hebrew, one-liners about the promiscuity of Israeli sisters or mothers and slurs about the ugliness or evilness of Jews. Sometimes just the word *Jew* was yelled, as if something so vile required no adjective. Ofir's Arabic was also made of one-liners: *hurry*; *show me your ID*; *go*; *halt*; *hands in the air*.

"I don't get it." Yaron, the soldier next to Ofir, a skinny kid of Iraqi Jewish descent, pointed his chin at the ground strewn with stones. "They must be dismantling their own homes to round up all these rocks."

Soon, Ofir thought. Soon this would all be over. A few months ago Arafat and Rabin shook hands in front of the White House, shook hands in front of the world, in front of his mother, who collapsed on the sofa in front of the television with her hand over her chest, while his stepfather, eyes shining, whispered, "Would you look at that? That's what three thousand years of fighting coming to an end looks like." Soon the army might be pulling out of Gaza City and Jericho. Maybe he wouldn't have to serve a whole three years?

Over the clamor of the square floated the *adhan*. The hallowed call to prayer fanned the riot's fire. More plastic bottles and cardboard boxes were thrown into the flames, and the noxious fumes thickened. Young men began pitching stones at the soldiers. Maybe that's what was missing from his composition: the sound of fear. Could that be it? It wasn't only about taking flight, but taking flight from something . . . Ofir rolled his head to release the tension in his neck. If it was the sound of fear, he had a lot more work to do. But he would do it. He wasn't aiming for good enough. Now every muscle ached to be at the piano. While he scanned the square, he hummed the melody, listening for where he could balance the—

Smack! Stone, just below the groin. Inner thigh. Ofir struggled to withhold a cry. God damn it. Fuck. He clenched his teeth. His whole body clenched, muscles gripping the bones. Tears escaped. He couldn't help it. Also, a little urine.

When his breath returned, and the world reemerged from behind a sheet of tears, his eyes picked out a Palestinian boy about his age, sixteen or seventeen, not thirty yards away. The boy stood still and looked right at him. His China-made fake American T-shirt read: I'M A HOT DOG, MAN! At the end of one of his long skinny arms was another stone. The boy smiled at Ofir, a smile that out of context might have seemed good-natured. Ofir, pretending not to notice, scanned the square without letting the boy slip from his vision.

Behind the boy, to his left, was the last entryway into the kasbah. He had only seen pictures of the kasbah's narrow, cobblestoned alleyways, the same *National Geographic*–type shots his American doppelgänger would have seen: women in headdresses milling past barrels of vivid spices; butchers' stands with raw carcasses dangling from hooks; silversmiths' workshops glistening in the shadows like polished buttons on a dark coat. It was so near, but so foreign. So near, but that entrance into the kasbah might as well have been on the other side of the world. It was strange living next door to the other side of the world.

The boy ran at Ofir, testing. Ofir lowered his head, leveled his eyes on him. The boy stopped. Now he was only twenty or so yards away. Ofir looked to his commander, but Dan squinted elsewhere.

"*Yalla!*" Ofir waved at the boy to move back. "Go back!"

The boy stood his ground.

"*Yalla*! Back! Back!"

The boy raised his arm and pitched the stone so hard and fast, Ofir barely managed to skip-dance out of the way. The stone whooshed an inch past his ear.

"Fucking asshole." Yaron shook his head.

Gadi, standing on the other side of Ofir, appearing even shorter in a lineup, said, "That was close, Ofi."

Ofir straightened his ammunition belt and took up his position again, widening his stance. The Arab boy laughed at him. Of course. He must have looked hilarious, loaded down with an M-16, a helmet, combat boots, pockets full of grenades, and dancing around a stone.

The frustration Ofir had suppressed all morning rose inside him, a tingling, angry upswell. It surged through every cell in his body and gathered in his head. He didn't want to be here. He didn't want to be here. He didn't want to fucking be here. Fuck this kid! If it weren't for fuckers like him and all this fucking bullshit, he could be in the dining hall right now working on his music, or, better yet, he could be packing for fucking university. Like his doppelgänger. He hated the Arab boy. He hated them for making him hate them—

No. Stop. He took a deep inhale. We are all human. An artist can't lose sight of that. An artist has to hold on to the humanity. We are all pawns of history. Aren't we? Are we? He couldn't think straight.

He pretended to survey the square, looking left and right, as if he could see anything other than the boy. They were two teenagers locked in a game, a game that might be photographed by an ambitious journalist and put on the front page of the *New York Times*. The paper would sit on his doppelgänger's kitchen table, next to a box of Kellogg's Corn Flakes, him looking like the bad guy. It wouldn't say underneath it that the only thing the teenager with the M-16 wanted to be doing at that moment was playing the piano. Ofir tried to remember: Arafat and Rabin shook hands. In front of the world. Peace was here. This was the last bang of thunder before the sky cleared. Six months in Nablus, though. He was so tired.

The boy, not taking his eyes off Ofir, crouched down and picked up another stone. He stepped forward. Ofir gripped his rifle, bent his knees, braced to dance around like a soldier-clown again. Face twisting from the effort, the boy hurled the stone. It flew. Ofir could see it. Then he couldn't. He jerked to the left, the right, and, jumping back, took it right in the chin.

He buckled forward, retching. No pretending it didn't hurt this time. Dark blood dripped onto the dirt, the dirt his stepfather liked to say these two peoples had been fighting over since the Book of Kings. He brought his fingers to his chin. He was going to need stitches.

Gadi laid his hand on his back. "Ofir, you all right?"

Ofir raised his head. The Palestinian boy came into sharp focus as the rest of the world, Gadi's voice, the burning tires, the wailing alarms, even the sun itself, receded. Now there really was only him and the boy. The Palestinian boy was everything. He fucked up his chin, killed his father, made his mom a fat tearful mess. Even put his grandmother in Treblinka. Why? Because the Palestinian boy in his stupid I'M A HOT DOG, MAN! T-shirt became the face of the undying hate for the Jews. Everything that kept him from his fucking piano.

Dan placed his hand on his shoulder. "Go to the police station and sit it out."

Ofir stared at the boy, and the boy stared back with an expression that said, *Your move.*

"*Nu,* Ofir. Go to the station . . ."

Dan's words trailed behind him. He was running. Running like water after a dam breaks. Running like blood through the veins. And it felt so good. Free. It took the boy three or four seconds to realize what was happening and make a break for it. If he was going to catch the boy, it had to be before the kasbah, and that wasn't going to be easy, weighed down by all this gear. The boy stumbled on a rusty exhaust pipe, and Ofir gained a few yards.

He was reaching out for the hot dog T-shirt when the boy ran into the shade of the kasbah. Ofir jogged to a halt and watched the boy beat it down the cobblestoned alleyway. He stood with his heart pounding, not ready to stop running, to calm down, to turn around and go back to the usual hell. He flipped out the rubber cartridges, chambered in a live round, and ran into the kasbah.

The shouts and sirens of the riot were dampened inside. The cool air smelled of cumin and wet stone. Ofir dodged a woman in a black robe and white headscarf. Otherwise the street was deserted. All the men and boys were at the riot, the women and girls indoors. Ofir didn't glance behind to see if he was being followed; he didn't want to know.

The boy was nowhere in sight. He must have taken the first turn off the alleyway. This lane was even narrower, cooler, covered by a blue tarpaulin that glowed with sunlight. The old stone walls and the steel grids lowered over the store entrances were scrawled with red, green, and black graffiti. Ofir glimpsed the boy disappearing to the left and charged, though he no longer knew what he was going to do if he caught up to him.

Shouts and footfalls echoed behind him. Ofir searched for a place to hide. He ran to a wood door that was slightly ajar. He ducked inside, praying no one was in there. He closed the door and, panting, tiptoed backward in the darkness. No windows, no lamps, it was too black to see. The sliver of brightness along the door's edge provided the only light.

He huddled in a corner. He was never going to catch the boy now, and he didn't care. He didn't want to fight him anymore, risk busting up his fingers. The anger was gone. The fear back. He'd never been so scared. The best he could do was wait until the footsteps passed and pray he made it out of the kasbah alive.

When Ofir's eyes adjusted, he found himself surrounded by mirrors—piled against the walls, hanging from the ceiling, skinny mirrors framed by iron vines, square mirrors bordered by tiles, round mirrors in brass fretwork. Ofir was wondering if he could take a small mirror as a memento of having been in this magical forbidden place, having survived it, when his gaze fell on the boy. He too was backed into a dark corner. His widened eyes reflected the door's sliver of light, the door that stood dead center between them.

The boy didn't move. Didn't even blink. Ofir kept equally still. The boy looked like he couldn't believe Ofir was here any more than Ofir could. They surveyed each other—the boy afraid Ofir would shoot, Ofir afraid the boy would scream and in moments he would be surrounded by Arabs.

He tightened his grip on his rifle. Oh, God. What should he do? He could shoot the boy and run for it. What if it were the other way around? What if he, the Jew, were unarmed in the corner and the Arab had the gun? What then? He would shoot him, wouldn't he? Would he? He didn't know. Didn't matter. He didn't want to shoot the boy. How had he ended up here? All he wanted now was to take a small mirror and get the hell out. He wanted to live. He wanted to finish his composition. But who knew what the Palestinian boy wanted?

Eyeing the boy, Ofir slowly rose from his corner. The boy stiffened. Ofir let go of his rifle and raised his palms in the air. The M-16 hung in front of him as they searched each other's eyes. The boy's face relaxed.

Ofir kept one hand in the air and reached his other hand into his pants pocket. The boy, nervous again, jumped to his feet. Ofir pulled out a twenty-shekel bill, and the boy watched with a furrowed brow as Ofir laid the money on the counter and picked up a mirror the size of a dessert plate. Ofir held the mirror up to the boy, as if to ask his permission, and the boy shook his head. With a raised finger, the boy walked around the darkness, inspecting the mirrors. He lifted one from the wall, one that was slightly larger, the size of a dinner plate, bordered by red and blue tiles, and held it out to Ofir. Ofir took it, tucked it under his armored vest, and stuffed his green army shirt back into his pants. He gave the boy one last look before slipping out the shallow door.

He bolted down the street, heart pounding against the mirror. Turning the corner, he found his unit holding back a small crowd.

"What?" Dan screamed at him. "Are you fucked in the head?"

Ofir had never seen his commander so incensed. Gadi's eyes shone with terror as he pointed his M-16 left and right at the shouting throng. Yaron's rifle trembled, and Shai's face was flushed, sweaty, as he squinted down his barrel; if he shot someone, Ofir would have that on his conscience. Dan ordered the soldiers to push through the people, but the angry mob wouldn't break apart for them.

People shouted: "Where's the boy? He's killed the boy!"

Dan's face reddened. "Don't make me shoot! I'm going to shoot! I'm about to shoot!"

The crowd broke open enough to let them through.

The soldiers ran behind Dan down the labyrinthine alleys. They didn't say a word. Just moved. As they bolted down the last passage toward the sunlight of the square and the noise of the riot, Ofir had to fight not to laugh. It was wrong to have endangered his unit, and the Palestinians they might have hurt to rescue him, but he loved the mirror tucked under his vest. He loved that moment he and the boy had in the dark room, as miraculous as that handshake on the White House lawn. He felt ready to inherit the world. The new century. His century, which promised to be so much better than the last one.

The sunburst at the end of the dim alley wasn't just the sunlight of the square, but life, and Ofir was running headlong into it, wishing time would hurry up already, the way his mother claimed only a seventeen-year-old would. It felt like if he just kept on running and breathing in the good feeling, he would soon outrun gravity and take leave of the cobblestones. His chest ached as if his soul were too big for his body, and all at once he knew what was missing from his composition. Not fear. It was this ache. The ache of feeling like you should be taking leave of the cobblestones, but you're not. The ache of gravity.

*A*dam wiped pasta sauce off a plate with a slimy sponge. His hands sweated inside his rubber gloves while the steam from the giant dishwasher made the walls perspire. Finally, the last plates were coming down the conveyer belt. In minutes he would be done with the dinner shift and heading to the old lady's apartment.

Yossi appeared on the other side of the belt, his face and hands red from unloading the scalding clean plates from the opposite end of the dishwasher, where it was even hotter. "You can go now, Adam. You did a great job again today. It's so much easier when I have a good teammate."

Adam peeled off the rubber gloves, flattered, unable to remember the last time someone had commended him on a job well done. He threw his apron into a hamper overflowing with dishrags and proceeded to the hand-washing stations, where he splashed water on his face and considered his reflection. Not great, but not bad, considering he'd only been sober for five days. The kibbutz hairdresser, a woman working out of her house, gave him more of a flattop than a pompadour, but it was still an improvement. The bags under his eyes had mostly faded. He gave himself a fake grin, checking once again that the black cavities only showed when he opened his mouth wide.

In the dusk, Ziva's window glowed on the other side of the square. Hers was the first apartment in the old age building, right after the bomb-shelter door. Passing the *kolbo*, Adam locked eyes with a boy strapped into a large electric wheelchair, his parent probably inside the shop. His arms were bent upward and his hands flopped forward as if his wrists were affixed to invisible puppet strings. Adam managed to give the boy a smile just before the boy's eyes and head rolled back. Adam walked on, feeling guilty that he could.

He knocked on Ziva's door. Inside he heard shuffling, followed by a shout in Hebrew with the cadence of "one minute." The muddy brown boots outside the door were identical to the ones on his feet. Adam had never been a part of anything with a uniform before—no school, sports team, fast-food joint—and it felt weird having the same boots as an old lady.

Ziva opened the door. Her eyes and lips tightened. Adam didn't know what to make of her strange expression. Why didn't she say anything?

"You're Ziva, right? Eyal's mom?"

"Yes . . ." Her voice came out slow, uncertain. Maybe the old woman still wasn't feeling well. Too bad; he couldn't wait any longer.

"Can I come in for a sec? I just wanted to ask you something."

She brought a hand to her forehead, looking dizzy. He hoped she wasn't going to faint again.

He stammered, "Eyal . . . said it would be okay."

"Well, it's not *okay*. I'm working on something."

He could hear the German accent now. He hadn't heard it outside the dining hall. He loved that accent. Some people might think of Nazis when they heard it, but he thought of Zayde and the other old people from their building.

"It'll only take five minutes, tops. I've been waiting three days to talk to you."

She took a deep breath. "And then you promise you'll go away?"

Go away? Eyal wasn't kidding: his mother was rude.

"Yes, ma'am. And then I promise to go away."

Ziva stepped back, allowing him inside. As soon as he was through the door, she turned and left, mumbling something about tea.

Adam edged into the room, hands clasped, feeling ill at ease. The place had little in the way of furnishings beyond the shabby green couch and chair, which were of the uncushiony variety found in waiting rooms. The walls were bare except for the yellowed banner that presumably said the same thing in Hebrew as it did in English: WORKERS OF THE WORLD UNITE! Aside from the well-used writing pad on the coffee table and the two picture frames on the wooden sideboard, the tabletops were clear, void of coasters, remote controls, magazines, bowls of candy.

It was so quiet. No sound of the old lady fussing in the kitchen. He wandered over to the old black-and-white portraits. One showed a smiling woman, thirty years old or so, with a storm of curly dark hair. She wasn't pretty exactly, but she had presence. She stood in short shorts—who knew people wore them so short back then?—meaty legs apart, one hand on one hip, the other grasping the rifle strap crossing her chest. Despite the youth, the smile, the vigor, Adam recognized this was the old lady. It was the eyes that gave it away, peering into the camera with confidence, excitement, like she had just dared the photographer to do something. The very handsome man in the other picture stared off to the side, as was the fashion for por-traits. A thin blond mustache traced a firm mouth, but his clear, light eyes were kind. This handsome man had probably been Ziva's husband, Eyal's father. He'd never seen a picture of Zayde young. Not one. He wondered what he and Dagmar had looked like at this age.

"All right, tell me why you're here."

Adam spun around. The old woman had returned without any tea. Had she gone into the kitchen and then forgotten why?

He gestured toward the armchair. "May I?"

"If you must." The old woman perched on the far end of the couch. "You said this would be quick."

Adam lowered into the chair, crossed his legs, then uncrossed them. This old woman really put him on edge. "I'm trying to find someone who used to live on the kibbutz. Someone named Dagmar."

Her gaze dropped from him to the ground. At first she seemed to be struggling to remember, but then her eyes became glassy. She offered no information. Had she forgotten what he asked her?

Adam tried to sound natural, as if he weren't feeding her the question again. "Do you know what happened to Dagmar? Where I might find her now?"

She raised her head, peered sideways at him. "Why are you asking me?"

"Because I know she lived here in 1947, and you've been on the kibbutz longer than anyone."

"I'm not sure that I . . . remember a Dagmar." She straightened the work shirt over her strange, pregnant-like belly. "May I ask why you're looking for her?"

For the last three days, Adam had been counting on this old woman remembering Dagmar. He should've known when he saw her blank out onstage that she might prove less than helpful. It wasn't fair to be frustrated with her—it wasn't her fault her mind was going—but frustrated he was. And what was he supposed to tell her? That he came all the way to Israel to give this Dagmar, his grandfather's long-lost love, their precious family heirloom? That made him sound like a saint, the very opposite of what he was. He answered through his teeth. "That's between me and Dagmar."

The old woman glared at him, and he regretted snapping at her. He softened his voice. "Dagmar was my grandfather's girlfriend. Or whatever you called girlfriends back then, after the war. Maybe you said 'sweetheart'? You might remember my grandfather, a Holocaust refugee. Franz Rosenberg?"

The old woman, eyes still beholding him with distrust, slowly shook her head.

He hated to push her, but he had hoped her face would light up at his grandfather's name, that she would have stories for him. "I know we're talking fifty years ago, but you must remember him. He was on the kibbutz for three whole years. Until 1947, when he moved to New York."

She said the name slowly, as if trying it on: "Franz Rosenberg."

Was it coming back to her? Adam sat forward. "He probably looked a lot like me. Thick black hair, dark eyes. Taller though. A real dapper guy. Always wearing a fedora, a straw one in summer, felt in the winter. I guess I can't say for sure that he wore one here, but in New York, always. Oh, and he worked in the cotton field. Said I wouldn't believe the way cotton grew on bushes, looking just like it did in the bags at the pharmacy. That always sounded very, I don't know, magical to me, cotton balls growing on a bush."

"He told you about the cotton fields?" Wearing a sad smile, the old woman's eyes gazed over his head, as if at the long-gone field.

"Yeah, a few times. Eyal said the field's gone, that there's a plastics factory there now."

"Your grandfather, does he like it in New York City? I'm only asking because . . . New York City, cotton fields, they're very different."

"He's dead."

"Oh."

"Died a month ago. I guess he liked New York. I mean, I can't picture him living anywhere else. It suited him."

"I'm so sorry . . ." She did look sorry, the corners of her lips pulling down. Sorrier than he would have expected for someone she didn't remember.

Was it just depressing to have everyone your age dying around you? He hoped Dagmar wasn't dead.

"So, Dagmar. That name really doesn't ring a bell?"

She closed her eyes and shook her head. "No. We've never had anyone named Dagmar on this kibbutz."

Adam wanted to ask how she could be so sure when she couldn't remember his grandfather, and he had definitely been here. "Well, if you remember her, please let me know. I work in the dishwash—"

"I won't suddenly remember her. There's nothing wrong with my memory. I have a perfect memory."

Adam insisted as gently as he could. "I don't mean to say there's anything wrong with your memory, but . . . there was a woman named Dagmar on this kibbutz. And she wasn't here temporarily as a Holocaust refugee. She was a kibbutznik. I know this for a fact."

The old woman bared her lower teeth. "Do you know how rude you're being, young man? And how ridiculous? Flying in here from New York City and telling me who was on my kibbutz thirty years before you were even born?"

He had hurt the old woman, and he was sorry, but the joke of *her* calling him rude!

"Thanks for your time." He stood. "And now, as promised, I'll go away."

He headed for the door, thinking there were still the archives. He'd call that Barry guy right now. He probably wasn't back from reserve duty, but he'd leave a message so that when he did come home, no time would be wasted.

The old woman hobbled beside him. "I am sorry, though, to hear about your grandfather. I hope he wasn't in too much pain in the end?"

Oh, he was in pain.

"No, he wasn't. He had a heart attack. Happened"—Adam snapped—"just like that."

Adam opened the door and found night had fallen, the lollipop lamps glowing. He walked away from the old woman's apartment with that pain in his breastbone again. How did disappointment, dread, regret, sadness, feelings that had no physical existence, press against the back of the breastbone like that, as if they were as real as tumors? He took a deep breath, but the air felt low on oxygen.

An eerie green light shone out of the bomb shelter. He slinked up to the open door and peeked down. At the bottom, above the second steel door, the safety lights had green bulbs, making the concrete stairwell glow.

The door opened and out came a young woman, as well as a thumping techno base and a walloping smell, the smell of trouble and intoxication and sweet numbing relief. The smell of the only thing in the world that could— in seconds—get those feelings to back off of his breastbone. The girl waved at Adam and stood on her toes to hook the door open to the wall.

Adam stepped back and raised his head to the sign above the bomb-shelter door. Three black letters on a blond piece of wood. He summoned what little he could remember from his bar mitzvah to sound them out: pei, aleph, bet. Pe . . . ah . . . bbb.

P-U-B.

Two guys in their twenties passed him on their way down the green-glowing hatch. They could. It was no big deal for them. This was probably where Ulya went every night. A bomb shelter—could there be a more perfect place to get wasted? Underground. Windowless. Shielded from the world. But he couldn't go down there, not even just to see the place. Tomorrow he'd have six days clean. Almost a week. How many chips for one week "Clean & Serene" were in his desk drawer back home? Fifteen? More.

The first time he got drunk was Passover 1980, a few months before his bar mitzvah. They didn't normally have a Seder, but Mrs. Silver moaned about being alone again for the holiday, and Zayde invited her to do it with them. Mrs. Silver was one of the few who hadn't fled the city for New Jersey over the last couple of years, who had stayed in the building and, like Zayde, bought her apartment for a song.

"Why couldn't you go to California for the holiday?" Adam had asked as they took their seats at the kitchen table. They almost never had someone in the third chair. Living up to her name, the old woman had silver disks pinned to her ears and silvery roots that betrayed her dyed black bob.

"I don't fly. My son knows that."

Zayde read from the English side of the Haggadah in his German accent: "Blessed are you, Eternal One our God, who gave us life, and kept us strong, and brought us to this time."

Adam sat with his elbows on the table, head propped in his hands. Other kids shared a Seder table with not only a grandfather and some old lady from their building, but a mother and father and sisters and brothers and aunts and uncles and cousins. Why had they no family? And what was going to happen in a few years? The old man wasn't going to live forever.

Zayde lifted his glass. "The first cup."

Adam raised his eyebrows at Zayde, making sure he was really supposed to drink.

"You don't need to drink it all. Drink a quarter."

Bringing the glass to his face, Adam got a waft of his mother, in bed, at night, making him feel guilty, because he never remembered her without also remembering how little he had mourned her. What eight-year-old didn't care that his mother had died? Before he'd even finished the quarter of a glass, a wonderful warmth was blooming in his stomach. It was that immediate.

The Seder continued—breaking the matzah, parsley dipped in metaphorical tears, talk of slavery, freedom. By the time Zayde invited them to drink the fourth glass, Adam couldn't understand why he had been so unhappy with this Seder. He brimmed with love for Zayde, a love he always harbored for him, but was usually buried under the sad promise of him dying some day. He had him now—that's what mattered. He even felt love for shiny Mrs. Silver, and why not? Didn't she always give him her leftover candy the day after Halloween? He loved this small kitchen, the old building, the lively street outside. He'd no idea how much dread he carried in his chest until, for the first time, it was dispersed.

The bomb-shelter bar switched from electronica to Bob Marley. A young couple skipped down the green stairs, the girl smoking, the guy with a finger hooked on her jeans. Adam delved his hand into his pocket, clutched the brooch, and turned away.

There, he thought, crossing the square. That wasn't so hard, was it? Though to be safe, he would avoid the main square at night, when the bar was open.

When he reached the bottom of the steppingstones, Golda charged at him and ran circles around his legs while he marched for his room to grab the phone tokens and directory. He ducked around the tree, all its flowers gone. Instead it bore greenish-brown balls, the size and shape of small lightbulbs.

The blue pay phone, shared by all the volunteers, hung on the wall outside the classroom where the Russians studied Hebrew. The phone token, a silver coin with a hole in the middle, reminded him of the subway tokens from his childhood with the Y of NYC punched out in the middle. He dropped the *asimon* in the phone and dialed Barry's number. Dagmar had to be in those archives.

An answering machine picked up. After a Hebrew message came an English one in a British-y accent. Maybe New Zealand?

"Lucky you! You've reached Barry Sloman. I don't need to tell you what to do after the beep, do I?"

Ulya and Farid lay on a maroon blanket in their usual spot on the hillside, just past the mandarin grove, on the other side of the cattle-wire fence that surrounded the back of the kibbutz. The spring wildflowers covering the hill, which were a splendid blur of blue and yellow during the day, lost their color at night, but were twice as fragrant.

Farid turned onto his side and looked down at her. "Maybe your cousin can lend me the money?"

Ulya, head resting on her purple vinyl purse, blew out smoke. "For what? Your little restaurant dream?" She tossed the cigarette, even though it still had a few hauls left. She refused to suck at butt ends. "Wake up. You're going to work on the kibbutz for the rest of your life."

"Why do you say that? Because I'm Arab?"

Ulya found Palestinians or Israeli Arabs or Palestinian Israelis or whatever the hell she was supposed to call them a lazy bunch, it was true, but that wasn't why she thought Farid was going nowhere. He just didn't have *it*—that hunger, that urgency, that willingness to do whatever it took.

"Yes, because you're a lazy *Aravi*." She said "Arab" in Hebrew to give it extra bite.

When she and Farid first started spending time together, he would get mopey when she teased him, but then he came up with his wishful theory that she was behaving like a love-struck schoolgirl, teasing a boy because she was frightened by her feelings for him. Ha! The truth was she couldn't care less if Farid ever got his restaurant. If he remained a fieldhand for the rest of his life, what did it matter to her? For selfish reasons, she even liked how easygoing he was. When she was with him, it made her feel almost easygoing. For the few hours, when she lay with him on the hillside, the future felt just a little less urgent. So the very reason why she liked being with Farid was exactly why she could never fall in love with him.

Farid picked a twig off the blanket and rolled it between his callused fingers. "Arabs are responsible for some of the world's greatest inventions, you know. We invented the concept of zero."

"Oh, I believe that!" Ulya tried to grab the twig from him. "If there's anything the Arabs could invent, it's nothing."

Farid climbed on top of her and poked her cheek with the twig. She wriggled her head and laughed under the delight of his weight.

"Say you're sorry."

"No."

"Say you're sorry!"

"Get off me!" she hooted.

"Have you ever said sorry in your life?"

Ulya gazed past Farid's shoulder at the stars. Just as she had to admit that Farid had striking eyes, she had to admit this sorry little country had a magnificent night sky. Every time she lay out here, she spied a falling star. In Mazyr, the gray smoke billowing from the orange and white stacks blanketed the sky, tucking its citizenry into the city the way her mother used to tuck her and her brother under the charcoal blanket they would spend the rest of the night fighting over.

She shrugged. "I've never had to."

"I'll make you sorry." Farid nuzzled his face into her neck and growled like a bear, tickling her, making her cringe and laugh. Then he rolled off and lay on his side again, resting his hand on her stomach, his fingertips under the hem of her cropped tank top. "I know why you can't ask your cousin for the money. He doesn't know I exist, does he?"

Of course he didn't know Farid existed. Ulya dreaded anyone finding out about them. She didn't want to see the knowing leers on the other Arab workers. She didn't want her fellow Russians making cracks about her giving it to an Arab fieldhand. And although the kibbutzniks might not say anything to her outright, they would certainly look at her askance, especially the girls in the dairy. She would rather sell *vobla* than have Jews looking down at her. And who was Farid to talk? Had he told his parents about her? No. He claimed he was waiting until she agreed to marry him.

"Forget my cousin. My *fourth* cousin or something like that. He may be a bioengineer, but he doesn't have any money. Doctors don't make real money in Israel. His apartment in Tel Aviv is a dump. And anyway, even if he did have money, he wouldn't give me any. He thinks I'm a user."

"What's a user?"

"He thinks I use people, you know, for my own purposes."

Farid's hand froze on her belly. Was he actually wondering if he were being used? What could she possibly use him for? Other than to pass the time. Or for that feeling of easygoingness. Or for his worship, his love.

He asked, "Do you?"

"My cousin is an idiot. When Israelis say the Russian immigrants have been good for the country—how it's all Russians in the symphony, the research labs, the universities, the Olympic team—they're talking about people like him. He's so grateful to Israel for getting him out of the Soviet Union, even though he can go to America now and make lots of money—people in his field are millionaires there, sometimes billionaires—he stays here and lights Hanukah candles. It makes me sick to see him turning into a big Jew."

Farid pressed on her nose. "The only thing I hear the Israelis say about the Russians is that they're criminals, that they brought the mafia with them. That they're *using* Israel to get to the United States."

"Firstly . . ." Ulya brushed his hand from her face. "I say Russian, because you all say Russian, but I am Belarusian. There is a difference! Secondly, you want me to say it? I'll say it. I'm a user. I'm not ashamed. Life is a game, Farid, that you can either win or lose. And if you don't win, it's not like you get to play again. You've got one chance. One! So if a person gets an opportunity to cheat, under those circumstances, who can blame them? You?"

Ulya did not like the way Farid regarded her with his bottom lip between his teeth. He had told her that he loved her for her fire, that he felt twice as alive when he was around her, but once in a while, like now, she could see her fire made him uneasy. One time, when she said something that disturbed him, he told her that according to the prophet Mohammad "the majority of the dwellers of Hell-fire were women," but he refused to believe women were corrupt or soulless, that he could sense Ulya's good soul beneath her tough talk, just as he could smell her skin under her perfume.

In order to change the subject—or maybe, Ulya thought, because he had wanted to ask all evening—he said, "So who was that person you were eating lunch with today?"

Enjoying his jealousy, Ulya pretended not to remember. She rolled on her side to face him. "Today? Lunch? Who was it?"

"He didn't look familiar. Didn't look Russian. Probably a Jew. Tanned skin. Black hair."

"Oh, him! Adam. Yes, he's a Jew . . . from Manhattan."

"Manhattan?" Farid raised his eyebrows.

Ulya smiled at his worry. She was glad he hadn't seen Adam until today. If he had seen her with him when he first arrived, a week or so ago, he never would've been jealous. He would have known that she couldn't possibly be interested in that bum with the shaggy hair. But Adam didn't look quite as sickly and unkempt now. From the distance Farid had probably seen him, he may have looked quite good.

"Yes, Manhattan. The real one, in New York. I don't know why he's on the kibbutz. His grandfather was here after the war."

"My grandfather was here before the war."

"Oh, God!" Ulya rolled her eyes. "Not this again. I can't hear this anymore. Everything was different before the war. Then Belarus had the Jews. Who knows? Maybe if there'd been no war, if the Germans hadn't destroyed every city in my country, and then the Russians, maybe I wouldn't be running away today."

Farid rested his hand on the dip of her waist. "And did this Jew try to convince you to go to Manhattan with him?"

Ulya wasn't going to tell him that even though Adam had seen her naked, he couldn't be less interested in her, that he talked to her as if she weren't the least bit attractive.

"I don't want to talk about Adam anymore."

"Me neither."

Farid pressed his lips against hers and pulled back his head to take in her face. Ulya met his stare with her blue eyes, which she knew Farid found as beautiful and exotic as she found his gold ones. He brushed a strand of hair from her face.

He said, "Chez Farid is going to be a very special restaurant. I can see the sign, very fancy. It's going to have the best hummus. Everybody—Jews, Arabs, even Russians—are going to come from all over for it."

Ulya stuck out her tongue. "I hate hummus. It tastes like whipped sawdust."

"And, of course, what I'm really hoping, Ulya, what I want more than anything is for you to be with me behind the counter. For it to be *our* restaurant."

Ulya managed to keep a cool face even though his words punched her in the gut and sent her soul, the soul he claimed to sense so well, reeling backward. How had she come to a place in life where such a proposal was possible from such a person? She couldn't imagine a worse fate than the one she'd just been offered. For a second she missed Mazyr and the smokestacks.

"That's sweet," she said, as if he couldn't possibly be serious.

But he either didn't hear the sarcasm or chose to ignore it. "I can't help it, Ulya. You're as important to the dream as the fancy sign and the hummus. I'm not even sure if I would want the restaurant without you."

As important as the hummus? If she weren't so horrified, she would laugh. And did he think it was cute that he wouldn't want the restaurant if it weren't for her? That's why he was never going to have one. He didn't want it enough. Farid didn't want anything enough. She couldn't even be sure he wanted her badly enough. Maybe she had come to him too easily. She rolled onto her back. A stone pressed into her shoulder blade, and she writhed to the side, away from Farid.

"I'm going to New York, Farid. Manhattan. I've told you that a hundred times. It's like you're deaf."

Farid shifted over to be near her again. "Do you know how many times you've said you never want to see me again, but then, the very next night, come crawling through that barbed wire?"

Ulya's face burned. The stars twinkled down at her, mockingly. She debated telling him, once and for all, that she never wanted to see him again. She rolled so that she was facing away from him. She really should get up. Go. Go talk to the American. Make herself see something in him, make him see something in her. Anything but keep wasting time here.

Farid laid his hand on her waist, tentatively this time. "Okay. I believe you. You're going to New York. But don't you think you're going to miss me? At least a little?"

Ulya's eyes roamed over the collapsed cattle wire fence and the fallen mandarins rotting on the ground and marveled that Farid could think for even a second that she would miss him amid the dazzling store windows and honking yellow taxis and elevators to the sixtieth floor and cocktails the color of gemstones and handsome young businessmen in Italian suits with platinum tie clips. Did he really think she was going to miss his farmer's hands with those flat fingernails packed with dirt when one of those suited men had his hands on her waist? She may have come to him easily while she was trapped on the kibbutz, but when she's in Manhattan she'll never think about this barbaric place and its lovelorn Arab. She probably won't even remember his name.

She sat up and reached for the second bottle of metallic cabernet. As she twisted out the cork, she noticed him watching her, head propped on his elbow, his glossy eyes like gold coins lost at the bottom of a lake.

She laid a hand against his cheek and covered his face in light kisses. Farid closed his eyes, and she kissed each lid. Why rub in how little she was going to miss him?

*A*dam walked down the hallway, looking for the archives office. Eyal's office door was open, revealing the secretary hunched over his desk, but everyone else had gone home early, as was the custom on Fridays, which sounded like a great custom to Adam until he found out Israel had a six-day workweek with only Saturdays off. Luckily, Barry, who had returned from reserve duty the evening before, wasn't making him wait until after Shabbat to go through the archives. He agreed to meet him the following day, as soon as Adam was finished with his dishwashing.

Adam knocked on the open door, and a stout man rose from behind a desk, extending his hand. "Shabbat shalom! You must be Adam."

Adam had expected a guy in his thirties, old enough to be in charge of the archives, young enough to be a soldier. How could this graying man with reading glasses tucked into the collar of his work shirt just have returned from reserve duty? They shook hands.

"Sorry about leaving you so many messages," said Adam.

Everything about Barry's face sloped down, his nose, the outer corners of his eyes, and yet he had a cheerful aura, a sense of humor under his clipped accent. "That's quite all right. It was nice to come home and have so many messages not from my mother. Last time, she forgot I was doing *miluim* and kept calling long-distance from Jo'burg asking why I wasn't calling her back."

"How often do you do reserve duty?"

"Every three years or so. This was probably my last. Funny, for years I hated going, and now . . ." He smiled, shrugged. "Well, I suppose we all get too old for something. So you're looking for a woman named Dagmar, eh? Who lived here in, what was it? Forty-seven? Dagmar, sounds Swedish. Or maybe German?"

Disappointed that yet another person didn't remember Dagmar, Adam said, "Not sure," before recalling the *liebster Liebling* and all the German in the goodbye note. "Sorry. Definitely German. Don't have a last name though."

"Not a problem. The kibbutz was tiny back then. We'll go through the papers of everyone who became a member in the forties."

Barry's sport sandals squeaked on the linoleum as he walked to the front of the room and ran a finger down a dusty cabinet. Tall metal filing cabinets lined every wall, most topped by cardboard filing boxes. Barry pulled out the bottommost drawer and returned with a stack of files. "Do you read Hebrew?"

"I can sound out the letters."

He jotted four letters on a scrap of paper. "That's 'Dagmar.' Look for it here, on the top line of each form."

Barry set half the stack down in front of Adam and took a seat with the other half. Adam dropped into a chair and eagerly searched the papers. Every time the passport-sized black-and-white photo stapled to the forms revealed a young woman, Adam compared the name to Barry's jotting twice, three times if she was pretty.

When Adam reached the last form without success, he looked to Barry, who shook his head. "No luck here either. We can check the files from the thirties, but those people, the pioneers who founded the kibbutz, are legendary. I would have heard of Dagmar if she were among them."

As Barry carried the file back to the cabinet, Adam contemplated Dagmar's name written on the scrap of paper. The four letters, though somewhat familiar from Hebrew school, were foreign enough for it to seem strange that these squiggles—דגמר—could represent a human being. Please, please, he thought, let these squiggles be in this next batch of files.

Barry settled behind his desk with a manila file too thin to need two people to leaf through. Adam, hands clasped on top of the desk, leaned forward while Barry's eyes skimmed the papers. A moment later, he removed his reading glasses and shook his head again.

Adam sat back. "This makes no sense. She was my grandfather's girl-friend when he was here. She was a kibbutznik. I have a letter from her, addressed from the kibbutz."

"I don't know what to tell you. I made aliyah in sixty-seven, after the Six-Day War, so I can personally say there hasn't been a Dagmar since then. And she just isn't in the records from before that."

Adam dropped his head. He had accepted that Dagmar no longer lived here, that it had been naïve of him to think that she did just because she had written she would be here "for the rest of her life." How many people lived the lives they planned for themselves when they were young? Now he had to swallow that she had never lived here. He would have to start looking for her elsewhere. But where?

Barry tapped the desk. "I have an idea. If you're sure she was a kib-butznik, you could write the United Kibbutz Movement. One letter, and you could find out if she's living on any of the three hundred kibbutzim in the country. Unless you think she might be religious. Religious kibbutzim are under a different umbrella."

In the note she had scoffed at the world to come, and he couldn't imagine his grandfather with an orthodox woman. He used to get a chuckle out of the wigged women fitwalking over the Williamsburg Bridge in their long skirts and opaque nylons. "No, she wasn't religious . . . Can we first look up my zayde's file? Franz Rosenberg?"

"Certainly. The DPs must be somewhere."

While Barry walked around the room, inspecting the file drawers, Adam closed his eyes and tried to stay calm.

"That him?"

Adam opened his eyes. Stapled to the form Barry held out to him was the oldest photo he'd ever seen of Zayde. By far. Any picture from before the war had been lost. The oldest pictures he'd seen were the faded Pola-roids from the late sixties, showing a man younger than the one Adam would come to love, but well into old age, his thick hair a gunmetal gray, his tall, thin body decked in fashions—high-waisted pants, fat ties—so out of step with his teenage daughter's mod minidress. But it wasn't only the youth that made this photo unique. He'd never seen Zayde so frail, even in old age. The hollows in his cheeks could hold water, as could the sockets housing his shiny black eyes. His hair grew in patches. Though Adam had long known his grandfather was a Holocaust survivor, he'd somehow never pictured what he must have looked like in the aftermath of those years. It occurred to him—he felt like an asshole making the comparison, but there it was—that he and Zayde had both arrived at this kibbutz frail, alone, with nothing but the brooch and a resolve to start over.

Barry pulled up a chair and began to translate. "It says he arrived February 17, 1945, and left . . . that's interesting. He never officially checked out. It says he—*ne'elam*. Disappeared. That he was last seen on the morning of November 30, 1947."

The date from the goodbye letter. So Dagmar knew he was leaving, but not the kibbutz.

"I wonder why he didn't check out."

Barry looked from the photo to Adam. "You know, you're the spitting image of him."

Barry left to xerox the picture for him and grab the address for the United Kibbutz Movement. After seeing that picture of his young, feeble grandfather, Adam felt closer to the old man, something he hadn't thought possible. So even though he was frustrated Dagmar wasn't in the archives, he also felt a tinge of excitement—he was on their trail: not only Dagmar's, but his grandfather's. He was getting a story about him after all. Why had he disappeared? And on the same day as Dagmar's note? In the note, she apologized for the night before. What could she have done?

Barry handed Adam some papers. "I also got you the address for the *Sochnut*, the Jewish Agency. They have immigration files on everyone who's made aliyah since 1930 or so. Between the *Sochnut* and the United Kibbutz Movement, you should get a good lead."

Adam headed for the general store to buy stationery and stamps, the papers folded in his back pocket. Outside, spring was putting on a show, the May sunlight compelling the square's bricks to sparkle, the same twinkling found on Manhattan's sidewalks on bright days. The leaves rustling in the trees flashed white, and the flowers in the cement planters bloomed a popping pink. The air smelled of fresh soil. Had it been this kind of ridiculously pretty day on the kibbutz when his grandfather first fell in love?

It was because of the brooch that Adam knew his grandfather had never loved his grandmother. One day when Zayde was cleaning it at the kitchen table—the second and only other time he witnessed his grandfather with the brooch—Adam leaned on a chair back and asked whether Bobbe had worn the brooch a lot. He wanted to sit down at the table with Zayde, but couldn't. Almost seventeen and home after his second stint at Lodmoor and third school suspension, he was trying hard to act normal, get things back to the way they were, but the old man wasn't softening as quickly this time. Without looking at him, Zayde dipped a Q-tip into a jar of jewelry cleaner and said he never gave the brooch to Bobbe, he had hoped that one day he would want to, but it didn't work out that way.

Adam gripped the back of the chair. He hadn't listened to the last story about the brooch, and this time he was going to fucking listen. "What do you mean it didn't work out that way?"

Still not looking at him, Zayde dabbed the brooch's tiny gold flowers. "Love isn't what brought me and your bobbe together. We were school-mates as little children. Not friends. We had some classes together. When I got to New York, she married me so I could stay here."

"You never loved Bobbe?"

"I loved her, the way you can't help but love someone in your family, the way you might love a sister you don't get along with . . . Your grandmother wasn't a bad person, Adam, but as the years wore on, we grew apart, not closer. She didn't like when I played my records. She never wanted to take walks, go to the movies. I had a hard time with her sleeping all day. All day, she slept. Never cleaned, never cooked. After a long day at Leo's, I had to come home and make dinner. She was a depressed woman, your bobbe. She had more than enough reason, but it was very hard for me the way . . . she slept."

Adam found it extremely romantic that after losing Dagmar, his grand-father had never fallen in love again. Adam had already been in love more times than he knew: Clara, the toothy registrar at Baruch, who'd sneaked him into the system after he failed to register on time; Suzie, the sullen Korean girl at the corner bodega, forced to work after school by her family; Stephanie, from that second time in juvie rehab, LOVE razored onto her arm, the embossed scar so poignant; and, of course, Monica Rivera of the pink velour track pants, the first girl he ever loved and hurt. Did having loved so many girls make each of these experiences something less than love? When he was with them, nobody else existed; and when it was over, usually after the girl tired of his bullshit, he was always shattered, convinced that he would never get over her. But then he would meet someone new. He didn't see how it was possible not to fall in love again. If you were paying attention to people. People were so heartbreaking, beautiful. Other people, anyway.

Bells tinkled as Adam entered the *kolbo*. Kibbutzniks filed in and out, hurrying to make purchases before the store closed for Shabbat. One-tenth the size of Duane Reade and not half as brightly lit, the store's shelves were sparsely packed with shampoos, cleaning products, and school supplies. Adam approached the cashier, a pudgy-faced woman with ratty, dyed blonde hair, and asked where he could find envelopes and stamps.

"How many do you need?"

"Two, I guess."

She laid two blue airmail letters on the counter. "They don't need stamps."

Adam pulled out his monopoly money, and she waved. "We give volunteers airmail for free. Just remember to tell your family how nice we are."

"I will." People always assumed you had a family. "I keep telling my mom not to worry about me."

"Worry—that's what moms do."

As Adam turned from the counter, he met eyes with Ziva, who stood before a wall of over-the-counter medicines. She quickly turned.

"Hey." He walked over. "I've got a picture of my grandfather, from back in the day. Maybe it'll jog your memory."

The old woman had taken down a bottle of calcium and was absorbed in its packaging. Adam pulled the papers out of his back pocket.

"Will you look at it?"

"Right now?"

"I wish it were clearer." He held it out. "It's a xerox of the photo in the archives."

The old woman pulled her eyes from the bottle and, barely turning her head, peered down at the picture. Adam, watching her face, thought he saw a spark of recognition in her eyes, but she offered nothing.

"Does he look familiar?"

"Hm . . . a little, perhaps, but . . . most of the survivors weren't here for very long."

"He was here for three whole years."

She went back to the bottle, turned it in her hands. "Three years might seem like a long time at your age . . ."

Ziva stopped talking when another shopper squeezed by them. Adam had noticed kibbutzniks acted like everyone was a potential eavesdropper and every conversation fodder for gossip. He pushed the photocopy at her. "I'd love to hear anything you can remember about him. Even if it's just something small, silly."

The old woman considered the small, fuzzy, black-and-white square—his hollow-cheeked grandfather.

"The hat. You were right about the hat. A brown fedora."

Excited, Adam pressed, "And what about a girlfriend? Do you remember him having a girlfriend?"

"No." She replaced the bottle on the shelf, turned from the vitamins. "All I remember is the hat."

"That's it—a hat?"

"I'm not even sure I remember that. You mentioned it first."

Ziva headed deeper down the aisle, away from Adam. He trailed her. "He disappeared on November 30, 1947. He didn't check out. Do you have any idea why he'd run away like that?"

The old woman stopped, turned her head to the side, giving Adam her profile. "How would I know?"

Adam returned the photo to his back pocket and headed for the door with the weird sensation that the old woman knew more than she was letting on. Maybe it was in his head.

He heard: "November 30, 1947 . . ."

He turned around. The old woman stood, clasping a shampoo bottle with both hands.

". . . is the day after the UN voted to partition Palestine."

"What? The UN?"

"Yes. Don't you know any history? It's the day after they voted to divide the land into two states—one Jewish, one Arab."

"Oh. And you think that could have something to do with my grandfather's disappearance?"

"I just thought you should know the date. That was a very important day."

Adam nodded, not knowing what to make of this information, and left the store. Why would a UN vote make his grandfather flee? Zayde was the least political person he knew. He didn't even vote for mayor.

And then, as if the spring day weren't already too much, as Adam was crossing the square, he spotted a rainbow in the middle of the green lawn, glowing in the sprinklers. A fat rainbow with a spectrum so bold and full, each color boasted three distinct bands. Adam felt a powerful urge to elbow someone and say, *Hey, look at that!* What if he never again had someone to elbow and say *Hey, look at that!* to? Maybe there were Tibetan monks out there who could enjoy a rainbow alone, but for him, if he had no one to say *Hey, look at that!* to, or *How delicious is this?* or *Aren't we having fun?* then it was all unbearable. He'd rather not notice the rainbow.

He lowered his head and hurried to his room to write the letters.

*C*laudette heard fumbling at the door and drew the wool blanket over her head so she wouldn't have to face her roommate. Ulya stumbled into the room and flipped on the light. Had she forgotten about her again? Claudette watched through the blanket's gray weave as Ulya drunkenly kicked off her high heels and tossed her purse at her bed. It missed and landed on the floor, coins jangling across the room. Swaying toward the purse, she stopped when she noticed the lump Claudette made under the woolen blanket. "Oops, sorry!" she snorted, returning to switch off the light.

Ulya made use of the bathroom without bothering to close the door. After a long urination, she blew a fart, laughed, and said again, "Oops, sorry." When she didn't come out after flushing, Claudette knew she would be in there a while, studying her reflection in the mirror. Claudette hoped that before Ulya came back into the room she would have figured out what she had been trying to figure out all night: Did she or didn't she molest a little girl today in the cafeteria at lunch?

Claudette closed her eyes, tried yet again to revisit the incident second by second. First she took a green tray from the steel trolley. Then a fork, a knife. A napkin from the dispenser. Had she already seen the girl with the wavy brown hair at this point? Maybe out of the corner of her eye? Maybe subconsciously? Did she hurry into the hot food line to make sure she would be behind the girl? She didn't remember walking faster than normal, but she couldn't be sure.

The skinny girl wore a heather gray muscle shirt and white shorts, even though it wasn't that warm. She looked eleven, maybe twelve. Buds for breasts. She was scooping mashed potatoes onto her plate when Claudette reached for the brussels sprouts ladle, and their arms brushed. Having left her brown cardigan on her chair at her table, Claudette wore only a T-shirt, so their skin touched, the soft skin of the girl's upper arm grazing the soft skin of her upper arm. Had she done that on purpose? And if she had, could the girl have sensed it? And if the girl sensed it, could this have traumatized her? Defiled her? In some unforeseeable way, ruined her life?

Claudette squeezed her eyes and rewound to just before she reached for the brussels sprouts. Did she have to reach for them right then? Could she have waited until there was no chance of touching the girl? Why didn't she go for the boiled carrots first? They were closer. What was going through her head? If only she could obtain a recording of what was going through her head! Then she could know for sure if she was a lesbian. A pedophile.

Ulya emerged from the bathroom and slumped on her bed, arms hanging between her thighs. Claudette observed her from under the blanket. Through the gray wool, which made it look like the crimson-headed girl were sitting in a fog, Claudette could smell the wine on Ulya's breath. The smell of Holy Communion.

Ulya leaned forward. "Hey? Are you asleep?"

Claudette stayed as still as possible. Why was she talking to her now? She never had before.

Ulya burrowed her fingers into her hair, massaged her head. "I can't even remember your name. Clara? Klavidya?" Did she know she was awake, or was she too drunk to care? Maybe she wouldn't have cared even if she were sober. "Chlamydia?" Ulya cracked up. "No? Cllll. . . audia?"

Claudette stuck her head out of the blanket. "Claudette."

"Right! Claudette!" Ulya, still dressed, lay down on her side. "Did I wake you?"

She shook her head.

"I used to have trouble sleeping." Ulya tucked her hands under her head. "After Chernobyl, I had nightmares. Terrible ones. Ah, but you probably don't even know what Chernobyl is. I was talking to Adam yesterday, Adam of Manhattan, and he didn't know. Said it sounded familiar."

Claudette didn't remember much about Chernobyl, only Sister Marie Amable, one of the oldest nuns at the orphanage, holding up *La Presse,* the large photo on its front page displaying an abandoned teddy bear on the asphalt in front of an empty Ferris wheel. Peering at Claudette and the other girls through her tortoiseshell glasses, the hoary sister said, too deaf to hear how loudly, *This is what happens to godless nations.*

Claudette pulled the blanket up to her chin. "I remember a picture of an abandoned amusement park."

Ulya rolled onto her back and gazed up at the ceiling, hands clasped over her stomach. "But don't pity Ulya. No, now I sleep like a dog in the sun. And for the rest of my life, free birth control. My uterus got dried up, like a potato in the microwave. But I don't care. I didn't want to have crying babies anyway."

Claudette didn't pity Ulya. She wished she could, but she never had space left in her head to feel pity. Now, having thought of Sister Marie Amable, all she could hear was the nun's booming voice. It echoed in her skull as it did in that office the morning Claudette finally mustered the courage to ask about her mother. *Recalcitrant girl.* The nun read too loudly from a brown folder. *Impossible to reform. Weak in the face of vice.* It wasn't what Claudette, thirteen at the time, had hoped to hear about her mother, though she shouldn't have expected much from a *fille-mère.* And then, pulling Claudette's folder closer to her eyes and lifting her steel-framed glasses, she said, "Oh. Oh no." What she read next, Claudette would not let herself hear again. She shook her head—in that office, and thousands of times since, including now on her pillow in the room on the kibbutz. Claudette did such a good job not hearing this part, it was almost as if she didn't know, except the feeling of knowing remained. She felt like a vile creation.

Ulya fluffed up the pillow under her head. "I guess I can't be angry with Adam. If I were American, I wouldn't care about Chernobyl either." She yawned. "It's not like I care about what's happening in Rwanda right now, the Hutus mass murdering the Tutus. Or maybe it's the other way around . . ."

Claudette whispered, "I don't know anything about Rwanda either."

Her confession landed on deaf ears. Ulya's eyes were shut, mouth slack. How could a person fall asleep that fast? One moment the girl was talking about nuclear fallout and genocide, the next she was sleeping. How would the sisters have explained that? They claimed only the clean of conscience fell asleep as soon as their heads hit the pillows.

Claudette reached for her rosary. Since she brushed the little girl's arm at noon, she would say twelve Rosaries. The clock showed 3:21 a.m. She wouldn't be going to sleep tonight. Working through the decades, she was bound to brush her finger against the blanket or touch a bead in a different way, necessitating an additional twelve Rosaries while brushing the blanket with her finger and another twelve touching the bead in that different way. Before long, in order to be sure she wasn't cheating, she would have to do twelve times twelve Rosaries.

Claudette made the sign of the cross. *Au nom du Père et du Fils et du Saint-Esprit. Amen.*

She didn't want to be doing this. It wouldn't bring her peace. As soon as she penanced this Bad Feeling about the girl's arm, another Bad Feeling would arise and need to be purged. Trying to rid the Bad Feeling was like walking toward the horizon; no matter how far or fast she walked, the horizon remained the same distance away.

Pray for us sinners, now and at the hour of our death.

The "obsessive thoughts" and "compulsive rituals," as Dr. Gadeau called them, began before Claudette could remember. At first, satisfying the Bad Feeling, the name she gave it as a child, was easy. At five years old all she had to do was eat her peanuts in even numbers or not step on the lines in the convent's speckled-tile floor. But as the years wore on, it took more and more to appease the Bad Feeling, and by her teens, it took every waking minute, and still it wasn't enough. Claudette suffered through the days, one after another. She had planned on suffering through them until God called her from this life, but then Sister Marie Angélique came halfway down the stairs and said someone was waiting for her in the foyer.

Mid-November, the Monday after the thirty-third Sunday, well into winter, Claudette worked alone in the basement's laundry, folding undershirts. "Are you sure they're here to see me?"

"Yes." Sister Marie Angélique smiled over the banister. The sixty-something nun smiled no matter what she was saying or to whom. Her cheeks possessed such perfect pink circles it was whispered the sister wore blush.

"Is it Dr. Gadeau?"

"*Non.* It's a young woman. *De l'extérieur.*"

The outside? Other than the Chinese who dropped off washing at the back service door, she never spoke to anyone from the outside. Claudette followed Sister Marie Angélique up the stairs, pausing when the sister did to catch her breath. All the nuns were old. When she was a child, the nuns came in all ages, but over the decades the old ones died, the middle-aged ones became old, and no young women came to replace them. The youngest sister in the convent was fifty-nine.

Sister Marie Angélique bid Claudette good luck, leaving her to walk down the long corridor to the foyer alone. Portraits of the mother superiors dating back to the order's founding in 1824 lined the wall, oil paintings giving way to black-and-white photos. Only the current mother superior stared out from a colored photograph, which still failed to capture the blueness of her eyes.

In the foyer, deaf Sister Marie Amable stood with a woman in an orange beret, a striking orange only someone *de l'extérieur* would wear. Claudette drew nearer, trying to look natural while making sure not to step on the lines between the tiles. Sister Marie Amable watched through her black bifocals, hands folded in front of her cardigan. The mysterious woman gave a big smile, and Claudette halted. She knew that smile. It was the one she used to see when she was a little girl playing with her reflection in the mirror. Claudette looked to Sister Marie Amable and back at the woman in the orange beret. Was this her mother?

The stranger in the parka opened her hands at her sides in a gesture that conveyed uncertainty about how exactly to do this. "I'm Louise!" she said. "Your sister!"

Of course, this woman was far too young to be her mother. Younger than herself by quite a few years.

"Don't act like you don't know how to speak, Claudette," said Sister Marie Amable. "Come closer. *Dis bonjour.*"

Claudette slunk forward, more careful than ever not to step on a line.

The young woman spoke uneasily. "I would have contacted you sooner. Much sooner. I actually found your record seven years ago, but it said . . . it said . . . I'm sorry, I'm being awkward. It said that you were certified insane in 1963, so *bien sûr* I thought it couldn't be you. You were only one year old in sixty-three. How could a one-year-old baby be certified insane? But when I had no success anywhere else, I went back to the file. And, well, here we are."

"Better now than not at all, *n'est-ce pas?*" said Sister Marie Amable.

Louise turned to the nun. "It doesn't make sense, though, does it? Certifying a one-year-old baby?"

The old nun lowered her eyes and said, for once not too loudly, "I am not a doctor."

After Louise assured Sister Marie Amable that she would bring Claudette back in time for dinner, they left the convent to find a café. The bitter wind prevented them from speaking as they scurried down avenue de la Miséricorde, holding their scarves in front of their faces. Louise stopped in front of a café Claudette had never visited despite having lived down the block her whole life. "This place looks nice enough."

Inside was all wood and warmth, much warmer than the orphanage, especially the basement laundry when the dryers were off. Louise peeled off her beret and ruffled her brown pixie hair. The girl behind the counter asked what she could get them, and Claudette, who had no money, averted her eyes. Louise ordered two cafés au lait and two mille-feuilles.

Seated at a booth by the window, Louise emptied a packet of sugar into her coffee and stirred in silence. Then she laughed as if someone had told a joke, apologized for being awkward again, and explained that their mother had died seven years ago of breast cancer, and on her deathbed she had spoken for the first time of the baby she had been forced to give up when she was fourteen.

Forced. Claudette latched onto the word.

"I'm sorry you never met her. She was a fun woman. Always singing songs she made up as she went along. She could rhyme any word in a heartbeat. Until she spoke about you I'd never heard of these orphanages where unwed mothers delivered their babies in secret. The church claims they were doing these women a favor, so nobody would know about their 'sin.' Otherwise, they say, these women's lives—our mother's life—would have been ruined. I don't know, maybe that's true." Louise clutched her scarf in front of her neck. "But you can imagine my surprise to find you still living in the orphanage."

Claudette needed to stroke the handle on her coffee cup twenty more times before taking a sip. "I'm not the only one. Children born to unwed mothers . . . aren't well."

"Yes, I saw in the records: you all have some kind of . . . mental illness. It's like all the children who grew up in this place developed problems."

"We didn't grow up to have them." Claudette looked from her sister back to the coffee mug. "Bastards are born sick."

Louise leaned back, mouth agape. Claudette considered her mille-feuille, so pretty with its hard sheet of black-and-white icing and the layers of yellow custard, but she couldn't eat. Louise hadn't touched hers either.

Louise sat forward again, leaned on the table. "We don't have the same father, Claudette. I tried to get my mother to tell me who your father was, but she wouldn't."

Claudette turned in shame from her half sister's eyes. Beyond the window, across the street, people walked down a snowy allée. The sky shared the same pale glare as the snow-packed sidewalks, and against all that white, the black branches of the trees looked like cracks in a pane of glass.

As it was in the beginning, is now, and will be forever. Amen.

6:10 a.m., and she was six Rosaries short of a hundred and twenty. In forty minutes the alarm clock would sound. How was she going to function on so little sleep? Even when she was well rested, Ziva yelled at her for being moony and inefficient. Ulya still lay on her back with her hands clasped on her stomach. She hadn't budged all night.

A month after meeting Louise, Claudette told Dr. Gadeau she was thinking of moving in with her sister. He didn't think that was a good idea. She'd only been on Prozac for a month. Prozac was an exciting new drug, but he didn't want her to have unrealistic expectations: OCD couldn't be cured, especially extreme cases like hers. The best they could hope to do was alleviate some of her symptoms. He even gave a number: forty percent. When Claudette said she didn't want to be ungrateful, but that left sixty percent of her symptoms, and she might live another fifty years, and she didn't see how she could cope with fifty more years of this, he assured her that clinical depression was a normal secondary diagnosis for people with OCD. She shouldn't feel bad about feeling bad.

Claudette's eyes, burning from exhaustion, stared into the first light starbursting through a broken slat in the blinds. This might as well be Hell. It was a profane thought—the mortal sin of Despair—but she couldn't imagine how Hell could be much worse. This past night she had been a lesbian and a pedophile; the night before, she wanted to have sex with a dog; the night before that, she lay awake scared that she hadn't washed her hands between going to the toilet and cutting vegetables in the kitchen with Ziva, and many people on the kibbutz were going to get sick and die because of her. What would it be tonight?

Yes, she was sure of it: better a lake of fire.

*A*dam followed the country road with Golda running ahead to sniff the trees and willow herbs. This was his first time leaving the kibbutz since walking up this road three weeks earlier. While waiting to hear back from those organizations, he figured he could use his day off to check if Dagmar lived on one of the two other kibbutzim on the hill. The more he thought about it, the more sense it made: maybe Dagmar and his grandfather, being in love, had visited each other's kibbutz every day. That would explain why she could refer to herself as a kibbutznik even though she wasn't a member of Sadot Hadar, and how she might still be reminded of her old lover wherever she turned.

The first kibbutz Adam called upon, halfway down the hill, sent him to their main office, where an old lady, hair yellowed from decades of smoking, rasped, "No, we've never had a Dagmar here." After she double-checked their files, she offered him a taste of chocolate made in their factory. Adam hoped he'd get a different answer at the second kibbutz, nestled at the bottom of the hill, not far from the bus stop at the road's end, where he recalled disembarking at a concrete shelter on the edge of a flaxen field.

The thirty-something woman in the guardhouse put down the phone when Adam approached her window. Hair tucked inside a light blue snood, she peered through what seemed to be a permanent squint.

"I'm looking for someone named Dagmar who might live on this kibbutz. Or used to live here."

She shook her head, lips curved down. "But you can check with Avi at the main office."

Adam glanced into the kibbutz: two men with yarmulkes stood talking, white strings dangling over their beige cargos, not over black pants like with the jeweler, but still, he didn't want to be around tzitzis. It was a religious kibbutz, and he really didn't want to go in there. And it probably wasn't necessary; he'd already decided Dagmar couldn't be religious. But he had to go in. It would be stupid not to. Maybe fateful.

"Can my dog come?" he asked, worried orthodox people had something weird against dogs. Had he ever seen a black hat walking a dog?

"Of course," the woman said, and directed him and Golda to the main office.

The peacefulness inside was similar to Sadot Hadar; old trees towered over small white bungalows. He passed a basketball court, the *kolbo*, and then something they didn't have on Sadot Hadar. It was an unimpressive synagogue, a boxy building covered in discolored stucco and topped by a large rusty steel menorah. Out of its open doors floated the sound of several men half singing, half mumbling an afternoon prayer.

Adam left Golda outside and stepped into the main office building, where it was cool and quiet. He poked his head in the first open door. "I'm looking for Avi."

"You've found him." A youngish guy with a scraggly black beard and silver-framed glasses put down his pen. Adam explained what he was looking for and Avi replied, "No, no one with that name lives here now, but if you follow me, we can check the older archives. Now I'm curious."

Avi touched the mezuzah as he passed through the door, but he didn't kiss his fingers afterward the way Mr. Weisberg had when he passed into the office in the back of the jewelry store. Adam accompanied Avi, who looked religious from the neck up—blue crochet yarmulke, beard—and totally kibbutznik from the shoulders down: threadbare T-shirt, khaki work pants, leather utility sandals. Mr. Weisberg would never have worn sandals. Would never *wear* them. He wasn't dead.

Avi ushered Adam into a room of filing cabinets and pointed at a beige computer monitor, orange Hebrew type glowing on its black screen. "We're slowly transferring the important files onto that computer, but it's taking forever. At the rate we're going we'll be in a perpetual state of data entry." He picked up a floppy disk. "It took six months to put six months of data onto this thing. What year were you looking for again?"

"Forty-seven." Adam didn't feel well. The windows in the room were shallow and high on the wall. He couldn't breathe in this drab office. Why did this guy also have to wear silver-framed glasses? Most of the time, when the jeweler popped into his head, he could push him out, but trapped in here it was impossible.

"Hey, do you mind if I sit outside while you do this? I can trust you to check, right? It's really important that I find her."

"Yeah. No problem. Do you mind if I ask you're relation to this woman?"

He'll look harder, Adam reasoned, if she's family. "She's my aunt. I mean, my great-aunt. She lost touch with the family during the war. And now, well, she's my only living relative."

"Oh. So you know her last name?"

"Um, actually, no. I know that sounds weird, but my grandfather's name was changed when he came to America, and I'm not totally sure what it was before. Oh, and I guess that doesn't even matter because she's an aunt on my grandmother's side, and I don't know what my grandmother's maiden name was. I don't think most people know their grandmother's maiden name, do they?"

Lies always snowballed into stupidity. Why hadn't he just told him that he'd rather not say why he was looking for Dagmar as he had with everyone else?

"Okay," Avi said, sounding suspicious.

Adam sat on a bench in the hallway, where at the far end, Golda peered through the glass doors for him. Was she afraid he wasn't coming back? He closed his eyes. He had never wanted to hurt anyone, physically or mentally, and yet that's all he had done with his life so far. The plan had been to get the brooch back peacefully. He'd figured it all out the same night the medics carried Zayde away. He had sat down at the kitchen table and done the calculations: if the jeweler agreed to keep the brooch until he could buy it back, for, say, fifty percent more than he had paid for it, then he could have the money—thirty thousand dollars—in a year. He still had four grand left from selling the brooch; and he could get the rest if he kept his monthly expenses on food and the apartment under five hundred a month and got a job as a bike messenger, mover, anything that paid a hundred bucks a day, six days a week. It would be hard, but not impossible.

The only potential hitch in the plan was the jeweler. Would he agree to hold it for him? A fifty-percent profit sounded high to Adam, but would the jeweler think so?

That next morning, he was waiting outside Weisberg's Gold and Diamonds when Mr. Weisberg arrived to open the shop. The jeweler bent over to unlock the rolling metal grate, his breath white in the cold morning air as he told Adam to wait a minute. Adam was too warm with drink to feel the cold. He knew he'd have to sober up to hold a job and save all that cash, not to mention the very idea of him drinking after what had happened was horrifying, but how else would he have gotten through that first night? Surrounded by Zayde's records and potted plants and the kitchen table where only that morning the old man had sat in his pajama set spreading marmalade on toast while the brooch was still safe in the shoebox? Adam, watching the jeweler unlock the door, couldn't believe that was only yesterday. Only yesterday that he had followed the sign in the store window: WE BUY GOLD, DIAMONDS, WATCHES, & ESTATE JEWELRY. Mr. Weisberg unlocked the door, hung his matching black wool coat and fedora, and steadied his yarmulke.

"All right, Ben," he said once he was behind the counter. He peered at him over his silver-framed bifocals. "What can I do for you?" When Adam explained that the brooch had belonged to his great-grandmother who died in Buchenwald and that he'd really like the chance to buy it back, the jeweler said his whole extended family had been wiped out in the Shoah, and that if Adam was serious about buying back his family's heirloom, he would hold it for him and sell it at the exact price he paid for it, twenty thousand, no interest. In the meantime, he would like to show the brooch to a jewelry historian because in his fifty-some years in the business, he had never seen anything like it. So, yes, the jeweler agreed to keep it for him, at no profit to boot, something Adam hadn't even thought to ask for. Adam left his shop, saying, "Thank you, Mr. Weisberg. Thank you, thank you."

Avi stood before Adam, shaking his head. "Sorry. I even found a map from 1946 showing who lived in what tent and house, and no Dagmar."

Adam got to his feet. "Thanks."

"Did you want to stay for lunch? You're welcome to have a bite in the dining hall."

"No, no. I have to go."

Adam rushed to get off the religious kibbutz, holding Golda in his arms so she wouldn't slow them down with her incessant sniffing.

"Bye," he said to the woman in the guardhouse, just as he had said "Bye, Mrs. Weisberg!" as he left the jewelry store that third time, that last time, as if nothing had happened.

Adam put Golda down and plodded back up the hill toward Sadot Hadar. Again the little dog ran ahead with her tail up. When he had followed this road from the bus stop, it had been twilight. Now the sun was high, the shadows short, the tall grass where the horses fed washed out by the bright light, like an old photograph. In the distance Mount Carmel loomed behind a haze.

This was the problem: a month after the jeweler agreed to keep the brooch for him, he was still drinking. He just couldn't stand being in the apartment without being drunk, and sometimes even then he couldn't bear it. He blew a lot of money on hotels and often followed people he met in bars back to their places. A couple of times he even slept in Penn Station like a bona fide bum. If it had been warm enough, he would have camped on park benches. The morning he went back to the jeweler for the last time, he had awoken on a mattress on a floor in Inwood.

The dump belonged to some kids he'd met the night before at the Aztec, the dive bar one block down on Essex. How he got to talking with them or how they got from the Lower East Side all the way uptown, he didn't know; all he knew was that the kids came from Wisconsin or some state like that to live out one of those dreams that drew people to his city—stand-up comedy or stockbroking—and that one of the guys had a pistol his dad gave him for his twenty-first birthday. While they were tweaking, the kid had been naïve enough to show the vintage gun to him, a total stranger.

Adam sat up on the mattress and looked at the black pistol still sitting on the coffee table, then at the two noobs sleeping, one on the couch, the other on a second mattress, both too wasted to be disturbed by the sun streaming through the curtainless bay window. Last night he'd squandered a hundred and fifty bucks on beer and his share of the eight ball. Not only hadn't he saved a dime since he spoke with the jeweler, he'd spent half of the four grand. It was a vicious circle: he was never going to save the money for the brooch unless he got his act together, and he was never going to get his act together until he'd done something right with the brooch. And any minute, the chance to get the brooch back might be gone forever. He'd been as naïve as the blond Midwesterner, believing for even a second that the jeweler would keep the brooch for him. For no profit? The guy was in the business of buying and selling estate jewelry. That's what he did. For all he knew, Mr. Weisberg might have sold the brooch already.

Within ten minutes, Adam was straphanging on the A train, crammed among the morning rush-hour passengers, the pistol under his leather jacket, stuffed into the back of his Levi's.

"I didn't expect to see you again so soon," said Mr. Weisberg when Adam came through the store's chiming door. "I've got a lot to tell you. Just let me finish up with these nice people, and we'll talk."

Adam was caught off guard by the young couple browsing wedding bands. He figured at this hour the jeweler would have been alone. He scanned for a camera. There didn't seem to be one, but just in case he backed into a corner. What in the hell could the jeweler have to tell him? That he'd already sold it? If the brooch was gone, he didn't know what he was going to do. He leaned on the mirrored wall and watched the jeweler tell the prospective groom, "That looks perfect on you."

"I don't know." The man considered his hand. "I was looking for some-thing flatter."

"What do you mean? It's flat! You want flatter than that? Let me get a calculator. I'll make you a good deal. And if you both get a ring, I can make you an even better deal. You know . . ." Mr. Weisberg smiled and pointed at the young woman. "She's going to need one too."

Adam grimaced while the yarmulked jeweler punched numbers into a small calculator. No wonder people thought we were money hungry. Who wanted "a deal" on their wedding band? The jeweler didn't have a senti-mental bone in his body. He was a two-bit salesman, and he had been right not to trust him. He better still have that brooch.

Mr. Weisberg turned the calculator around to show the couple the dis-counted price. When the woman said they were going to continue looking elsewhere, the jeweler shrugged and replied okay in a way that suggested they were wasting their time.

When the door closed behind the couple, the jeweler turned to Adam. "The brooch is in my office. We'll talk in back."

Adam exhaled. He still had it. He was both relieved and nervous. The jeweler never would've taken him into the back room if he weren't a Jewish kid whose great-grandmother died in Buchenwald. The jeweler called for someone to watch the front, and an elderly woman, presumably Mrs. Weisberg, shuffled out of the back in a wig too thick and black for her pale shriveled face. She touched the mezuzah, kissed her fingers. Adam smiled at her, and she returned a look that left no room for misunderstanding how unimpressed she was. Adam realized that he hadn't showered or changed his clothes in days.

"Come, come." The jeweler squeezed past his wife, the space behind the counter too narrow and the jeweler's belly too big for them to pass each other comfortably.

Mr. Weisberg also touched the mezuzah as he passed into the back office, which reminded Adam of *Barney Miller*, one of the shows his mother used to watch from her bed: drab green walls, papers piled on a metal desk, a word processor collecting dust on a filing cabinet. The room's only splash of color was a stylized, almost cartoonish painting of Jerusalem in a brass frame.

"Sit down. Sit." The jeweler gestured at the visitor's chair.

Adam took the seat in front of the desk and checked that the back of his leather jacket concealed the gun.

"So, you're here to buy back the brooch?" Mr. Weisberg turned the knob on one of the three safes stacked in the corner.

"Yes." Adam barely got the word out.

"Good, good. I have so much to tell you, Benjamin. It's as I suspected. This isn't any vintage brooch. No, it's even more valuable than I could have imagined. Infinitely."

"Oh, yeah?" Adam shifted in his seat. Heart pounding in his head, he moved his hand back, readying to grab the pistol. "It's worth more than the twenty grand?"

The jeweler carried the faded blue felt bag, the one that had been in Zayde's shoebox, to his desk. He pulled out his chair, sat down. "Don't worry, I'll sell it back to you for the twenty, like I promised. I'm a man of my word. But before I do, Benjamin, I'm hoping to convince you of something. I have some very important things to tell you about this brooch."

Adam's hand remained tense, trembling, by his hip.

The jeweler pushed up his glasses. "Listen, Benjamin. I'll tell you up front what I'm hoping. I'm hoping after I tell you everything I know about this brooch, why it's so special, you and your family will be convinced that the right thing to do would be to loan it to a museum, preferably the

Jewish Museum, but maybe the Met. That's what I was going to do if you never came back for it. To be frank, I doubted you would. Tell me, Benjamin, do you have any idea how your family came to have this brooch?"

The sea of rubble. A city turned to rubble? A house?

"No." Adam shook his head. Realizing he wasn't going to make a move until he'd heard about the brooch, he relaxed his hand, brought it back in front of him. "Why? What's the big deal?"

"What's the big deal?" Mr. Weisberg emptied the felt bag onto a black velvet display box and picked up the brooch. Head tilted back, a small appreciative smile on his face, he peered at it through the bottom half of his lenses. "This brooch was made in the thirteen hundreds, that's the big deal. It's almost seven hundred years old!"

Adam couldn't wrap his mind around that much time. Their apartment building was a hundred and twenty years old, and the city had been poised to designate it a historical landmark before the Mexican restaurant downstairs knocked out the old storefront to put up a flat glass window.

"How do you know it's that old?"

"How do I know? Well, I had my suspicions straightaway. I've been in the jewelry business since I was thirteen years old, Benjamin, and my family, the Weisbergs, have been jewelers, maybe not as long as some, but since at least 1656, when the Jews were kicked out of Lithuania, so I know a little bit about jewelry. As soon as you brought this in I knew we were dealing with something from the Middle Ages. But just to be sure I took it to the jewelry historian at the Cloisters, and oh, you should have seen his face! I thought he wasn't going to give it back! I'm sure you know, Benjamin, that during the Middle Ages, Jews couldn't own property, that we were banned from all the professions except moneylending and gem cutting, but either way, we dealt with jewels, right? I'm sure you know all that. But what you probably don't know is that although the Jews made jewelry, we couldn't wear it. Sumptuary laws forbade us from wearing nice clothes. We couldn't look better than the goyim, right? But this brooch, this magnificent brooch, was made for a Jew. This wasn't the main thing that impressed the historian at the Cloisters, but I . . . I was moved by that. That someone would make something so magnificent that could never be worn in public."

"How do you know it was made for a Jew?"

"Benjamin, did you even look at the brooch?" Mr. Weisberg turned it over in his hands and pointed with his thick pinky finger at an engraving on the back. "Look what's inscribed here: *B'ahava*. At first I thought, well, maybe your grandfather had this inscribed for your grandmother, but the historian ran tests, and it can be dated by the patina and debris deep inside the engraving. It was inscribed seven hundred years ago to a Jew named Anna. 'To my dear Anna, with love.' This Anna, Benjamin, could have been your great-great-great-great-I-don't-know-how-many-greats-grandmother."

If this Anna was his great-great-who-knew-how-many-greats-grandmother, then he hadn't only betrayed his grandfather, but seven hundred years of his ancestors. How many generations was that? Forty? Fifty? Seven hundred years of the brooch getting passed down, all for him to sell it to get some money to pay off a fuckhead named Bones?

The jeweler, having turned the brooch back around, now pointed with his pinky at one of the little jester heads. "I was also moved by these little pomegranates, this nod to the Holy Land. I mean, think about it. The goldsmith who made this brooch, probably in some cold, miserable city in Eastern Europe, most likely had never even seen a pomegranate in real life, and yet there he was, fifteen hundred years after the Jews were expelled from the Holy Land, still putting pomegranates on his brooch, like a little wish. You know, these stylized pomegranates look exactly like the ones on the ancient shekel. Exactly. It's unbelievable."

The jeweler appeared pensive, affected; Adam wished he would just stop already.

"No." The jeweler polished the sapphire with a chamois. "I didn't need some lab results to tell me this brooch was special. You see, this pearl, Benjamin, this was my first clue. The pearls are fastened with a pin through them. That's a medieval technique. And then the gemstones, they're all in their natural shapes. They aren't cut to be symmetrical in size, or faceted to better reflect the light. Nobody would have done that after the seventeenth century. The goldsmith obviously didn't have the know-how, the tools. And this . . . you see the way the stones are held into their beds by a thin string of gold across them? Like little seat belts? I've never actually seen that, only read about it in books. The historian said the quatrefoil style of the brooch was popular in the thirteenth century, but they only know that because of images in manuscripts and tapestries. This brooch, this brooch, he said, is one of only two surviving examples. Two! In the world, Benjamin! I can't tell you how much the Cloisters wanted this brooch. He was willing to pay a lot for it, let me tell you. He said it could be the most prized piece in the treasury."

The office door creaked. Adam hurried to sit up and make sure his jacket still covered the gun. What if he'd lost his chance to be alone with the jeweler? He should have made his move already.

Mr. Weisberg looked toward the door. "What is it, Miri?"

Then again, wouldn't it have seemed suspicious to the wife if he'd gone into the back office with her husband and then come right out again? Adam realized the wife was a real problem. How was he going to stop the jeweler from screaming at her to call the police? He hadn't thought about that. He had expected the jeweler to be alone in the store.

"What's taking so long?" Adam heard her ask.

The jeweler gestured at Adam. "This is Benjamin, the brooch boy."

Adam forced himself to turn around. Mrs. Weisberg stood in the doorway, hand resting on the knob.

"Yes, I guessed as much. You're so excited about the brooch, Avrom, you're not thinking." Mrs. Weisberg dropped her gaze to Adam. "He's been going on and on about this brooch since you sold it to him. You know, it's worth a lot of money. I told him not to give it back to you."

"Please, Miri, don't rush me. If we're busy and you need my help, I'll come out. But otherwise, please, don't rush me. This is really important."

The wife said something in Yiddish, and Mr. Weisberg glanced behind him. When Mrs. Weisberg closed the door behind her, he got up, taking the brooch. He shut the safe he'd left ajar and turned its lock. Adam sucked in air while the jeweler's back was to him. He couldn't make his move right now, not with him having just told his wife he needs time. And what should he do about the wife, right there, outside the door? Could he wait until she went for lunch or something? Should he point the gun at the jeweler and tell him to call her in here? Jesus, did he have it in him to do that?

Back in his seat, the jeweler straightened his vest. "If I were you, Benjamin, I would give the brooch to the Jewish Museum, not the Cloisters. Gems are an extremely important part of our history. We say the world is getting smaller because of television and telephones and all that, but for the Jews the world's been a village for over three thousand years already. When this brooch was made, Benjamin, Jews in India sold gems to Jewish caravans from the Middle East who brought them to Jewish merchants in Venice.

These merchants then sold the gems to Jewish goldsmiths in Antwerp and Lithuania, and they turned the gold and gems into crowns and swords for the princes in England and elsewhere. Jews were constantly being expelled from one country and fleeing into another and then being allowed back into that other country again, so we had the languages and the connections to pull off this international business. Not to mention, Benjamin, and this is important, so pay attention, when you constantly have to get up and go at a moment's notice, jewels can be a good means of preserving wealth. They're easy to carry and have value anywhere. Without gems, you'd have to flee with nothing. There are cynical Jews today, and I am one of them, who think this is still a good idea, even in America. Even in Israel. Who knows what *mishigas* could happen tomorrow? Tomorrow Andy Martin could become president. And Israel, I don't think there's anyone who really believes it can last. Before, Europe held up signs saying GO BACK TO PALESTINE! Now it's GET OUT OF PALESTINE! Israel is just the latest ghetto, and sooner or later they'll liquidate that one too. If there's anything history teaches us, it's that everyone hates the Jews, always have and always will. Remember that, young man, everybody hates you. You must always be ready to run."

Adam, trying not to let fear contort his face, moved his hand back toward the pistol again. "Listen, Mr. Weisberg, I do appreciate the history lesson. I really do. If you knew me, you'd know that I love history, but we should get down to business." He stalled. He couldn't quite do it yet. "So, um, how much did you say the brooch was worth?"

"Worth? You heard my wife. A lot! But I'm a man of my word. How many times do I have to say it? I'll sell it back to you for the twenty."

Adam's hand calcified in a twisted claw at his side. It felt like it wasn't attached to his body, his brain. Until now it had only been about him and his zayde. He hadn't thought about the line of ancestors. He hadn't thought about the jeweler. Not as a person anyway, only as an obstacle. Not only was Mr. Weisberg about to lose a lot of money, but he was going to be made a fool, a fool for trusting him.

"I know. I know you said you would do that, Mr. Weisberg. And . . . and I think that's big of you. I mean it. I just want to know how much it's worth, you know, just because."

Come on, Adam thought, do it. Now. If you don't do it now, you're never going to do it. Come on, grab the gun! Though he still didn't know how he was going to keep the jeweler from calling out to his wife as he left the store. Maybe he could tell him that if he didn't stay quiet, if he heard him crying for help before he was out the door, he'd shoot Mrs. Weisberg. Fuck. That sounded terrible. And what if he said that, that he would fucking shoot Mrs. Weisberg, and the jeweler still didn't stay quiet? He'd go to prison and the brooch would be lost.

"Well, sticking a price tag on a thing like this isn't easy, Benjamin. It has sentimental value, which is difficult to quantify, but not impossible; it had great sentimental value for you, and you were willing to sell it not so long ago for twenty thousand. Then we have the value of its raw materials, which is easy to calculate. How much is a sapphire worth of this size and clarity? After that, there's the workmanship, which is sublime, although one floret is irregular, missing a petal. And lastly, there's the rarity of the piece, which in this case is extraordinary. If I were forced to make an estimate right now, I'd say, oh, three hundred thousand dollars, or thereabout. But it could be worth three million. Of course, you will need—"

Mr. Weisberg's eyes raised to the pistol. Adam was on his feet, holding the gun, shakily, very shakily, pointed at the jeweler's chest. The jeweler remained still, looking up at Adam. "You don't want to do this, Benjamin."

"I don't." Adam's voice shook as much as the pistol. "But I have to. Give me the brooch."

"You don't want to do this. I can tell. You're a good kid at heart. The kind of kid who wants to get his grandmother's brooch back."

Instead of calming him down, the kind words enraged him. He was a good kid at heart! He did hate doing this! He fucking hated it! He extended the gun. "Put the brooch down on the desk, Mr. Weisberg. And your hands in the air."

"Why don't you go home, Benjamin, get some sleep, and then come back, and we'll talk? We can figure something out."

Adam wished the jeweler would take him seriously. It would go a lot quicker if he did. If the old man were being held up by a black kid, he'd be pissing in his wool pants right now. Adam needed him to be pissing in his pants. He needed him to hurry.

"I mean it, Mr. Weisberg. Put the brooch down and your hands up! Or I'm going to have to shoot."

"Come now." Only Mr. Weisberg's mouth moved, the rest of his body frozen, including the hands that held the brooch. "I'll keep it for you as long as you need. I told you that. Didn't I?"

Please please please please please, he couldn't take this, he needed this to be over. "Put down the fucking brooch!"

"Didn't I say that? Didn't I say I'd keep it for you, Benjamin?"

"Now!"

When Mr. Weisberg opened his mouth again without handing over the brooch, Adam swung the pistol. The steel butt smacked the side of the old man's head.

Adam stepped back, clutching at the chest of his T-shirt.

The jeweler leaned on his desk, blinking behind his bifocals, before going down like a trapdoor.

Adam swiveled, pointed the gun at the office door in case the wife heard the thud and came running. He waited. She didn't come. He heard voices in the front shop.

He scrambled around the desk and grabbed the brooch from the floor. He crouched beside the jeweler. His yarmulke had fallen off. Blood seeped into the white hair. Adam whispered, "I'm sorry, Mr. Weisberg. I'm so so sorry. It wasn't even loaded. It wasn't even loaded!"

He headed for the door, afraid he might faint before he got there. He paused before opening it, trying to calm his breath, trying to look normal. The calendar on the back of the door still showed the month of March, a photo of matzah on a pink background. A heart was drawn around March 21st, Yiddish scribbled inside it. Adam stuffed the gun into the back of his jeans. Natural, he had to act natural.

He pushed open the door, saying, "Thanks, Mr. Weisberg! I'll be back."

He walked down the narrow store toward the glass door through which he could see yellow cabs stalled in traffic. Watching the back of Mrs. Weisberg's shiny black wig, he had to use all his willpower not to run. She was showing a businessman a watch. Would it be more or less natural for him to say goodbye to her? He had to think quickly.

"Bye, Mrs. Weisberg!" He glanced back as he pushed open the door. Her small eyes in her white face regarded him, but she said nothing.

As soon as he was on the sunny sidewalk and out of sight of the store, he walked as fast as he could, afraid that breaking into a full-on run would draw suspicion. Maybe plainclothes officers lurked all over the Diamond District. He pushed past suited men and high-heeled businesswomen and dodged Mexican delivery guys carrying half a dozen plastic bags. He shoved against the flow of people pouring out of the Rockefeller Center subway stop. He had the brooch. He had it. Now he'd go home, grab his passport and Dagmar's note, and head straight to the airport.

Adam and Golda reached the gate of Sadot Hadar. Recognizing him, the woman inside the guardhouse waved him in. He reentered the kibbutz, thinking he had to find Dagmar for the jeweler's sake too. He was sure he'd only knocked him out, at most given him a concussion—he hadn't hit him that hard, had he? People didn't die from a minor blow to the head. Still, the jeweler's suffering would be for nothing if he didn't get the brooch into Dagmar's hands. He had to do it for Mr. Weisberg, for Anna and his ancestors, for his grandfather, for himself, and, he was increasingly coming to believe, for the brooch itself. Once he'd done that and was back in New York, working and making money, he'd send the jeweler anonymous envelopes of cash. Yes, that's what he was going to do. He'd send cash until he was all paid up. And even after that.

"We'll start with the pillowcases," Ziva said, pushing a canvas cart loaded with linens toward a folding table.

Today they were working in the laundry house. On one side of the room hummed washing machines and dryers the size of jet engines; on the other side, rows of cubbyholes filled with folded clothes and sheets awaited pickup. The middle of the room, where most of the work got done, was a jumble of blue ironing boards, steamers, wooden folding tables, and carts overflowing with clean laundry to be folded.

Dana, the kibbutz's head laundress, turned the knob on an old radio. A Queen's English filled the room: *Russia qualified for the World Cup and will be competing independently for the first time since the dissolution of the Soviet Union.* Dana smiled at Claudette. "For you, the BBC."

"Never mind the radio." Ziva held up a yellow pillowcase and pointed at a small blue iron-on with the number 37. "You see this number, Claudette? Every towel, every T-shirt, everything has a number and has to be folded so that the number remains visible. I hope you can handle that. Because I've had enough of your staring into space."

Claudette nodded. In the three and a half weeks they'd worked together—picking avocados, chopping vegetables in the kitchen, weeding the sidewalks, feeding the heifers—not one day had passed without Ziva losing patience and upbraiding her. Claudette hoped today would be different. When it came to laundry, she should be able to keep up no matter what was racking her mind.

Yesterday, South Africa held its first multiracial election, marking the final end of apartheid . . .

For the last twenty-four hours Claudette's mind had been on her bathroom sink. Since washing her hands in the sink after working with Ziva in the cowshed, she had disinfected it six times with rubbing alcohol, sticking Q-tips into the ridges around the taps, but what if she had missed a spot? Left a trace of fecal matter that could poison Ulya? Maybe even kill her? It didn't make sense—if manure were so dangerous all the kibbutzniks would be falling sick—but she still felt the need to go home and sterilize the sink again.

Dana helped Ziva and Claudette carry the folded pillowcases over to the cubbyholes, explaining, "This is where people come to get their clothes, Claudette. Everyone has a number assigned to them. Put the pillowcase in the cubbyhole with the corresponding number." She set her pile down on a table and picked up the topmost pillowcase. "This one, you see, is 64. That's Talia, Shlomo's daughter. I don't want to know how many boys have had a good time on the 64 sheets!"

Ziva snatched the pillowcase from her. "Really? It seems to me you do. Go check the dryer. It's beeping."

Dana lifted her eyes to the ceiling and stomped off.

Ziva took the pillowcase to cubbyhole 64. "That woman is intolerable. Of all the things she could have told you. She could have said: 'Isn't it nice, Claudette, how a member of the kibbutznik doesn't have to come home after a hard day's work and do his laundry?' No, he just comes here and picks up his clean clothes. He doesn't have to cook his dinner, either, or do his dishes. Until recently, he didn't even have to raise his children. All this, of course, is most liberating to women. I understand in the United States, career women still do all the house chores."

Claudette wasn't sure she had put the right pillowcase in cubbyhole 19. Actually, she was sure, but she had to double-check anyway. She walked back and peeked in: yes, that was pillowcase 19. The second she turned away, however, the feeling of uncertainty reappeared. She would have to check one more time. As she peered into cubbyhole 19 for the third time, she heard Ziva gasp. Afraid she had been caught being inefficient again, she turned. The old woman was buckled over with her hand on her back.

Claudette took a step forward. "Ziva, are you all right?"

Ziva didn't move.

"Ziva?"

Ziva exhaled through her teeth and slowly straightened. Limping to the pile of pillowcases, she spoke as if she'd never been interrupted. "Not so long ago, Claudette, we didn't even have these numbers on the clothes. We didn't have our own clothes. When the pants you were wearing were dirty, you traded them in for a clean pair. If you were a size 6, you got any size 6 that was available. We had no private property. None. Everyone had the same pillowcase. A nice clean white. Now look at this stupid—"

Israel and the Palestinians are moving forward with their peace plans—

Dana turned up the radio, and Ziva paused to listen, the Mickey Mouse pillowcase in her hands.

Both parties signed the Cairo Agreement this week, establishing the Palestinian Authority and outlining Israel's withdrawal from the Gaza Strip and Jericho. Israel will remove all of its forces from these areas immediately and will soon pull out of other Palestinian cities in the West Bank. In New York, the Dow Jones . . .

Ziva shook her head in wonder. "The Iron Curtain's fallen. Apartheid is over. The Jews and Arabs are making peace. Things are really coming together in time for the next century, aren't they, Claudette?"

Knowing next to nothing about any of these things, Claudette remained quiet as she reexamined cubbyhole 37.

After the pillowcases, Ziva and Claudette folded jeans at a wooden table. The hedge outside the window glistened under a sunshower. Ziva noted how swiftly Claudette folded the jeans into tidy piles and assumed she was responsible for this marked improvement. She had been hard on the girl, but look how much better she worked. She hoped her article "Utopia on the Auction Block" would be as motivating. If she ever finished it.

Every day after work, she sat down to write, but in the middle of a sentence, her mind would wander, always into the past, leaving her depleted and drowsy. She had even taken a few afternoon naps. She, who had never taken a nap in her life. It didn't help having that boy lurking about the kibbutz, Franz's mirror image, confronting her with old pictures. For decades she had gone without seeing a picture of Franz, having only her memories; and it had been powerful to see that xeroxed square and find her memory had not failed her, that all these years, when she would envision Franz on the day he arrived—concave temples, thin, playful lips, his emaciated body swimming in that beige suit—she'd had it right. Only the xerox couldn't capture the light in his eyes. It had been so long since she was Dagmar, it didn't feel as if she had lied to the boy. She despised lying, but he had been so fierce, so upset, when he asked about Dagmar's whereabouts. "That's between me and Dagmar." Well, she didn't want to hear what he had to say, and he couldn't force her. For fifty years she had lived without knowing how Franz felt about her, and now he was dead. Not knowing at this point was better. And she couldn't afford the distraction right now. The last person she should be thinking about was Franz, who wouldn't have given a damn if the kibbutz lived or died. Better to remember Dov, the man who gave the kibbutz everything.

Dov and she had been doing the laundry that sweltering day everything changed between them. Nothing but a tin vat near the river, lines for hang drying, a canvas tent for escaping the sun. No big machines. No stupid Dana. No Mickey Mouse pillowcases. 1935. They were nineteen years old. Ten years before Franz. She told the boy, Adam, that a few years was nothing at her age, but she didn't explain that only the later years seemed short, negligible; the young years didn't shorten along with them. When she and Dov were preparing the vat that afternoon for the dirty clothes, it had been two years since they'd come to Palestine. Those two years had been long and hard; and in her memory, they still were.

"We need one more," she said, after he dumped the bucket of water into the tin vat.

He wiped his brow. "I was hoping you wouldn't say that."

She should have known then that something was wrong. Dov never groused about work. While he headed back to the river with the wooden bucket propped on his shoulder and his white shirt wrapped around his head like a turban, she stoked the fire under the vat.

Half an hour later, while the two of them shaved palm oil and lye into a bucket of water, a drop hit its surface. Ziva looked up hoping for rain, the fields could use it, but the only drop of water dangled from Dov's chin. His eyes glowed so blue in his red, sweaty face. She'd never seen her friend perspire like that, but they were squatting near a fire and a tub of boiling water on a hundred-degree day.

The soap prepared, Dov stood and unwound the shirt from his head, revealing a mess of sun-bleached curls. He slipped his arms into the sleeves. "I'm freezing."

"Of course." Ziva shook her head at him as she used to shake it back in Berlin when on the coldest day he would strut without a scarf and gloves claiming he was hot. She circled around the vat with a pitchfork. "You're so blond now, you know, you could go back and join the Hitler Youth."

Dov flicked hot water from the tank at her. She laughed and flicked him back.

He squeezed his eyes. "I have to say, I don't feel very good."

"Do you want to go sit in the tent?"

He shook his head. "No, I think I'll be all right."

Ziva dug the pitchfork into a pile of dirty clothes. While she heaved up a load, Dov dropped behind the vat. Too quickly.

"Dov?"

He didn't answer.

She let go of the pitchfork, walked around the vat, and found Dov convulsing on the dirt, the seat of his khaki shorts soaked brown. She scanned for help, but everyone else was in the fields, no one moving about the cluster of white tents up the hill. She would just have to handle this alone. She hooked her arms under Dov's armpits and dragged him toward the tent, leaving a trail of watery stool in the dirt.

It was barely cooler inside the white tent. Dov curled on the ground, clutching his stomach, while she knifed a hole in the canvas cot, as she had learned to do from a cholera pamphlet distributed by the Jewish Agency. She felt nothing as she stepped over Dov to fetch a bucket. There was no time for feelings. The pamphlet warned that in high heat a cholera sufferer could die of dehydration within hours. She had to keep him hydrated. That was her one goal. She returned with an emptied bucket and placed it under the hole in the cot.

"Come." She strained to help him up. When they arrived on the kibbutz, he hadn't been much taller than her. A late bloomer, in his seventeenth year, he had shot up. Once he lay on the cot, buttocks over the carved-out hole, she hastened to unbutton his shorts and pull off his underwear, keeping her eyes averted from his penis. As soon as they were removed, diarrhea spouted through the hole, splashing into the bucket. The tent filled with the smell of rotting fish.

Dov wheezed, "I'm sorry, Ziva."

Even so sick, he didn't call her Dagmar. Ever since that first night on the *Kampala*, when she told him she never wanted to be called Dagmar again, he had never once faltered, even though he had known her as Dagmar nearly as long as he had known his own name. He understood how much she no longer wanted to be Dagmar Stahlmann of the velvet hair bows, daughter of a weak, humiliated people, but Ziva Peled, descendant of Judah the Maccabee, intrepid pioneer.

"Don't be silly." She drew a sheet over his body, covering the thatch of ash blond pubic hair. She hadn't known a man's pubic hair could be so light.

She hurried to fill a canteen with boiled water from the vat. How lucky they hadn't yet added the soap or dirty clothes. She had to replace his fluids as fast as he lost them. The pamphlet cautioned that most cholera patients refused to drink, that she would have to force him. Kneeling beside him, she brought the canteen to his lips. "I know it's hot, but please take a sip." Dov's face twisted from the effort, but he did sip.

For the rest of the afternoon, as the sun traveled from the ridge of the tent down its western slope, Dov never refused to drink, except when he couldn't help but throw up. His milky vomit expelled in violent convulsions. His diarrhea also resembled skimmed milk, speckled with grains of rice. Both reeked of fish.

"Hey!" Danny, the American pioneer, poked his head into the tent, the sky behind him a dusky rose. "We were wondering why—"

He stopped midsentence.

Ziva held a cloth against Dov's forehead. "Get salt and sugar!"

Danny returned with tins from the kitchen and two other pioneers. Darkness fell with the three men waiting outside the tent for Ziva to hand them buckets of waste to dump and canteens to fill. When they struck matches to light their cigarettes, their figures flared on the tent's inner walls like shadow puppets. She asked them for a lamp.

Dov lost consciousness. Stopped sipping. Ziva poured water into his mouth, but it filled like a bath and overflowed. His face wizened in a matter of hours: the eyes retreated into their sockets, the cheeks and temples caved, the lips shriveled. When two hours passed without a canteen needing to be refilled, Danny peeked into the tent.

Ziva stepped outside. "Please, go to bed. We can't all be too tired to work tomorrow."

"Are you sure, Ziva?"

"Yes. Dov wouldn't want us all standing around."

On her way back from dumping yet another pail of milky waste, Ziva thought: nobody dies of cholera in Berlin anymore. Dov could have lived out a long life surrounded by his family. Does he regret coming here now? *Better to die like a man than live like a dog.* That was something they both liked to say, and Dov didn't waver, didn't change his mind when it was convenient. She was sure even death couldn't get him to back away from his ideals. That's why she loved him.

Love? She stopped and stood with the emptied pail, staring at the tent glowing in the darkness. How could she have not realized it before? What else could it be? This terror she felt at the prospect of the sun rising from behind the hills tomorrow morning and shining down on a world without Dov? This feeling that if Dov died the Promised Land would lose some of its promise? This difficulty she had believing that any two people had ever been as close?

Ziva reentered the tent where Dov lay still as a corpse. She sat on the floor, ready with the water. The blackest hour of the night passed, and the hour after it. She laid her head on the cot, closed her eyes. Within seconds she was in Frau Kessler's dance class, waltzing with a Dov not much taller than her, laughing as he kept stepping on her toes.

She scrambled to her feet. Had she fallen asleep? While Dov needed her? Unforgivable. How long had she been out? The bucket under the cot didn't contain much waste. Did that mean he was getting better or worse? She paced the tent. This night felt like a battle between her and fate, and she wasn't sure who was winning.

She shook Dov. "Wake up!" His eyes fluttered. "Wake up!" She brought the canteen to his mouth.

He sipped.

Eventually the sun crested the hills and glowed through the hem of the tent.

Dov squinted at her through one eye. "I hope you didn't forget the laundry."

She laughed. She adored him for his sense of humor. His perseverance. She wrapped an arm over his chest and rested her forehead on his. They remained like that for a long time.

When she finally lifted her head, Dov said, "Ziva, will you marry me?"

What marriage was going to look like in this new society, they didn't know, only that it was going to be nothing like traditional marriage, the family unit being a form of exclusivity that undermined the health of the larger community. But whatever marriage would mean, obviously there was no man she should be wedded to more than Dov. They were going to be the kibbutz's very first couple.

She kissed his cheek. "I was going to ask you the same thing."

Ziva looked around the modern laundry. The large washer in a spin cycle rattled and shook like it was trying to escape. Outside, the sun-shower had become a downpour, blurring the windows. Dana had changed the radio station and was singing along to a pop song, bopping her head and shoulders as she ironed. Claudette was halfway through a new cart of jeans. Yes, the young woman was much better today. The happy pop song was followed by a lovesick one: *Baby, baby, I'll never get over you, baby.*

Dana asked Claudette if she had a boyfriend back home.

Claudette shook her head without taking her gaze off her folding.

"Oh, I bet you're going to meet a nice Israeli boy!"

Claudette ignored this, and Ziva considered whether she might have misjudged the young woman. Now that Claudette wasn't driving her to distraction, she could see her more clearly, and she wasn't like the other volunteers. For one thing, she didn't wear makeup and hoop earrings and T-shirts that were either ridiculously large or desperately tight.

Dana smirked and raised her eyebrows. "What do you think of Israeli men, Claudette? Do you think they're handsome?"

Claudette shrugged, eyes remaining on the jeans in her hands.

"No? You don't think Israeli men are sexy? Too macho?"

Claudette finally raised her head, and Ziva was taken aback by the terror in her eyes. Terror was the only way to describe it.

"Oh, leave the girl be," Ziva said. "Not everyone is as sex-crazed as you, Dana."

Dana laughed. "I don't believe it! Some people just aren't in touch with what's going on in their mind and body. My mother once told me you used to listen to your body, Ziva. Hmm? She said you had quite a few lovers. Is that true? Come on, it's such a long time ago, you can admit it now. Did you?"

"The apple doesn't fall far, does it? Your mother was the kibbutz gossip, and now it's you. You know, I heard you the other day, Dana, spewing your *shtuyot*. And so did Eyal. You should be ashamed."

"Eyal, poor man, I don't think he's had sex in ten years. Not since Orna left him."

"Dana! What makes you think I want to hear this? And besides, *he* left her. She wanted him to leave the kibbutz, and he wouldn't go."

"Well, doesn't it bother you that you're not going to have any grandchildren?"

"All the children on the kibbutz are my grandchildren, Dana. I don't care about passing on my bloodline. I care about passing on my ideals, my hard work. If the kibbutz dies—if you people kill it—then I'll have no lineage."

Dana cocked her head, pursed her lips. "You still haven't answered my question, Ziva. Did you have a lot of lovers?"

"What I can't understand is what difference it makes to you."

"Just curious. Did you?"

"No, Dana. I did not. There was my husband, Dov. And that's it. I know your generation must find that shocking. Now will you leave it alone?"

Dana smiled and shook her head. "One person your whole life! I don't know how you people did it. And the kids today aren't having much fun either, aside from Talia. Oh, the sixties, now that was a good time!"

The three women folded in silence. As Claudette worked through the jeans—a fat woman's elastic waist, a young man's faded Levi's, a little girl's pink pair—she thought: other people had boyfriends, husbands, mothers, friends, children. They snuggled under blankets, hugged in metro stations, kissed goodnight, walked hand in hand. That's what other people did while she disinfected the sink.

When Dana left for the bathroom, Ziva said, "Are you all right, Claudette?"

Claudette nodded.

"You looked scared before. You look a little scared right now."

Claudette shook her head.

"Well, speak, Claudette! If you're okay, say so."

"I'm okay. Thank you."

"Dana is always bullying people to talk about their private lives. She's so stupid she can't help it."

"I understand."

"You know, if you're ever scared, you can tell me. I'm very good at toughening people up."

Dana returned and fidgeted with the radio antennas, but all she got was static. She turned it off. "Fucking rain."

Ziva folded, remembering how scared she had been that first night she and Dov were expected to sleep together. The group voted to give them a private tent every Shabbat, saying, "Make the kibbutz's first child!" Every other day, so as not to undermine the supremacy of the group, they would sleep with the others in one of the main tents. To this day, the smell of kerosene brought her back to that first Shabbat, lying in the darkness after Dov snuffed the lamp. Outside the others sang around a campfire. *No more tradition's chains shall bind us. Arise, you slaves, no more in thrall! The earth shall rise on new foundations. We have been naught, we shall be all.*

Dov perched on the edge of her cot, carefully, as if he didn't want to wake her. The awkwardness was upsetting. Until now she had always felt as comfortable around Dov as she felt by herself. With a serious expression on his face, he gently laid a hand on her shoulder. She wanted to laugh, but was afraid that would ruin what was supposed to be a romantic moment. She'd never stifled a laugh around him before. As Dov's familiar face came toward her, she assured herself that this made sense. Who else was she supposed to make love to if not the person she loved the most?

Their lips met. She felt little. She kissed him back, feeling as if she were playing make-believe, pretending that she was married, pretending that she was being swept off her feet. Having never made love before, she didn't know if it always felt like pretending, if everybody pretended to feel what they read in books and saw in the moving pictures. Dov's hand moved up her thigh and inside the leg of her shorts. She braced, and yet it still surprised her, the jolt she felt when his fingertips grazed her there. Just a soft, quick touch and his hand retreated down her thigh.

Unease gave way to curiosity. When his hand once again crept up her thigh, she nearly moaned, but caught herself in time. How embarrassing, to moan like that in front of her friend. His hand did not venture any closer. It loitered, hesitant, inches away. Holding her breath, Ziva reached into her shorts and laid Dov's hand between her legs. His lips stilled on her mouth. His hand froze. Was he unsure what to do? Too self-conscious? Uninterested? Repulsed?

He withdrew his hand, leaving Ziva feeling like an idiot, unsure why she had gotten it into her head that her ugly vagina was something someone would want to touch.

He turned his back to her and unbuttoned his shirt. "I suppose we should undress."

Ziva unbuttoned her shorts to boisterous singing. *We shall not cease, for still our strength is rising higher. For dauntless is our will, and our hearts are on fire!* She laid the shorts on the floor and started undoing her shirt. Last she peeled off her underwear. The summer night was warm but her skin still goosebumped.

She lay back on the cot and considered her body: pale breasts falling to the sides, brown nipples, smooth belly, mound of black hair, strong, tanned thighs, much tanner than her chest. Did she glow like her mother's favorite painting, the uniformly pale *Nude Maja*? She would know perhaps when Dov turned around.

"Ready?" he said.

"Ready."

He tossed his work shirt and, without so much as a peek at her body, climbed on top. What she saw of his body did resemble the marble statues lining the main hallway of the Alte Nationalgalerie, but she found it off-putting that Dov had a body. She would have loved him without it. There was a poking at her vagina.

"Here?"

"Yes."

As a schoolgirl, changing for gymnastics, she had heard another girl reading aloud from a novel to her enraptured friends. She vaguely remembered the novel saying it felt like a dam rupturing, sending a wave rolling over the woman, engulfing her, making her feel as if she needed to come up for air, making her gasp.

"I'm not hurting you, am I, Ziva?"

"No."

He pushed in and out while Ziva thought: For this, all the fuss? The banned novels? The giggly whispers? The bawdy innuendos? The dirty photograph Danny the American kept under his mattress? The scandals? Betrayals? Rabbinic obligations and condemnations? The Song of Solomon?

It chafed. She closed her eyes. *Away with grief and pain, for hope does sorrow mend. Around and round again, for the hora has no end!* At last Dov's panting loudened, quickened. She hoped this meant it would soon be over.

He grunted, said, "I love you, Ziva."

"I love you, too."

He returned to his own cot, and she rolled to face the other side of the tent. What did she care if sex wasn't all that it was trumpeted to be? That only made it easier to concentrate on the important matters. The cotton and peanut fields needed water before this heat wave shriveled the fledgling plants. She had to practice her rifle shot if she was going to be of any use to the Haganah. According to yesterday's paper, Jews were being stripped of their German citizenship, meaning she had to try harder to convince her parents to come to Palestine; though how they could travel without a passport now she wasn't sure. And Dov, dear, dear Dov, was alive and deserved to be loved.

Ziva put down the jeans in her hands and rubbed her arthritic knees. She could no longer bear so much standing. Her ankles ached too. She could sit on a stool to fold the laundry, but she didn't want to sit all day. She would rather take anti-inflammatories. She limped over to her bag hanging on the wall and pulled out the plastic pill organizer. She might as well take the blood pressure capsules, too. Weren't those the ones that had to be taken between meals?

Dana looked up from her ironing. "That's a lot of pills, Ziva."

Ziva's hand shook as she extracted a red tablet. "Yes, my bathroom looks like a pharmacy."

Heart pounding, Claudette watched Ziva shamble over to the kitchenette, pour a glass of water, and swallow a handful of pills. A bathroom like a pharmacy. When that orphan boy had killed himself with stolen medication, she had condemned him. Twelve years old and she already spent most of her waking hours trying to appease the Bad Feeling—counting tiles, washing her hands—but she wasn't yet wondering the worst about herself, whether she wanted to have sex with Sister Marie Amable or burn down the orphanage. She had been horrified when she heard how the boy did it. After swallowing the pills, he pulled a plastic produce bag over his head and held a rubber band around his neck. As he lost consciousness, he let go of the band. That way, if he didn't take enough pills to die, only to pass out, he would still suffocate. For years she pictured him in the Hell of the Damned, eternally suffocating on a produce bag. Now she understood that the boy simply could not take it anymore.

The rain clattered against the windowsills while Ziva and Claudette spent the remainder of the afternoon folding towels. Claudette pressed

Christina the Astonishing, patron saint of the insane, against her chest, trying to push her into her heart, but even Christina couldn't prevent Claudette from trying to get to Ziva's bathroom. When the wall clock showed half past five, Ziva folded one last hand towel and headed for the door, eager to work on her article.

"You did all right today, Claudette."

Claudette consulted the window. "Shouldn't we wait until the rain calms down?"

Ziva pushed open the screen door. "It's only water."

Claudette paused in the doorway as Ziva hobbled into the downpour. If she wanted the pills, she would have to go after her.

Dana lit a cigarette. "Haven't you figured it out yet? The eleventh plague couldn't stop that old hag."

Claudette ran into the rain and joined Ziva on her journey down the path, making sure to take two steps in each sidewalk square. In seconds, they were both soaked, Ziva's bra straps showing through her white shirt, Claudette's brown hair hanging in thick wet strands. This time when dizziness rushed up at Ziva, she slipped her arm through Claudette's. To give the impression this was merely a gesture of goodwill, not of necessity, Ziva kept her chin raised. Now Claudette felt dizzy: their skin touched. She didn't know the word for lusting after the elderly, but that didn't mean such a deviance didn't exist. She desperately wanted to retract her arm.

"I lied."

Claudette looked over at Ziva. The rain had matted down the wild white hair, exposing its actual thinness and the mottled scalp beneath. "What?"

"I've told two lies recently, and I'm not a liar. I despise lying."

Claudette nodded. "Lying is a sin."

"I just couldn't bear that horrible woman asking me any more questions, but the truth is I've been with two men." Ziva kept her head up, making no effort to avoid puddles. "I know it must be hard to imagine anyone wanting to sleep with me."

Claudette was besieged by fear: fear of the old woman's freckled scalp, the warmth where their elbows met, by what she was going to do in her bathroom, by the thought of being with a man as the old woman had been, by the requirement that she respond to her confession. What could she say?

Claudette stammered, "I've never . . . been with anyone. Kissed, I mean."

Ziva turned to Claudette, her sparse eyelashes in small wet clumps. "Once I would have said you weren't missing much, but now, I have to say, Claudette, you must try it."

Claudette, having forgotten to watch the sidewalk, witnessed her foot landing on a line between the concrete blocks. More fear bloomed in her chest. No, she would never kiss anyone. She couldn't even walk down a sidewalk.

When they arrived at the old people's quarters, Claudette hesitated while Ziva opened her door. If she wanted the pills, she would have to ask to come in, but wouldn't it seem odd to ask to use the bathroom when hers was only a minute away?

Ziva turned in her doorway. "Claudette, why don't you come for tea this Shabbat? Friday night after dinner?"

Claudette nodded. "Yes. Thank you."

If God didn't want her to do this, why was He making it so easy?

"My son, Eyal, the big shot, will be here."

As Claudette walked back to the volunteers' section, where she would spend the next few hours sanitizing the sink again, she dodged all the lines in the path, thinking, Friday Friday Friday Friday. Now that she wasn't going to have to do fifty more years of this, the three days until Friday seemed a long time.

*O*n his way to lunch, Adam stopped by the office building and pulled out the letters in the mailbox for the foreign volunteers. Once again, they all hailed from the former Soviet Union: Russia, Ukraine, Russia, Lithuania, Russia . . .

The Jewish Agency.

He tore open the envelope. Please, please, let her be alive. Inside was only a short letter directing him to fill out the attached "Search Form for Missing Relatives." It was disappointing, but he supposed it could have been worse. It could have said they couldn't find a Dagmar, or wouldn't even look for her without a last name. He folded the form back into the envelope and headed for the dining hall.

The crowded tables were covered in glasses, plastic water jugs, bowls, trays of food, all the crap he would spend the rest of the afternoon washing. Today he had the second shift, the latter half of lunch and dinner.

"Adam! Adam!"

Ulya stood behind a table, waving him over. Why did she always want to eat with him? He pointed at the food bars, indicating he still needed to get his lunch, and wandered over to them. Their steel containers offered the same bland crap as every meal: potato or rice, chicken or turkey, boiled vegetables. Adam loaded a plate with French fries, squeezed on some ketchup, and scanned the hall for a place to sit undisturbed with the form.

"Adam! Adam!"

He'd forgotten about Ulya. She had taken off her blue work shirt, stripped down to a white tank top. He walked over and laid his tray across from her.

She eyed his fries. "You have to be careful. It's so boring here, even though the food is blah, you stuff your face and get fat. You've already gained weight, but you needed to. I don't."

Why did girls always count calories? She looked fine: arms weren't skinny, but nowhere near fat; full boobs, nipples hard little bumps under the white Lycra top; a plump face, but in a good way. Her blue eyes were amplified by her dark eyeliner, but not as boldly as when she went out at night. She couldn't be going to the bomb-shelter pub after all, because it was closed Sunday through Wednesday, and she still left her room all gussied up.

Adam dipped a fry in ketchup. "You don't need to worry about your weight."

"Why? You think I look good?"

He popped the fry into his mouth. "Did you know you're always fishing for compliments?"

"Did you know you're very stingy with them?"

"Wrong. I'm known to be pretty generous with the sweet talk."

"Then it's just me, I guess. I don't look good."

He didn't mean to make the girl feel bad. "No, it's not you. I'm just not my complimentary self lately. You're very pretty."

She looked away. "It doesn't count. I forced you to say it."

"You did. But it's true, okay?"

Ulya smiled, took one of his fries. "I always think about the restaurants in New York. I want to eat in the Rainbow Room. Tell me what it's like in the Rainbow Room."

"The Rainbow Room? How would I know?"

"You've never been to the Rainbow Room? Why? The restaurant is round and on the top of a tall, tall building. It's surrounded by windows so you can see the whole of Manhattan. It has a dance floor with a giant chandelier. I have seen the pictures. When I live in New York, I'm going to eat in the Rainbow Room once a week."

Adam noticed a swarthy guy, a few tables behind Ulya, staring in their direction.

"Well, you'd have to be pretty damn rich to eat in the Rainbow Room once a week. Or even once a year. Personally, I've got no desire to go to that place. I mean, I'm happy it's there, 'cause all that glitzy shit is part of what makes New York New York, but that's not my New York. I'd rather eat at Moishe's."

"Moishe's? That sounds like it could be in Israel."

Adam stared over Ulya's shoulder. "Okay, there's a dude over there, like three tables away, who, I swear, has been eyeballing us. He's got crazy gold eyes."

"So?"

"So, turn around and look. He's probably got the hots for you."

"I don't care. Let him stare."

"Should I wave at him?"

"No!"

The man in question seemed to realize they were talking about him and went back to his plate of food.

"I think he's an Arab worker. I think everyone sitting at that table with him are Arab workers."

"Enough! I don't want to talk about this person anymore. I want to talk about the Rainbow Room."

"Never mind, he's leaving now."

"Good."

"Handsome guy."

Ulya took another one of Adam's fries, but didn't bring it to her mouth. "You look better."

"Better than him? You didn't even see him."

"No, I mean better than you when you first got here. You used to look terrible. Now you look," she paused, "good."

"Yeah?" Adam raised his eyebrows, nervously patted his hair, though he knew his looks were back. "Thanks. I was having some health issues when I got here."

It always surprised him how quickly he recovered his looks whenever he jumped back on the wagon. His face had filled out, and once again his skin was a warm olive. If anything, his complexion looked better than ever thanks to the Mediterranean sun. The kibbutz dentist had filled his cavities, enabling him to talk and smile with ease. Older addicts always warned him that one day his body would stop bouncing back—that is, they liked to add, if he didn't OD before then. He knew they weren't lying because he had seen the forty-year-olds picking up chips for a year clean still looking like garbage.

Adam spotted Claudette setting her tray halfway down their table. He waved at her, and the old woman, who was taking a seat across from her, leaned forward to see whom Claudette was waving to. Adam gave the old lady a smile, and she scowled back. What did she have against him? He got that creepy feeling again that she was hiding something. Maybe she hated his grandfather? Maybe he spurned her? Maybe his imagination was running wild because he really wanted her to remember him or Dagmar. The truth was all the kibbutzniks were standoffish. They invited people to volunteer on their commune and then ignored them. Did they think they were too superior or were they scared of talking to strangers?

Ulya asked if he was going back to Manhattan soon.

"Hope so."

"You could take me with you, you know. We could get a fake marriage."

"Once upon a time—and by once upon a time I mean last month—I would've jumped at that chance, as long as you paid me enough. But now I'm done with scams."

"How much do you have to pay someone to be your green-card husband? I know people who've done it, paid someone, but I don't know how much."

"I know people who've done it too, I mean been the husband or wife. One girl I know got ten grand up front and her rent paid for two years. They were roommates—I think the guy was from Romania—and he paid all the rent, because, you know, it's best if you live together. It makes the marriage seem more real, all the mail going to one place and that kind of thing. Also they ask you all these questions at the interview to make sure you're really married. What shampoo does your wife use? Does she brush her teeth before or after breakfast? If you've been sharing a bathroom for two years, you know."

"How much is rent? How much all together did this Romanian pay?"

"They were in Queens, so the rent wasn't too bad. Probably eight hundred dollars, maybe a thou. So let's say a thousand times twenty-four months, plus the ten grand. He probably paid thirty-five thousand dollars, something like that."

"So much money." Ulya pushed away from the table. "I have to go. My stupid job. I hate making cheese."

Adam watched Ulya walking off, thinking, the fucking Rainbow Room. How funny that she thought he might be a regular there. If she saw where he had eaten most of his dinners, that small kitchen table with only three chairs. And imagine if she got a load of where he used to eat with his mom: the coffee table, after pushing away weeks-old fast-food wrappers.

They'd had no kitchen, only a kitchenette, its counter covered in dirty dishes and sticky coffee and syrup rings. One morning he climbed onto the counter to get the box of Fruit Loops from the top of the fridge and his mom appeared, her skinny, unshaven legs sticking out of her baggy T-shirt.

"What the hell are you doing up there?"

"The Fruit Loops."

She stomped over, grabbed the box off the fridge. "Jesus Christ, Adam, stop feeling so sorry for yourself. You think you've got it bad? Try growing up with Holocaust survivors. Holocaust survivors who fucking hate each other."

Adam, confused, climbed down the footstool he'd made out of phone books.

"Are you fucking kidding me?" His mother stared into the fridge. "We're out of milk already? Go to the couch, Adam. I'll bring you the cereal in a second."

Adam waited on the couch, singing under his breath a song he'd recently learned in school—*Oh, Susanna! Oh, don't you cry for me*—until his mother came over with a bowl, no milk, piled high with Fruit Loops, picked free of the green ones. She kissed him on the head. "I know you don't like the greenies."

Adam stood, picked up his tray and the search form. The dining hall was clearing out. He headed for the dishwashing room, where he would scrub and sweat until late tonight.

Ziva opened the door to find a bright-eyed Claudette standing on her step wearing a white eyelet sundress.

"You look different!" Pretty was what she thought, but she didn't believe in complimenting women on their appearances.

Claudette entered the apartment, her hands in nervous fists. It wasn't good that Ziva found her different. Different was suspicious. Why had she bought this dress? She had gone to the *kolbo* to secure the plastic bag and rubber band and ended up at the clothing rack in the back. She spent half the money Louise had given her for the summer on this sundress.

Ziva had no idea now why she had invited the young woman over. She untied her apron. "The cookies are almost done."

"They smell delicious." Claudette tried not to sound nervous as she set her bag against the wall next to the bathroom door. She had placed a work shirt inside it so she wasn't carrying around an empty plastic bag. The plan was to grab the bag when she used the washroom, preferably just before leaving, and to load it with pills.

Not knowing what else to do, Claudette gravitated toward the pictures on the sideboard. Grateful to have something to talk about, Ziva walked over. "That was my Dov."

Claudette considered the blond man in the shirt and sweater vest, his handsome face staring off to the side. So this, she thought, was one of the two men.

"That photo was taken for a fake German passport. Dov and two others from a nearby kibbutz snuck back into Europe to help Jews escape. We wanted to start an underground railroad to Palestine, but all they managed to do was save five people. It's not six million, but five lives are still five lives, and quite a few people are walking around today because of Dov." After repeating this phrase as she had for decades, she paused, realizing the boy, Franz's grandson, wouldn't exist if it weren't for Dov. "He was gone for three months. No letters. I barely slept."

Claudette tried to imagine how the young man must have felt posing for this picture. "You must have been very scared for him."

"Yes, scared. And jealous. I wanted to be on that mission. But everyone thought I looked too Jewish."

"Isn't this you?"

"Yes, that's me, young and beautiful." Ziva handed Claudette the picture. "Well, young at least. About your age."

It was true young Ziva didn't have the delicate features Claudette normally thought of as beautiful, the dainty features of the Virgin Mary: her cheeks were fat, nose strong, hair wild, eyes close-set, she looked, yes, too Jewish, though technically wasn't the Virgin Mary Jewish? And yet, Claudette did find Ziva beautiful. What's more, she thought Ziva had carried that beauty into her old age. All the women in Louise's photo albums, which Claudette had scoured for glimpses of their mother, appeared trapped in their snapshots, their smiles wary, as if they feared having their imperfections immortalized. There was nothing wary or apologetic in Ziva's portrait. Both her smile and stance were wide, her eyes glinting like the steel rifle peeking over her right shoulder. What did it feel like to stand and stare out at the world like that? Did such a person even know about the fear in other people?

"Shabbat shalom!" Eyal came through the door. Surprised to see the strange volunteer, he added, "Oh, hello."

"Look who's here!" Ziva took the photograph from Claudette and returned it to its place next to her late husband. Claudette noted she had no pictures of her son.

Eyal sniffed the air. "Is that the chocolate-ginger cookies I smell?"

"I've got to go check on them." Ziva walked toward the kitchen, hands pressed into her back to support the belly. "Have Claudette tell you what we've been doing on our assignments. She was an appalling worker when you first sent her to me. A real disgrace. But she's been better these last few days. You see, some people get better, Eyal, not worse."

Eyal sighed as he sank into the armchair. In a low voice, he said, "I hope it's not too terrible working with my mother."

Claudette sat on the couch, sweeping her white dress under her. "Actually, Ziva has been very kind to me."

"Kind?" Eyal raised his eyebrows. "I think you're the first person in the history of the world to call Ziva Peled kind."

In the kitchen, Ziva peered through the oven window. Back when her mother made cookies, ovens didn't have windows. Her mother would have to open the door and take a peek before her reading glasses steamed up. The cookies needed another minute, so Ziva went to the windowsill to pick leaves off the mint plant. Outside a gibbous moon glowed over the cedars behind the dining hall. Unlike ovens and most everything else, the moon looked exactly as it did when she was young. Had people really walked on it since then? Those three months Dov was in Europe, she lay in bed at night staring out the window at the moon, watching it get larger and larger until it was so full she knew Dov must be noticing it wherever he was, if he was still alive. It comforted her to think their eyes were on the same thing. Then for the next two weeks she would watch it get smaller and smaller.

She had been close to losing hope of ever seeing him again when one lunch he came through the dining hall door. She didn't notice the stranger beside him in the baggy beige suit. Only Dov. She sprang up and ran past a row of tables and into his arms. Breathing in his familiar smell, she squeezed him as tight as she could as if to prove he were real. "You're home."

"This is Ziva," Dov told the man in the baggy suit. "My best friend. My wife. Ziva, this is Franz."

Ziva let go of Dov. She would meet many camp survivors over the next few months, but this was her first. If he hadn't been standing and giving her a rusty, rather grotesque smile, she might have thought this was a body that had been wasting in a coffin for some time, shrinking inside that beige suit. The whole dining hall—the kibbutz had fifty-some members now—had stopped eating to stare at the walking corpse.

"We'll have to think of a Hebrew name for you," she said in German, trying to give the man a welcoming smile. "How about Adam? I love that name. And we don't have an Adam on the kibbutz."

"What do you mean?" He had a Dresden accent, heavy on the *v*'s. "He just told you my name. It's Franz."

Though his black eyes were sunken into his skeletal face, they were not the eyes of a corpse. They were black—irises almost as dark as the pupils—and somehow still bright.

Ziva canted her head, confused. "Franz is a German name."

"I'm German."

How could she pick a fight with a man barely able to stand? But then how could she let such a comment go?

"Well, then," she said, "you must be sad your country is losing the war."

Dov snapped, "Ziva!"

Franz smiled, revealing once more his turmeric-colored teeth, the ligaments in his meatless cheeks. His black eyes shone with amusement. "It seems you and Hitler have something in common. He also thinks I can't be German."

Ziva blinked at Franz in disbelief. "Did you just compare me to Hitler?"

"All I'm saying is that the Nazis tried their damnedest to do away with Franz, and if it's quite all right with you, I'd prefer to not lend them a helping hand."

Dov squeezed Ziva's shoulder before she had a chance to respond. "Franz, I'd have thought after all the stories I told you, you'd have known not to get on the wrong side of this woman."

Franz nodded. "It's true. I was warned."

Dov kissed Ziva on the forehead. "Now I have to rush back to Haifa with the truck. Four others are waiting there. Would you please take Franz to his tent? Nicely? Without making him want to turn around and go back to Europe?"

Dov hurried off and Ziva tried to sound nice. "Where's your bag?"

Franz shook his head. "No bag."

"Not a problem. We have soap and some clean clothes for you."

They hadn't even made it out of the dining hall before Ziva regretted putting the refugees' tents on the outskirts of the kibbutz. The man's gait was slow, jerky. They had been afraid to build the tents too close because who knew what diseases the refugees might be bringing with them. Rumors described people dying of typhus in the ghettos too fast to be buried, their corpses rotting on the sidewalks. Ziva held the door open for Franz and he stepped out of the hall as if his hips might break. How had Dov ferried this man across Europe?

"That's the children's house." She pointed at a white building, where the sound of children singing the Hebrew alphabet floated out of the windows. "Eight babies have been born on the kibbutz."

She pointed out everything, in part to make their plodding seem more natural, in part because so few Jews from Europe had ever come to see what they had built. She pointed out the new water tower, the banana fields in the distance, the health clinic, the young eucalyptuses. A regrettable I-told-you-so feeling rose inside her. She didn't want the feeling, but she had cautioned her fellow Jews that Europe could never be a real home, and they had laughed at her, called her a fanatic.

"Where's the dance hall?"

"Dance hall?"

"You know, where people do the jitterbug?" He smiled, the ligaments in his neck and cheeks popping again. "Loosen their bow ties?"

Ziva didn't know what the jitterbug was, only that she didn't like it. "We don't have jitterbug here. Or bow ties."

She didn't talk to him the rest of the way. She had shown him where they had drained a swamp to build a health clinic, and he asked about bow ties? Ever since she first laid eyes on this frail man, she had been feeling ashamed, because the truth was she hadn't just voted to put the tents far away: she had been the only one who voted for no tents. No refugees. She didn't want them on the kibbutz. Not because of their physical diseases—she didn't fear that—but their mental ones. This question about jitter-whatever dispelled that shame. She had been right. These refugees weren't socialists. They might not even be Zionists. Dov, of course, had voted to house them, and as soon as he heard the Jewish Agency had asked the settlements to prepare for a million more, he would telegram to offer Sadot Hadar as a refuge. People, he argued, were more important than ideals. But how was that possible? How could the two be separated? People were their ideals, and ideals only existed in people.

At last they reached the four tents halfway down the hill from the rest of the kibbutz. Beside the tents shimmered two twisted old olive trees. At the bottom of the dusty hill a streamlet babbled over white rocks. Ziva tied open a flap. "Welcome home."

Franz bowed into the white tent and considered the four military-style cots waiting on a dirt floor. "This isn't my home." He sat on a cot like an old man, hands on his knees. "Though before you start up again, don't worry, I'm not insane enough to see Germany as my home anymore. I have no home."

"Palestine can be your home."

Franz gazed at her, standing in the tent's entryway. She felt increasingly uncomfortable as his focus traveled from her unruly hair to her face, chest, tanned thighs. She pulled down on the hem of her shorts.

"It's been a long time since I've seen a healthy Jewish woman. It's beautiful."

Ziva's face warmed. She had to think quickly: Was there anything wrong with what he'd said? He hadn't called her beautiful. He said "It's beautiful," and it was, wasn't it? A healthy Jew—that was the whole point of the kibbutz.

She crossed the tent. "We have some books here on the table." Having no idea where the refugees would be coming from, they had collected books and pamphlets in Polish, Hungarian, Greek, French, Dutch. She handed Franz a German copy of *The Old New Land*. "Have you read it? This book can help you understand some of what we're trying to do here."

With a small smile, Franz rested his hand on the book.

Ziva narrowed her eyes on him. "Why are you smiling like that?"

"Like what?"

"That."

Franz shook his head with the smile still on his face.

She grabbed the book back and hugged it against her chest. "This isn't funny. I should think that would be apparent by now."

He shook his head again. "I'm sorry. I didn't mean to be rude. I guess I don't know what to make of your . . . type anymore."

"My type?"

"Yes, ideologues. Before the war, to be honest, I merely found you people funny with your sashes and slogans. As long as you didn't try to censor my swing songs . . . But now, of course, you're right, it isn't funny anymore, and . . . I'm confused. I think it makes sense, after the Nazis, that I would have a . . . distaste for any sort of . . . movement. And yet, I know, don't think I don't know that if it weren't for people like you and Dov, I wouldn't be here right now. I wouldn't be alive."

"I can't understand what's so confusing. Not all ideologues are the same because—obviously—not all ideologies are the same. And you know what? I don't care if you think I'm funny, if I'm a fanatic with my

Altneuland. Everything truly great has happened because somebody was a fanatic, because somebody was brave and obsessive enough to fight for their beliefs."

Franz rubbed his knees. "I would take up this conversation, but I think I'm too tired."

"Of course." Ziva realized she should have waited until he felt better, that she should let the refugees discover the books, discover everything, on their own. The place would speak for itself. She placed the book back on the table. "You need to rest. Here's a jug of boiled water. I'll have someone bring you something to eat. Do you want me to leave the flap open?"

"Yes, I like the light. And the view of those ugly trees."

"Ugly? Those are two-hundred-year-old olive trees."

As Ziva was ducking out the tent, she heard: "Wait. Before you go, can I ask you a question?"

She held open the flap, stuck her head back in. "Yes?"

"What was your name in Germany? Surely it wasn't Ziva."

Was he trying to belittle her? Make it seem like she was someone other than who she was? Ziva debated saying nothing at all, just turning and walking away.

Her voice came out low, threatening. "Don't ever ask me that again."

That night she and Dov lay on the bed in the bungalow they had been sharing for six years. She was sad to find that after three months of living in fear that Dov was dead, she still didn't want to make love to him and was relieved when he never crawled on top of her. Sitting against the headboard, chain-smoking, he told her the rumors weren't true. It was much worse. The three of them had rented a room in Bergen, and all day ashes fell like snow flurries, dusting the streets, while the people went about their business amid the stink of burning bodies. He had no problem passing for an Aryan because no Jew could be as healthy as he anymore.

"One night, in a bar—we would go to pick up information—I ended up talking to a doctor's assistant from the camp. At first I thought, stupid me, that he was there to treat the sick. With his hand on my shoulder—I can still feel his hand there, Ziva, I don't think I'll ever stop feeling it on my shoulder—he told me about this experiment, how they were sewing the legs of Jewish men onto Jewish women and vice versa. I know; it takes a second to sink in. And I had to keep a straight face, keep a charmed face and drink my beer. I even smiled at him. Oh God, I feel sick. But I got something for that smile. He told us 'Jewish cockroaches' were hiding in the rubble of Dresden."

"Is something burning?"

Ziva turned to see her son entering the kitchen.

"Oh!" She rushed to the oven. "The cookies!"

Eyal stood next to her, looking down at the smoking tray. "They look all right. Just the edges are black."

Here again was her middle-aged son. And this apartment in the old people's building. Was she losing her mind? It was disorienting enough, feeling these last few weeks as if events from sixty years ago had happened yesterday, but tonight was worse. Tonight it felt as if there was no such thing as today and yesterday. It felt as if the past were happening right now, and right now had been there in the past, that this moment with her fifty-year-old son and the burned cookies was already there with her on the boat to Palestine, when she and Dov leaned on the railing and gazed out at the waves. She asked Eyal to please go keep Claudette company while she salvaged the cookies.

Minutes later, Ziva carried the tray of hot tea in her shaky hands. She could see how much Eyal wanted to spring off the couch to help her. The tray clattered as she laid it on the coffee table. "I hope they're edible. My mother used to make chocolate-ginger cookies. I never helped her or got the recipe, so I've spent the last fifty years trying to re-create them. Nutmeg, vanilla, more ginger, less ginger. It seems I'll never get it right."

Ziva poured the mint tea while Claudette took a mangled cookie. Was this the last thing she would ever eat? She was tempted to go to the washroom now, to get it over with, but Ziva had just sat down. She had to wait.

"So I noticed something the other day when Claudette and I were in the avocado orchard," said Ziva, leaning back with her tea. "There were more Arabs picking fruit than kibbutzniks."

Eyal, cookie at his lips, paused. Years ago it had occurred to him that these chocolate-ginger cookies tasted like heartache to both him and his mother. "Don't start, Ima."

"Cheap labor, that's what it is. Even in the worst of times, when a few extra hands would have stopped us from going to bed hungry, we didn't hire help. No employers or employees: that was the idea. Next thing, you will find Arabs too expensive and start importing workers from Africa."

Claudette stood up. She shuffled between Ziva and the coffee table. "Excuse me. I'm just going to the washroom."

"Palestinians need work, Ima, and we need help in the fields and factory. If I could pay them more I would—these are things you don't think about, these are things you didn't have to deal with when you were secretary—but we have to compete with China. China, which is practically giving away their fruit and plastic. And to be fair, these Palestinian workers bring home more money from the kibbutz than they otherwise would. A lot more."

Claudette, relieved they were so absorbed in their argument, grabbed the bag from the floor and hurried into the bathroom. She locked the door and then leaned against it for a second to steady herself. Through the wood she heard Ziva shouting: "Do you even hear yourself, Eyal? Do you? They're better off? That's what all exploiters say and have said throughout history!"

Claudette opened the medicine cabinet's three mirrored doors and was greeted by a wall of medications—glass bottles of pills, pills in orange plastic containers, boxes with sheets of tablets. What should she do? She didn't want to endanger the old woman by leaving her without some important medication; and, anyway, wouldn't she be more likely to notice something was wrong if she found a bottle empty or missing? Not to mention, if all she did was grab a bottle or two, she might end up with vitamins, because everything was in Hebrew, and the few names in English she didn't recognize. The only thing to do was to skim a little of everything. Six of each. A good round number. She reached for the blue container in the top left corner, planning to work her way across. When she saw its orange sticker with the black skull and crossbones, she took eight.

"Goodnight, Ima." Eyal pushed himself out of the armchair.

Ziva pulled on the armrest and shuffled after him. "My son, the feudal lord."

Eyal opened the door and walked out the apartment.

Ziva called from her doorway. "Slave driver!"

He didn't look back, and she watched him walk to the administration building and disappear into its back door. After a minute, his office window on the second floor lit up.

Ziva closed her door. Was Claudette still in the bathroom? She knocked on it. "Claudette, are you okay?"

"Yes!" Claudette was on her hands and knees, scrambling to pick up all the tiny pink pills scattered about the tiled floor. Everything had been going smoothly until then. She had feared her OCD would keep making her reopen the same bottle or recount the same pills, but that never happened. The Bad Feeling was quiet. Eerily so. In her haste, though, she had forgotten to stuff back a wad of cotton and had to reopen a number of bottles to find the one missing it, and when she finally did find that container, she was shaking so badly she dropped it.

Claudette hurried to her feet, put the bottle of pink pills back, and grabbed the next in line. She had made it through two rows of bottles. She struggled to open the childproof cap—each one was secured differently— and eased six yellow pills into her palm. She dropped the pills into the plastic bag, replaced the bottle, and grabbed another.

"Claudette?" Ziva spoke through the door again. "I'm starting to worry about you."

"No, no, I'm fine. I'm coming out now."

That would have to do. The bag contained a rainbow of pills. She hoped this and her two-month supply of Prozac were enough. She stuffed the work shirt back inside and flushed the toilet. She ran the water while dabbing her sweaty face with the hand towel. She took a deep breath and emerged from the bathroom, holding the plastic bag behind her.

"Are you ill?"

"No." Claudette felt the sweat returning to her face. "Well, a little."

"The mint tea will help. Come, come sit down."

Claudette couldn't bring herself to say no. She set the bag back down on the floor and took a seat again next to Ziva on the couch. It was getting late. If she took the pills tonight, her roommate might come home in time to save her. It would be safer to wait until tomorrow, right after Ulya left for the night. She sighed at having one more day.

Ziva tasted her cookie. "My son's still mad that I didn't give him his own birthday presents when he was a boy. On his sixth birthday, he threw a fit when I gave all the children in his year a sun hat. He wanted me to give only him a sun hat."

Claudette forced down a sip of tea. "I can understand wanting your mother to give you your own birthday present."

She could. Her whole childhood she had wanted a present bought just for her, a mother to love her especially. Over the years she had met many women she had hoped would take a motherly liking to her: doctors, nurses, nuns.

Ziva put Eyal's uneaten cookie on the tray. "Of course you can understand it. People are naturally selfish. They don't want to share. It's an instinct that has to be fought." She stood. "Well, I think I should go to bed now. I want to get up early tomorrow and finish my article."

Claudette rose to her feet. Since she couldn't thank Ziva for the pills or for the kindness she had shown her over the last few days, she said with emphasis, "Thank you, Ziva, for the cookies. Thank you so much."

"No need to make a fuss, Claudette. They're just cookies." Though as soon as she said it, she knew that wasn't exactly true. "But I'm glad you enjoyed them."

t was six o'clock in the morning, the kibbutz still asleep, when Adam headed out to mail the search form. He knew the mail didn't go out on Saturday, but he awoke at 5:45 a.m. as if the alarm had gone off. He had lost the ability to sleep in.

As he crossed the great lawn, dew wetting his sneakers, Golda in tow, he spotted Ziva on a bench in the square, writing. Half of him wanted to prod her again for information; the other half prayed she wouldn't notice him. Yesterday, while he was wiping dishes, she stood on the other side of the conveyer belt berating two teenage girls, pointing from their plates to the garbage, where they had been about to dump their uneaten sandwiches. The harangue continued until the girls, under her watch, stuffed the sandwiches into their mouths. To think he had once hoped this woman was Dagmar. His gentle grandfather never would've fallen for such an ogress.

"Golda! Come back here!" It was too late. The little dog bulleted across the square.

Ziva looked toward the shouting. She missed the little dog, low to the ground, only saw the young man and his familiar gait. Was he coming toward her? She had risen at the crack of dawn to concentrate on the article. And now here he was, like a revenant. What was he doing about at this hour?

"Oy!" The chihuahua pounced at her shins, surprising her. She moved her aching legs away, but the dog continued to paw at them. Leaning over her sore belly, she tried to shove it away.

"Sorry." Adam nudged Golda aside with his sneaker. "Guess she just wanted to say hello."

Ziva forced herself to look up. "I never understood the point of breeding them so small."

He shrugged, gave her that closed-lip smile. "Small things are cuter. I don't know why. Just a law of nature. Say, did you happen to remember anything more about my grandfather, Franz Rosenberg? Or his girlfriend, Dagmar?"

She spoke with her lower jaw extended. "You must stop asking me about this."

"I just thought something might have come to you."

"You're a little pest. I told you I'm not going to suddenly remember something. My memory is fine."

A little pest? Fuck her. "If your memory's so fine, why don't you remember anything?"

The old woman leaned forward. "Your grandfather . . . he obviously didn't teach you any manners."

"Actually, he did. He had better manners than anyone."

Franz, manners? Ziva had no great esteem for manners, but the boy didn't understand the difference between manners and charm. She shook her head. "Well, I'm afraid to say whatever graces your grandfather had didn't rub off on you."

"Maybe they didn't. Maybe a lot of good shit didn't rub off on me." Adam looked off to the side, pissed that he had proven her point by swearing. Why did this woman get under his skin so badly? He turned back to her. "You know, I get this weird feeling about you . . . like . . . like you're not telling me something."

Ziva gripped her writing pad. "Why would you think such a thing?"

"Not sure. A look in your eye."

"And what do you think I'm not telling you?"

She waited, heart pounding. She didn't want this. All she wanted was to be left alone. To work on her article. Save the kibbutz. His presence felt like a revenge.

"I don't know."

She exhaled. "You see, you're being absurd."

Perhaps it was absurd, but Adam wasn't going to say sorry to this woman. He held up his letter. "Well, I got to go mail this. The Jewish

Agency is going to check their files for Dagmar. You were right about one thing: she didn't live here."

Ziva struggled to think of what the *Sochnut* could have on her. If she'd arrived with all the refugees after the war, they'd have papers for sure. But she came when the agency was what, one or two years old? And from the minute she stepped off the boat, she had been Ziva. If she had filled out a form back in 1932 in Berlin, and by some miracle it made it to a bureaucrat in Tel Aviv, could they really trace it to her?

"Young man, can I ask you a question? I don't know why you're looking for this Dagmar, and I don't want to know; it's none of my business. But have you thought about whether this Dagmar wants to be found?"

"What do you mean?" Adam tapped the letter against his palm.

"What do I mean? That's exactly my point. You're young, so you're thinking like a young person. Young people like to shake the snow globe. But old people, they've worked hard to put things exactly where they are, and maybe this Dagmar doesn't want you coming along and stirring things up. Maybe she doesn't want to hear what you have to tell her. You hadn't thought about that, had you?"

It was true. He hadn't given a second's thought to Dagmar and what all this would mean to her. He tried to picture it: If a woman died fifty years from now with his goodbye letter in her hand, would he want to know? Would it make him happy to learn such a thing, or unbearably sad? He shrugged. Because it didn't matter. There was no one else to give the brooch to.

"I hate to say it, but I guess I don't care. I'm going to find Dagmar, and that's all there is to it."

Ziva shook her head. "There we go. It's the me-me-me generation from the me-me-me capitalist culture. You're very selfish."

True. If he hadn't been a selfish fuck his whole life, he wouldn't have to find Dagmar. But this old bitch didn't know that. If she weren't a hundred years old and the secretary's mother, he would tell her to fuck off.

He turned for the mailbox. "Come on, Golda."

*C*laudette lay on her side, pretending to nap, while she waited for Ulya to leave for the night. Normally her roommate would have set out an hour ago, but she hadn't even begun getting dressed. Instead she also sat on her bed, smoking a cigarette and flipping through a fashion magazine. What if tonight were the one night she didn't go out?

The sun set. The room darkened. At last Ulya rose from her bed. This was it. She was leaving. Claudette's heart thumped. After flipping on the ceiling lamp, Ulya returned to her bed and magazine.

Claudette sat up. "Aren't you going out tonight?"

Ulya looked over. "Yes. Why?"

"I just wondered. Normally you would have left by now."

Ulya sensed something strange. Why was Claudette anxious for her to go? What did the weirdo do at night while she was out? Masturbate? No, she had probably never masturbated in her life. She probably wanted the privacy to say a million Hail Marys or do one of those bizarre rituals of hers, tap her fingers together or open and close the closet door. Well, it was none of her business why she was leaving later tonight. She wouldn't have told her best friend, if she'd had one, that her Arab lover wouldn't bring her to his father's fiftieth birthday party, not unless she put on more clothes and could be presented as his fiancée. He claimed it wasn't worth the drama of introducing her otherwise—a Russian immigrant, a non-Muslim, an unbelieving Christian, a fake Jew, a woman with obscenely red hair. It was pathetic and unmanly to be so afraid of his parents, but what did she care? More proof that he wasn't a man to be taken seriously.

And besides, she wouldn't have gone to the party anyway. And so she had agreed to meet him afterward, as she preferred to meet him: in secret.

"I'm going out a little later tonight, that's all."

Claudette rested her hand on her roiling stomach. "How much later?"

Ulya regarded her suspiciously. "Nine o'clock."

Claudette lay back down and did the calculation. Ulya never came home before two in the morning, leaving a window of five hours. It wasn't any more time than she would have had after leaving Ziva's last night. But it would have to do. What was she going to do with the next two hours though? The Bad Feeling hadn't said a word since she stole the pills— didn't accuse her of any wrongdoing, didn't demand any penance. It was silent for the first time in as long as she could remember. Claudette knew why: it couldn't accuse her of doing anything worse than what she was about to do. Even a murderer could later repent and be returned to God, but a self-murderer was lost forever. Claudette closed her eyes and listened to the strange quiet in her head. She heard Ulya flip a page of her magazine. Then the chitchat of people walking along the path behind their window. A bird. Another, higher-pitched bird. Her stomach calmed a bit.

At last Ulya tossed her magazine aside and padded off to the bathroom. Claudette rolled onto her back to wait out the final minutes while Ulya put on her makeup. The ceiling lamp stared down at her, its light dotted by a graveyard of flies. She hadn't noticed that before. Ulya stopped humming, let out a toot, and resumed humming. Could she not hum and toot at the same time? It was the silliest thought, and Claudette felt close to laughing. Laughing? Here, now, on the edge of perdition? She couldn't help it. She felt giddy. Free. Her mind was free. Why did she have to experience, just before she died, how easy and enjoyable life was without the Bad Feeling? How easy and enjoyable it was for other people?

Ulya came out of the bathroom and wiggled into a black minidress. She slipped on her high cork-wedge sandals and, taking a last look in the mirror, fluffed up her hair and gave her reflection an approving smile. She headed out the door, leaving behind a sweet, powdery scent of vanilla. "Ciao!"

Claudette sat up and listened to Ulya turning the key. She rose from the bed and turned off the ceiling lamp. The streetlamps provided enough illumination. It would be easier if she got this over quickly. She retrieved the bag of pills from the blue backpack she kept under the bed, the backpack her brother-in-law had lent her for the trip. She emptied the pills onto the gray blanket and swept them into a colorful heap. She laid out the instruments: bottle of Prozac, rubber band, new plastic bag. It was all there. Except the water.

The water bottle was too big for the bathroom sink, so she held it up to the showerhead. She slowly turned the faucet until the water trickled. The showers here were so strange: no tub or curtains, only a showerhead and a drain in the middle of the bathroom floor. As the bottle filled, she took in the rusted shower basket laden with Ulya's shampoos, body scrubs, shaving creams. Ulya always complained about having no money, but every day she came home with new lotions and tank tops.

When Claudette turned off the shower, she heard music. Carrying the water back to the bed, she remembered Ulya asking her a few weeks ago if the piano wasn't driving her crazy. When she told her roommate she hadn't noticed it, Ulya gave her an incredulous look. But she hadn't heard it. She had been too busy trying to work out whether she'd been aroused that morning while milking the cow. Again and again she had forced herself to picture the cow's long rubbery teats in her hands.

Claudette perched on the edge of the bed, water bottle in hand, and listened to the piano. She wanted to hear, to feel, what other people did when they listened to music. She waited. The first thing she noticed was a change in the pale light pouring through the window, what it seemed to do to the room. Ulya's green high heels, lying haphazardly on the floor, appeared strangely poignant. The colorful pile of pills popped against the gray wool blanket. The air thickened with all the disappointments and dreams of the transients who had lived in this room. Including hers.

The notes ascended, and Claudette remembered an icicle. It appeared in her head. She saw it through the rusty bars on the window, hanging from a lintel, at once clear and opaque, full of fairy light, muted pinks and blues. She reached through the bars for it—she must have been four or five years old—and broke it off. When later she tried to show it to the beautiful and older Françoise, the prettiest girl in the orphanage, the icicle was gone. Françoise laughed at the puddle in her drawer: "Silly-head, you can't own an icicle!" That was years before Françoise lost her mind completely, before she harbored the most evil delusions about one of the younger priests, accused him of doing unspeakable things to her in the broom closet. After months in the pink-padded quiet room, Françoise disappeared, but by then Claudette was too busy counting tiles to notice. She hadn't recalled trying to show Françoise the icicle in twenty years. She hadn't recalled anything.

Half an hour later, the piano still hadn't released her. She felt as if the music might lift her, as Christina the Astonishing had risen toward the rafters during her requiem. Was God reaching out to her, asking her to reconsider? Could that be? Why would He wait until the last second to show He cared?

Claudette put down the bottle of water. She had to make sure. She covered the pills with a shirt and went outside. The music came from somewhere behind the classroom. As she climbed the stones, the music grew louder and her heart beat faster. What was she going to find? What if it were a vision of Christina? Or the Son Himself? On the main road, she found the music emanating from the darkened dining hall. She scurried to its back door.

Ofir was exhausted, but he couldn't stop playing. For three weeks Dan and the others had given him hell for running into the kasbah, and tomorrow he would stand before army court and get sentenced to at least six weeks in jail, but he didn't regret it. The only thing he truly cared about was his music, and his composition was infinitely better thanks to those minutes with the Palestinian boy in the shadowy room of mirrors and the race back toward the sunlight of the square. The melody had turned out sadder than he had expected. The ache of gravity. It carried this fear that life could never quite slake your thirst for it. Strange considering he'd never felt more optimistic, but he didn't force it. He stayed honest to the piece, more honest than he'd ever managed before, and it made him feel like a true artist, not the sham he always feared himself to be.

Usually he played with reservation, careful not to get too loud. If his music carried too far, the next morning there would be teasing: *Ofir thinks he's Beethoven. Oh, here comes our little Mozart!* Growing up in a children's house, where he had to line up to take a shit at an assigned hour, had taught him it was best not to stand out, even in a good way. Tonight, though, he didn't care who heard him.

Had someone come to complain? Sensing a presence behind him, he glanced back—

His fingers froze. A ghost haunted the doorway, a wide-eyed ghost in a moonlit white dress.

"Oof." He laughed. "You scared me."

Claudette leaped sideways and stood with her back against the wall. She didn't know what to think. Could that Jewish teenager be a messenger of God? Pimples riddled his cheeks. A hideous gash crossed his chin. His T-shirt bore a cartoon mouse in a big yellow hat.

When the piano started up again, she held her breath to listen. It was as beautiful as before.

To Ofir's relief, he got right back into it. His fingers moved over the keys as if guided by instinct. He forgot about the girl in the doorway.

Claudette slid down the building until she was sitting on the cool cement. The music came through the wall, vibrating against her back. She must have cried before, when she was a little girl, but she couldn't remember it. It felt different, crying, than she had imagined. She clutched at the front of her dress, where her chest hurt, as if it might bust open. But it also felt good, the tears and mucus running down her face. A relief.

"Hey, hello. Hey, wake up. *Boker tov.* Good morning."

Claudette felt herself being shaken. She opened her eyes.

"You better get up now. People are going to start coming for breakfast."

The teenager who had been playing God's music looked down at her, the sky behind him a pale yellow. Had she taken the pills? The boy's gray eyes were bloodshot, the raised red scar on his chin flanked with black perforations. Would an angel have such an ugly scar? Was this Hell? In her grogginess, Claudette allowed Ofir to clutch her upper arms and help her up.

"Sorry about shaking you like that. But you wouldn't wake up. I've never seen anyone sleep that hard."

Sleep? Claudette blinked. Through the night? Outside? Without medication?

He brought his hand up to cover his chin. "I got scared for a second. I thought I might have to call the nurse." He couldn't decide how old this girl was. Most volunteers were in their twenties.

"It was like you were playing that music just for me. I thought God was playing through you. Yes, I think He was."

Ofir stared at Claudette, joy burgeoning inside him. She stared back, face stern. It was the best thing anyone had ever said to him. All at once, she had dispelled the doubts that had arisen with the morning light. He must have captured something universal if it affected someone so different

149

from him, this girl from, he wasn't sure, France? His eyes stung with excitement and pride. He blinked back the tears. The girl didn't need to see that.

"Thank you." He flipped open his pack of cigarettes. "How long are you going to be on the kibbutz? I would love to play for you again, but . . ."

He paused to light his cigarette, and the girl took off. It was so odd. He watched her run across the lawn in her white sundress and bare feet and hoped she would still be here when he got back from army jail.

*O*fir waved at Gadi from his seat at the back of the bus. Gadi pushed through the people, mostly taller than him, standing in the aisle. When he got to where Ofir was saving him a seat, he said, "I don't know what you're smiling about. Your chin looks Frankensteinish, and you're on your way to jail."

Ofir hadn't realized he was smiling. "Never mind my chin. I almost lost an eye saving this seat for you."

He gazed out the window while Gadi stood on his toes to stuff his duffel in the overhead shelf. The Haifa bus station was coming to life, starting the workweek. The CD store blasted electronica out of giant black speakers. Vendors replenished their bins of candy and nuts. Couples kissed in front of bus doors, and parents hugged their adult children goodbye. Gadi barely sat down and secured his rifle between his knees before the bus backed out.

"Sorry I was so late. I didn't think I was going to make it. Every time I was halfway out the door, my mom remembered something else she wanted to give me: new underwear, potato chips."

The bus descended through the hill city, winding its way to the seaside highway. They passed more CD stores, shoe stores, falafel stands. Soon they were past the city center, driving by residential buildings, three- and four-story white apartment houses yellowed by the sea air. Every car, telephone booth, scaffold was plastered with banners and bumper stickers. They'd proliferated over the last year: PEACE NOW!; NO ARABS, NO BOMBS!; THE HOLY ONE, BLESSED BE HE, WE VOTE FOR YOU; NATIONAL SUICIDE IS

NOT A PEACE PROCESS; THE NEW GENERATION WANTS PEACE; RABIN
IS A MURDERER. Gaps between the white buildings provided glimpses of
the Mediterranean. A year into his army service, Ofir still wasn't used to
being off the kibbutz.

Before Gadi had a chance to start talking about yet another girl he had
met this weekend and almost, just almost, fucked, Ofir said, "I had a good
Shabbat."

"You?" Gadi opened a bag of peanut-flavored puffs and held it out to
Ofir. "I thought you'd be crying the whole time. That's what I would've
been doing if I were headed to army jail. But it could have been worse, I
guess. We could all be dead because of you. It's weird Dan let you go on
leave first. He must have a crush on you."

"You know that composition I've been working on all winter? I finished
it. And, I feel kind of weird saying this, but I think it's good. I mean, really
good. Like maybe I can use it to get into a top-notch music school."

"It must be fucking good, 'cause this is the first time I've ever heard
you say anything positive about your music. Usually you're like, 'I wanna
be good, I wanna be good, but I suck I suck I suck.' Does this song have
a name? I'd love to hear you play it. Though, honestly, I don't see that
happening anytime soon. My weekend leaves are turning into jail. If I just
mention going out, my mom starts crying. If we don't leave the West Bank
soon, I think she's going to go crazy."

"And there was this girl, a French girl. She was really moved by my
piece. I'm too embarrassed to even tell you what she said. She said—no, I
can't. Anyway, I'm not sure what I'm calling it yet. Maybe—"

"A French girl?" Gadi raised his eyebrows, decidedly more interested.

"I think she's French. She was weird. She had this necklace with a big . . .
I don't know, like a woman with a halo. A saint or something Christian."

"Oh my God, this kid won't stop kicking my fucking seat." Gadi turned
and stilled the little boy's leg with a gentle hand on his knee. The child, his
pudgy face smeared in chocolate, grinned, and the young mother whispered, "Sorry."

Gadi, settling back, dug into his bag of peanut puffs. "So the French
girl? *Nu?* Did you—"

A loud crack split open the world.

A wall of hot air rushed at Ofir, slamming him hard, sending him flying,
flying back as if the seats and windows of the bus had disappeared.

What was the sound of fear?

The air sparkled with glass as the gray asphalt rushed up on either side. He landed on his back, the smack driving the air out of his chest. Blackness.

He wheezed for breath. Was it seconds later? An hour? He tried opening his eyes. The left eye—no, fuck, pain. Glass, something, in his eyeball.

He opened his right eye. Red strobe lights revolved, but the only siren he heard was in his head. That's all he heard: a high-pitched whistle. EMTs and civilians waved and soundlessly called to one another in front of the charred shell of the bus. The cool May morning blew on Ofir's legs and chest like when his mother would blow on his fingers after he burned them on the toaster. He smelled burning—hair, flesh, gasoline.

A medic kneeled beside him, her eyes darting over his body. Her lips moved, but he couldn't hear her above the whistle. It was the whistle that pained him the most. More than anything, he wanted a stop to that incessant high-pitched C. The medic's lips moved as she wiped his face with a cool cloth. He knew, having been trained to treat shock, that she was talking at him for the sake of talking at him, saying calming things like, "Everything's all right. You're all right. Everything's all right."

He lifted his head. Thank God, he wasn't paralyzed. He squinted down at his body. His khaki shirt had blown open and blood streaked his torso, but it didn't seem to be his blood. He had all his limbs. He moved his fingers. Oh, they were fine.

Gadi. Peanut-flavored puffs. Annoyed at the chocolate-faced boy kicking his seat. As the medics lifted Ofir onto a stretcher, he covered his painful eye and searched for his friend.

He had been right beside him. A red mess pooling out of his side. It was probably his blood on him. His brown eyes were open but unseeing. His friend would never almost fuck a girl again.

Dresden,
1945

Franz, limping past darkened townhouses, breath clouding in the cold March night, checked with trembling fingers again that his false papers were still in the top-left pocket of the beige suit. In one hour, he had to be at the train station. They would be waiting for him, these crazy Zionists who had returned to Europe, risking their own lives to help other Jews get out. They had secured him this suit, the fake papers, a railway ticket, and it was wrong of him to chance missing that train for a brooch.

The bombs that had shattered most of Dresden had missed Kaitzer Street. It was ghostly the way the residential boulevard and the surrounding blocks stood amid a sea of rubble. The streetlamps were unlit, and the dome of the Church of Our Lady no longer rose in the distance, but otherwise the street looked as peaceful and lovely as it did when Franz would practice his swing outs on the way home from a night at the Manhattan Mayhem. Now, four years later, he had trouble walking, knees buckling under his meager weight.

Franz stopped before townhouse 5. Aside from the missing mezuzah, it too looked the same: red brick, the two dormer windows in the roof that belonged to his room. The new inhabitants must have liked his mother's stained-glass hummingbird, for it still hung in front of the white curtains in the bay window.

Franz glanced in either direction, pulled open his pocketknife, and limped up the steps. He could do it. He could be in and out in five minutes. How many times had he arrived home after a night at the Mayhem and found he'd forgotten or lost his keys? He always got the door open without waking his parents. Even if the lock had been changed, the latch was loose.

Franz held his breath as he slipped the blade between the doorjamb and the frame. The latch might be the same, but his hands were not. They were nothing like the hands that used to do little more than lead a girl into an underarm pass and later that night, if he was lucky, unbutton her blouse. These raw, bony hands shook uncontrollably, making the knife rattle inside the doorjamb like a Purim grogger.

He paused, scoped the street. Look at him—a burglar breaking into his own home. A window lit up two houses down. Frau Gaertner's house. Did she still live there with her three cats? He turned back to the door. To hell with his shaking. He had come this far, and he wasn't leaving empty-handed. He would either leave with the brooch or be killed in his home. He reinserted the knife and pressed down, ignoring the rattle, putting all his weight in his arms. They burned with fatigue, but he had learned to live with pain.

The latch gave, and Franz nearly fell over. The door opened halfway with barely a creak, as if the house were on his side. He tiptoed into the foyer, it too almost unchanged: the brass chandelier, the red oriental runner ascending the stairs, the worn-down depression in the middle of the landing. Franz half expected Bennie Goodman to come running out and do panting circles around him. Thankfully whoever lived here now didn't have a dog. There was no barking, no sound of someone getting out of bed upstairs. It was quiet except for the tick of the pendulum clock, the clock his father had brought home the day his firm made him a partner. Franz clenched his jaw.

He crept, bringing down his feet as lightly as he could. When he spotted an oak chest, he paused. He had been sure he remembered the house perfectly—he would walk through it hundreds of times, room to room, while lying in the barrack—but he had forgotten this chest with the inlaid vines along its edges. It scared him, made him wonder what else he had forgotten.

Above the chest, he saw a man in the mirror. He jumped.

The man in the beige suit jumped too.

That pale scrag with shadows for eyes was him. He had seen his reflection a couple of times since escaping, but it was different to see it here, in the mirror where he had watched himself grow up. The last time he straightened his tie in this mirror, he had been a handsome twenty-six-year-old with thick black hair and broad shoulders, a man all the girls wanted to dance with because he lifted them so high their skirts flew.

When he reached the kitchen at the back of the house, the smell of home walloped him. He stopped, inhaled it. This he hadn't been able to relive hundreds of times; one can picture a place, but not its smell. What was it exactly that had steeped into the walls? His mother's Friday-night brisket? His father's turpentine shoe polish? Every morning his father used to shine his shoes at the kitchen table over yesterday's newspaper. Franz headed for the sink, thinking, please be here.

He counted nine tiles to the left of the faucet. Please, please. He jammed the knife in the groove between the tile and the grout. Please. Long before the Nazis, Franz would watch his mother unpin the brooch from her dress and carefully store it behind this tile in the wall. As a teenager he used to laugh at how easy it was, despite his mother's velvet theater dresses and rouged cheeks, to see the shtetl in her when she was hiding the brooch in its special place like a peasant hiding a groschen under the bed. He would tease her—"Why are you so paranoid?"—and then not listen when she launched into the history of the brooch. His mother claimed she could recount the provenance of the brooch all the way to before the Black Plague. Franz wished he'd listened. He always figured he would pay attention next time. When his mother used to stow the brooch, the tile came out more easily, but his father had filled in the grout when it became clear things were going to get worse before they got better.

Franz chipped away at the mortar, heart pounding in his ears. Sweat ran into his eyes even though a wintery wind whistled through the window over the sink. Please, let this be the grout my father filled, he thought. Look, Mother, I've come back for your brooch. The tile loosened. Easy, easy, he tried to coax it out with the knife, but his hands were even shakier now, and he lost control. The tile fell. Clanged onto the counter.

Worried about the noise, Franz ducked, scanned for a place to hide. He crawled across the checkered floor and huddled under a rolling server, against the icebox. He gripped the open pocketknife. He felt like a scared animal backed into the corner of a cage, the shining knife his claw. He listened to footfalls upstairs. Then the stairs groaned. Somebody was coming.

A blonde woman in a satiny black nightdress crossed the kitchen, her pale bare feet padding against the checkered tiles, toenails painted glossy red. Franz hunched up, breathed as quietly as possible while her lilac perfume displaced the smell of his past. It was hard to believe the world still contained women who wore perfume and nail polish. She filled a glass at the sink and drank it, her back to him, staring out the window. How thirsty he had been for four years while this woman drank from his sink. Her nightie scooped low in the back, a glow tracing the satin over her buttocks. The fear Franz had that she might turn around and see him was replaced by the fear that he would kill her. Oh, to see the fear on her face.

The woman picked up the fallen tile, turned it over in her hands. Franz stiffened, gripped the knife. She leaned forward to inspect the hole. Franz could hear her thinking: What's this? One of those exciting stashes? Everyone knew the Jews had hidden their watches, wedding rings, kiddush cups under floorboards and in the walls of their houses, planning to come back for them one day.

The woman turned in the direction of the foyer, offering a view of her wary face. She tiptoed toward the front of the house, disappearing from Franz's view. Her voice echoed in the darkness, a tentative "Hello? . . . Hello?" A silence followed, and Franz held his breath. The wooden floor creaked as she walked around, looking into the parlor, the dining room.

When she reentered the kitchen, her gait was relaxed again. She returned to the hole. As she slid her white hand and red nails inside, Franz readied to spring if she pulled out the brooch. The woman felt around, her blonde head turned to the side. Her shoulders fell. She pulled her hand out and balanced the tile against the wall as if planning to deal with it in the morning. Franz held his breath again as the woman and her lilac scent turned and left the kitchen.

Why hadn't she found the brooch? He remained huddled, listening to the woman climbing the stairs. He waited for it to go quiet, eyes on the black hole. It looked like the missing piece in a puzzle. He had tried so hard over the last few years to remember what his mother had told him about the brooch. His grandmother, her mother, had given it to her on her eighteenth birthday. He was almost sure of that. Though maybe it was her wedding. The rest of the brooch's past was even hazier. He could call up only snippets from the centuries: a consumptive deathbed, Cossacks on horses, an elopement, a knife peddler wandering across the Pale. There was the dramatic story of how their family came to possess the brooch in the first place, an incredible story—something to do with a housemaid and a magical army of yellow butterflies. This was the story Franz tried the hardest to remember, hoping it had been stored somewhere in his subconscious, but after being passed down for six hundred years, it was gone. All that remained was a strange image of a sky filled with yellow butterflies.

The only thing Franz recalled with certainty about the brooch was his mother's response to his youthful questions, not about its past, but its future. *What if I don't get married, Mutti? What if you don't like my choice of wife? What if she's a horrible, unworthy woman, but outrageously beautiful? Can I still give her the brooch?* His mother never laughed at these questions. She would say in a grave voice: "I wouldn't give this brooch to just anyone, Franz. She'd better be special."

With the house hushed again, he rushed at the hole and reached inside. Nothing. He patted around. The hole curved to the left. He didn't remember that. Had his mother, shortly before the family was ripped from their beds, chipped and chipped into the wall, trying to make the hiding place more secure? Franz leaned over the counter, stretched his arm as far as he could. If only he could cry out, maybe he could stretch his arm some more. His fingertips brushed something hard, cold, pushing it away. He went back in with the knife and tried to edge it out. Please be the brooch, please be the brooch. Beyond the kitchen window, the sky paled over the rooftops. Morning. He was lucky to see morning. Ten people were shot or starved in a barrack for every one that escaped. But they were going to die anyway, right? They should have made a break for it too. Run like hell through the evergreens. He wasn't the only one who'd seen their bunkmate throw himself at the electric fence and not die. They had all seen him hanging onto the wires until a guard had to come and shoot him in the head. Still: What would those ten men think of him jeopardizing his life now for an object?

Come on! He almost had the damn thing. If he got it now, he could still join the Zionists on that train for Vienna. Then the boat down the Danube to Odessa. And from there, a smaller boat across the Black Sea, followed by an illegal ship traversing the Mediterranean. His chances of making it to a kibbutz were laughable; but at least if he were seized at sea, he could toss the brooch overboard. Better an eternity at the bottom of the sea than pinned on a Nazi's breast.

He felt the knife catch.

When Franz would daydream about this moment—and he had day-dreamed about it countless times, it was the only dream he had left—he'd been careful to warn himself that if, by some miracle, he did get to come back for the brooch, it might do nothing for him. It might turn out to be so ludicrously inadequate that it would only kill whatever little scrap of hope he had left.

He pulled out the brooch. He didn't have the time to look at it now. He stuffed it in his breast pocket between the fake papers and his heart. If his luck held up, in a couple of hours he would be able to take a long look at it in a bathroom on a train headed north, but as he headed for the front door he already knew that it had been worth coming back for. He felt less alone with it in his pocket. He took one last glance around his old home before limping into the street, not bothering to close the door behind him.

Part Two

*A*dam sweated in front of the messenger boxes, squinting at the names in the letter: *Dagmar Stahlmann, Dagmar Gopstein, Dagmar Aisenthal.* The last day in June, a strong sun still beamed in the sky at five o'clock in the evening, blinding him as he scanned the white paper. He had waited a month to hear back from the Jewish Agency, and it was worth it.

Dear Mr. Soccorso,

We have three Dagmars in our files and the forwarding addresses for two of them. Their information is below. Be advised, however, that the address for Mrs. Dagmar Gopstein hasn't been updated since 1969. We hope this proves helpful. We wish you the best of luck with your search.

Sincerely,
Lymore Mendelsohn
Associate Archivist

The Aisenthal one from the UK, he could forget. Born in 1971. But the other two were perfect—both around eighty, originally from Germany, and living in Israel in 1947. He was down to two people with last names. And one had a phone number and an address where he could knock on the door and place the brooch in her hand.

When he got to the volunteers' phone, ready with the letter and the tokens, another foreigner was chatting on it. He waited, leaning on a pillar.

Although the girl was gabbing in Russian, he could tell by her gossipy tone and mindless toying with the cord that the conversation was trivial. Come on, get off, get off, he thought, eyes darting from the girl to the quad and back to the girl. The solitary tree's hard fruits, which were an orangey-red for a few weeks, were light green again, and rounder, larger, the size of baseballs now. At last the sun was softening, bringing a slow close to the third day in a row topping ninety degrees.

The girl was in the middle of one of those long drawn-out goodbyes—"*Okay, okay, da, da, pokah, da, ya tozhe, chao, okay . . .*"—while another Russian approached the phone. Adam readied to pounce. If he'd learned one thing over the last few weeks, it was that Israelis and Russians didn't give a shit about lines. As soon as the girl moved to put down the receiver, he grabbed it from her hand.

She screwed her face. "Excuse me."

To Adam's relief, the other guy waved his hand as if the phone weren't worth the wait and walked off with the girl.

The letter shook in his hand as he punched in the number. Hopefully this one with the contact information was his Dagmar. The phone played back the melody of numbers, hummed, and clicked into a connection.

One ring. How should he introduce himself? Two rings. Should he tell her everything on the phone, or just ask to meet her? Three rings. He really should have decided that beforehand. Four.

Twelve rings and no one had picked up, not even an answering machine. He wondered if he should hang up and try again later, or if he should stay on the phone, letting it ring and ring until someone answered, even if that was five hours from now. Then came the crackle of someone lifting the receiver, followed by more crackling.

"Hello?" Adam said. "Hello?"

The rustling continued until an old man offered a slow, shaky: "Shalom?"

"Shalom, may I please speak with Mrs. Gopstein?"

"Dagmar? You want to speak with Dagmar?" His German accent was sluggish, heavily aspirated.

"Yes, that's right. Thank you."

"I'm sorry. Dagmar died three years ago."

"Oh." Adam revisited the letter, praying now that his Dagmar was the other one. "Can you tell me, did Mrs. Gopstein live on a kibbutz?"

He leaned on the phone, squeezed his eyes, waited for the answer.

"Dagmar?" The old man chuckled. "On a kibbutz? Ho, that's funny. My wife was a real city girl. Barely made do with the theater scene in Tel Aviv. She would have been Europe's greatest theater critic if things had gone differently in the world. Every Saturday she went to the theater and . . ."

Adam couldn't bring himself to interrupt. He fed tokens into the phone while the old man, happy for the chance to talk about his Dagmar, droned on about how his wife always picked up on things in plays or movies that he missed—so why would he go to a show now alone? There would be no pleasure in it, none at all. But back in Berlin, when they were young, and Dagmar dreamed of writing reviews for the *Berliner Tageblatt* . . .

After Adam inserted his last token, he explained they were going to get cut off soon, and the old man said, all right, he would let him go, and then hung up without ever asking why the young American had been inquiring about his wife.

Adam walked toward his room, taking heart in having at least a full name now: Dagmar Stahlmann. It had to be her. But now what? He could write to the United Kibbutz Movement again with the updated information, but he couldn't bear sitting around for another letter, and that office never even wrote him back the first time. Next Tuesday, his day off, he would go to Tel Aviv. He would show up at their office with her full name. *Dagmar Stahlmann.* The more he said it, the more sense it made. It just sounded right.

"Adam, Adam!"

Ulya stood outside her door, beckoning him, her messy hair matching her red terry short shorts. Walking toward her, he had to admit she was a cute girl. It wasn't the first time he'd had to admit this over the last few days.

"Come, hurry." She drew him into her room. "The boy is back."

He followed Ulya to her back window, the window that framed her nakedness that first night. Claudette already stood there, craning to see the medics pulling a stretcher out of an ambulance. Adam remembered his first glimpse of the young soldier poring over his music sheets in the guardhouse.

The medics rolled the stretcher along the path behind their building, toward the teenagers' section. The boy was wheeled right past their window, his body covered by a white sheet, his head swathed in bandages. An obese woman jogged alongside the stretcher, struggling to keep up, her T-shirt soaked through with sweat. She talked nonstop at the medics.

Ulya shook her head while Claudette remained stock-still, unblinking. For five weeks she had waited to find out the boy's fate. At first she couldn't understand why God would have allowed this to happen to the boy who had played His music; but then she surmised, of course, it was her fault. The boy had been fine until her. She had allowed him to help her onto her feet, to clutch her arms—she, who had been planning to kill herself—and just a few hours later, he boarded that bus. She had infected him with her death wish. She knew it made no sense, but the feeling of guilt was undeniable.

Adam turned from the window. "Doesn't look good, head bandaged up like that. I wonder what's wrong with him."

"I know what's wrong," said Ulya. "His mom comes to the dairy every day. She's good friends with my boss."

Adam sat on Ulya's bed, shuffling until his back was against the wall. "So, is he going to walk again?"

Claudette didn't breathe as she waited for the answer. Every day she had wanted to ask Ziva about the boy, but the question lodged in her throat, held back by the fear that if *she* asked about him, spoke his name aloud, it might bring him bad luck and change the answer for the worse.

"His body was covered with—I can't remember what it is called—the little pieces of the bomb that get stuck in your skin . . ."

"Shrapnel?"

"Maybe, yes. And his face and chest were burned, but this will be okay. He will walk and talk. One eye is ruined. But the thing everyone in the dairy is talking about is his ears. The blast burst the eardrums. And the boy loved music. He was the one who was always playing the piano."

Claudette turned back to the window and gripped the sill.

"So he's deaf?" said Adam.

Ulya lit a cigarette, shook the match. "I think he can hear, but not well. They tried to make new drums from the skin on his arms or neck or somewhere, but it didn't work. They are going to try one more time."

Claudette dropped her forehead against the pane and rolled her head back and forth. She had to ensure the boy's next operation worked. But how?

Adam pulled his gaze away from Claudette's strange rocking. "You know, I never paid attention to the wounded. Whenever we hear about these suicide attacks, we always ask how many people died, and then we judge how bad the attack was by that number. Three dead, that's sad; twenty dead, that's fucking horrible. I've never read 'seventy wounded' or whatever and thought, holy shit, that's seventy people who were now going to have to live without a leg or their hearing."

"Wounded, killed, war, terrorism, I'm so fucking tired of it." Ulya sat on the bed with Adam. "Are you sure you don't want to take me to the States?"

"No, my little babushka. I'm only going to marry for love."

Ulya blew smoke rings that dissipated against the languid sweep of the standing fan. She pictured Farid, how he lay in the heat the night before, talking about his big fancy restaurant in his sad little underwear. She smiled to herself.

"Is there something funny about me getting married for love?"

"What? No." She turned to Adam and noticed his hand fussing in his pocket again. "Why do you always have your hand in your pocket?"

Adam's eyes went down to his pocket. He hadn't realized he was grasping the brooch. "I don't."

"Yes. You're always playing down there, and it looks like you're playing with your dick."

Ulya pulled her feet onto the bed and sat facing him, cross-legged. Adam glanced, instinctively, at her soft inner thighs and the band of red terry just wide enough to cover her crotch. He felt himself getting hard. His first spontaneous boner in months. He crossed his legs.

"It's not my dick, okay. It's nothing. I mean, it's not nothing, but . . ."

"But what? What do you have in your pocket?"

He arched his back, felt his hard-on press against his pants. Then, more for himself than Ulya, wanting to be reminded of why he was here, he pulled out the brooch.

"This." He held it against his palm, the first time he was showing it to anyone since the jeweler. He immediately went soft.

Ulya had expected something different. She didn't know what, maybe some kind of good-luck charm a man might carry around, a rabbit's foot or skeleton key, not a piece of old-lady jewelry.

"And why do you carry this thing around?"

"It's complicated."

The way Adam regarded the piece of costume jewelry piqued Ulya's curiosity. "People always say that. Just tell me."

He couldn't tell her the whole story—the old Florsheim shoebox, Bones and his hoods, the heart attack, the yellowed goodbye letter, the jeweler's blood. But without those details, how would the story make sense?

"You know my grandfather lived on this kibbutz fifty years ago, right? Well, when he was here he tried to give a woman this brooch. She turned it down, turned him down, and it broke his heart. He never got over it. Now I want to find this woman and give her the brooch."

"Oh, God!" Ulya leaned over the bed to stub her cigarette in an ashtray on the floor, giving Adam a close-up of her ass, the red short shorts hugging the roundness, riding up the crack. "You and your fucking grandfather again. Why do you want to give the brooch to somebody who didn't want it in the first place? This makes no sense."

"Because I do. This woman is the only person my grandfather ever wanted to have it."

Ulya shook her head. "No. There's something weird here."

Claudette glanced at the brooch but hardly registered it. She turned back to the window, where the medics were returning down the path with an empty stretcher. She had decided to walk around the perimeter of the kibbutz for the injured boy. But how many times? The number of pills he stopped her from taking? That was impossible. It couldn't be done in a month. She might still be walking when he went into the operation.

Ulya brought her face closer to the brooch. Adam smelled her vanilla perfume and strawberry shampoo and a tangy trace of BO. He stared down at her bowed head, the light blonde roots in the red, and had a flash fantasy—his libido was definitely back—that she were giving him a blowjob. Jesus, not now, he thought, not while talking about the brooch.

"All these gems," she said, "they can't be real."

"Oh they're real. It's real."

She had difficulty believing it. She could picture this kind of brooch in the treasury at the Kremlin. "If it's real, how much is it worth?"

"I don't know. A lot."

She looked at him, her face so close to his. "How much is a lot? Five hundred dollars?"

Adam snorted, shook his head.

"More?"

"Yeah, a little."

She sat back. "Five thousand?"

He made a sweeping motion upward with his hand.

Her eyebrows arched. "How much more?"

He turned his gaze to the brooch. "I don't know exactly. Probably worth more than my apartment. This brooch has been in my family for almost seven hundred years. Can you imagine that? Seven hundred years."

Ulya turned back to the brooch. More valuable than an apartment in New York? Then it had to be worth at least a hundred thousand dollars. Since stealing the magazine in the train station, she had stolen many, many things, but nothing so valuable as this. The most expensive was a dress with a price tag of four hundred shekels. Some would say, she supposed, that it was stealing from the State of Israel to pretend she was a Jew, but stealing from a state didn't count. Even stealing a dress from a store like Mango wasn't really stealing since it didn't hurt any one person. It wasn't like stealing from a neighbor or a friend. Or even a stranger. From actual people, she'd taken nothing, except maybe a lipstick here, a scarf there, some kopeks off a table. The magazine. But a family heirloom? If she needed it to survive, fine. But otherwise, she wasn't sure she wanted to do that.

"And where do you keep this thing all the time if it's worth so much?"

Adam patted the front pocket of his jeans and, seeming to have heard her thoughts, said, "Never leaves me. Ever. I even sleep with it. I take it into the bathroom when I shower. Someone would have to kill me to get this brooch."

Ulya smiled. "And how do you know I won't kill you?"

"Don't get me wrong, Ulie, I think you're badass, but I don't think you have murder in you. Anyway, it shouldn't be long until I've gotten it to Dagmar. This Tuesday I'm going to Tel Aviv and—"

"Tel Aviv?" Her face lit up, and she jumped onto her knees, shaking the bed. "I'm coming!"

"I'm not sure I invited you," he said, though he liked that she wanted to come.

"It's going to be so fun! Tel Aviv isn't Moscow or New York, but at least it isn't the kibbutz."

The ambulance pulled away, and Claudette turned from the window. She would walk the perimeter of the kibbutz five times, because it had been five in the morning when the boy shook her awake. She headed for the door. It was going to be a long, long night. If only she had ignored the music, taken the pills. She didn't think she could be in a hell worse than the one she had tried to escape. She still had the pills, hidden in the backpack under the bed, but she couldn't escape before the boy's operation.

Adam said, "Where you going, Claudette the Astonishing?"

"To walk around the kibbutz."

When the door closed behind her, Ulya pointed at her head and made crazy circles.

*Z*iva admired the final draft of her article, painstakingly rewritten onto the pages of a new legal pad. "Utopia on the Auction Block" had taken her far too long to write, but in the end she hadn't let any of it stop her—her deteriorating body, the specter of Franz's grandson, her wandering mind, the fatigue. She wielded the pen ruthlessly, erasing and reworking every sentence, every argument, until she was left with her most inspiring rhetoric yet.

She turned in her chair as if she would find Dov sitting on the couch, waiting to share in her triumph. After all these years, she still felt in these moments his pride in her. Her eyes wandered to his portrait, obscured by the glare on the glass, and then to the wall clock. It was almost three in the morning.

Too exhilarated to go to sleep, she would immediately walk the article over to the library, where that young woman—Mara? Maya?—edited and printed the newsletter. She would take the long way, posting the SAVE THE KIBBUTZ! flyers she had made over the last week. They weren't fancy, just blue marker on white paper, but sometimes simple hit hardest. And it was best to spread posters at night, so people woke up to them in the morning. That's how they did it when she was a student.

Stepping out her front door, she saw the light on in Eyal's office. What could he be doing in there at all hours? Brainstorming new ways to ruin the place? He hadn't had a girlfriend since that artsy-fartsy Orna woman, ten years ago already. Why hadn't he just gone and lived in Tel Aviv with her? Why did he refuse to leave the kibbutz if all he was going to do was try to destroy it? It didn't make sense. Maybe he was subconsciously seeking revenge on his mother.

Such a muggy, quiet night. She would wait until she had passed the old people's building before hanging up a sign. No use wasting posters on people who, aside from her, didn't work anymore; they would never vote for salaries. It was the future she had to convince. Walking with her article, her stack of signs, and a roll of scotch tape, Ziva felt very much in her element. In the eighties, she drove around Galilee gumming up posters for the Labor Party. During the wars of the sixties and seventies, she hiked about the Jezreel Valley with heartening images of dancing children and homegrown watermelons. There were a few posters, she was proud to say, she had nailed up at great risk to herself. In 1936, she and another woman, dressed as British officers' wives, marched up to the British police station in Haifa and hammered a sign to its door with the warning: GO HOME OR ELSE! And three years before that, while still a girl in Berlin, she pinned to the school's bulletin board a drawing of a buck-toothed Hitler Youth under the dictum: ONLY COWARDS JOIN THE HITLER YOUTH! Dov and another freckled boy from their Maccabi Hatzair chapter, a *mischling*, as the Nazis would have called him, a half-breed, whose name she hadn't been able to recall for decades, stood guard on either end of the hallway. Wait! His name was David. And they called him Bloomie. Funny, for most of her life she couldn't remember, and now there it was, both his real name and nickname.

Ziva reached the smaller houses belonging to young couples without children and stopped to tape her first poster to a lamppost. While breaking off the tape, she heard a rustle behind her and quickly turned around. Just a rabbit darting out of a bush. She exhaled and went back to taping the poster. Instead of having to watch out for Nazis or British patrolmen or Arab raiders, she had to beware of busybodies who would ask her if she thought it was a good idea to be out at this hour. And where was her helper from Canada? they would say. It was sickening the way people treated someone like a child as soon as they reached a certain age. She wanted to shout into their concerned little faces that she was taking on the world before their parents had even fucked, but her bluntness, a point of pride her whole life, was now shrugged off as crotchety old-ladyhood. Fuming, Ziva scanned about for another good place for a poster and, lo and behold, there was her son's bungalow. She would stick one to his front door.

By the time Ziva reached the western edge of the kibbutz, she had posted all her signs and was out of breath. Her skin prickled from the heat, and her knees smarted with every step. She wheezed up the path to the library, which had a banner along its white wall, faint ink on continuous computer paper: WELCOME BACK, OFIR! She paused at the door to savor the moment before slipping the article into the metal slot.

With only the roll of scotch tape left, she hobbled over to a wooden picnic table to rest before starting the trek back. Nestled in a patch of pines, the table overlooked the bank leading down to the plastics factory. An ugly but practical factory. Corrugated steel, cement, a parking lot. That boy was right about one thing: the cotton fields had been magical. In September, before the harvesting, a sea of white fluff glowed in the sunlight. Ziva exhaled deeply, trying to expel the nostalgia. Nostalgia was an idle person's ailment.

She took a shorter route back to the old people's quarters, cutting across the parking lot and its flock of white Subarus—compacts, hatchbacks, minivans, some new and shiny, others beat up. Look how many cars the kibbutz had now. She paused to count the keys in the cabinet. Twenty-three. One missing. Why did people need their own cars when they had twenty-four sitting here waiting for them?

"Ziva?"

Two teenage boys and a girl stood beside her. The handsome boy with the thick dark eyebrows held the missing key. She didn't know any of their names—when had she stopped knowing everyone's name?—though she could guess who their parents were.

"Yes?"

"It's late," said the girl, glittery purple stars hanging from her ears. "Is everything okay? Can we help you?"

"Can *you* help *me*? How dare you tell me it's late. If one of us should have a bedtime, it's you, don't you think?"

The teenagers exchanged looks. The handsome boy, smirking, reached past Ziva to return the key to its hook. Then they walked off, waiting until they were a couple of meters away before bursting into laughter. She heard the shorter, gingery boy call her a witch.

She arrived at her apartment in nearly unbearable pain. Her joints burned. The marrow in her bones throbbed. She leaned on her desk to read her article one last time, the hand copy she had made to later verify the newsletter hadn't messed with her words. Was it indeed a tour de force? She found that it was.

Reassured that her pain was worth it, she changed into her nightie and limped to the bathroom to take her nightly muscle relaxer and opioid. Removing the cap from the opioids, she found only a couple of pills at the bottom of the bottle. Hadn't she picked up a two-month supply only a month ago? She was sure of it. Was she losing her mind? Fear fluttered in her chest. A deteriorating body she could handle, not a failing mind.

She climbed into bed. At least tomorrow was Shabbat, and she could rest. She rolled onto one side, and then the other. It was impossible to fall asleep before the pills carried away the pain. It wouldn't be too long. As much as she hated relying on so many pills, she was grateful for them. Without them, she might not have been able to keep working. Oh, yes, she could feel the sharp pain softening to a mild throb. Hmm, very good. Soon even the throbbing would disappear. When the hurt lifted, it always left her with a strange floaty feeling. Like lying on a stockpile of cotton.

That field of white. She remembered walking through it, the dusty path puffing under her boots. All around her, ripe white fluff, and the sky above a perfect blue, as if all the clouds had fallen to the ground. Her mind was at peace—it always was when she was heading into the fields. Her whole life she had watched people look for that peace—on psychologists' couches, at ashrams, in nightcaps—when all they had to do was give themselves over to honest labor.

"Hello, Ziva."

Startled, she turned to Franz, who was short of breath from jogging to catch up. It crossed her mind to pretend not to remember his name. But why would she do that? Sometimes she had to wonder if she were the one making things needlessly awkward.

"Hello, Franz."

"I'm also working in the cotton fields. It seems I've been deemed well enough to work outdoors."

He did look healthier, the tendons in his face no longer visible, though the cheekbones were still too sharp. His black hair didn't grow in patches anymore; it was thick and combed back with pomade. Who wore pomade to work in the fields? He was as clean-shaven as if he'd stepped out of a barbershop. Most men on the kibbutz shaved only on Fridays, but come to think of it, she had never seen Franz with bristles. His ironed shirt glowed as white as the cotton fluffs. And yet, for all the newfound health and careful grooming, the hue of someone recently sick lingered, an ashen cast.

"Don't you have a hat?"

"No."

Should she tell him that she knows very well that he does have a hat? A brown fedora with a black ribbon—a green feather reserved for Shabbat and holidays. But to say so felt like an admission, while not saying so also felt like one. She decided, no matter, a felt fedora wasn't appropriate for picking cotton.

"You could have requested a tembel hat from the clothing house."

"Today's my first day in the fields. I didn't think of it. I'll be fine."

She couldn't let this pasty man, still too thin, work all afternoon in the sun with his head uncovered. She took off her own hat and held it out.

"Take mine."

Franz stopped walking, forcing her to stop. He looked down at the beige bucket hat.

"That's kind. But, of course, no thank you."

"Why? Are you afraid of messing up your hairdo?"

He smiled and touched his hair. "No, it's not that."

She gazed off to the side, holding back her own smile. She had really embarrassed him. When she had regained the air of a person who only happened to know better and was just doing her duty, she turned back to him. "You don't understand what it's like in the fields. You're going to get sunstroke. You must take my hat."

"Then you won't have one."

"I'm used to the sun. And, let's be frank, I'm in better shape than you."

He nodded. "Yes, you're in great shape."

Was that a lewd remark? Pretending not to have heard it that way, she proffered the hat. Franz's shoulders dropped in mock defeat. He reached for it, and Ziva let go of it too early. Why did she do that? She apologized, diving to catch the hat, while Franz lunged for it too, and they knocked heads.

Laughing, Franz swept the hat from the dusty ground. Ziva straightened up, her face warm as if the midday sun were already here. Franz brushed off the hat, pulled it onto his head, and gave her a wide closed-lip smile. The floppy thing looked so wrong on him, she couldn't help but snort and shake her head.

All day Ziva and Franz picked cotton off the dry bushes one row down from one another, along with five or six other pickers. She kept messing up, plucking the stalks off with the bolls. Then she had to waste time picking the brittle twigs off the cotton, cutting her fingers in the process. The fluff stuck to the blood. The day before she'd only pulled off a couple of stalks.

Why had Franz broken their months of awkward silence? Or was that awkward silence just a figment of her imagination? No, she had caught him watching her many times, hadn't she? On Friday nights, while everyone sang around the campfire, she would catch him observing her from the other side of the flames. If he kept his eyes on her when she caught him, then she could have chalked it up to mere lechery. If he had tried to speak to her sooner, tried to flirt with her, this too would have defused everything. Instead, he always turned away, which Ziva found disconcerting, so she tried not to look at him. To do this, however, she had to keep track of his whereabouts, and that made his presence loom even larger, so that in the end their eyes met less often, but when they did, the effects were keener.

Ziva discreetly looked over at him now and found him doing the same. This time when their eyes met, he didn't look away. He gave her another wide smile and a tug on the hat's droopy brim. Should she smile back? What for? No, she should make no response at all, just go back to work.

The day wore on, and the sun grew vicious. Eventually, Ziva got into the right mind-set, picking the cotton efficiently and gracefully.

When the sun dipped behind Mount Carmel and the other pickers ambled toward a well-deserved dinner, Franz hung back. Was he waiting for her? He kept glancing in her direction.

"Go ahead!" she called. "I'm going to work a little longer."

Tembel hat in his hands, he walked over to where she stood at the end of a row of harvested plants, not a boll to be seen.

"I'd say we worked enough for one day, don't you think?"

"I'd feel better if I did one more bush."

She wanted to insist that she usually wasn't this slow, but she couldn't risk giving him the impression that he had distracted her.

"Do you want me to help?"

"No. Really, I'm fine."

"Well, thank you for your hat." He held it out and then withdrew it. "Actually, it's rather sweaty. I'll wash it first."

She extended her hand. "Don't be silly. Give it to me. I'll drop it in the laundry."

He hesitated, as if unsure what would be the mannerly thing to do.

Before he had a chance to decide, she whisked it from his hands. "Anyway, I didn't lend you *my* hat. It's the kibbutz's hat. I personally don't own anything."

"Nothing? Not one little thing?"

She shook her head.

"Don't you want to own something? Just one little thing that belongs to you and nobody else?"

"No. Whatever I want for me, I want for everybody."

Franz buried his hands in his pockets and regarded her, pensively. "You have a real sense of purpose, Ziva. That must be nice."

Ziva started on a new bush while Franz walked back toward the kibbutz. Every once in a while, she would look up and find him farther down the path. After she picked the bush clean, she walked down the rows the others had picked, gleaning the missed fluffs.

When it was well into twilight, she started back toward the kibbutz. As she walked down the dirt path between the cotton, she turned the hat in her hands. Sweat darkened the band. His sweat.

The path grew dimmer and seemed to lengthen with every step.

At last sleep descended on Ziva, with the kibbutz as it used to be, just up ahead, a few lovely lights on a dusky plateau.

"**O**fir-chik!"

At least that's what Ofir thought he heard. He turned to see who was coming through the door. He had never been a popular kid, and yet every afternoon a different delegation of his peers stopped by his studio apartment, leading him to believe they were taking turns. On visiting duty today was Hadas the guffawer, Gingi of the orange Isfro, and handsome, cooler-than-thou Ido.

Hadas, dark hair pulled into a ponytail to show off her feather earrings, came up to the side of his bed, saying, "Hey there, Ofir." Ido stood next to her. "What's up?" Gingi stationed at the foot of the mattress.

After the hellos always came the uncomfortable silence while his visitors scrambled for conversation, something other than what would've been the go-to topics, his music or their army service. Ido said something about it being hot, though his tanned, chiseled face showed no sweat. He tapped a pack of red Marlboros against his palm.

The same kids who used to tease Ofir for his Mozart and pimples now regarded him as a hero. But what had he done? In the hospital, when he told the other patient in his room, a middle-aged man who'd also been on the bus, that it didn't make sense that they were being treated like heroes when all they had done was be at the wrong place at the wrong time, the man, staring down at his missing leg, claimed it was heroic that anyone in this country boarded a bus. He had a point, but then the people visiting him were also heroes. He wanted his specialness to come from his music.

Ofir pointed at Ido's pack of Marlboros. "I'll have one."

Ido shot a look at the other two visitors. "You sure you can smoke?"

"What?" The *what* came out before he had a chance to catch it.

Ido raised his voice: "Your mom said not to give you cigarettes."

Ofir still couldn't hear him over the whistle in his head, and he seemed not to have said the same thing. He nodded. "Yes."

Ido shrugged and lit a cigarette for him. Ofir took a drag while Gingi straightened the mirror from the kasbah. That dark room full of mirrors felt like it belonged to a past life.

Hadas perched on the edge of his bed. Enunciating each syllable, she shouted: "IRIT was seen SNEA-KING out the BACK DOOR of YOSSI's HOUSE. Everyone says they are ha-ving AN AFFAIR."

Ido sat in one of the visitor chairs. "You're KIDDING! IRIT? Which Irit?"

"Which Irit? One of them's TWELVE YEARS OLD."

The strained shouting at each other reminded Ofir of the Purim plays they put on as children. No one could relax and have a real conversation when they had to talk like that. It was never long before his visitors gave up and gabbed amongst themselves while he sat there, nodding, pretending for their sakes that he could follow along. Ofir watched Hadas's head kick back as she laughed. He didn't even have quiet amid all this *ha ha ha*. He had the fucking whistle. And the doctors said the ringing would only worsen as his hearing diminished with age. By forty he could be completely deaf, alone with the whistle.

Fed up with everyone small-talking around him as if that were some kind of cure, he said, "I'll never hear music again."

The three of them stopped talking, turned to him.

Gingi leaned on the bed. "Don't be silly, Ofir! Of course you will!"

"Or compose."

Ido shook his head like someone privy to secret information. "Believe me, Ofir-chik, you will play in the greatest halls in Europe. I know it."

Gingi said something else, which Ofir couldn't hear, except for "Beethoven," which made him the hundredth person to say if Beethoven could do it, he could.

Hadas nodded, her feathers shimmying. "YOU—should—be—HAP-PY—you're—ALIVE!"

Ofir looked from one visitor to the other, debating whether to tell them that without music, he wasn't sure why he was alive. He decided against it. It would only lead to more inane lies and maxims and false cheer.

After they left, Ofir rose to open the blinds. He wasn't allowed direct sunlight on his skin, but it was late in the afternoon and none of the light fell directly on the bed. He climbed back under the sheets and stared at the golden square of light the window cast on the wall. The square faded as it ascended toward the ceiling. What was the sound of sunlight dying on a wall? A cello? He stopped the train of thought. What if he really couldn't compose again? How would he appreciate afternoon light?

"My son! My little boy!"

Ofir was startled to see his mother and stepfather standing at the end of his bed. His mother, seeming to have gained another twenty pounds, wore that maniacal smile she acquired the day of the bombing. She had never been a smiler. His reticent stepfather appeared as he always did, red faced, paunch pressing against his Haifa football shirt.

"We brought you dinner," his mother said. "All your favorites."

His stepfather slumped into a visitor's chair while his mother turned on the lights and placed one Tupperware after another onto the bed table: raisin and carrot salad, spicy black olives, couscous with pine nuts, roasted chicken. She laid out a napkin and fork with the flourish of a high-class waiter and settled into the seat next to her husband. Ofir suppressed his nausea to pull a string of meat off the chicken breast.

His mother, inappropriate smile in place, watched him chewing. Her eyes welled. Unable to stop herself, she asked the universe again: "My son? My only son?"

"Ima, I'm fine."

"What did I do? Everyone I ever loved."

Ofir glanced at his stepfather, who stared into space.

"Other people died, Ima. I'm not dead. I'm right here. I'm ... I'm lucky to be alive."

Tears streamed down her cheeks. She apologized, said she shouldn't let him see her so sad, that she should be cheering him up, not the other way around. She wiped her eyes and said through that smile: "Yes, yes. It could have been much worse. You can see out of your left eye. It's just your hearing, *some* of your hearing, but you are here. Here you are."

"Here I am." Ofir tore off another string of chicken.

His stepfather cleared his throat. "Eighty-five people were killed yesterday in that JCC in Argentina. Eighty-five!"

His mother nodded as if this should make them all feel luckier. Desperate to return the string of chicken to the Tupperware, Ofir struggled to find something to say that would distract his mother. "So do you know which way you're going to vote?"

"Vote?"

"Equal pay or salary scales?"

His mother shrugged, though Ofir knew she was going to vote for the status quo. His whole life he'd heard her say that she didn't know what she would have done if she hadn't lived on a kibbutz, having a baby without a husband or parents. And now he could imagine what she was thinking: that it might be hard for Ofir to hold a job with his impaired sight and hearing, that the kibbutz would take care of him for the rest of his life. His nausea swelled at the idea of spending the rest of his life working in the plastics factory. A far cry from Juilliard.

He turned to his stepfather. "And you?"

"Keep things as they are."

His mother heaved herself out of the chair. She never stayed long. She did a terrible job hiding how hard it was for her to be around him.

"We'll ask for a TV," she said.

"What?" He caught himself too late again.

"We'll—get—you—a—television!"

"You know I don't watch TV."

"Maybe you will now. *Seinfeld* is funny."

His mother pressed the lids back on the Tupperwares of untouched food and waddled over to his minifridge. Her rolls bulged against her T-shirt as she bent over to find room for the containers. He could always tell how his mother was doing by her weight, and he'd never seen her fatter.

His stepfather patted the bed. "Keep your chin up, Ofiri."

His mother stood by the door. "Whatever you do, don't go in the sun: the burns need to heal. Don't open the blinds during the day. Don't get up, except to go to the bathroom. Don't touch the bandages. And don't stay up all night. Get some sleep. And you're going to need to start eating."

His parents pushed through the screen door, leaving him alone for the remainder of the night, alone in the room where everything looked exactly as it did that morning he set out for army jail, exhilarated from the best night he'd ever had at the piano. The kasbah mirror hung where he'd nailed it. The information packets from the best conservatories in the world still sat on his desk: the navy folder from Yale, Juilliard's red glossy booklet, the catalog of classes from the Royal College of Music in London. The Speedy Gonzales T-shirt he'd taken off to put on his army uniform was still draped over the back of his chair.

How many visitors did he have today? Twelve. Nine if he counted his mom's four visits as one visitor. Nine visitors and zero connections. Every day it became more obvious that no one could hear the whistle in his head but him. That no one else would ever hear it.

It was nine in the morning and already sweltering, even under the eucalyptuses that shaded the modest graveyard. Ziva and Claudette began the cleanup by tackling the weeds growing around the recumbent tombstones.

"I'm the only one who wants to work here." Ziva tugged on the yellow star thistle sprouting around the only English gravestone: *Daniel Birnbaum, 1924–1989, Born in Cincinnati, Ohio.* "But there are more people here I want to be around than in the dining hall."

Claudette, attempting to pull out each weed with an even number of tugs, couldn't have imagined a cemetery more different from the one covering the slope of Mount Royal, where Louise had taken her to visit their mother's snowcapped headstone. At the bottom of that sprawling cemetery hummed the gray city. When Claudette returned in the spring, the stone angels and crosses basked among green grass and giant leafy oaks. This cemetery had no snow, no grass, no sprawling city, no angels. Its few dozen graves rested among parched cacti, dusty earth, and white gravel paths. The limestone tombs lay flat like white stone beds.

"Come see this grave, Claudette."

Claudette joined Ziva in front of a slab of weathered white stone, its recessed Hebrew letters packed with dirt. Ziva had explained that Jews left a rock on the grave when they visited, but this one had none.

"That's Ziva Peled's grave."

"Your mother's?"

"No. My mother died in Theresienstadt . . . I think. And Jews don't name their children after themselves. There's no such thing as Shmulik Goldberg the third. Look at the date of death, Claudette."

There wasn't one. It read *1915–*

"This grave has been waiting for me for forty-six years. People say it's morbid, that it's against Jewish tradition, blah, blah. I think they're being ridiculous: there's a bit of land waiting for everyone, whether your name's on it or not. And it brings me great comfort to know that I will lie next to my best friend." Hand on her back, she grabbed a stone from the ground and added it to the pile on the grave beside hers. "My dear Dov."

Claudette recalled the face from the black-and-white photo, the clear eyes, the serious mouth under the thin blond mustache. The dates on the grave—*1915–1948*—revealed that he had died not so long after that picture was taken. She had assumed Ziva had lost her husband only a few years ago, when they were both old.

"How did Dov die?"

"In the War of Independence. After working so hard to create the Jewish state, he only lived in it for two weeks."

Claudette was confused: Hadn't this always been a Jewish place? What about Jesus? She lowered her eyes. "I'm sorry."

Ziva shook her head. "Don't be. Dov died fighting. Israel declared independence, and the next day we were attacked by five Arab armies. Can you imagine that, Claudette? The country wasn't a day old and we were fighting Iraq, Syria, Jordan, Lebanon, and Egypt. Two weeks into the war, the Syrians made it to Sadot Hadar, and all we had were Molotov cocktails, a few grenades, and one, just one, antitank gun. Dov was shot over there, where the mandarin grove is now." She pointed at a shallow hill covered by lush green trees. "I got to him within seconds, but he was already dead. The bullet went right through his head." She continued to gaze in the direction of the grove. "But no, don't be sorry. There are worse ways for a Jew to die than fighting. People won't like me saying this, but in a shower, for instance."

While they weeded, Claudette asked herself: Was there a more shameful way to die than with a plastic bag over your head and veins surging with medicine stolen from a sick old woman? These days the Bad Feeling was more demanding than ever, telling her to do this and that and if she didn't the boy's operation wouldn't work. Tolerating the Bad Feeling was even harder after experiencing what it felt like to live without it, if only briefly.

Ziva tugged the thistle from Dov's tombstone. "When we buried Dov, it was very simple, very dignified. After lowering him into the ground, we all stood around in silence for a minute or two, each of us left with our own thoughts, and then we started shoveling the dirt on him. No prayers. No *Blessed art Thou, O Lord* claptrap. Now everyone says the Kaddish. We tried so hard to keep religion out of the kibbutz, and for the most part, we did, except when it came to death. Even the most rational people can't seem to bury their loved ones without some hocus-pocus. I know you're religious, Claudette, and probably don't like me calling it all hocus-pocus, but I can't pretend to respect something I don't."

Claudette was too distracted to be offended. She had pulled out a weed on the seventh tug—an uneven number. Now, to even things out, she had to make sure it took seven tugs to pull out the next weed, or the boy's operation wouldn't work.

With the weeding finished, Ziva and Claudette watered the cacti and the eucalyptuses. The day had grown even hotter, and the tin watering cans were too scalding to handle without wetting their hands first. Claudette had to give each plant eight spills of water, no matter if it was a tall tree or a wee flower. To give a plant the right amount of water, she had to adjust the lengths of the spills. If she made a mistake and splashed a plant a ninth time, she had to give it an additional seven teeny pours. All the while the idea of a dignified death hung around her like the heat. Even if she never swallowed the pills, was it possible to have a dignified death after an undignified life? Look at her, pouring seven extra drops on a cactus as if it mattered.

She rested the watering can. "Ziva, how do you want to die? If you could choose?"

Ziva laid a hand against a eucalyptus. What a question. Most people refused to talk about such things, but not this girl. She had to give her that. Leaning on the tree, she surveyed the fields unfolding from the shaded cemetery, the dark green mint, the purple rows of cabbages, the yellow lines of the flowering peanut plants.

"Working," she said. "I would like to die working, preferably in the fields."

Claudette noticed the old woman appeared very yellow against the tree. Not olive, but unquestionably yellow—her face the ochre of old scotch tape, blue veins bulging on mustardy calves.

"I don't want to die in bed. I've never been lazy, and I don't deserve to die with my head on a pillow. It wouldn't be fair, Dov in battle and me in bed."

After lunch, sandwiches eaten in the shade of the largest eucalyptus, the women wiped down the dusty gravestones. The midday sun bore through the trees, leaving dazzling flecks of light on the limestone and white gravel paths. Every now and then, while the women dunked their rags in buckets of bath-warm water, a breeze blew through the trees, bringing momentary relief and making the flecks of light dance. Somewhere in the sky, military planes broke the sound barrier.

"That's a sad one." Ziva pointed at the grave Claudette was wiping down. "You know that boy who was in the bus bombing? Ofir? That's his father's grave."

Claudette froze, her rag over the inscription.

"That boy's poor mother. First her parents starve in the Łódź ghetto while she's hiding in a convent in England. Then her first husband's killed in the Yom Kippur War, while she's pregnant with the boy—which, by the way, I can relate to, because I was pregnant with Eyal when Dov died. And after all that, the boy, her only child, gets blown up on a bus."

"The boy . . . do you know how he's doing? Is he going to be all right?"

Ziva shrugged. "Depends on how you define all right. If I were him, I'd be all right. He has his legs, his hands, his brain. Personally, I think hearing is the least important of all the senses. But the boy really lived for music."

"But the operation . . . I heard they were going to do the operation again. Did they?"

"They did. It failed. They tried to graft him new eardrums three times. The skin doesn't stay. And now they think that maybe the little bones deeper in his ears are too damaged anyway."

"So he'll no longer be able to play music?"

"I don't know."

Claudette traced the foreign letters on the father's grave with her finger. She would trace the father's name a hundred times—no, two hundred. She would trace the father's inscription two hundred times to make sure the boy could still play his piano.

She finished a third tracing. The prospect of doing this a hundred and ninety-seven more times—assuming she traced them all perfectly—was unbearable, but if she refused, wouldn't it seem like she didn't care about the boy's plight? What if her lack of caring was taken into account by God and this affected the boy's chances of being able to play music? She saw Ziva carrying her bucket to a new grave.

She had lost count. Or rather, she hadn't lost count, but worried that she had anyway. Just in case, she would have to start over. Even though she didn't want to. Even though she didn't truly believe it would make any difference. If these rituals made a difference, why after six weeks of saying Hail Marys for the boy and counting the leaves in the trees and chewing her food in even numbers did the operation not work?

Before she fully understood what she was doing, she was standing up and backing away from the grave. She walked backward with the heavy pail of water, eyeing the white grave as if she were afraid to wake it up. Her fists were clutched so tight, the nails dug into the skin of her palms, as she whispered, *Ce n'est pas vrai.*

It isn't true. She whispered it again and again as she knelt before a different grave with the rag. *It isn't true.* Her heart beat in sharp painful bursts. Was she really going to refuse to do a ritual? Disobey the Bad Feeling? She would keep repeating the phrase until she left the cemetery. *Ce n'est pas vrai.* She had to fight so hard not to return to the father's grave that she shivered in the heat, felt close to throwing up.

Ziva noticed Claudette looking ill and supposed the Canadian wasn't used to the high temperature. "Claudette, have you been drinking enough water?"

"I think so."

"Your pee should be clear."

Ziva felt a little queasy herself. She hoped she wasn't suffering from mild sunstroke. She used to handle the heat with ease. Maybe it was the drugs that made her more sensitive? Some warned of photosensitivity, whatever that was exactly. Her sweaty cotton shirt stuck to her back and bulging belly, which got a painful squeeze every time she bent over. It had only been three weeks since she'd had the fluid pumped. It used to take four months before she noticed any discomfort. Ziva arched her back, and the blood rushed from her head. Her vision darkened. She leaned on a grave and lowered herself to the ground. And she had just been worrying about the girl. She would sit down for just a minute. Just until everything stopped spinning. She closed her eyes, but still the graves circled her. All those graves, all her old comrades.

"Ziva! Ziva! Your hands!" Dov shouted as he danced past her. She was dancing in the inner circle and had once again failed to clap her hands. She was wretched at the hora. Dov, face illuminated by the campfire, shook his head at her in mock disappointment as the dancing pulled him away.

Round and round—it was dizzying—and when she next had to clap hands, this time with a Hungarian refugee, she failed once more. A strange sound floating over their singing had distracted her. She broke from the hora and stood between the two circles listening for the source of that sound. What was it? Jazz music? Others stopped to listen too, and the hora circles slowed to a halt.

After you've gone and left me crying, after you've gone there's no denying . . .

A wind-up phonograph with a large brass horn sat atop a wooden vegetable cart, Franz grinning beside it. Seven months had passed since he had arrived on the kibbutz. He had regained his health and good looks, and tonight something extra seemed to be back.

"What is *this?*" Ziva stamped toward him, while everyone else watched.

"It's 'After You've Gone' sung by Bing Crosby. Written by Turner Layton and Henry Creamer."

Ziva marched so forcefully toward the phonograph that Franz jumped in front to protect it. Pointing at the machine behind him, she spat in German, "I mean, this thing! Where did you get the money for it? Out of the money coop? Was there a vote?"

There'll come a time, now don't forget it, There'll come a time, when you'll regret it—

"Listen." Franz raised his hands. "I bought it with my own stipend. It didn't cost much. It was abandoned by a British officer. I just thought it would be fun for everyone."

"Fun? We don't want commercial music. We sing our own songs! You can't ignore the will of the people."

Ziva turned with an open arm to reveal the indignant people and found many had paired off, both kibbutzniks and refugees. American Danny spun a giggling Polish girl. A Litvak with a ginger beard led a shy Dutch woman in a floral dress. Men leading, women following—it was repulsive. Women being scarcer, some men laughed and danced with one another.

Franz winded the phonograph. "I believe the people have spoken."

Ziva, speechless, scowled at the dancers swaying around the campfire as if it were a chandelier. "An hour of jazz won't kill us," joked one of the survivors as he shuffled past.

Dov sidled up to Ziva. "Don't get too worked up about it."

"They aren't here because they love the land. They don't care one bit about Eretz Israel."

"Come now, Zivale. Be fair. I think some of them love Palestine as much as we do now, which makes sense after what they've been through. If it comes down to it, I don't think anyone will fight harder to have their own country than this frail lot."

"Yes, but what kind of country? Another England? Or United States? It's seditious. Franz is staging a coup d'état with this music."

"A coup d'état?" Dov laughed. "It was inconsiderate to play it while we were dancing, you're right, but . . . Zivale, you're reading too much into this. Don't worry, we'll make him get rid of the phonograph first thing tomorrow morning."

The people have spoken. It was sacrilegious to think it, but sometimes the people didn't seem to know or care what was good for them. The same song started up again. Did he have only the one record? *You'll feel blue, you'll feel sad, You'll miss the bestest pal you've ever had . . .*

Dov took Ziva's hand and tugged her toward the makeshift dance floor. She shook her head, eyes wide with warning.

"In honor of Frau Kessler," he said.

Ziva caught one of the survivors watching them, and she realized she wasn't going to win this battle with inflexibility and fury. Tomorrow the phonograph would be gone, but tonight she would show the people what it meant to follow the group. "One dance."

It had been fifteen years since she and Dov had been the worst pupils in Frau Kessler's dance studio, but they immediately fell into their old habits, Dov leading, not on the beat, Ziva following, only when she felt the beat had arrived. She remembered how Dov used to mimic Frau Kessler's high-pitched voice in her ear: *One two three, and one two three.* Not only were those younger versions of her and Dov gone, but it was all gone—the dance studio, bombed with the rest of central Berlin, the boys who'd grown into German soldiers, and all the Jewish children that had waltzed around them, as well as their parents who would wait in the hallway. Frau Kessler herself had probably been fed to an oven.

"Sorry, my friend." Franz tapped Dov's shoulder. "There's only one woman to every three men."

Dov released Ziva and, stepping out of the way, extended an arm like a maître d'hôtel. "She's all yours."

"I'm all nobody's." Ziva turned to go. "I've had enough dancing."

"One dance." Franz grabbed her wrist. He pulled her in and wrapped his other arm around her back. *There'll come a time . . .*

Behind Franz's head, Dov gestured with his hand that it was going to be all right.

Ziva kept her head stiff, eyes fixed over Franz's shoulder, as he guided her around the dirt with a slight press on her back, pull at her waist, gentle push on her hand. He was such a competent lead, he swept her around the campfire, making other couples seem stationary, making it look as if she knew how to dance. Was she being paranoid or were people observing them with knowing eyes? *Knowing?* Why would she think such a thing? Franz's breath tickled her ear as he crooned along, "Babe, think what you're doing, You know my love for you will drive me to ruin . . ."

"You have a voice made for Hollywood," she said sarcastically.

"Thank you." He swung her out and drew her in again.

When the song came to an end, he flamboyantly dipped her, drawing applause from all around. He smiled over her horizontal body at their admirers. When he pulled her back up, a wobbly Ziva turned to leave, but he wouldn't release her hand. With his other arm bracing her back, he kept her facing him. Someone started the record again, and Ziva jerked to get away, but not too violently. She didn't want to draw attention. Franz held on, forcing them to sway side to side.

"Let go."

"I wish you were all mine."

. . . After you've gone away . . .

Ziva's heart thumped against her ribs so hard she feared Franz could hear it. Since that afternoon in the cotton fields, he had given her a compliment here and there, a friendly wink, but always in a way that allowed room for doubt, for her to act as if she simply didn't take it the way he might have meant it. His neck smelled warm and brackish, like the sea. Maybe he had taken a dip after buying the phonograph in Haifa or Tel Aviv. Why had she allowed him to force her to dance? She lifted her hand from his shoulders and pinched his neck. Hard.

"Ow." Franz let go, and rubbed his neck.

She strode away from him and straight through the joggle of dancers, past Dov, laughing and dancing with David, a newer member from Paris. She had to get away. She left the light of the campfire behind and climbed up a knoll into the surrounding darkness, toward a half-built schoolhouse.

She ducked through a doorless doorway and stepped among the planks and piles of bricks on the unfinished floor. In a few weeks, the school would be ready for the kibbutz's handful of children and the more to come, but in its incomplete state, it felt abandoned, private. From here, she barely heard the stupid Bud Crosby or whoever it was. She stood before a wall of wooden beams, not yet covered with planks, facing away from the camp-fire and the dancers, toward the black silhouette of Mount Carmel. The stars twinkled above the mountain.

A wobbling light illuminated the wooden framing, and behind her she heard someone stepping on planks.

"I think you drew blood."

She turned. "You should have let go."

Franz wasn't wearing his usual smile, but his black eyes still flickered with amusement. He set his gas lantern on a worktable.

"The phonograph isn't the only thing I bought in Tel Aviv." He dug his hand into his pocket and retrieved a small black box tied with a silver bow.

Ziva eyed the box. "Gifts to individuals are against the rules."

"So we better not tell anyone." He held it out to her.

What could be in that tiny box? It wasn't square like a ring box, but the shape and size of a finger. "If you want to buy me a gift, buy the kibbutz a gift."

"My God, Ziva, some things can't be given to a whole kibbutz."

"Why not?"

"Take it and see."

She shook her head. "There's no point. I'm not going to keep it."

She couldn't remember the last time she'd been given a gift. Not since Berlin anyway. Fourteen years? The silver bow pulled at her—the selfish, undignified pull of gifts. Maybe the gift giver had dignity. Maybe not. Giving a gift was also a manipulation.

Franz kept holding out the box. "What do I have to do to get you to take this?"

"There's nothing you can do."

"What about seeing you in it? Just once? And then I'll take it back."

Seeing her in it? Was it a pair of earrings? A necklace? She hated wanting to know. And she hated how being alone with him in this room made her nervous, parched her mouth, muzzied her thoughts. She didn't feel in control.

"I'll tell you what . . ." She grabbed the small box. "I'll put on whatever's in here if you promise to never—never—try to do this thing that you're doing right now. Wooing me, I suppose. If you promise to never woo me again."

Ziva waited while Franz, staring at the box in her hand, made up his mind. For a second she hoped he would choose to take back the box, so he could woo her again tomorrow, but no, this needed to end.

"Fine," he said. "Put it on."

She almost didn't want to know what was in the small box now, to keep it a mystery. She pulled the silver ribbon. Having no use for a silver ribbon—just a waste—she handed it to Franz, who nervously fingered it as she lifted the box's black top. Inside was more silver. What was this trinket? Looked like a mezuzah. She picked it out and found it to be another finger-shaped box with a silver snap on its side. Franz took the gift box so she could unsnap the flap and pull out—

"Is this lipstick?"

"It's from the Kaufhaus Louvre in Tel Aviv, a new store, as beautiful as any in Berlin. Well, maybe not, but as fancy as you'll find in Palestine."

She held up the silver tube as if it were court evidence. "You thought *this* would make me happy? All *this* does is show how little you know me. The women of the kibbutz, we're trying to throw off our old shackles. And you know what's the saddest part? You don't even know you're giving me a shackle. Why didn't you pick me up a pair of high heels while you were at it?"

Franz's gaze dropped to her scuffed brown work boots. It was a pensive gaze. Was it dawning on him that if she did put on this lipstick, wore high heels, she would cease being the woman he was falling in love with? *Falling in love*—how could she think something so ridiculous? He was a playboy. She was merely a conquest.

He spoke slowly, hesitantly. "I guess I wouldn't mind seeing you in high heels . . . Not every day. But maybe once in a while, on a special occasion. Is that wrong? Maybe it is."

"There's no maybe." She held the lipstick out to him. "Go."

"You said you would put it on."

"I'm not putting on lipstick."

"Come now, Ziva. You would go back on your word?"

Ziva glowered at him, kept the lipstick extended.

"That was the bargain." He shook his head, smirking. "If you don't put it on, then I get to keep wooing you."

She drew back the lipstick. Clenching her teeth, she pulled off the cap and peered into the tube.

He pointed. "You twist the bottom."

She twisted out a bright crimson, the shade worn by young women who slept all day and let men buy them drinks all night. She wasn't even so young, thirty years old.

"There's a mirror in the top flap of the case."

"Enough with your *gottverdammt* instructions." She lifted the lipstick and mirror to her face. The sliver of mirror reflected only her mouth. She drew the brilliant color across her bottom lip, as she had seen her mother do many times. The effect was dramatic. Even with only the bottom painted, the jolt of red ripened her lips. She felt Franz watching as she painted the top. Being a perfectionist, she couldn't help but go back and dab the tips of her Cupid's bow. Her lips bloomed in the mirror, the juicy, glistening red of ripe pomegranate seeds.

She twisted back the stick, eyes on the tube, unable to look up at Franz. She knew he would find her attractive, and the idea brought back that wooziness. She had never felt anything like this—a fog that made it impossible to think. She only worsened the tension, though, by shying away from him. She raised her head. "Now you can go."

Eyes on her painted lips, he said, "You think we're so different, but we're not."

She inhaled, grateful for his pronouncement. As powerful as smelling salts—it cleared her head, returned her senses. "You and I? You must be kidding. We're as different as can be. You're a . . ." What was he? A loafer? No. And then the perfect word came to her. "You're a leisurist."

"I don't work as hard as you," Franz admitted. "Maybe I'm not as good a person in some ways. But we both refuse to be bound by fear. To be told what to do. We both insist on being true to ourselves. We do share that, Ziva."

"The most fearless person I know is Dov Margolin. If it weren't for his bravery, you wouldn't be standing here today. Trying to seduce his wife."

Franz half nodded. "Dov's part of the reason I'm still alive, it's true. But not all of it. And you don't love him the way I want you to love me."

"You obviously don't know how much I love Dov." She managed to keep her eyes on him. And why would she look away? What she had to say was true. "I couldn't love anyone more than I love him. Now it's your turn to fulfill your promise. Please go."

Franz hesitated, and Ziva wondered if he was going to try to kiss her, if he was going to rush forward and take her in his arms like the fiery couples in the moving pictures. And she wanted him to, because if he attempted to kiss her now, she could push him away. She hadn't been so sure a few minutes earlier, but now she could easily turn him down. Deridingly. Come on, she thought, try to kiss me.

"That's something else we share." He picked up his lantern. "I keep my word."

He navigated between the wood panels and bags of cement toward the doorless doorway. He stopped before it and took one last look at her before going through. Ziva continued staring at the empty doorway, the dusty ground and night sky it framed, confounded that such a man could affect her so. She didn't admire him. He wasn't a serious thinker or man of action. He had no honorable ambitions, wasn't a part of any important movement. He seemed immune to the sweep of history. Whatever was happening in the world, he would have given her this lipstick, which she found was still in her hand. Franz would have been Franz no matter when or where or to whom he had been born.

Ziva grabbed a knife from the worktable and sawed the corner off a burlap bag. She rubbed the scratchy cloth on her lips and checked the mirror. A red stain persisted. She rubbed at them again, but it was no use. No matter: it wasn't enough color to make anyone think the unthinkable, that she had been wearing bright red lipstick. It was only enough color to make her look perhaps a little, inexplicably, prettier. She left the half-built schoolhouse, tube of lipstick and smeared scrap of burlap in her pocket, chin raised. She had nothing to be ashamed of. Everyone had uninvited thoughts and feelings; the only thing that mattered was whether one acted on them.

The dancing had ended. Franz was folding down the phonograph while stragglers sat around the dwindling fire smoking cigarettes and passing a flask. Ziva walked up to Dov and held out her hand. He took it, and she helped pull him to his feet. Together they ambled up the dirt path to their bungalow. Seven years had passed since the days of the communal tents, when she and Dov would only have privacy on Shabbat. Everyone had assumed theirs would be the first child born on the kibbutz, to grow up never knowing what it was to be a persecuted minority, a wandering Jew; but people had long ago stopped teasing them about babies. Although no one had said it to her face, she had the feeling most blamed her for their sterility, that she was the barren prig.

She hooked her arm in Dov's. "Did you tell him to get rid of it?"

"Not exactly. Wait before you get upset, Ziva. I said he couldn't play the phonograph as long as he was on the kibbutz, but that he could keep it under his bed and take it with him when he leaves."

"Leaves? Did he say he was leaving?"

"No, but he's not exactly the type to live the rest of his life on a kibbutz, is he, Ziva?"

Ziva stopped walking and turned to Dov. She wanted him to look at her, while her lips still bore a hint of red. She wanted to see if his crystalline eyes would have even a fleck of the desire that had burned in Franz's black eyes as he contemplated her lips in the unfinished schoolhouse.

Dov looked confused. She smiled, sadly. He said, "What is it, Ziva?"

It was shortsighted of Franz to not want the love she felt for Dov. It didn't make her dizzy, but it made her steady, made her feel like herself in a way that nobody else did. Franz wanted a carnal love, but that dizziness couldn't last forever, and what she had with Dov would.

She shook her head. "Nothing."

Dov pinched her cheek. "Don't worry, Zivale. Everything will be back to normal in the morning."

Ziva opened her eyes and saw Claudette wiping down a grave at the far end of the cemetery. How long had she been sitting here with her eyes shut? She held out her wristwatch far enough to make out the hands. Three o'clock? Could she have been daydreaming for nearly an hour? Wouldn't the girl have noticed? Claudette seemed to be in her own world again, wiping down the grave and—was she talking to herself? Ziva got to her feet. She would just have to work twice as hard to make up for the lost time.

When they finished cleaning the cemetery, Ziva and Claudette returned the tin buckets, watering cans, and rags to the garden shed, where shovels awaited a more gruesome chore. Walking away from the graves, Claudette couldn't believe she still hadn't given in. As they walked through the fields, her body itched to run back and finish tracing the father's grave. She kept repeating in her head *It isn't true, it isn't true* while putting one foot in front of the other, letting the foot land where it landed, even if, once they were back on the cement paths between the houses, it landed on a line.

As they were passing the *kolbo*, Ziva stopped Claudette with a hand on her arm. Claudette assumed the old woman needed a rest. It wasn't hard to see the walks home were getting harder for her. Last week, Ziva had been given an electric golf cart, which was how members ten years younger than her buzzed about the kibbutz, but she refused to use it. The cart sat in front of her apartment, only brought to life once a week when Eyal came around to make sure the battery was charged.

"I would like to buy you something, Claudette."

"Buy me something?"

In front of the store, a spotted dog panted in the shade under a tomato stand, and children leaned on a crate of oranges, licking yellow popsicles.

"Yes, Claudette. A little gift."

Claudette followed Ziva through the chiming door and into the air-conditioned store. The plump, ruddy-faced cashier acknowledged Ziva with a nod. When Claudette was a child, she used to wish someone would give her a gift. At Christmastime, she rummaged through the bins of donated dolls, sweaters, and kaleidoscopes, imagining the girls who'd been given these things when they were new. Over the last half a year, Louise had bought Claudette a bra, a toothbrush, and the costly airplane ticket to Israel. She didn't mean to be ungrateful, but none of these things gave her the silly delight she had imagined those girls felt ripping away the festive wrapping paper. Louise gave what her poor half sister needed. It wasn't Louise's fault—she meant well—but if anything, these handouts made Claudette feel like a burden.

"Where are the lipsticks?"

"Lipsticks?" The cashier gave Ziva a bemused smirk. "For you?"

"Just tell me where they are."

The cashier pointed down the middle aisle, and Claudette followed Ziva to a small shelf space reserved for makeup. Eye pencils stuck out of a tin canister, and a repurposed shoebox held a disarray of blushes, lipsticks, and mascaras.

Ziva rooted through the shoebox, disappointed by the plastic cases of these mass-produced lipsticks. No silvery elegance. At least back then capitalists had some concern for workmanship. She held up a green-tubed CoverGirl between her misshapen fingers. "Do you like this one?"

Claudette took the tube and turned it around in her hands. Ziva told her to pull off the cap and turn it. Claudette did, and Ziva crumpled her face.

"Blech. Pink is such an insipid color."

While Ziva fished again in the shoebox, Claudette spied Ulya standing in front of a shelf of shampoos. Ulya's eyes were on the cashier as she slipped a purple bottle into her work shirt. So that was how her roommate brought home so many new beauty products.

"How about this one?" Ziva inspected under the tube. "Oh, but look at its stupid name! *Rosy the Riveting*! Isn't that offensive? Sickening?" Ziva tossed the lipstick back in the box. "You know, I really don't know what we're doing here. Let's forget it."

"Okay." Claudette tried not to sound disappointed. "I don't deserve lip . . . I mean, I don't wear it."

Ziva could see the girl was crestfallen. How had she gotten herself into such a predicament? "Well, maybe we can find one without such an offensive name."

She picked up a white plastic tube. *Tropical Sunset*. She twisted out a stick the hue of ripe papaya and held it out. "What do you think?"

Claudette nodded. "Yes, that's very nice."

On their way to the mirror at the back of the store, they passed Ulya, coming in the opposite direction, arms crossed over her work shirt. Ulya gave a curt "Hi" as she went by.

At the mirror, the old woman stood in back while the younger one painted her lips. Ziva found the effect to be as immediate as it had been with her, so long ago, in the dimly lit schoolhouse. The bold coral brightened the girl's complexion, brought out the russet in her eyes and hair.

Standing next to the healthy young woman, it was impossible for Ziva to miss how much she'd yellowed, like an old newspaper. Claudette blinked at her image. Ziva smiled.

"I never thought I would ever write 'lipstick' next to your name," said the cashier, jotting down the purchase in the logbook. "I just read 'Utopia on the Auction Block.'"

"What? I didn't know it was going to be in today's newsletter. I was told next week."

The cashier put down the pen. "It was well written. But that kind of thing, you know, is out of style."

"What kind of thing? You mean, social responsibility?"

"Well, yes. Today people want to know—have the right to know—what's in it for them. All this talk about the common good, it's up in the air. It's like . . ." The cashier rubbed her fingers together as if feeling for something that wasn't quite there. "It's like fluff."

Ziva left the store, having trouble breathing. Claudette hurried after her. Fluff? She leaned on Claudette's shoulder.

"Do you want to sit down, Ziva?"

She shook her head.

Claudette regarded the lipstick in her hands. "I'm very happy with my present."

Ziva nodded, unable to care about the lipstick now. She turned and walked in the direction of the old people's quarter, leaving Claudette in front of the store with the small white tube. Claudette patted her lips together to feel the softness. And—

The boy.

The guilt winded her. She had forgotten about him as soon as Ziva said the word *gift*. She had walked into the store feeling sorry for whom? Herself. Because nobody had ever given her a present. While the boy suffered in bed with burns and blindness and deafness, she reveled over lipstick.

You could go back to the cemetery. The Bad Feeling was right. She could still go back and trace the inscription on the father's grave two hundred times. Three hundred times to make up for not doing it right away. Unable to read Hebrew, how could she be certain which was the right grave? She would have to trace the markings three hundred times on all the graves in its general vicinity.

Claudette brought a hand up to her throat. "It isn't true."

Two women seated on a bench watched her warily.

"It isn't true," she repeated aloud as she walked away from the store, not toward the cemetery, but in the direction of the volunteers' section. "It isn't true."

When she reached her room, she closed the door and backed into a corner. Everything in the room accused her: the chests of drawers, Ulya's orange dress crumpled on the floor, the white walls. She hunched down and, wrapping her hand around her waist, clawed at her side as if she were trying to rip herself out of herself. *It isn't true. It isn't true. It isn't true.*

The rosary beckoned from her bedside table. She rushed at it, thinking she would say three hundred Hail Marys instead of tracing the grave. How could saying Hail Marys be wrong? She balanced the lipstick on the bedside table and picked up the rosary. She held it in her hand, the sacrificed Son dangling. If she wanted to say Hail Marys, that would be all right. But she couldn't say them for the Bad Feeling anymore. She shuddered as she lay the rosary back down.

"It isn't true." She paced. "It isn't true."

Night fell. Ulya came home, and Claudette intoned *It isn't true* in her head while they crawled into their respective beds. All night she spoke over the Bad Feeling's protests. *It isn't true, it isn't true.* The fan whirred back and forth, fluttering the pages of Ulya's magazines, the corners of their bedsheets. They had failed to close the blinds, and the white lipstick tube on her bedside table glowed in the pale light. Ulya got up to go to the bathroom once.

At last the birds were cheeping. The rising sun, coming through the open blinds, striped the room in a smoldering coral, like her lipstick. Feeling feverish, Claudette trembled under the wool blanket. She never even closed her eyes, but she had done it. She hadn't returned to the cemetery or reached again for the rosary.

She had defied the Bad Feeling.

The quad was still in the blue half-light of morning while Adam waited for Ulya at the picnic table, next to the strange tree, its fruits having transformed again, the green balls now flecked with red, the flower at its end, desiccated, woody. If she didn't come out in five minutes, he was leaving without her. He hoped if he got to the United Kibbutz office early enough, they would check their files before he left Tel Aviv at the end of the day.

Ulya emerged from her room, red plastic bangles on her wrists, eyeliner as bold as ever. She came forward swinging her purse like a little kid. "Let's go!"

Adam had never seen her this happy. He pointed at her sandals. "Can you hightail it in those things? The bus comes in fifteen minutes."

"No problem. I wore platforms today because I want to walk all over the city."

Adam and Ulya scampered down the road, away from the kibbutz. They reached the bus stop at the bottom of the hill just as the bus was coming around the bend.

"Will you pay for my ticket?" said Ulya.

"What?"

"I don't have any money for the bus."

Adam groaned. "Fine."

A half hour later the bus was climbing through the hill city of Haifa, making its way to the central bus station at the top of the mountain. Adam couldn't believe he was finding five-story buildings tall. Two months on a kibbutz had warped his perspective. Ulya seemed impressed too, staring out the window, watching the small city start the workday.

It was the heart of rush hour at the central station, where they needed to switch buses to Tel Aviv. They disembarked into a chaos of blaring CD stores, competing food stands, people running for the green buses. Ulya paused in front of a kiosk to study the covers on the fashion magazines. She pointed at a picture of a girl wearing only white cotton undies, her small breasts hidden behind a spindly arm. "Kate Moss is so skinny. Do you like it?" Adam grabbed her arm. "We can look at magazines all you want in Tel Aviv. We can't miss this bus."

On the bus, Adam extended his hand, offering Ulya the window seat. He had enjoyed how keenly she had looked out the window. Her curiosity made everything they passed seem more interesting. Waiting for the bus driver, it occurred to Adam that this might be the same bus route Ofir had been on.

"Yes," Ulya said. "An early bus from Haifa, heading in the direction of Tel Aviv."

Adam observed the next few people to board. A darker guy climbed inside, and once again Adam found he couldn't always tell if someone was Jewish or Arab. So many of the Jews here came from Iraq or Egypt or Yemen. If the person wore a keffiyeh or kippah, easy, but this guy in a T-shirt waving at someone through the window, no idea. He figured people who lived here must have no problem telling each other apart, just as he could nail someone down the second they stepped on the subway, gleaning their background by the cut of their jeans, the trim of their beard, the way they took their seat.

The express bus drove without break down a highway alongside the Mediterranean. The sea appeared more gray than blue, its modest waves frothing onto the sandy shore. Ulya bopped her head and sang along to the pop music blaring out of the bus driver's radio. She wondered what they would do after Adam's office errand. Tel Aviv had an American-style mall with the Levi's store and Zara. It would be fun to go shoplifting, but that was impossible with Adam in tow. Still, she was glad for his presence. Walking around a city was more fun with somebody else. And he paid for the bus.

The music was interrupted by the long beep that heralded the news. Adam liked the female broadcaster's sonorous voice and was pleased to be able to pick up a word here and there: *boker tov*, good morning, *Byll Clyn-tonn*, Bill Clinton. He unfolded the map Yossi had lent him to figure out the quickest way from the bus station to the office. The streets formed squares within squares, like a giant Pac-Man board. Having never left New York City, this was his first time needing a map. Even if Manhattan hadn't been a numbered grid, he knew the place too well to ever get lost. Every block was familiar all the way up to 148th, where he would meet Bones. On those rare occasions when he got turned around, he only had to look up, see the twin towers, and that was south. Adam returned the map to his back pocket, a little excited to be visiting a new city.

The bus wound its way up the ramps of Tel Aviv's central bus station and dropped them off on the fifth floor. Under an enormous departure board hung a banner: TEL AVIV'S NEW CENTRAL BUS STATION—BIGGEST BUS STATION IN THE WORLD! Adam couldn't understand why such a tiny country needed so many buses. Did no one have a car? Along the walls, soldiers napped on the floor, heads on their duffel bags, M-16s under their arms.

They pushed through the front entrance and were greeted by a square full of homeless people and street vendors. It was a lot hotter and more humid here than on their hilly kibbutz in the north. On the other side of the square, taxis and scooters whizzed down a street lined with white buildings, discolored by exhaust and packed with restaurants and shops. Ulya gave the urban scene a huge smile, and Adam consulted the map. "It shouldn't take more than half an hour to walk there."

They ended up on a pedestrian road closed to traffic and flanked by open-air stalls, tables laden with sunglasses, pyramids of colorful spices, knockoff designer underwear, the brands misspelled: Calbin Klein. "Come, come!" vendors called. "Special price for you!" Adam would have liked to explore the *shuk*, but there was no time, and it was annoying the way Ulya, hand shading her eyes from the sun, stopped at every second stall. Now she fingered a beaded necklace while the huckster said, "Beautiful necklace for beautiful girl." Adam grabbed her hand and pulled her along.

They arrived at the office later than planned, but it was still earlyish and the air-conditioning gave Adam solace. A directory in the foyer sent them up an open staircase to the third floor. Climbing the last flight, Ulya said, "After this let's go for a drink. We can have piña colada on the beach."

Ignoring this suggestion, Adam opened the office door and walked up to the reception desk while Ulya took a seat behind him in the waiting area.

"I'm looking for information on someone named Dagmar Stahlmann. She lived on a kibbutz in 1947, and I'm here to find out which kibbutz and if she's still living there."

The receptionist put a finger on her place in her book. "Do you have an appointment?"

"No, but I wrote you guys a month ago and—"

"You can't expect me to drop everything. You need an appointment."

"Please, I've come all the way from a kibbutz near Haifa to ask you to look this woman up."

The receptionist adjusted her ponytail. "It's not my job to look people up. I don't even know whose job that would be. You need to request an appointment."

"Can I make an appointment for today?"

"Today?" The receptionist snorted and handed Adam a form.

"Last time I wrote you guys, I never even got a response. If I fill this out, how long will it take to get an appointment?"

The receptionist shrugged.

"You can't tell me how long?"

"Two weeks. More, perhaps."

The woman returned to her book, and Adam walked the form back to Ulya.

"Are we done?" she asked, checking her face in a compact mirror.

Adam shook his head. "I'm going back to the kibbutz. That bitch won't do anything. She says I need to make an appointment. And who the fuck knows when they'll give me one. And all she's doing right now is reading a fucking book."

Ulya wasn't going back to the kibbutz. She dropped her compact into her purse and marched to the front desk. Adam followed, unsure what was happening.

"Shalom." Ulya rested her arms on the reception desk.

The receptionist lifted her eyes. "Yes?"

"I'm sorry, but you're going to have to do what he asks."

"Excuse me?"

"Yes, I am sorry, but we can't take no. He has come all the way from the United States of America to find this person."

"I already told him that he needs an appointment."

"And what are you doing that's so important that you can't help? I'm going to stand here watching you do this important thing until you look this woman up."

Adam grinned at Ulya's chutzpah. He knew some guys didn't like strong women; they wanted to be the only strong one. But maybe because his mother was such a weakling, so incapable, never coming through for him on anything, he didn't see the charm in it.

"If you don't turn around and go right now," said the receptionist, "I'm going to call the police."

Adam raised his hands. "Whoa, there's no need to call the cops." He turned to Ulya. "I really don't want the police coming."

Ulya didn't even look at him. "Fine, call the police."

Adam looked from Ulya to the receptionist and prepared to bolt as soon as the latter made a move for the phone. But she didn't. Ulya had called her bluff. The receptionist rolled her eyes, stuck out her lower jaw, and went back to her book, pretending to read.

"Police!" Ulya yelled. "*Mishtara*! Yoohoo, *mishtara*!"

"Okay, okay." The woman turned over her novel. "I'll do it. What's the name?"

Ulya turned to Adam.

"Dagmar," he said. "Dagmar Stahlmann."

"Write it down." The receptionist passed over a paper and pen. "Come back at three o'clock."

Adam skipped out of the office and down the building's stairs. "That was amazing, Ulie! You're fucking amazing! A fucking dynamo."

Ulya laughed. "I am molten lava."

"Okay. Molten lava. That works."

Outside, the old, tarnished Bauhaus buildings appeared almost white again under the bright midday sun. The air blowing off the sea, only two blocks away, was briny, fresh. "We have three hours," Ulya said. "Let's get a drink and walk around the city tipsy."

Adam rolled his head as if he had a crick in it. How good that sounded: getting stupid and wandering around a foreign city with this gorgeous woman. But he couldn't.

"Let's get ice cream. We can probably find some on the beach."

Ulya gave him the same big smile she gave her first glimpse of Tel Aviv. "Okay. Ice cream first."

They walked down a residential side street, the sand and sea visible at the end. Cats lurked everywhere, walking along the white concrete fences, sleeping in packs on the sidewalk. They arrived at the beachside boulevard, which had a wide esplanade across the street from rental car offices, travel agents, and high-end stores for foreign tourists.

"Look at those shoes! So beautiful! Can you see me walking down Park Avenue in them?" She twisted her foot this way and that, envisioning the fuchsia pump on it, and then returned her focus to the real pumps behind the glass. "Vivienne Westwood. That's a very fancy designer."

Adam saw both the shoe behind the window and Ulya's reflection in the pane. It broke his heart how far she was from owning those shoes other people could waltz in and buy without a thought. He wished he could do that for her, as a thank-you for sticking up for him back in the office.

"You think that's a nice window? Wait till you see the ones on Fifth Avenue. Especially Bergdorf's Christmas windows—even I have to stop and stare at them, but you, you are going to die."

Ulya closed her eyes. "Yes, I am going to die."

They crossed the street to the esplanade, where Adam bought ice-cream bars from a shirtless old man rolling a cooler around in a shopping cart. They walked alongside the beach, biting through the chocolate shell into the vanilla ice cream, taking in all the people on the sand, women reading under umbrellas, children running into the waves. Some college-aged kids—tanned girls in stringed bikinis, buffed guys wearing wraparound sunglasses—played volleyball, calling out to each other before they dove for the ball.

He was young, thought Adam, but he wasn't like them. He would never be a guy playing volleyball with his buddies. Why did only the most normal people seem to have a crew of friends? Would he regret never having tried to be like those guys? Why did people say time flew, that youth was wasted on the young? It felt like he'd been young forever, after all he'd been through, and he was still only twenty-six.

"Do you find it hard to believe you're not always going to be young?"

Ulya sucked a dribble of ice cream off her thumb. "Never thought about it."

"It's funny. Even though everybody grows old—I mean, everybody who doesn't die young, of course—somehow I feel like it's not going to happen to me, like I'm going to be the only person in the history of the world that it just doesn't happen to."

"When does someone become old?"

"Forty, I guess."

Ulya stopped and turned to him, the sea breeze tousling her hair. "Can you picture me forty years old?" She didn't say it coquettishly, fishing for a compliment, but holding her half-finished ice cream off to the side, solemnly offering herself for consideration.

Adam tried to picture an old Ulya, not merely an Ulya with wrinkles around her eyes and fallen jowls, but an Ulya whose spirit had been eroded by time, a tired Ulya, an Ulya too exhausted to covet fuchsia pumps, New York City, anything as badly as she wanted them now. It seemed to Adam only the young claimed they were "going to die" if they didn't get the thing they wanted, and Adam couldn't picture Ulya without that kind of wanting.

"Can't do it," he said. "I just can't picture someone like you ever being forty."

She smiled, and they walked on. Ulya could tell Adam was starting to have feelings for her. Could she pretend to have feelings as well? For two whole years? Maybe that wouldn't be so horrible. People had boyfriends and girlfriends for that length of time, longer, that they said "I love you" to, when they weren't sure they did, when they knew they were going to leave them some day. Would it be so different from that?

They came upon a trendy beach bar. On a black wooden deck that extended into the sandy shore were low white wicker couches with bright red pillows and matching sun umbrellas.

"Is it time for our drink now?"

Adam scraped his Converse against the ground. "We just finished our ice cream."

"So?"

He looked into the place: young people relaxed on the red cushions, smoking cigarettes, chilling out to the ambient house music. It'd be so nice to sit like that with Ulya.

"I'll sit with you, but I'm just going to have a Diet Coke."

This was too close. He felt it the moment they entered the bar. He wasn't scared enough. He needed to be so scared of relapsing that he kept a safe distance. The danger didn't begin with the first sip, but when you stopped being scared that you might take a first sip. You're scared, he told himself. You're fucking scared.

They took a table at the far end of the deck. The sea waves roared under the electronic beats. Ulya crossed her shapely legs and fished lip balm out of her purse.

"Have you noticed Claudette wears this bright lipstick now?"

Adam laughed. "She's a weird one."

Ulya rubbed the balm on her lips as the waiter set two menus on the table. A scared alcoholic would leave the menu alone, thought Adam, picking it up. He read the small selection from the English panel. Two local beers. Herzl would be proud: Hebrew menus, Jewish beer. A nation like any other now. If he wanted to taste Israeli beer, he could just swish it around in his mouth and spit it out. What? Stop. That was crazy thinking. Think scared.

"Shalom." The waiter stood over them.

Ulya handed back her menu. "I'll have a screwdriver without the orange juice."

Adam opened his mouth and now he was scared, scared of what was going to come out. "I'll have a Diet Coke."

He exhaled as the waiter walked away. He did it.

Ulya lit a cigarette and raised her head to blow out smoke. "Diet Coke? That isn't fun."

Adam lowered his eyes and fingered the wicker handrest. "I'm an alcoholic. And, I guess, a drug addict. But the cocaine, that was mostly so I could keep drinking."

"Alcoholic? Doesn't that mean you *do* drink? A lot?"

"I'm a recovering alcoholic. It means I can never drink again."

"Oh." She turned to the beach. Was she embarrassed for him? Sorry? Did any interest she might have had in him dissipate? She pointed at a woman in a gold bikini and wide-brim straw hat. "I love that girl's bikini. She looks like a movie star."

Adam didn't know what to make of her changing the subject. He supposed he should be glad for the nonchalance.

The waiter brought their drinks. Ulya sipped. "Blah!" She scrunched her face. "This vodka is disgusting. I'm not even sure it is vodka."

Adam, wanting to show Ulya that he too could be nonchalant, said, "So where do you go every night? I promise it won't change my opinion of you. I'm just curious."

He knew for sure now that she didn't want people knowing about her nightly excursions. He noticed that she didn't take the steppingstones up to the main road but went in the opposite direction, as if she were taking some furtive exit off the kibbutz. She had to be working in one of the nearby towns, because she wasn't buying all those clothes and makeup with the kibbutz's monthly stipend.

Ulya drank the awful vodka, surprised by his words. Wouldn't change his opinion of her? Where did he think she was going?

"It's none of your business."

"Come on, tell me."

"Maybe later," she lied.

When it was time to pay, Ulya pulled a twenty-shekel bill out of her purse.

"Hey," Adam said. "I thought you didn't have any money."

"I never said I didn't have money. I said I didn't have money for the bus."

After strolling along the boardwalk some more and wandering into the nearby streets, it was time to head back to the office. As they came through the door, the receptionist shook her head.

Adam pushed on the desk. "What? How is that possible? I gave you her full name, and she most definitely lived on a kibbutz."

The receptionist shrugged. "Dagmar Stahlmann, it's such a German name. Maybe she changed it. At that time, after the war, a lot of people changed their names to something more Jewish."

"What? Are you saying she might not be called Dagmar anymore?"

"Or Stahlmann. Stahlmann isn't a Jewish name. All these names people think of as Jewish are just German. At some point Jews were forced to take on German names. A lot of people when they got to Israel changed their names back to something Hebrew. Shimon Peres used to be Szymon Perski."

Adam's head was spinning. "Okay. There must be somewhere I can go, some records office where they keep track of name changes. I mean, you can't just change your name. It's like a legal thing, right?"

The woman shook her head. "What office? Israel didn't even exist in 1947. People just started going by something else, and that was that."

Adam staggered out of the office building and onto the sidewalk.

"Fuck fuck fuck fuck fuck." He paced back and forth while Ulya leaned on the cement building. "This is a fucking joke. Who ever heard of people changing their names to something *more* Jewish? That's fucking hilarious. Why is this so hard? There's like twelve people in this country, twelve people who all fucking know each other, and I can't find this one woman. Fuck! I don't even have a name now."

Adam's pacing and cursing slowed until he stood, silent, head bowed.

"Are you done?" said Ulya.

Adam turned to her. "What?"

"Are you done with your little boy tantrum? Good. Now you think of some other way to find her."

"Little boy tantrum? Fuck you, you Russian bitch. Oh, excuse me, Belarusian bitch. Are you fucking hearing me? I don't even have a fucking name!"

"Don't shout at me! Think, you American bitch! We're in Tel Aviv, and tonight we have to go back to the kibbutz. Stop crying, and make the most of that. Maybe Tel Aviv has an office—"

"Fuck offices!" Adam paced again. "I've had enough of fucking offices and their fucking forms. I mean, I could go up there and murder . . ."

His eyes fell on a man, seated on a bench, legs crossed, reading a newspaper.

He spun to face Ulya. "Hold on . . . What does everybody do in this news-obsessed country? Read the fucking paper! All the newspaper offices are probably here in Tel Aviv. Make the most of Tel Aviv, you said. I'm sorry for calling you a Russian bitch, Ulie. Come on, let's go ask that guy what's the most popular paper in Israel."

The man looked over his paper at them, seemingly amused by the foreigners and their question. "Well, it's not this one, *Haaretz*. I would say *Yedioth Ahronoth*."

"Which paper would a kibbutznik read? I want to use the classifieds to find a woman who lives on a kibbutz."

"Well, a kibbutznik might read *Haaretz*. It's the most left-wing of the papers. But I would go with *Yedioth Ahronoth*. It's everywhere. That way even if she doesn't see the ad, someone she knows will."

"Do you know where their offices are?"

"How should I know? Call 144. There's a pay phone over there."

Luckily their offices weren't far. It took them fifteen minutes with Adam checking and rechecking the map to make sure they were heading in the right direction. The newspaper's red logo was emblazoned across a a building of pristine Jerusalem limestone. Inside a security guard checked Ulya's purse and pointed toward the ad office.

Adam approached the counter, panting. "How much is a classified? Or maybe it's a personal. Are personals only for lonely hearts? What if you're looking for an old lady? Not for sex, I mean. Like you're trying to find a specific old lady."

The clerk put on her reading glasses. "What day do you want to run the ad?"

"What day do you get the most readers?"

"Friday."

"Friday then. Actually, how much would it cost to have it run a whole week?"

"Depends on the number of characters. Write it here."

"Can I write it in English and you translate it?"

"I'll do my best."

Adam wrote: LOOKING FOR DAGMAR STAHLMANN, APPROX AGE 80. I AM ADAM SOCCORSO, GRANDSON OF FRANZ ROSENBERG, A HOLOCAUST SURVIVOR WHO LIVED AT KIBBUTZ SADOT HADAR. PLEASE CALL—

Adam asked Ulya to fill in the number for the foreigner's pay phone. If this ran for a whole week, it was bound to get to Dagmar. It gave him honest-to-God goosebumps to picture the old woman confronted with her original name alongside the name of her old lover.

The clerk reached for her calculator. "A hundred and thirty-two characters is . . . a hundred and sixty-two shekels for the Friday paper. It won't appear in this Friday's, but the following one. And to run all week would be . . . three hundred and ninety shekels."

A hundred dollars. Adam opened his wallet. He'd have only five bucks left. He would have to rely on the kibbutz stipend from here on out.

Out on the city sidewalk once more, Adam thanked Ulya for her help. "I don't know what I would have done without you."

"Maybe now you'll marry me and take me to America?"

Adam definitely felt tempted in a way he hadn't before.

He smirked. "Do you have my thirty-five thousand dollars?"

"No, but I would get it. If you say you'll do it, I will get it."

He believed her. She had mettle. And Ulya believed by the way he looked at her that she had won him over. She hooked her arm in his.

After she bought them each a falafel, Ulya was out of money too. They had barely enough left to pay for their bus tickets back to the kibbutz, and yet they still wandered around until well after dark. The stores lit up, and the sidewalk cafés filled with people. They ambled up a ramp onto an elevated pedestrian plaza that had at its center a large, cylindrical sculpture striped in a rainbow of faded colors. A concrete basin under the wheel revealed it was meant to be a fountain. Beside the broken fountain, Hare Krishnas sang and tapped on drums. Adam and Ulya continued down a busy sidewalk, where a street violinist drew a small crowd and bouncers guarded unmarked dance clubs. The buses stopped running at midnight, and they caught the last one returning to Haifa.

"I hate to go back to the kibbutz," Ulya said, staring out the window, though she was excited for one thing. When she had told Farid not to wait for her tonight because she was going to Tel Aviv with the American boy, his eyes clouded with jealousy. She smiled at this, and Adam gently poked her in the arm, as if he had something to do with her smile.

The bus sped down the highway, desolate at that hour, the Mediterranean and farmlands a swath of darkness. Adam had heard that one of the highways in Israel could double as a landing strip during a war and wondered if this was the one. The light bobbing on a distant buoy gave him the strange, irrational feeling that it was the light of home, so far away. Talk radio mumbled at the front of the bus.

Ulya had fallen asleep, her head back, mouth hanging open. How vulnerable she looked, and kind of ugly. If he'd had a camera he'd have taken a picture to tease her with, though he wouldn't even have the money to develop the film. Her bare thighs splayed on the seat, her knees having parted in her sleep. He pictured his hand slowly grazing up and up until he felt her warm pussy.

Beyond the big windshield, the headlights illuminated the highway and the occasional road sign: CAESAREA, 5 KM. He had never loved a girl he hadn't ended up hurting, beginning with Monica of the pink velour track pants. After an agonizing year of waiting to lose their virginity together and much masturbating, two weeks before their anniversary, he wound up drunk on the couch with someone's older sister. He didn't even remember it, how they got from the couch to the girl's bedroom, the feeling of slipping into a vagina for the first time. When he confessed to Monica, around the back of their school, her big brown eyes filled with tears. "We had only two weeks to go, Adam."

Ulya lifted her head and asked for the time. Adam held up his wristwatch. 1:08 a.m.

"You looked cute, sleeping." He imitated her, dropping his head back and opening his mouth.

Ulya hit him. "Oh no! My mom sleeps like that. Actually, I dreamed I was in Mazyr. I've been in Israel for a year, but my dreams never take place here. Sometimes the people in the dream are from here, but we're always in Mazyr."

"Have I ever been in one of your dreams?"

"Not telling."

Ulya's face was pale in the dim bus. His gaze darted from her eyes to her lips as he debated kissing her.

She realized what he was thinking, and he saw her realize it. Her lips parted slightly. She didn't look away, and he took that as a yes. He leaned in, slowly, while her eyelids dropped halfway. His body hummed as, drawing closer, he smelled the coconut sunblock on her neck, the tobacco on her breath. Just before contact, she turned her head, his lips skidding against her cheek.

"Sorry," she said.

She didn't know what happened. She had braced to kiss him. While he debated whether to kiss her, she debated too and decided that until she had made up her mind about faking it, she should fake it. But at the last second, she saw Farid and couldn't do it. She laid her head on Adam's shoulder. "Maybe we can try again later."

Adam's heart and groin ached from the refusal. They didn't talk much the rest of the way home. In Haifa they caught a van running the bus routes after hours. It was two in the morning when they walked through the kibbutz gate.

At the bottom of the steppingstones, Golda darted for Adam. He lifted the dog to his chest and carried her.

As they passed the tree, he said, "Do you know what kind of tree this is?"

Ulya, turning for her room, shook her head. She looked back at him over her shoulder. "I'll see you tomorrow, Adam. Okay?"

He nodded. "Yeah. Okay."

*C*laudette was crossing the main lawn when she heard the piano. A few weeks ago, when she began these nightly walks, finding it easier to still her mind while her body was moving, she wouldn't have heard the faint plinking. She would see and hear little as she roved, repeating *It isn't true, it isn't true.* Then one night, as she was walking past the pine trees beside the library, she noticed she wasn't repeating the mantra, that her mind had strayed. She didn't know where her mind had gone, only that the pines smelled wonderful. She hadn't known that was possible, not to monitor your thoughts, but every night more and more of her walk was spent simply taking in the kibbutz while wondering about Ziva or the orphanage or the boy. Tonight she had been wondering what the boy did all day in his room when she heard the piano. She hastened toward the dining hall and crept up to the doorway, the same one she had stood in seven weeks ago.

Ofir twisted the volume on his hearing aids with the hopes that turning them all the way up would enable him to hear the softer notes over the ringing in his head. Nothing could be done about the loss of silence. He knew rests were important to music, but he had never appreciated just how much sound was in that quiet. He stretched his fingers and, sweat trickling down his face, started once again. Now the low notes, meant to be solemn certainties, thundered like a volatile storm. Was that the hearing aids? Was he coming down too hard on the keys? Had the notes always been wrong?

He bit his lips and played on. Maybe it was only a matter of loosening up after being away from the keys for two months. He had never been away that long. Even during basic training. If he kept playing, by the end, the music might flow out of him as it had that last time, as if the melody had its own need to be heard.

That didn't happen. He got worse. Fast. The notes grew increasingly angry, loud, incoherent—the stammering sounds a person makes when he's desperately trying to explain himself, but keeps failing.

Claudette watched Ofir slam two fists down on the keys. The dissonance spread through the dining hall, humming in the plates and glasses, while Ofir sat dead still. When the last shred of sound left the piano, he dropped his head on its shelf. Though Claudette couldn't hear him sobbing, she saw his back rising and falling. She had her answer: the boy would live, but not with music. She could turn around and go now. Or—the thought turned her cold—she could try to help him.

How? What if she said the wrong thing? What if he touched her again? She could already hear the Bad Feeling preparing to accuse her of violating a young boy. But she couldn't let the Bad Feeling be the only reason for not going to him. *It isn't true. It isn't true.*

She stepped into the unlit dining hall and tiptoed down the alley between the long cafeteria tables. Nearing the piano, she heard the boy's sniffles, gasps for air. She edged closer. He continued sobbing, having no idea she was there. Maybe she had been too quiet? She stood next to him, paralyzed, afraid to startle him.

Turning his head to rest on the other cheek, Ofir saw a white blur through the tears. He raised his head, and there was a face. Annoyed, he sat up, wiped his eyes. He didn't want to see anyone. He had waited until two in the morning, played as quietly as possible, so nobody would hear him and offer their fake praise and bullshit encouragement.

When he recognized the girl he had been daydreaming about when the bus blew apart, he felt sick, like he might throw up. She wore the same white sundress. It was disorienting, things being just as they were, as if nothing had happened—his room, the dining hall, the trees outside his window, the same leafy green as last summer. If anything, the girl looked prettier, her lips painted a bright coral.

"Did you feel as if I were playing just for you again?" he said sarcastically, though part of him hoped that maybe, just maybe, he hadn't been hearing himself properly. "Like God was playing through me?"

Claudette shook her head.

He turned to the keys. Her answer hurt, but at last someone had been honest with him. Not cruel. The downward curve of her bright lips when she shook her head revealed how sorry she was. Ofir closed his eyes, making Claudette wonder why she had thought for even a second that she could help anyone.

She said, "I'm sorry. I'll go now."

"No." He opened his eyes. "Don't go. I like that you told me the truth."

Claudette fidgeted with the waist of her dress as Ofir wondered what to say next. Maybe nothing. What right did he have to ask the girl to stay with him? She had been drawn to his music. Now the music was gone, and he was just a charity case.

"I mean, of course you can go. I couldn't tell how loudly I was playing. Sorry if I woke you up."

"I was awake."

"At two a.m.?"

"I take long walks at night."

Ofir lowered his head, contemplated the black-and-white keys. Should he keep playing? Or, rather, keep failing to play?

"If you don't want me to, all you have to do is say so, but if it's okay, can I walk with you a bit? This is the first time I've left my room in twenty days."

Claudette felt the Bad Feeling awakening, stretching its arms, but she couldn't say no because of it.

Outside the dining hall, Ofir glanced left and right to make sure the coast was clear, then beckoned Claudette around the side of the building, hemming close to the wall. "If I'm seen out late with a foreign volunteer, there'll be talk. When you live somewhere this small, you learn the less people know, the better."

Claudette, having also grown up in a closed community, understood this, but recoiled at the idea of there being anything to "know" about her and the boy. They were doing nothing wrong. *Nothing wrong.*

"Have you been to the spearmint field?"

"I only wander among the houses."

Claudette tried to stay calm as they walked past the feathery cedars looming against the night sky and down the dirt path to the fields. The rusted rod gate that opened onto the fields was draped in pink and purple bougainvillea. The lush mint plot, just up ahead, beckoned with its heady, sweet fragrance.

When they reached the mint, Ofir waded into the dense green foliage. "You won't believe the smell when you're standing in the middle of it."

Claudette followed him through the plants, their leaves and branches brushing up to her waist. She remembered seeing this dark green square of field from the cemetery, when she had asked Ziva how she wanted to die, and she had said working.

Ofir grabbed her hand and pulled her along. Claudette panicked. She had to assure herself that *he* took *her* hand. What could she do? Yank her hand from a sick boy? It was no different than when Ziva slipped her arm through hers. *No different.*

When they reached the heart of the field, Ofir turned to her. "I keep telling myself: I don't need music to make life worth it. This smell should be enough."

Claudette tried to ignore Ofir's warm hand still gripping hers.

"The thing is . . ." His face twisted. ". . . I can't quite convince myself. I just don't know what to do with the smell of things now. How to enjoy it."

Claudette shook her head. "Me neither."

Ofir regarded her with interest, and she noticed now that his right pupil wasn't round. Both his pupils had been round when he shook her awake that morning, his bloodshot gray eyes the first things she saw, informing her she was still alive. Now the right pupil was shaped like a teardrop, giving his eyes a sad beauty. No, not beauty, she thought, afraid. But beauty didn't have to be sexual. *There was nothing wrong with beauty. Nothing wrong.*

Ofir had the same sensation he did the first time he spoke to her, the rare sensation of not being alone, of being understood. "Let's take as big a sniff of the mint as we can and see if we can enjoy it, okay?"

Claudette agreed, and at the count of three, they both inhaled deeply, smiling at how silly they looked, nostrils flaring, straining to smell together. Claudette's gaze fell from the boy's mismatched eyes to his mouth, where the moonlight glowed on his lower lip. The world reduced itself to the flare of moonlight on the boy's bottom lip.

Ofir looked down at Claudette's lips, the color of the ripe pitangos he used to hunt for in the bushes near the schoolhouse, popping them in his mouth while they were still warm from the sun. He leaned forward.

Claudette saw his face coming toward her but didn't believe it, couldn't believe it.

When his lips touched hers, she screamed—a scream amplified tenfold for Ofir by his hearing aids. She pushed him with surprising force. His balance no longer what it was, he stumbled and fell back into the bushes of spearmint.

Claudette pressed her hands against the sides of her skull as if that could control the insurrection forming inside.

Ofir scrambled to his feet, hurried to apologize. "I . . . I guess I misread you."

She crushed her head as hard as she could. "No, no, no, no, no, no, no."

"I'm sorry!" He stepped toward her, then stopped himself. "I'm so sorry."

"It's vile. I'm vile. I'm thirty-one. You're too young. Too, too young. I can't. I can't."

Ofir figured she was older than him, but thirty-one? That was old. Two months ago he might have balked. But this wasn't two months ago.

"I don't care if you're a hundred and one."

"I want to go back. Now."

"I'm not twelve, you know. I'm almost eighteen. I patrolled the West Bank for six months. I've been through a hell of a lot. I think I can be considered an adult."

Claudette hugged herself and rocked. "I've never kissed anyone. Never. And I never will. I'm sick. Please, leave me alone. I'm sick. Very, very sick."

Ofir gaped at her. Did she have AIDS? Or some other STD? Is that why she couldn't kiss anyone?

"What do you mean? Sick?"

She kept rocking, bowed her head. "Mentally."

He didn't know what to say, but he wasn't going to do what others did to him, downplay her pain.

"That must be terrible."

"Sometimes I think . . ." She brought her clasped hands up to her mouth and looked up at him. "I think it was because of me . . . that you were in the bombing. That I'm a conveyor for evil."

Ofir looked at her sideways, wearing a small smile. "That makes sense. It's because of you, and not the jihadi with the bomb strapped to his chest."

Claudette's mouth twitched a little. She was shocked to find that she did see the humor in it. The idea still hurt, but it was also a little funny.

They stood in silence.

Ofir imagined that far beyond the mint field right now, on the other side of the world, yesterday's sunlight still shone on his American alter ego as he practiced the piano. He had to try to let that guy go. They weren't in competition anymore.

He said, "I really don't want to go back to my room yet. I can only go out at night because my skin and this eye still can't take the sun. If I promise not to try to kiss you again, can we keep walking?"

Claudette nodded.

"Have you been to the old olive trees? They're two hundred and fifty years old."

Claudette shook her head.

"Do you want to see them?"

She nodded again.

Halfway into his shift Adam decided that as soon as he'd wiped off the last dish he would walk over to the dairy house and ask Ulya on a proper date. Ever since their day in Tel Aviv, he could feel her toying with the idea of being with him. At dinner, she watched him from across the table as if waiting for him to do that one thing that would help her make up her mind. Last night she had a good laugh at the only joke he knew about Russians. *How did Russians light their houses before they started using candles? Electricity.* He hoped they could go out tomorrow night. The next morning the ad would appear in the paper, and after that, he was going to want to stay near the phone.

He pulled down his yellow rubber glove to check his watch: 2:40 p.m. Exactly twenty minutes to go. After two and a half months of standing in the dishwasher's foul steam sponging off egg yolk and baba ghanoush, twenty more minutes felt like forever. How the hell did people do it? Wash dishes, or fold clothes at the mall, or cross off to-dos in a cubicle, or endlessly snap pieces of plastic together on an assembly line? All day, nearly every day, for fifty years. It was fine for the few who had interesting jobs. Civil-rights lawyers, Martin Scorsese. But most people weren't Martin Scorsese.

Zayde used to wake up three hours before his shift at Leo's! so he could drink his coffee and eat his marmalade toast with an unhurried grace. Then he'd take his time to shave properly, comb his thick, silvery hair, polish his shoes, slip horn stiffeners into his collar. All that prep to earn chump change selling twenty-somethings futons and laminate bookshelves. And yet Zayde did this job with grace, always walking his customers up and down the floor with a smile and friendly conversation. At night he'd come home and tell Adam what he'd noticed about the young people that day: "How come you don't have an earring, Adam? All the other boys do."

Why was Zayde able to do it but not his mother? She used to hit the snooze button twenty times before finally staggering out of her bedroom toward the kitchenette. There, leaning against the counter as if she didn't have the strength to stand, she would drink a cup of microwaved coffee through a scowl. One time, while Adam was waiting by the door to go to school while his mother leaned on the counter drinking her coffee, hours after they should've left the apartment, the phone rang. She didn't pick up. It rang and rang, stopped for a few seconds, and started again: *brrring, brrrring.* She grabbed the handset. "I can't. I just can't, Mike." A pause while she chewed her lip. "I don't give a fuck! Tell the bitch to clean her own fucking toilets!" After hanging up, his mother slunk down to the floor, repeating, "I just can't do it anymore."

At last it was time to take off the rubber gloves. Adam walked around the washing machine, asking Yossi if he had a restaurant he could recommend.

A smile spread on Yossi's sweaty face. "This for a date? Who's the lucky girl?"

"Yeah, it's a date. I need a nice place. White tablecloths, candles."

"Around here?" He heaved a stack of plates onto a steel trolley. "I'll have to think about it."

Adam freshened up at the hand-washing station, splashed his face, tweaked his hair. On his way to the dairy, he passed the laundry house, the medical center, the swimming pool with its rumpus of children on summer vacation, running and cannonballing into the water. When he arrived at the whitewashed dairy house, he was grateful for its lack of windows. Ulya couldn't see him pausing to take a fortifying breath. You're just asking someone on a date, he told himself. Straightening his shoulders, he pulled open the door.

Inside four women wearing latex gloves sat at four separate tables pouring yogurt onto cheesecloths. More people wasting their lives on drudgery. Three of them looked up to see who'd come through the door and then rotated in their seats to watch him walking down the center of the room. Only Ulya, at the far right table, took no notice. She worked, lost in some daydream, only noticing him when he stood over her table.

"What are you doing here?"

The other girls didn't turn back around. It creeped Adam out the way people openly watched each other on a kibbutz. People watched each other in New York, but people they didn't know—the crazy guy taking a shit between parked cars, the couple engaged in a shouting match on the subway platform—and then forgot about them as soon as they looked away. Here everyone had front-row seats to a never-ending soap opera starring their neighbors. Adam gestured with his head toward the door. "Can I talk to you outside for a second? In private?"

Peeling off her gloves, Ulya smirked at the other girls and then strutted out the door, Adam tailing. Outside, she pulled out a pack of cigarettes. "So? What do you want?"

He rubbed the back of his neck. "What exactly are you doing in there? Making cheese?"

"Labneh. I have to boil the milk, cool it, mix it with old yogurt, make these disgusting pouches."

Ulya wasn't wearing makeup for once, her skin clean and fair in the sunlight. Without mascara, the lashes framing her cobalt eyes were blond.

Adam mindlessly kicked the dairy house. "My job sucks too. Wiping off all that soggy half-eaten food. Sometimes it actually triggers my gag reflexes. But these shitty jobs, they're just for now. We're not going to be doing them forever."

Ulya eyed Adam as she took a drag—studying him again. She blew smoke, lips pursed off to the side. "Not me anyway."

"What? You think I'm going to wash dishes for the rest of my life? As soon as I'm done here, I'm going back to school, finishing my degree—"

"Adam, I can't leave the yogurt out. What do you want?"

He dug his hand into his back pockets, stretched his chest. "Well, I'm here to ask you something."

Ulya's shoulders fell slightly, her head too, as if she anticipated what he was here to ask and didn't want it. Hoping he was misreading her, he plowed ahead. "I'm here to ask you on a date. A real date. To a nice restaurant."

Ulya observed her cigarette smoldering between her chipped red nails. She should do it. Fake interest. Later fake love. It could be nice to go on a real date, to a restaurant, instead of lying on a hill with rocks digging into her back.

"How are you going to take me to a restaurant? In Tel Aviv, you didn't have money for a bottle of water."

"We got our stipends. I'm willing to blow all of mine on you."

"When?"

"Tomorrow night."

Thursday nights she got to spend a little more time with Farid. Fridays being half days, she could catch up on sleep in the afternoon. Sometimes she stayed out until four in the morning.

She shook her head. "Not Thursday. Maybe Tuesday?"

"Why, 'cause you have that secret thing you do at night?" He worried about missing that phone call. Then again, by Tuesday night the ad would have run for five days already. Surely she would have called by then. Or he'd be going crazy. "Okay. Tuesday. On the later side."

Ulya looked down at the dusty ground. As soon as they settled on a plan, she knew it was no use. She could lie to her mother, steal clothes, fake being a Jew, but she couldn't pretend to like someone she didn't. Maybe for a night, but three years? She'd never make it. She'd get to New York, but not like this.

She raised her head. "Actually, no." She threw down her cigarette and squashed it under her boot. "I can't go on a date with you."

"What? You just said you would." He felt whiplashed. "Why *can't* you? Do you have a boyfriend or something?"

"No," she sneered as if nobody around here were good enough.

"Then what's the problem? Think of it this way: you get a free meal, a night on the town, and I get a chance to change your mind about me. Nothing more. If you never want to do it again, fine."

Ulya shook her head, unable to stop herself from smiling. She felt lighter, freer now that she had made up her mind.

"Why? We eat dinner in the dining hall together every day. What's the difference?"

She never understood this: why guys pressured a girl who didn't want to go on a date with them to go on a date with them. So stupid.

"Because it's a waste of time, Adam. I will never ever ever ever be your girlfriend."

Shocked by the certainty, the callousness, Adam couldn't find his voice.

"Sorry," she said, turning for the door. She smiled widely before disappearing inside.

Adam stood in front of the closed door, taking a different kind of forti-fying breath. What was with that smile? Did she get off on hurting people? Why did she say she would never ever ever ever be his girlfriend as if she were talking about eating a cockroach? Was it now obvious to anyone who looked at him that he was a cockroach?

He left the dairy house, gripping the brooch. Never mind. He had to suck it up. Maybe he deserved this. It would have been wrong, starting up with Ulya, moving on with his life, before he'd taken care of the brooch. If all went well, in two or three days, the brooch would be safe with Dagmar and he would be on a plane back home, never to see Ulya again.

*Z*iva, seated on a stepladder, chopped her umpteenth onion. Through the tears in her eyes, her hands appeared the same color as the onion skins. The steam belching off the industrial pots compounded the sweltering August forenoon, and yet her short-sleeve shirt remained bone dry. She had forgotten to tell the doctor about the lack of perspiration. She turned her attention to the ponytailed cook, a Jew of Yemenite parentage, rolling dough at the other end of the steel table. "Who told you we wanted to eat egg cylinders?"

Claudette, peeling carrots across from Ziva, was relieved to hear the old woman's voice. Ziva hadn't said a word all morning, not since they first arrived and Claudette offered to fetch her a stool. Claudette had expected the old woman to say no, as she always did, claiming she liked standing up, that it was more efficient to work on one's feet, but instead she had muttered "All right" and then remained silent for the next three hours.

"Firstly," the cook said, pushing his wooden roller, "they're called egg rolls. Secondly, I make whatever Mr. Margolin orders."

"*Mister* Margolin?" Ziva smacked her hand on the steel table, rattling her tin bowl and cutting board. "What *Mister* Margolin *orders*? Don't call my son *mister*."

Ziva wiped away the onion tear streaming down her cheek. She knew it was unfair to berate the cook, just as it made no sense to scowl at the hired fieldhands. They couldn't be blamed for accepting jobs. But the anger got the better of her. Where was the difference between this man hired to cook for the kibbutz and the housekeeper who used to prepare her family's dinners back in Berlin? A servant was a servant.

The cook muttered "Fine, fine," and everyone went back to working in quiet. Claudette peeled her carrots, exhausted from walking with Ofir until three in the morning, but this languor was different from the kind of exhaustion that followed a night of counting bathroom tiles. Over the last week, she and Ofir had walked together every night, around the fields and along the stream, each time saying goodbye just a little later. The Bad Feeling still accused her of lusting after a child, but just as she had been fighting the Bad Feeling before their walks, so the fight continued. As Claudette placed the last peeled carrot into the steel tub, she remembered the first time she worked in this kitchen, how she had to wash the vegetables over and over again, afraid she missed a bug or a spot of manure, or that the very hands she used to wash the carrots were poisoning them.

"No *mister*, no *sir*! We do not use honorifics here!" Ziva spoke as if an hour of silence hadn't gone by. She halved an onion with her knife. "Why? Because the fieldhand who digs up the onion, and the kitchen worker who cuts the onion, and the cook who boils it, and the person who eats it and uses its energy to invent better ways of growing onions are all equally important."

The cook raised an eyebrow at Claudette, who turned back to Ziva. Ziva lifted the hand with the knife and wiped her tears on her forearm. Claudette asked if she needed a tissue, and Ziva shook her head. "No, no. The more I wipe them, the more they tear."

Claudette carried the carrots to the cook, thinking she should probably tell Eyal that Ziva wasn't well today.

Ziva squeezed her eyes as she scraped the diced onions into a bowl. It was impossible to cut onions gracefully. She remembered Franz's joke: "That's something I never thought I'd see—Ziva crying." He had been dicing tomatoes on the other side of the table, where Claudette cut the carrots, except the table had been wood and the kitchen half the size. She had smiled at him. With the adrenaline from the night before still surging through her, she couldn't quite stifle her excitement at finding Franz also on dinner duty.

"Ziva doesn't cry. She's a national hero!" piped the eleven-year-old boy helping Franz cut tomatoes. Also in the kitchen were two women from Poland, plucking chickens at another table, and a former psychotherapist from Belorussia, one of the few Jews to survive the Minsk ghetto, scouring pans at the sink.

Ziva pinched the boy's cheek. He wasn't her biological child, but he was hers the way all the children were. She loved how the children had no memory of any other world, and she took great pains to never speak in front of them about death camps or pogroms or anything that might give them a sense of victimhood. "If anyone is crying today, it's King George, right?"

The boy nodded, and Franz said, "I've never seen you this happy. You're so—"

He shook his head, went back to his tomatoes. Ziva, returning to her onions, wondered why he didn't finish his sentence. What was he going to say before he stopped himself? Franz's restraint over the last year had surprised her. She hadn't thought him capable of restraint, but he had kept the promise made in the half-finished schoolhouse, giving them room to build a friendship. They talked quite a bit, around the campfire or when they shared a work shift, Ziva often surprised by what he would tell her—about the casual sex he had before the war, how he knew the electric fence behind his barrack wasn't strong enough to kill, how he went back for his brooch. Sometimes she suspected his restraint was part of a plan, that he nurtured this friendship assuming she would eventually grow too fond of him. At other times she believed what he told her not long after the lipstick incident, that he would rather have her as a friend than not have her in his life.

A bang shot through the kitchen. Ziva spun around, holding up her knife.

"Sorry." The former psychotherapist picked up the skillet he'd dropped.

Ziva exhaled and, heart still pounding, returned to her onions.

Franz leaned forward, spoke a little quieter. "Last night, I didn't sleep a wink. I was so worried about you."

"Worried about me? You just said I've never looked happier."

But she had known Franz would worry about her. While driving down the dark road toward the Syrian border, she pictured him lying in his barrack, worrying about the explosives taped to her legs. It was the same thrill she used to feel when their illegal Zionist meetings would run late, and she knew her mother was on the other side of Berlin pacing the kitchen. How Franz had come to know about the operation, he wouldn't say, but she wasn't surprised someone had let him in on it. Everybody liked Franz and wanted to be liked by him. By the big day, he knew everything, including who was in charge of bringing the dynamite to the Yamruk Bridge, where others waited in the thicket along the Jordan River. She had been chosen because a British patrolman was less likely to body search a woman, to check under her skirt. In one night, the resistance movement managed to blow up seven bridges connecting the British Mandate to the surrounding countries. The British were going to have a hell of a time getting supplies and reinforcements into Palestine.

Franz laid down his knife and leaned on the table. "I know, but—"

Once again he stopped midsentence. Pretending not to have seen the hesitation on his face, she blinked back the tears and said, "The British need to be driven out of Palestine. I still can't believe they're forcing boats of refugees to sail back to Germany."

Franz glanced at the boy and then proceeded to speak in German so he wouldn't understand. "Ziva, I know you're not going to like this, but I'm going to tell you anyway. When the radio reported that fifteen Jews had been killed on one of those bridges, I didn't care what happened to the rest of the operation or the British Empire or even the Jewish people. The only thing that mattered to me was that you weren't one of those fifteen."

Ziva stared at Franz, trying to decide if he had just crossed a line. And what if he had?

The boy broke the silence. "I hate cutting vegetables! It's boring."

"Quiet!" Ziva slapped the boy's shoulder. "All work is ennobling. It's complaining that demeans you. You've just demeaned yourself!"

The boy pouted and sullenly took another tomato while Ziva went back to work. She needed to think. Franz assumed she would find his worry despicable. Well, didn't she? Wasn't it low of him to care only about her well-being? She had recently learned how the guards at Buchenwald deterred escapees: Franz had to have known that ten people would be publicly shot or starved to death when he ran away. Instead of saving only himself, why hadn't he led an uprising? Of course, he never would have survived then. Never would have made it to Palestine to lie in a barrack worrying about her. Dov must have worried about her last night while he waited with the others in the shadowy brush by the bridge. But he would never have chosen her well-being over the success of the mission, over the well-being of the whole Jewish people. Nor would she want him to. Not since her mother and father had somebody cared for Ziva the way Franz did—so exclusively. Selfishly.

Finished with the onions, Ziva wiped off her knife to help with the tomatoes. As she reached for a tomato, Franz did too. Their fingers grazed. His touch jolted her and quickened her heart. Trying to feign indifference, she picked up a tomato and placed it down in front of her.

Franz must have felt something too, because in a hushed German he said, "Ziva, I know I'm going back on my word, and I'm sorry. I really am. But after what I went through last night, thinking maybe I was never going to see you again, I just can't pretend anymore. I can't pretend that . . . I don't love you."

Ziva looked behind her at the other table, where the psychotherapist had joined in plucking the chickens. Even if one of them understood German, the taller Polish woman blathered too loudly and incessantly for them to have heard anything. The boy obliviously hummed as he chopped.

She turned back to Franz, whose black eyes held a mix of apology and hope. She shouldn't feed that hope. She had to tell him not to talk that way, that it couldn't end well, but instead she said something equally true.

"I don't want you to pretend anymore."

They both lowered their heads and returned to their work. What would happen next? Ziva didn't know. When the shift was over, after the dinner was cooked, eaten, cleaned up, would they remain in the kitchen while the other workers left? Where was this going?

When it came time to break for dinner, they brought their trays to different tables. Ziva joined Dov and some other pioneers while Franz sat with fellow survivors. All through dinner, her table discussed how the Brits were going to retaliate: they had already instated a curfew in Tel Aviv, and soon—maybe tonight—they would raid the kibbutzim. Between this urgent talk and what transpired between her and Franz, Ziva couldn't eat.

Dov rubbed her back as he told eager listeners: "We chose Ziva not because she could wear a skirt, but because we needed to know the dynamite would get there. No one would be more fail-safe."

Ziva smiled, pushed away her uneaten plate. "My job was the least dangerous. I didn't lay down any explosives. I just waited in the car."

Dov smiled. "The getaway car."

Ziva remembered Dov's face, looking at her from the passenger seat as the car squealed away, a brilliant fire raging in the rearview mirror. His blue eyes beamed with pride and collusion. They were a team, she and Dov. A very special team. She shouldn't ruin that.

Those on dinner duty reconvened after the meal to clean up the kitchen. Ziva and Franz washed pots in the farmer's sink while the psychotherapist dried. Ziva feared Franz might reach for her hand under the sudsy water. Instead he barely looked at her. Had he too changed his mind? After walking to the edge, maybe he no longer wanted to step off. They skirted one another as they put away the pots and pans. Ziva felt more and more certain that Franz was going to be relieved to leave things alone. While she mopped the floor, Franz helped one of the Polish women return food to the fridge. The woman laughed, slapping his arm, and Ziva seethed, thinking for a moment that having won her over, he was bored and already onto someone new. By the time the other workers were removing their aprons and departing with cigarettes in their mouths, she was ready to tell him she had no intention of taking this any further. It was going to be hard for her to say, but not impossible.

When the door closed behind the last worker, she stopped pretending to clean the floor. Holding onto the mop, she said, "Franz, I've made it this far in my life without doing anything I regret."

A hanging lightbulb buzzed between them. The dank smell of the wet cement floor mingled with the piney breeze billowing the curtains over the sink.

Franz stood with one hand on the prep table. "I don't want you to do anything you'll regret."

Was that why he hadn't moved toward her? Maybe he was terrified of getting what he wanted? Maybe she was. She didn't see how their coming together could possibly live up to a year of yearning. It might be no better than it was with Dov.

She laid the mop against the counter. When she started walking toward him, Franz took his hand off the table, straightened. She stood as close to him as she could without touching. Her chest trembled. He gazed down, breathing heavily.

She closed her eyes as she raised her face. Her lips, her whole being, pulsed with anticipation. Their mouths met, and she felt a surge of life, like she did when she saw the bridge explode. Franz clutched her arms and pulled her into him with a startling violence. He kissed her, hungrily, as if he couldn't quite get enough, but not in the way she had feared, not because she was disappointing, unsatisfying, but because the more he had of her, the more he seemed to want.

He lifted her onto the table, clasping her ass so hard it smarted. He unfastened her fly while she hurried to unbutton her shirt, hoping he would take her nipple in his mouth, something Dov had never done in all their years together. He did. As soon as her breasts were freed. She groaned as he sucked on one, then the other. Pushing her breasts together, he said, "So much whiter than the rest of you."

When Franz pushed into her, Ziva's thoughts fuzzed while the kitchen— the world—crystallized, as if for a moment existence had dropped one of its pretenses. It was for this, all the fuss. The poetry, taboos, rabbinic obligations and condemnations, the hidden photographs, the promises. And the betrayals.

Afterward they held each other, Franz standing, Ziva sitting on the table, head resting against his chest. She wanted to tell him that she loved him as much as he loved her, but how could she? How could she feel this oneness with Franz when there was Dov?

"Dagmar."

He toyed with her hair. "What's that?"

"My name was Dagmar."

"Dagmar." Franz said it slowly, as if conjuring a spell.

Fifteen years had passed since she or anyone had uttered her old name, and for Ziva it did conjure an apparition. She seemed to see the idealistic German schoolgirl standing behind Franz on the cement floor, dark hair in two unruly braids, hands folded in front of her navy tunic. Her girlish, close-set hazel eyes stared back at the thirty-one-year-old woman embracing a man under a naked lightbulb. Her younger eyes bore no judgment, just curiosity, as if after being shut out for so long, she only wanted to see what had become of her.

"But don't call me Dagmar when anyone else is around."

Franz nodded. "I promise, Dagmar."

"Ziva!"

Startled, Ziva gaped at Claudette running around the cutting table. Claudette reached for Ziva's bloody knife, but the old woman, bewildered, trembling, jerked her hand free and went back to dicing the onions with the tip of her index finger missing.

"*Mon Dieu*! Your finger! Ziva! We need to wrap your finger!"

The cook rushed over, others too. They stood around the table as Ziva scooped the blood-splattered onions into a bowl. Blood smeared the plastic cutting board, the steel table, Ziva's chin.

"Ziva, we have to go to the hospital!" Claudette laid her hands on the old woman's bony shoulders and felt the skin broiling beneath the dry white shirt. "Now!"

"Nonsense." Ziva pushed Claudette away with her bloody hand. "I'm working."

Claudette shouted at the cook to call Eyal. The cook, already at the phone, hung up. "Mr. Margolin is on his way."

"*Mister* Margolin!" spat Ziva. "Fuck *Mister* Margolin!"

In seconds, Eyal bounded into the kitchen and ran toward his mother. "Ima! We have to go to the hospital!"

Ziva leaned forward on the stepladder, pointing her knife at him. "Stay away from me."

Eyal crept forward, palms raised. "Ima, please."

Ziva swung the knife at the air between them. "You, you who give orders, you cannot order me! I want to keep working!"

The kitchen workers gawked while other bystanders gathered at the kitchen's back entrance and the doors onto the dining room. Eyal inched toward Ziva, trying to keep a calm face, but Claudette could see his distress.

"I called 1-0-0, Ima. They're going to be here in a few minutes."

Ziva thrust the knife toward him. He stopped, waited, and took another step forward. She lunged with the knife again and toppled off the stepladder, landing on the cement floor hip first. The crack was audible. She howled in pain.

Eyal kicked the knife away from her and roared at the bystanders: "This isn't a show! Go away! Go away!"

Cheek against the cold cement floor, Ziva sobbed, tears no longer from the onions. "I want to keep working."

*A*dam stared at the ceiling as the afternoon sunlight drained from the room. Golda had tried to snuggle against him, but he kept pushing her away until she curled into a ball at the bottom of the bed. It was a new Friday. A new paper without his ad sat on newsstands and doorsteps all over the country. A week of ads, and nobody had called. Now all those papers were in the garbage, and he was all out of ideas. Over the last few days he had tried to think of another way to find Dagmar, or whatever she was called now, but nothing came to him. Meanwhile the brooch sat in his pocket like a bona fide mark of Cain.

Golda sat up seconds before there came a knock at the door. Adam rolled off the bed. He'd called in sick today and assumed this was Yossi coming to check on him. He walked toward the door, bending over, preparing to feign he had a bad stomach bug.

It was one of the Russians, the skinny kid with the mullet and square glasses—all he needed to look like the perfect computer nerd was a computer. He even had the name.

Adam dropped the sick act, straightened up. "What is it, Eugene?"

"Phone call."

"Phone? For me?"

"Yes."

"They're on the line right now?"

When Eugene nodded, Adam pushed past him, not bothering to put on shoes or close his door. He bolted across the quad, his bare heel landing on one of the hard fruits hidden in the overgrown grass. He hopped in pain up the stairs and down the veranda toward the dangling receiver.

"Hello? Shalom?"

"Shalom. *Sprechen Sie Deutsch*? Or English?"

It wasn't Dagmar. A man. Traces of a German accent. He must know her.

"English, English," Adam said. "I'm American."

"Good. I'm calling from Toronto. A friend told me about your ad in *Yedioth Ahronoth*."

"Great." Of course this is how it would go: a turnaround at the eleventh hour. Adam felt light, rescued.

"I know a Dagmar Stahlmann who would be around eighty today. We were in a Maccabi Hatzair chapter together in Berlin. Did she contact you?"

"No. Can you give me her number?"

"Oh." The man clucked his tongue. "I was hoping you would give that to me."

Someone else looking for Dagmar? Adam leaned on the phone.

"Hello?" said the old man.

"Yeah, I'm here."

"So you haven't found her?"

"No. All I know is that she lived on a kibbutz in forty-seven. After that, I've got nothing. You? Do you have any idea of where she might be?"

"Well, I can't imagine Dagmar ending up anywhere but on a kibbutz. She was obsessed with the Land of Israel and the kibbutzim. Of course, I'm talking about a sixteen-year-old girl I once knew. People grow softer as they age. They give up. Though I can't picture the Dagmar I knew giving up."

"So you think she's still on a kibbutz?"

"That would be my guess . . . if she's still alive."

"Thing is she's probably not even called Dagmar anymore. Apparently, everyone changed their names in Israel to something more Jewish. Hebrew."

"Well, I might be able to help you with that. We all had Hebrew names we used at the meetings. My name, David, was already Hebrew. Maybe that's why I got a nickname, Bloomie. Now what did Dagmar go by? God,

I haven't thought about it in decades. In school, everywhere else, she was Dagmar. But . . . it's right there, on the tip of my tongue."

Adam waited. Come on, come on.

"She did all the translations, and she would sign them with her Hebrew name. Vera? No. Tsvia . . . Yes, something like Tsvia . . . But it's just not coming to me."

Adam squeezed the handset. He had to use all his willpower not to slam it against the wall. He spoke through his teeth. "Okay, thanks."

"If she contacts you, will you let her know I called? David Blumenthal. Are you writing this down? Do you have a pen?"

"Yup."

Adam felt terrible about lying to a Holocaust survivor looking for an old friend, but he just didn't have it in him to go fetch a pen.

"I live with my son now." He gave the phone number. "You can tell Dagmar that Bloomie said he should have listened to her, that he should have followed her to Palestine. You can tell her my brother died in Auschwitz. She knew him. He was also in Maccabi Hatzair."

"Got it."

"May I ask you why you're looking for Dagmar?"

"It's a long story."

"All right," said the old man. "I really hope you find her."

Adam banged down the phone, hard, half hoping to break it, and stormed back to his room. Unaware Golda was following him, he slammed the door, nearly crushing her, but she jumped through in the nick of time.

Fuck, fuck, fuck. He kicked the dresser and looked around his room, heart beating too fast. Through the window he saw Ulya leaving her room, all gussied up in a short orange tube dress. He watched her teeter down the path in her stupid high heels.

Where the hell did she go every night? What was the big fucking secret?

He headed for the door. Golda made a dash for it too, but he couldn't trail Ulya with the dog running ahead. He slipped outside, closing the door on her round pleading eyes.

He hung back while Ulya climbed the back stairs out of the volunteers' section. Once she'd reached the top and turned behind a wall of bushes, he started for the stone steps. He walked slowly to give her time to get ahead. When he peeked around the bushes, he feared he'd waited too long.

She was nowhere to be seen. And then she reappeared for a brief second, crossing the gap between two white bungalows.

He kept a good distance as he followed her down the path away from the kibbutz's center. The kibbutz did feel different on Friday evenings. Serener. Women chatted on porches. An older man watered his modest flowerbed. A younger man headed home with plastic bags full of sodas and snacks. The way Ulya walked past these people, swinging her silver purse as she did that morning they set out for Tel Aviv, made her seem like one of them, just another person excited for the weekend, not somebody on her way to a second job.

When she reached the dirt road encircling the residential part of the kibbutz, she didn't turn in the direction of the nearby towns or the bus stop, as Adam had expected. Instead she made a left, toward the fields and orchards. This made no sense. Where could she be going?

He waited, allowing the distance between them to grow long enough that if she happened to turn around, she might not spot him in the half-light. At this point, he'd have a hard time pretending he was going any-where believable. She crossed the road, leaving behind the white houses to walk alongside the open fields.

She continued along the road for a good five minutes before veering off behind a long shed. Adam jogged to catch up. When he reached the corrugated steel shed, he knew she couldn't have gone inside it. The clamor behind its walls—high-pitched squawks, countless beating wings—was frightening, and the stench unbearable. Hand on his mouth, pinching his nose, he crept along the chicken house. When he reached the end, he saw Ulya walking across a dusky cabbage field.

Grateful for the near darkness, he abandoned the cover of the chicken house and followed her down a path between the purple heads, ready to duck if she looked back. She seemed to be slowing, so he did as well. She ceased swinging her purse, and even from a distance, he sensed her mood had taken a downturn.

She stopped, and Adam dropped to a squat, balancing himself with one hand on the dirt. She didn't turn around. Head tilted toward the eve-ning sky, she stood very still, reminding him of those scenes where an alien spaceship descends from the sky and lowers its ramp for one special human being. He hated to admit it after the way she had treated him, but he believed Ulya was special.

She set off again. At the end of the field, she began ascending a hill covered with mandarin trees. Adam followed and, feeling safer in the shadows of the orchard, closed the distance a bit. A bright citrusy smell pervaded the darkness. He quietly plucked a mandarin and peeled off its rind as he walked down a parallel path through the trees, watching Ulya appear and disappear behind the trunks like a flickering film.

"Hey."

Both Ulya and Adam halted, the crunch of the wood chips under their feet replaced by the faint squeak of bats.

"I'm over here," a man called. His accent was thick.

What kind of accent was it? Not Russian. Or Hebrew. From behind a tree, Adam surveyed the clearing beyond the orchard, the uncultivated hillside strewn with limestone boulders and clusters of wildflowers. Two legs—dark jeans, brown shoes—extended from behind a large, white boulder. Ulya awkwardly stepped over collapsed cattle wire and sashayed toward the hidden man. His hand came out, and she took it. He said something—Adam couldn't make it out—and she laughed and tried to tug her hand free. Why did she say she didn't have a boyfriend? Was she being paid for this? Was he married? The man tugged back. Ulya stumbled toward him then leaned backward with all her weight. "Let go!" she said through more laughter. No, she wasn't getting paid for this. This was real flirtation, not the sad imitation she'd been giving him, not some kind of tease. "Enough!" the man cried with that accent, yanking hard. Squealing, Ulya let herself fall forward onto her hands and knees. The man's hand clasped her orange back, and they switched places; she lay on her back while he emerged from behind the boulder.

Holy shit. It was the guy who'd been eyeing them in the dining hall. Here he'd been wondering if he was too poor, too Jewish, and all the while she'd been screwing around with an Arab fieldhand.

The Arab leaned toward Ulya, and she tweaked his nose. He smiled, and their lips came together. Adam held his breath while their faces remained locked as if they hadn't seen each other for months. A mandarin fell out of the tree and landed beside Adam with a hollow thud. Jesus, were they ever going to separate? Their motionless kiss seemed unending.

He emerged from the trees, stepping over the fallen cattle wire. "Hi."

The couple looked up.

"Adam!" Ulya screamed, adjusting her tube top.

Adam was as surprised as they were to find himself standing before them. He hadn't planned on coming out of the trees. He just had.

He stood over their maroon blanket, their shocked faces. The bottle of wine. "I thought you didn't have a boyfriend."

Ulya clambered to her feet. "Fuck you, Adam! Get out of here!"

In her bare feet, she seemed so much shorter, more vulnerable.

"Funny. I thought you were stripping."

Farid had gotten to his feet and was looking from Ulya to Adam and back to Ulya.

Ulya waved Adam away. "Get out of here! Go! Go where someone wants you!"

Where someone wanted him? Nice. Adam cocked his head, pointed between her and the Arab. "So is this something I should keep to myself?"

Ulya breathed heavily.

"'Cause you're definitely keeping this a secret, right, Ulie?"

She shook her head, smirking as if he were so clueless, but her eyes gleamed with fear and hate. So different from the gleam he had wanted to see in them. He turned to the Arab.

"If you think she takes you seriously, you're crazy. You're nothing to her. Soon as some rich guy comes along, you're gone. You know that, right?"

Ulya waited to see what Farid would do. Adam was right: in the grand scheme of things, Farid was nothing to her, but that was beside the point. He should still stand up for himself, but all the coward did was gape at Adam.

She waved her hands. "Hello, Farid! Defend yourself! Tell him to get lost. Do something!"

Barely making eye contact with Adam, Farid said, "Get lost."

Ulya looked from one man to the other, not sure whom she loathed more: the Jew, always feeling sorry for himself, but who at least had the passion to make this move, or the lazy, daydreaming Arab, standing like a frightened puppy caught peeing on the rug.

"And if I don't?" Adam opened his arms at his sides, a gesture that said, here I am, come and get me, though really he didn't want to be come and got. He knew from too much experience that he was a sorry fighter. He'd had his lights knocked out more than once. Though getting his lights knocked out didn't sound so bad right now. Sounded great actually.

Farid glanced at Ulya. Ulya, realizing a fight over her was imminent, couldn't stop the grin from blooming on her face. A duel—like in the novels she'd been forced to read in school. And why not? Why should her life be any less exciting than Pushkin's wife's? The threat of violence—violence over her—electrified the night.

"Go on, Farid. Do something!"

Farid raised his fists. Adam did the same, widening his stance, bending his knees. Farid brought one leg back. Waiting for the Arab to take a swipe, Adam changed his tactic; he straightened up and offered his chest, again daring Farid to punch it. Farid licked his lips and rocked his weight back and forth, back and forth. Adam had been right: this guy was never going to swing. And Farid, as if he saw Adam understand this, sagged.

Trying not to sound too relieved, Adam said, "A real man you have there."

Ulya shot Farid a black look and charged at Adam. She pushed against his chest with all her might again and again. Adam stumbled backward as she shoved and shouted: "Go! Go! Go! Go! Go!"

The Arab's head was down; he wasn't even watching. They were both losers now, but that didn't make Adam feel any better. He turned. "Okay, I'm going."

Once he began his retreat, he couldn't retreat fast enough. He headed for the orchard as fast as he could without breaking into a run. He climbed over the cattle wire and weaved his way down the darkness of the mandarin orchard and out onto the flat, open cabbage field again, where the moon beamed down on him like a spotlight. He'd been so focused on Ulya, he hadn't noticed how enormous the moon was tonight. This must have been what she had stopped to look up at.

Back among the white bungalows, he couldn't stand the laughter and chitchat floating out of the cozy-lit windows. Everybody having a nice Friday night with everybody else. Coffee, cake, small talk, arguments about the peace process, thighs secretly squeezed under the table, please pass the sugar. He couldn't be more alone. It was his fault: he killed his grandfather, hurt every girl who ever loved him, betrayed every friend. But that only made the loneliness harder.

Descending the stone steps into the volunteers' section, he nearly collided with Claudette. He looked up, and her painted lips formed a smile, the first smile he'd ever seen on her. She apologized and hurried past him. Even Claudette had plans.

He dreaded the long night ahead, cooped up in his depressing dorm room. If only he could take a benzo and be out until morning. When he opened the door, Golda spun in circles and pawed at his legs, but he ignored her. He flipped on the light, but this only made the room appear more jail-like. Fuck it. He couldn't do it: sit here all night with himself. Wished he could—it was the fate he deserved—but he couldn't.

"Come on, come on, come on," he said, waving Golda out the door.

He crossed the quad with the little dog hurrying to keep pace. He marched up the steppingstones and past the jasmine hedges and across the main lawn. He headed toward the bomb shelter, its door wide-open, insides glowing like a traffic light. Go.

Adam hesitated in the doorway. The steel door at the bottom of the stairwell held back a pounding bass. He could still turn around. Turn around and go where? He needed distraction. That's all. Not alcohol. The distraction. He'd order a Diet Coke. He did it in Tel Aviv.

Inside, he was enveloped by a thumping techno beat and a haze of cigarette smoke streaked with green and blue lights. And yet the vibe in the concrete bunker was mellow. On a shabby couch, two army-aged guys bobbed their shaved heads to the repetitive beats. Some teenagers sat around a table, leaning precariously back in their chairs, cracking jokes. At another table four Russians played poker while a fifth stood over them like a referee. Did people hide in here from Iraqi scud missiles?

He climbed onto a barstool and lifted Golda onto his lap. A skinny girl in low-slung jeans came for his order. An inked peace sign adorned her bony hip. Adam asked for her name.

The girl rolled her eyes. "Talia. What do you want to drink?"

Israelis really got on his nerves sometimes. He wanted to tell her to calm down, she wasn't that hot. And that all he wanted was a Diet Coke.

The girl crossed her arms when he failed to order. "*Nu?* Goldstar's half price tonight."

He lowered his head and scratched the wooden bar as if it were a lottery ticket.

"*Nu?*" she repeated.

"*Nu, nu, nu.* Just go fucking get it already."

"Go fuck yourself." The bartender walked off on her pin legs.

Did that mean she wasn't going to bring him a beer? That would make things easy. But no, she grabbed a bottle from the minifridge. That's fine. He was still okay. No harm in ordering it. Only drinking it. He'd leave it sitting in front of him so he looked like a normal dude at a bar. What did he care if after he left the bartender found it full? Maybe he could empty it in the bathroom. Bomb shelters had to have bathrooms, right? People couldn't be confined in here without a toilet.

The girl popped off the cap and placed the bottle before him. Beads of condensation trickled down its brown glass and red and gold label. She leaned on the bar. "I'm going to kick you out if you keep being an asshole."

Adam nodded. "You're totally right. I'm sorry."

The girl left to take someone else's order and he eyed the bottle without touching it. Until he'd taken a sip, he hadn't taken a sip. He'd just sit here with the bottle and his aching breastbone. Ten seconds. He still hadn't taken a sip.

Why don't Jews drink? went the old joke.

Because it interferes with their suffering.

His heart pounded wildly as he clasped the bottle. So cold in his hand. So familiar, he could practically taste it by just holding it. His mouth dried.

Was he doing this? He lifted the bottle, brought it to his mouth. Even with the cool glass rim against his lips, he wasn't sure. Or maybe that was bullshit. Maybe the only thing he wasn't sure about was whether he was truly unsure.

Was he?

Yes. Because he could still put down the bottle.

He tilted back his head and the cold, fizzy lager poured into his mouth. He held it in there, tongue absorbing the taste, not swallowing. He still hadn't swallowed, he still hadn't swallowed, he—

So fucking swallow and get it over with, you fucking loser.

Done.

Unsure of his unsureness? What a fucking joke he was. He knew he was going to drink from the minute he left Ulya and her Arab on the hillside. No, before that. He knew when he didn't go get a pen for the Holocaust survivor. Bloomie. Jesus, was there anything more depressing than an old pet name?

Yes.

He chugged the rest of the bottle and called, "Another one!"

He was going to get plastered tonight. Only tonight. Tomorrow, he'd stop. Tomorrow, he would be sober again, ready to push on. To think of a new way to find Dagmar. He just needed help getting through this one night.

Claudette sat on her bed, the fax in her hands. The room had darkened in the two hours it had taken her to read it. She was supposed to have met Ofir at the car lot five minutes ago, but she couldn't help but reread her sister's note again.

Salut ma chère Claudette,

You must read this article from *La Tribune*! Didn't I tell you it made no sense that you were certified insane at one year old? Call me collect as soon as you read this!

XOXO,
Louise

Before the man from the office had knocked on her door with the fax, saying it must be important because her sister had called long distance to make sure it was hand delivered to her, Claudette had been brushing her hair, thinking she never could have imagined herself this content. It had been a month since she last wiped a doorknob or wondered if she'd molested a farm animal. Instead, her days were spent by Ziva's bedside, drinking mint tea and listening to her memories of surviving cholera and blowing up bridges. At night, she explored the fields and the surrounding hills with Ofir. She had been especially excited for tonight. He had planned on driving her to the Sea of Galilee to ring in her birthday. No one had ever planned something special for her birthday before.

She turned again to the newspaper article, the sea of small print that had taken her so long to understand. Each letter had to be sounded out and threaded into a word; the word strung into a sentence; the sentences looped together into something that made sense. But nothing did.

"DUPLESSIS ORPHANS" VICTIMS OF CHURCH-GOVERNMENT SCAM

BY JEAN CLOUTIER

Before Paiement Bottling Company would employ Michel Brossard, a paranoid schizophrenic, they required that his doctor provide a written statement that he was fit to work. Imagine Mr. Brossard's surprise when Dr. Pierre Maisonneuve, the psychiatrist who diagnosed him with schizophrenia thirty-three years earlier and had been treating him ever since, informed him that he didn't have the brain disorder and never did.

Mr. Brossard is one of several thousand victims of a long-term scam by the government of Quebec and the Roman Catholic Church to steal money from the government of Canada. Since provincial governments were financially responsible for orphanages and the federal government for insane asylums, Quebec had up to 20,000 orphans falsely certified as insane. In order to secure the cooperation of the Church, which ran most of the province's orphanages, Quebec offered the church nearly three times as much to care for psychiatric patients than orphans, $2.75 versus $1.00 a day.

Overnight, orphanages were converted into insane asylums, and many healthy children were shipped to existing mental hospitals. The orphans were slapped with diagnoses ranging from antisocial disorder to mental retardation, including infants far too young to be diagnosed. Most of these fraudulent diagnoses, beginning in 1949 and continuing until 1967, were never corrected. Thousands of orphans spent decades confined to institutions or were released in early adulthood poorly equipped for regular life.

Now the Duplessis Orphans, named after Premier Maurice Duplessis, who reigned from 1936 to 1939 and again from 1944 to 1959, are demanding an apology and compensation for the alleged mental, physical, and sexual abuse they experienced at the hands of psychiatrists, priests, nuns, and lay workers. The allegations include unwarranted electric shock treatments, days in isolation cells, lobotomies, beatings, and rape. Some of the orphans claim they were used for drug tests and are calling for an excavation of an abandoned cemetery in the east end of Montreal to autopsy the remains of children who purportedly died from these trials. Their lawyer, Robert Néron, points out that the Church and government made still more money by denying the children an education and using them as forced labor.

Mr. Néron is seeking permission to file a series of class-action suits against the Quebec government, the Sisters of Charity, the Sisters of Mercy, the Sisters of Providence, the Brothers of Notre-Dame-de-la-Miséricorde, the Little Franciscans of Mary, and the Brothers of Charity. In addition, Mr. Néron is preparing a suit against the College of Physicians of Quebec for their cooperation in falsifying medical records.

"We were easy targets," says Geneviève Tremblay, who grew up at Mont Providence orphanage in Montreal. "They could do whatever they wanted. We were children, had no families to stand up for us. But now we can stand up for ourselves."

Technically, most of the Duplessis Orphans, including Mr. Brossard and Ms. Tremblay, were not orphans. They were born to unwed mothers sent by their families to the Catholic cloisters so they could carry and deliver their babies in secret. Afterward, the babies remained in the Church's care. Few orphans were ever reunited with their biological parents, and a number of the orphans maintain the nuns viewed them as "living sins."

Mr. Brossard says, "They punished us as if we had been the sinners."

The current Quebec government of Robert Bourassa said it would be inappropriate for them to comment while the investigation is under way. The Roman Catholic Church promises to do their own internal investigation but for now insists it has "nothing to apologize for." The College of Physicians of Quebec said they were prepared to hand over their patients' files for inspection of forgery, but all files over twenty years old have been discarded.

When Dr. Maisonneuve was asked why he finally told Mr. Brossard the truth after thirty-three years, he said, "I'm an old man now. I have lung cancer. I didn't want to die with the lie. I had to confess if I wanted God to forgive me."

Claudette rose from the bed and switched on the light. After a week of agonizing over whether or not to wear Ulya's bikini, she numbly put it on. She painted her lips without feeling them. In the mirror, she contemplated the metal pendant hanging over her white dress: Christina the Astonishing's haloed head, modestly lowered, her lissome hands hugging the book to her breast. What would Christina have done if she had read that fax? She wouldn't have believed it. Her faith would have been too strong.

Ofir knew something was wrong as soon as he saw Claudette coming across the car lot, her gait even more robotic than usual. For half an hour he had lurked around the cars, nervous that any second someone would ask where he was going and with whom. He had begun to think Claudette wasn't coming, that she didn't want to go, and now it looked like that was precisely what she was on her way to tell him.

"Are you okay?" he asked, glancing around, hoping no one was seeing them together.

"Yes. I'm very sorry I'm late."

Claudette reached for the passenger door, and Ofir, relieved she still wanted to go, hastened to open it for her. He understood Claudette didn't see tonight as a date, but he did, even if it wasn't going to include kissing. He held the door ajar as she ducked inside, revealing the red bikini strings in a bow at the nape of her neck. He imagined pulling on one of those strings, the bow falling open.

To avoid the prying eyes of the guard at the front gate, Ofir drove the car along the road behind the kibbutz, descending into the fields and winding along the bumpy dirt paths between crops until they entered the back of a different kibbutz. They drove through that kibbutz's front gate onto the country road.

"For security reasons," Ofir explained, "the only way to get onto the main road is through one of the kibbutzim's front gates. It sucks having someone always seeing you coming and going. If we'd gone through our front gate, by tomorrow everyone on the kibbutz would've been talking about us."

"Hmm," said Claudette, staring out the windshield. Lighting a cigarette, Ofir decided to keep quiet for a while. Hopefully she would emerge from her funk before they got to the lake.

The car traveled down the dark highway, occasionally passing a gas station or illuminated junction, but for much of the drive the car's headlights were all that kept the valley and the hills and the night sky from melding into one darkness. Ofir was halfway through his second cigarette when the headlights illuminated a signpost he hoped might shake Claudette out of her daze. He pointed. "Hey, look, only fifteen miles to Nazareth. Isn't that where Jesus was born?"

Claudette eyed the sign. "No. Bethlehem."

"Oh, yeah, that's right. I always get that mixed up because he's called Jesus of Nazareth."

"That's where He lived."

Ofir would have thought she'd be more excited to be so close to where Jesus lived. Instead she sounded emotionless. Frighteningly so. Was this a hint of the madness? She had warned him that she was mentally ill, and though he had found her very odd, he hadn't yet witnessed any break from reality.

He switched off the brights for an oncoming car. "But the Sea of Galilee is where he supposedly walked on water, right?"

Claudette turned to him, gave him a dark stare. "'Supposedly'? You didn't have to say 'supposedly.' The Sea of Galilee is where He performed many miracles. Walked on water. Fed the multitudes. Calmed the storm."

Ofir lifted his eyebrows and, smiling uncomfortably, crushed his cigarette in the ashtray. Well, at least now she was talking.

"Why are you laughing?" she said.

Ofir shook his head. "I'm not laughing."

"Yes, you are."

"I don't know. I guess . . . I guess the idea of miracles makes me feel weird. I just don't believe in them."

"Then what do you believe in?"

"Um . . ." He scrunched his face as he searched for an answer. He used to believe in music. But what now? There had to be something.

"Humans?"

"Humans? What do you mean you believe in 'humans'?"

"You know, just humans. Their perseverance. Their ingenuity. Yeah, definitely human ingenuity. We've come up with some pretty amazing things, don't you think? For an animal. Languages. Airplanes and heart transplants." He paused. "The piano."

Claudette shook her head. "I don't like that. That is arrogance. That is . . . no."

She was tempted to point out that human ingenuity came up with the bomb that blew open his eardrums, but she didn't, because it would have been cruel and beside the point. Even if humans hadn't invented bombs, it would still be arrogant to worship their ingenuity over God's, as if their ingenuity hadn't been given to them by God.

Ofir could have said more too, but he didn't want to delve any further into this discussion, especially not when Claudette was already in a bad mood. He supposed religion would come up again sometime in the future, but he didn't focus on the future anymore.

They drove in silence once more, the humid air blowing through the open windows. Ofir tried to ignore the dial tone in his head, the phone that could never be put back on the hook. This evening wasn't going at all to plan. Could it be her birthday that was upsetting Claudette? Any birthday after thirty, he supposed, had to be a little depressing.

The quiet became more and more unbearable to him. He even considered turning on the radio. He reached for it, but then returned his hand to the steering wheel. How could he enjoy listening to music knowing he couldn't compose his own? He had never understood how people listened to symphonies, admired paintings, read books without feeling the need to contribute their own works of art.

He peeked over at Claudette, still staring vacantly through the windshield. His eyes roamed down the front of her body to the hammock of white dress between her thighs, the red swimsuit bottom showing through the white cotton. How could the Orthodox go on believing in *shomer negiah*, that being forbidden to touch a member of the opposite sex was an effective way to avoid sexual tension? His inability to touch Claudette intensified the yearning. It made the curve of her shoulder surprisingly erotic.

After still more silence and yet another cigarette, he reached for the radio and hurriedly turned the knob. A Coca-Cola commercial burst into the car: *Can't beat the real thing!* Claudette watched out of the corner of her eye as he turned through the stations. She knew he hadn't listened to his tapes or the radio since the bombing. He landed on a staticky classical-music station and massaged the knob until the piano came in clear. It was a Chopin Nocturne, one of his favorites. He sat back, clenching the steering wheel.

Despite the hearing aids, the high-pitched tinnitus, the music still translated the night for him. It isolated the moment—he and Claudette driving through this dark valley—and filled him with sad wonder, wonder for how much had to happen for this dark valley to exist and for them to be driving through it. He still felt jealous of Chopin, but he also felt him commiserating with him across the centuries. Was it possible the Nocturne moved him even more now?

Claudette saw Ofir's lips quiver into a sad smile. Could she do what he was doing? Learn to live without the one thing that had given her life meaning? Learn to live without God? She didn't think so. She watched him listening to the music, his eyes—one teardrop eye—on the road, and felt an urge to reach out and touch his gentle face, to feel the scar on his chin. *No, it isn't true.* She turned toward the window so the wind whipped her hair against her face. *It isn't true.*

Ofir parked the car in an empty lot beside some stone ruins, and they followed a path beneath a bower of palms toward the lake. The warm air smelled of fresh water and wet reeds. Ofir stopped and read from a historical marker. "It's one of the oldest synagogues in the world."

Claudette's eyes widened. "This is the synagogue of Capernaum?"

"You've heard of it? We can walk around the ruins a bit. Your birthday isn't for half an hour."

Ofir followed Claudette through a calcareous arch. Her white sundress swayed as she walked, running her hand along the remnants of walls, white stone battered down by thousands of years. Faint patterns still adorned the broken columns. She paused, looked around with a contemplative expression. Ofir, sensing she wanted to be alone with the place, hung back, then left to wait for her outside.

Claudette watched her blue flip-flops walking on the worn stones. Were these the very stones Jesus had walked on? It was here that He began His mission, choosing John, Peter, and Matthew to be His disciples. She might be standing on the very spot where He had healed the paralytic, who had to be lowered through the roof because the synagogue was so crammed with believers and naysayers. He told the cripple that his sins were forgiven, and the man got up and walked away as if guilt had been his only handicap. At least, that's what she had been taught.

She raised her head and looked past the missing roof to the night sky. She whispered: "If You are true, please send me a sign. I am going to wait for Your sign."

Claudette emerged from the ancient synagogue noticeably calmer. When they reached the placid lake, Ofir laid a white bed sheet on the grainy shore. Trying to ignore the ringing in his ears, to not let it ruin the quiet of the spot, he sat across from Claudette and unloaded from his backpack what he hoped was romantic French fare: a bottle of red wine; a baguette, albeit slightly stale; grapes; and a wedge of Roquefort cheese, which handsome Ido—who secured all this stuff for him and had promised on his mother's life that he wouldn't tell anybody about Claudette—swore was supposed to be riddled with mold. Ofir filled two plastic cups with wine and pulled the blue cover off a Tupperware box, revealing a chocolate cupcake bedecked in rainbow sprinkles. He stuck in a pink candle and checked his watch.

"Only one minute to go."

Claudette smiled down at the cupcake. Heartened by the smile, Ofir took a sip of wine and struggled to keep his face from betraying how bitter he found it. Ido asked the owner to recommend a good affordable bottle, but could this really be the taste of good wine? He knew it was lame, but he preferred Manischewitz. Claudette was also used to a sweeter sacramental brand, but she recognized and liked the warm feeling in her stomach.

At last Ofir's watch showed 12:00 a.m. He struck a match and lit the candle. While he sang "Happy Birthday," Claudette wondered if it were possible, despite what she had learned today, for this still to be the nicest birthday she'd ever had.

"Okay, make a wish."

"A wish?"

Ofir gave her a questioning look. "You don't know about making a wish? I thought they did that everywhere."

She shook her head. Ofir explained the tradition and then watched as she squeezed her eyes to think of a wish. The next time he blew out his candles, he too would have to come up with a new wish.

"If you don't hurry up, the candle will go out on its own. Just wish for whatever you want the most."

Claudette bit down on her lip. She looked like a child to Ofir, agonizing over her birthday wish, not like a woman turning thirty-two years old. If anything happened between them, the world would condemn her. All they would see was a thirty-two-year-old woman debauching a wounded seventeen-year-old boy. But that was not how it felt to him. To him it felt like he was the experienced war vet taking advantage of the fragile ingénue.

"This is ridiculous!" He laughed. "Just wish for the next thing that comes into your head."

You. That's what came into her head. *No, no. It isn't true.* She had to say something. She had already decided that she wouldn't wish for faith, that she would wait for His sign. So she said the only other thing she knew she wanted.

"I wish your ears would be healed."

Ofir was touched by her gesture. Too bad he'd forgotten to tell her that the wish wouldn't come true if she said it out loud.

"Now blow!"

Claudette blew out the flame moments before it reached the cupcake. Ofir clapped, and she held out her plastic cup for more wine. Ofir refilled her cup, wondering whether he should have borrowed money to buy a second bottle. He forced down another bitter swig and wiped his lips.

"I want to know everything about you, Claudette. Is that weird? Tell me something I don't know."

Claudette stared into her wine. It felt as if he were asking about the article.

"You know enough."

"Tell me a secret. I want to know something that nobody else knows."

Claudette saw Sister Marie Amable, standing in the office that morning almost twenty years ago, reading from her mother's dossier. *Recalcitrant girl.* And then, *Oh. Oh no.* Had Sister Amable been a part of the scam? Was that possible? Gaping at her through her steel-frame glasses, she had said, *No wonder you are so sick.*

Claudette swilled down more wine. Normally at this point she would shake her head, shake the memory off, do anything to not think about it. Count, touch, pace, clean, repeat.

"There is something."

Ofir leaned forward. He had that rare feeling of being with someone, not just being in the same vicinity, but truly being *with* them.

Claudette found she was having trouble holding up her head. It felt both heavy and light, as if filled with lead and helium. Her fingers tingled. How much did one have to drink to be drunk? She'd only had two glasses.

"But if I tell you, you have to promise me that we won't talk about it afterward. Not a word. I just want to be able to say it and then never talk about it again."

Ofir nodded. "Okay. I promise."

She had never repeated what Sister Marie Amable had told her, not to Dr. Gadeau, not to another girl in the orphanage, not to another nun, not to Louise, and not to herself, though she might as well have been repeating it every second of her life. The secret had followed her, silent, unthinkable, obscured, but no less incriminating. She had walked through rooms and years believing she was a hideous creature whose very existence offended God. Say it, she thought. Say it. Could she really say it?

"My father was also my grandfather."

Ofir blinked at her, confused. She watched as he worked out the riddle, saw his eyes widen when he understood. He stared at her, wordlessly. He didn't have the face of someone beholding a monster. He looked sad for her, concerned.

She let out a small groan. She remembered the man from the article saying they had treated them as if they were the sinners. It seemed so obvious to her now that her young mother had been raped, that she hadn't been "weak in the face of vice." Even if she had willingly submitted to her father, if that were possible, it had nothing to do with Claudette.

Ofir looked to the lake. "The water's been baking in the sun all day. It'll feel great. Are you going in?"

"Yes!" Claudette jumped to her feet, grateful he had kept his promise. "Let's go!"

He shook his head, pointed at his ears. "I still can't go swimming. They get infected too easily. I can't even shower without wearing these giant rubber earplugs."

"But you told me to bring a swimsuit."

"I want to watch you go in. It's as close as I can get to going in myself."

"But I don't know how to swim."

"It's safe. There's no undercurrent. Just don't go deeper than your head."

A wooden boat floated in the darkness, its cabin light reflected on the still water. She pulled her sundress off over her head. The warm, windless night touched skin that had never before been uncovered out of doors. She tossed the sundress onto the sheet beside Ofir, too tipsy, too elated, to feel awkward in Ulya's bikini.

Ofir watched her lope toward the lake. He felt bad to think it, but did inbreeding cause mental damage? Was that why she was so strange? She looked fine. Lovely, actually. A second red bow tied in the middle of her back. Two plump white crescents peeking out of the red bikini bottom.

Claudette stood at the water's edge. She had never bathed in a lake. Or ocean or pool. She hadn't taken a bath since infancy. Only showers, which couldn't be too long, especially in the winter when the water quickly ran ice-cold. She dipped her toe. Warm. She waded in until the water reached her shins, and then looked back at Ofir. He waved, and she walked in deeper. The warm water soothed her calves, her thighs, the curve of her back. Her body loosened, like a fist opening up to reveal something hidden in its palm. She walked until her breasts and shoulders were immersed, everything but her head. She jumped. The weightlessness made her laugh. She jumped again and looked to see if Ofir was watching her. He was. He waved once more.

She dipped her head under the water and emerged again in the world. She looked around at the dark hills, the fishing boat, its cabin light off now, the ruins of the ancient synagogue, and Ofir on the shore with his glowing cigarette tip. The glowing orange dot reminded her of the "You Are Here" on the map inside the Sauvé metro station, down the street from her sister's apartment, where she would catch the subway to work at the orphanage. Yes, Ofir's cigarette tip looked like a small insistent orange spark, a tiny "You Are Here" on the black map of existence.

I am here, she thought. She had never felt so *here* before, so existent, like she wasn't only floating in the dark warm lake, but floating in a moment of time—a moment that in a few heartbeats would be gone, never to be had again.

She didn't want that. To think she had almost killed herself. She had never feared time or death before, but now, feeling so here, so alive—as if she couldn't have one without the other—she also felt with a terrible keenness how one day she wouldn't be here, wouldn't be with Ofir.

She hurried for the shore, splashing through the water. Ofir jumped to his feet. She ran out of the water and up the sand, teeth chattering. Did everybody live with this feeling, this knowing that one day they were going to die and not wanting to? How did they do it? She grabbed the towel Ofir held out to her.

"You look like you've seen a ghost."

"No, no, it was wonderful. Too wonderful."

Ofir sat back down on the sheet and Claudette rubbed the glistening water from her chest and arms. She didn't know what to do with this sense of urgency. Even if the Hereafter wasn't another lie, the Hereafter wasn't Here.

She caught Ofir studying her thighs as she toweled off. She stopped, held the towel in front of her. She wasn't drunk anymore. It was a different light-headedness. She sat down on the white sheet, closer to him than before. Ofir met her gaze with a quizzical look. She saw her reflection in the teardrop pupil. You are here, she thought, as her eyes dropped to the scar on his chin. She reached out and ran her fingertips along his jaw until they reached the scar and then she lingered there.

Ofir leaned toward her, scared. He brought his lips close to hers and paused to make sure she wasn't going to scream, push him away. He felt her breath on his face. Heart pounding, he gently pressed his mouth against hers.

Claudette fell back onto the sheet, the rough sand beneath it cradling her body as Ofir climbed on top of her. He was heavy. She felt pinned to the earth. She tasted the wine on his lips, the tobacco on his tongue, and in her own mouth the algal from the lake Jesus had walked on when He was Here.

By the time they were driving through the kibbutz's back gate, the sky had yellowed over the avocado orchard. Ofir was thankful Claudette's birthday fell on Shabbat, when everybody was still in bed at this early hour, not headed out to the fields or factory. He pulled up to the volunteers' section, and Claudette climbed out of the car. She knew Ofir didn't want to idle there, but she still hadn't managed to ask the question she'd wanted to the whole ride home. Leaning on the open door, she lowered her head back into the car. "Did we have sex?"

Ofir regarded her with disbelief.

"I think we did," she said. "But I'm not sure."

The Christina the Astonishing pendant hung below her sheepish face, a faint lipstick smear around her mouth. Ofir felt odd being the authority given he'd only had sex with two other girls, both at music camp, and those times had felt nothing like tonight. Throughout those other brief, awkward encounters, he thought about later when he could enjoy knowing he'd had this experience, as if the whole point of having sex was for the knowledge later that you'd had it. Tonight with Claudette he forgot about later.

"Yes, we did. I hope that's okay."

She nodded that it was.

"Good. Because I liked it a lot."

"Me too."

She closed the car door and walked back toward her room. This was the most fragrant hour on the kibbutz, when the daylilies opened while the scent of the nocturnal flowers still lingered in the air. From the treetops came the first chirps of the dawn chorus.

She unlocked the door to her room and found Ulya, who hadn't gone out these last few nights, asleep, her red hair fanned over the white pillow. All those times she had been in bed when Ulya came home, she never could have imagined it being the other way around. She felt tenderness for this room—the tube of lipstick on her dresser, the creaky oscillating fan, Ulya's magazines on the floor.

She crouched by the bed and pulled out her brother-in-law's backpack. She unzipped it without worrying about waking Ulya. She knew now that nothing could wake her roommate, that a person didn't have to have a clean conscience to sleep well. She removed the sock filled with Ziva's medication and took it to the bathroom.

Standing over the toilet, she shook out the pills, tablets, and gelcaps. Soon the white bowl resembled Sister Marie Angélique's dish of licorice allsorts. She turned the sock inside out to make sure she hadn't missed any and flushed.

Next she fetched the bottle of Prozac. This was harder to do. When she told Dr. Gadeau that her half sister had convinced her to try living outside of the convent, he had warned her that no matter what, while she was gone, she mustn't stop taking her medication. Sitting in his office overlooking the inner courtyard, mustache covering his upper lip, he said people often stopped their medication when they felt better as if it weren't the medication making them feel better. Claudette felt certain this happiness wasn't Prozac. She pressed the flush button and watched the green pills whirl away.

Ulya placed another cheesecloth into the yellow bowl, scooped yogurt out of a big bucket, and poured it onto the cloth. She then gathered the edges and tied them with a string. After setting the pouch next to the fifty other pouches on the colander tray, she placed another cheesecloth in the yellow bowl.

It had been two weeks since she stopped seeing Farid, and it bothered her how much she still missed him. She was sure it had more to do with the boredom of this place than Farid himself. The main thing that got her through the endless hours at the dairy house was the anticipation of seeing him later that night. Now the sweltering nights were as tedious as her days. But he'd left her no choice. When he leaned in to kiss her after failing to stand up to Adam, her whole being recoiled. She walked off, not even bothering with her usual "I never want to see you again." She didn't bolt through the orchard, though; she stomped off slowly enough for him to run after her, grab her by the arm, whip her around, beg her not to go, to do something—anything—to prove he had a little oomph. He didn't. The lazy coward. She was sure he had waited for her the next night, thinking it was another false alarm. And the night after that. How many nights had he gone to their spot before he realized she wasn't coming back? At least she derived some pleasure from picturing him standing by the barbed wire, waiting for her in vain.

She carried the tray of yogurt pouches to the walk-in fridge, where one of the girls came up to her and asked if she had a spare tampon.

"No," said Ulya, sliding the tray into a rack.

"Argh. I'll have to ask Irit."

While the girl approached their boss, a wiry woman in her forties, Ulya carried a new tray back to her table, thinking it did seem like a long time since her last period. She sat on her stool and tried to work it out. Had she needed to throw a tampon into the bathroom bin since Claudette had moved in? She didn't think so. How long had Claudette been here? She arrived near the end of April. Almost four months ago. Was that possible?

Placing a cheesecloth in the bowl, Ulya remembered how she didn't wear her cropped pink T-shirt yesterday because her stomach wasn't so flat anymore. She had chalked it up to eating more at dinner now that she wasn't seeing Farid afterward, but wouldn't her belly be much bigger if she were four months pregnant? She had no idea. She knew nothing about pregnancy. She wasn't even sure how regular her periods were. When she felt a cramp, she prepared to bleed in a couple of hours. She'd never paid attention to dates. Didn't need to. She could still see the mint-green clinic where she had sat on an examination table, stringy blonde hair hanging over her hospital gown, while the doctor told her and her mother that her eggs were cooked. Those were his words: *eggs were cooked*. She would never have a baby.

"See you tomorrow, *chamudot*," said Irit, standing up from her table. It was the same every day: as soon as she was out the door, the other three women gathered their things and left. This time, Ulya waited until they were all gone before rising from her stool and grabbing the canvas tote bag that had been hanging in the back of the dairy house for as long as she worked there. She preferred not to depend on a bag when stealing—her theory being store owners felt more comfortable looking in your bag than on your person—but a pregnancy test might be too bulky to slip in her pants or under her shirt.

When Ulya entered the *kolbo*, she was disappointed to find the cashier with the shabby blonde hair on duty. This one seemed to be onto her. Not only did she keep the eyes in her pudgy, middle-aged face glued on her, but the other day, when Ulya plunked a pack of gum down on the counter, the cashier said: "You always look around the whole *kolbo* and then buy a pack of gum." And she was exactly right. Ulya always bought a small something before leaving, figuring it would look suspicious if she came in here every other day and never bought anything.

Ulya gave the cashier a cursory smile, which the cashier did not return, then made her way down the center aisle. Unfortunately the feminine hygiene products were on the far wall, putting her back to the cashier. She wouldn't be able to watch her for the best time to make the swipe.

She scanned the boxes of tampons and panty liners until she came across Dr. Fischer's Pregnancy Test with the picture of a laughing baby. Twice as big as a box of tampons, it was good she had brought the bag. But how was she going to nab it? Maybe she would have to buy the damn thing. Without taking the box off the shelf, she searched for its sticker and found it on the side. A hundred and twenty-eight shekels! More than a month's stipend. She supposed she could get a test for free at the medical center. But then what if by some crazy miracle she were pregnant? The whole kibbutz would know.

She wandered away from the women's products, pretending to be interested in a barrette, a bottle of aspirin, until she reached the farthest aisle, where she had a clear view of the counter. She was feigning to read the back of a shampoo bottle, considering her next move, when the door chimed. A man approached the counter with a loud, friendly voice. "Shalom, shalom!"

The man struck up a conversation with the cashier, asking if her son were planning to play basketball this fall because his son was and wouldn't it make sense if they took turns driving them into town. Ulya drifted back toward the pregnancy test. The cashier kept glancing in her direction, so she paused to inspect the hats hanging on the wall. She pulled on a wide-brimmed straw hat and stood in front of the mirror. Oh! Why hadn't she thought of this before? She could see the cashier in the mirror. The man requested a pack of Marlboros, and Ulya, knowing the cigarettes were stored behind the counter, braced. As soon as the cashier bent down to get them, she glided to the pregnancy test and swatted it into her bag.

Ulya felt a swell of pride. Quick and graceful as an athlete. They had talked of basketball; well, she had just executed the perfect dunk. Only this sport had no audience, the pleasure and fear belonging only to her. She had never told anyone about a single stolen trinket. Most experiences lost their power with repetition, but not this. Every time was as scary and satisfying as the last. She loved the things she stole in a way she never loved anything she had bought or been given. When later she would pull the objects from her sleeve, they had the magic of something smuggled, something she shouldn't have. Like that first magazine.

The man left with his cigarettes, door chiming behind him, while Ulya strode up to the counter and surveyed it for something small to buy. Feeling daring, feeling like it would be a nice little fuck you, she placed a box of Chiclets in front of the cashier.

The cashier looked down at the gum. "All that browsing, and you're buying another pack of gum."

Please don't check the bag, please don't check the bag.

"I browse here because there is no Macy's on the kibbutz."

The cashier spoke through clenched teeth: "One shekel."

The elation dissipated as soon as Ulya was outside the store. A pregnancy test was hardly a fun nab. She walked toward the volunteers' section, trying again to pin down the last time she'd had her period. She could picture shaking her head at Farid and telling him he couldn't go down because of it. He loved burying his face there. With other men, she'd never been sure, but Farid left no doubt, by the unhurried way he did it, responding to her every twitch and moan, and because he would crawl on top of her afterward as hard as could be. But the last time she could remember shaking her head at him she'd been wearing a sweater and the mandarins were still green.

Coming down the steppingstones, she saw Adam slumped at the picnic table with that ridiculous dog seated beside him. She didn't have the patience for him right now. Ever since he barged in on her and Farid, he'd been trying to apologize, but she refused to acknowledge him, not even to say, "Go away." She hadn't failed to notice, however, that he was falling apart. Every evening he carried a six-pack of beer into his room and didn't come out again. Any doubts she'd had about not pursuing him for a green card were gone. Even if she could have faked love or convinced him to marry her for money, it would have been too risky. How could she depend on him for two or three years? He would have gotten drunk and not shown up for the most important interview; or worse, he would have shown up tanked and said something stupid, and next thing she would have been in jail awaiting deportation to Mazyr. She had heard from a Russian who worked in the kitchen that the man in charge of dishwashing had lost his temper when Adam didn't show up for work again yesterday. It wouldn't be long before he was booted off the kibbutz.

"Ulie, please, please." He blocked her from walking toward her room. His eyes were puffy, his hair greasy. "Just give me a chance to say a few words. What I did was totally asshole-ish, I get it . . ."

She couldn't bear to fight her way around him. She only wanted to get to her room. She didn't care anymore. Faced with pregnancy, Adam's lovesick prank wasn't a big deal. If anything, it seemed kind of sweet now, like it belonged to an easier time when she was young and boys fought over her.

"Fine, I forgive you."

"Really?"

He blew through his lips, breath reeking of booze.

"Yes, yes, I forgive you, but only if you get out of my way now."

"Okay, okay." He stepped to the side. "It's a start."

Ulya hurried to unlock her door. Thankfully, Claudette wasn't home. That weirdo used to always be home, and now who knew what creepiness she was up to. Finding the room too quiet, she switched on the transistor radio. A crackly dance hit came through the speaker, but the happy party song only made the small sweltering kibbutz dorm seem that much farther away from the discotheques in Manhattan, or even from the one she used to go to in Mazyr. She was both eager to do the test and hesitant, terrified that it would be positive. But it wouldn't be. Couldn't be. And the sooner she did it, the sooner she could relax.

She locked herself in the bathroom, tested the door, and ripped open the box with its picture of that dumb baby. Imagine if Farid could see her now. She rifled through the instructions, looking for the Russian.

It was simple enough: a blue plus sign or minus sign. She pushed down her pants and sat on the toilet, recalling how she used to sit on the toilet back home with the door locked flipping through the stolen magazine. Eight years, one magazine. Right now, if she wanted to, she could mentally flip through every glamorous page by heart. She dipped her hand between her thighs and held the strip of paper under the path of her urine. Warm piss splashed onto her hand. How was that for glamour?

She placed the tester on the edge of the sink and steeled herself for a long five minutes. Through the door came the beep that preceded the news. It was so annoying how often people listened to the news here. Every fifteen minutes, that ominous *beeeeeep*, and the music would die, and everyone in the dairy house or on the bus or wherever would fall silent, listening, hoping for no real news. No news was good news. A blue minus sign would be no news.

After twelve years of running the PLO from Tunis, Arafat's first month back in Gaza as head of the new Palestinian self-rule authority has already left some Israelis doubtful that he will prepare the Palestinian people for peace. Yesterday he drew cheers from a crowd with a speech that boasted, "With our spirit and blood we shall redeem you, Palestine. The battle is on the land!" Prime Minister Rabin, however, remains hopeful . . .

Ulya cringed when Arabs spoke in that theatrical way of theirs, as if they were prophets in the Bible. *With our spirit and our blood.* When Farid complimented her, he often evoked the moon and honey and eternity, and it was cute in a way, but it also made her want to scream at him, oh please, wake up and join the modern world. And then a terrifying question came to her: Could a woman even get an abortion in this country?

If she couldn't get one in Israel, no country on this medieval continent would give her one. Syria? Egypt? What would she do? She didn't have the money to fly to Europe. And even if she did, what European country would give her a tourist visa? They were too afraid she would stay, which infuriated her, even though, of course, she would.

She reached for the tester.

It was a little exciting, the idea she could have a baby—someday with a rich, handsome man who could put an end to this nonstop struggling—but not now, not now, not now.

A plus sign.

She stared at the tester a moment before throwing it at the cement floor. She wrapped her arms around herself and doubled over.

In school they had been taught that at six weeks it had a heart. The fucking thing had a beating heart. Her mother had warned her there was no such thing as a better life somewhere else. Sitting at the kitchen table, drinking what amounted to hot water, the tea bag having been used so many times, she said, *Ulya, if you were meant to be happy, you'll be happy. If you were meant to be sad, you'll be sad. The place doesn't matter.* Ulya still believed that was bullshit, still believed if a person wanted a better life, they had to go out and get it, but that said, could she be any further from the better life she had imagined?

She was a fake Jew with an Arab growing inside her.

Holy Roman Empire, 1347

homas threw open the door, sending a rimy gust through the room. "Did you see the yellow butterflies? Scores of them, flying out of the Jewish quarter!"

Margaretha continued stuffing sausages, ignoring the brewer. She hated when he dropped by. He never knocked and always brought a bottle of ale, which meant the night would end with her husband, Peter, missing the chamber pot. Peter, seated at the dinner table, crumpled his brows as if he needed to think about whether he saw a swarm of yellow butterflies in the dead of January.

"Margaretha, did you see anything strange when you were with them today? Claudia, the Beckenbauer girl, saw the butterflies. And so did my sister-in-law, Nichola."

The tall brewer filled their entryway, snow whipping around his legs and in the darkness behind him. At least he didn't have a bottle. Margaretha wiped her hands on her apron. "Please, Thomas, come inside before we all catch winter fever."

Thomas stomped the snow off his boots and closed the door. Removing his felt hat, he took a seat near the fire. "A butterfly landed on Nichola's little boy, and his coughing stopped. Just like that. There are miracles happening all over town."

"I noticed nothing unusual with the Jews today," said Margaretha, laying out a casing. She didn't like the sound of yellow butterflies; it was an alarming flourish.

Peter poured Thomas a glass of cider. "Every day I ask her to stop working for those Christ killers. For over twenty years, she has swept and cooked and scrubbed for that Jew, one of the richest in the *Judengasse*, and look at us, we eat sausages stuffed with grain."

Margaretha raised her eyebrows. Yes, it would be nice if the Jew paid her more, but it would also help if her husband spent fewer nights throwing dice at the White Swan. Once in a while, like now, she felt a touch of relief that God hadn't granted them children; but then, on the heels of that relief, as always, came the sad idea that if they'd had a brood, Peter might have been less interested in ale and dice.

Thomas downed the cider. "The prince has no honor. He'd rather collect taxes than let us get rid of them. He's gilded his carriage with their blood money."

Pouring another glass, Peter said, "I think he'd be glad to see them go. He owes them so much money. Margaretha's Jew has one of the prince's belt buckles as collateral. Doesn't he, Margaretha?"

Thomas banged down his hand, sending a cork rolling off the table. "I'm sick of it! It's time we drove them out of Terfur! Out of the Rhineland! Margaretha, are you sure you didn't see anything suspicious today?"

Hunching over to retrieve the cork, Margaretha wished they would stick to the standard bellyache about the Jews and drop the worrisome butterfly business. She was too tired for this. Her neck was stiff in the mornings, her shoulders sore. She was getting old, her honey-brown hair fading fast. The days bore nothing sweet. "I told you, no."

Another cold wind blew through the house when the door swung open without warning. The cooper and his two sons entered bearing axes and saws.

"Everyone's heading to the Jewish quarter! They're torturing the host!"

"Ha!" Thomas jumped to his feet. "There you have it! I told you something was awry."

Margaretha gaped at the sharpened blades. She had been right to worry about the butterflies. "But how did they get one?"

The cooper shook the snow off his bushy, red beard. "Who knows? Maybe they bribed a Christian who owed them money. Maybe one of them pretended to be Christian and smuggled it off in his vile Jew mouth."

"What do we know then? How can we be sure they're torturing a host?"

Peter shot her a silencing look while the younger of the cooper's sons stammered with excitement. "Fräulein Claudia saw a ray of light shoot out of the Jew Lippmann's house into the sky. She peeked in the window and at first it was too dark to see anything, but then all the candles in the house kindled at the same time, by themselves, and there was Lippmann and two others standing around a table with a Eucharist. One of them said something like, *Let's see if what they say about you is true*, and then came down on it with a hammer. But the Eucharist didn't break. Another stabbed at it with a knife. And still it didn't break. Only bled. The table flooded with blood."

The other brother, visibly annoyed at his younger sibling for hogging the story, interjected, "The Jews panicked. But instead of being convinced, they tried to get rid of the host. One of them threw it at a pot of boiling water, but the host floated above the pot."

A rabble and their horses could be heard gathering outside, beyond the wooden shutters. Margaretha's heart pounded so hard her chest hurt. Well, what did God expect? How could she not care for that family at least a little? She had worked for Meister Goldsmid since she was a young girl, and though it was degrading to call a Jew a master, aside from a general irascibility, he had been good to her. Once he called her "an ignoramus" in his thick French accent, but what were a few ugly scenes in twenty-four years? She was in the house when most of his children were born, and some of the grandchildren. Just last week, she helped deliver baby Jonah, her mistress Anna's late bloom, she being a frail forty-four, a whole three years older than sturdy Margaretha's forty-one. At one week old, the baby already looked like Meister Goldsmid. Same eyes.

Unable to keep the shaking out of her voice, Margaretha said, "Why go after the lot of them? Why not just kill the Jew Lippmann and the other two?"

The cooper switched his axe onto the opposite shoulder. "They all have to go. While Claudia was running away from the first house, bright lights shot out of all their houses. They must have divided the host. Probably charged each other a pretty sum."

"Lights? I thought it was yellow butterflies."

"Lights, butterflies! What difference does it make?" Thomas pulled his hat back on. "They're torturing a host! They're a pestilence! We must be rid of them!"

"Hurrah!" cheered the younger son. "Before the cock crows, not one will be left alive!"

They marched out of the house chanting *They will pay!* while Peter hastened to don his coat. When Margaretha rushed for hers, he grasped her arm. "Leave it alone. It's dangerous."

Margaretha realized he knew she was going to warn Meister Goldsmid before she did.

She shook her hand free. "I have to get there before you."

At this hour in winter, the street was normally dark and quiet with everyone tucked behind their wooden doors and shutters, nestled around their hearths, but tonight the street glowed with torches. Men mounted their steeds or marched off with hatchets to the cheers of their women and children. Margaretha darted down the cobblestones, skirting carts and crowds, taking a route she had traveled thousands of times. Was this mad dash the last? In nearby Düsseldorf, the massacre following the desecration of a host had been thorough. While the Jews were still alive, they ripped off their flesh with iron pincers and fried it on pans like rashers of bacon. Margaretha hiked up her heavy skirt and ran faster.

When the *Judengasse* came into view, the thick wooden doors that usually locked the Jews in from sunset to sunrise were wide-open, revealing darkened alleyways flecked with fire. It looked like a giant stone oven. Margaretha didn't give up hope though. There was a chance that the violence hadn't reached her Jew's house at the far end of the ghetto. If she got there in time, she knew he would be ready to flee, that he had always been ready. One summer afternoon when the jewels in his workshop gleamed with sunlight, he told her that he loved gemstones, not only for their beauty, but because they were small enough to conceal on one's person and had value in any country. At the time she took this for avarice, but now she understood. Meister Goldsmid had been evicted with all the Jews from France, and his father before him had been forced out of England; she had seen the papers in his desk with the name Gold*smith*, not *smid*. Oh well, he would have to fly again. And then she had the uncomfortable thought that whatever the family left behind should go to her, she who had spent her days in that home, not some random pillagers.

When Margaretha passed through the low, arched gate, she found the massacre had started. Fire raged out of the windows and doors of the mossy stone rowhouses, and the streets, the narrowest in the town, were thick with smoke and the stench of burning flesh and hair. In Düsseldorf some Jews supposedly set fire to their own homes, preferring to perish in their own flames than risk being disemboweled. A Jewess, chased by two men with axes, ran past Margaretha, screaming, "I did nothing! I did nothing!" while another Jew came in the other direction, crying, "I want to convert!" When his pursuers caught up to him, mere yards in front of Margaretha, the Jew backed against a wall: "I saw the miracle! I believe in Jesus Christ now!" It was like watching pigs running from the slaughterer. Margaretha realized that even if she got to the family in time, the walls of this pen were too high to scale. And yet, she pressed on.

She removed her hood so she wouldn't look like a fleeing Jew. She wasn't much afraid for her own life—she was too fair-haired, ruddy, and tall to be mistaken for a Jewess, and she would only have to rattle off the Supplication to Mary to dispel any doubt—but just in case, she steered clear of the marauders, turning onto quieter side streets even if they took her slightly out of the way. If anyone looked in her direction, she planned to raise a fist and cry, "Death to the Jews!"

At last she arrived at the untouched part of the ghetto. It was good she knew these laneways as well as the cracks in her bedroom ceiling, otherwise she never would have been able to find her way in such darkness. The moonlight didn't reach these cramped and crooked alleys, and not a candle flickered. Fear and dread resounded in the unnatural quiet. She could feel the Jews listening behind the walls, holding their breath, hoping her footfalls would pass them by.

She knocked on her Jew's door. Nothing. She listened for movement and heard only the scared stillness. She banged again and then understood she must be terrifying them. She took a quick glance around before calling, "Meister Goldsmid! It's me, Margaretha!"

The door cracked open, and a round black eye peered at her from the shadows. Meister Goldsmid grabbed her by the hand—it was something he had never done before, touch her. He led her through the unlit front shop and into the back workroom. As he bolted the door between the two chambers, Margaretha's eyes adjusted, and half-finished candelabras and pendants shone in the gloom.

The goldsmith's face glistened with sweat. "Anna and the children, God protect them, are hiding in the cellar."

"I came to warn you, but I'm too late."

He wore the yellow circle badge on his black cloak and on his head the pointed yellow *Judenhut*, with the brim twisted to look like horns. She had rarely seen him in the marks of shame; he'd always whipped them off as soon as he entered the house. Why had he donned them now? To appease the mob? It was a mistake. He looked so Jewish in that hat. He looked like someone who'd desecrate a host. They were going to descend on him with zeal.

"First they accuse us of torturing Christian children, using their blood in our rituals. And now, now they are killing us because of a . . . a cracker."

Margaretha shook her head. "It's not a cracker. It's the body of Christ."

The Jew raised his eyes to the wood ceiling. "Dear God, how much longer until You gather us back in the Promised Land?"

"Give me Jonah." Margaretha was shocked by the offer—plea—that came out of her mouth. Had that been her plan all along?

"No." The goldsmith shook his head but Margaretha saw the cogs turning behind his eyes.

"Meister Goldsmid, the synagogue's burning. Everything's burning. People are . . . I'm sorry, but you're all going to die." She heard how odd she sounded, as if she were saying she was sorry but the bakery was out of bread. "But I can save Jonah."

"And have him baptized? Have him become one of the people who killed his family? Better he were burned at the stake."

A cannonade of galloping hooves. Screams. The marauders had reached the far ends of the ghetto. Margaretha had to think quickly: Could she bring up a boy in her house who wasn't Christian? There was a pounding at the front door.

"Fine! I won't baptize him!" It sickened her to make such a promise, even though she had no intention of keeping it.

"And you will tell him when he's old enough who he is?"

"Yes!"

With the thud of axes chopping at the door, the Jew fumbled into the leather pouch hanging off his belt and pulled out the brooch, which Margaretha had watched him craft over the last year to give to Anna on their twenty-fifth anniversary. Nothing could distract the goldsmith when he worked with his gold, squinting and breathing heavily as he twisted threads of what he called the "noble metal" into elaborate filigrees, but never more so than when it came to this brooch. Every gulden he could spare had been put into it, and even in the shadows its sapphire, rubies, and garnets smoldered with color. If not for the fleuron missing a petal, the brooch would have been faultless. The missing petal was Meister Gold-smid's signature; he made a "mistake" in all his jewels so he never risked thinking in vainglory that he had made something perfect. Now Anna would never see her brooch, never even know of it.

"Give this to Jonah when you tell him he's a Jew. Tell him he can sell it if he needs the money."

Margaretha grabbed the brooch and stuffed it in her pouch.

"Jews! Jews! Where are you hiding the host?" The clamor was in the front shop. "Ah, behold! Another jeweler's house!"

Without saying goodbye, Margaretha hurtled for the kitchen, where she had spent much of her life. With shaking hands she grabbed the iron ring and heaved open the heavy trap door. As she scrambled down the narrow stone steps, she heard Meister Goldsmid begging, "Take, take what you want! All the gold and jewels! My family has fled."

Margaretha would never be able to clearly recall what happened in the cellar. The family's eyes must have gaped at her in the gloom, but she could never quite picture it. Could she really have said nothing, nothing at all, as she took Jonah from Anna's arms? Could Anna have handed over her baby without a word? One of the boys prayed in their exotic tongue. Could she have taken this boy too? Could she have grabbed one or two of the grandchildren by the hand and led them up the stairs and out into the night and back to the safety of her house? It would have been too hard to explain to the neighbors. One could pray for and be granted the miracle of a newborn, not a twelve-year-old.

Margaretha hastened out the back door and into the night, cradling Jonah beneath her cloak. If she were stopped, she could probably get away without revealing what was under her robe, but she didn't want to chance it, so she weaved her way back taking streets that had already been ravaged. Running as fast as she could, she dodged the bodies splayed on the cob-blestones and the flames leaping out the windows. A dismembered man dangled from an eave. She passed a wall smeared with human entrails, grateful her baby was shaded from these sights. She peeked at him only once, and he looked happy nestled in her arms. And why not? He knew her arms as well as anybody's.

She ran through the gate out of the *Judengasse* and into the quietude on the other side. As she stumbled back toward her house, gasping for breath, she wondered if there was any chance that in fifteen years she would give her son the brooch and tell him that he was a Jew. She didn't think so, but she couldn't be sure. When the peddlers brought the stories of torture and death from Düsseldorf, Margaretha had asked herself what she would have done had it happened in Terfur instead. She had decided she would have done nothing. What reason had she to believe that a woman like her, too meek to ask her husband to stop gambling away her hard-earned guldens, would behave any differently than the thousands who either butchered the Jews or silently watched the blood seep into the snow? But she had surprised herself. In fifteen years, she could surprise herself again.

Part Three

Part Three

*Y*ossi held a dinner plate covered in hardened yolk before Adam's face.

"Look at this! This is the third time I'm telling you: you have to do a better job scraping off the food! You're giving us twice as much work to do, Adam."

"Okay." Adam steadied himself on the edge of the conveyer belt.

Yossi set the plate down in front of him. "Don't make me tell you a fourth time."

Adam waited until Yossi rounded the dishwasher before bending down to take a swig from the water bottle hidden beneath the conveyer. He was only breaking his rule about drinking before dusk this one time. Until now he had always come to the dishroom sober, hungover but sober. But when he woke up this morning he knew he wasn't going to get to work without some help. He could barely sit up after a night of the most brutal, vivid nightmares. He would have called in sick, but Eyal told him if he missed one more day, he would get kicked off the kibbutz. He just needed this one bottle of vodka to get through this one shift.

He snatched the incriminating plate just before it disappeared into the washer and scrubbed at the yolk with a disgusting clump of steel wool, its grooves packed with soggy old food. Egg, more than any other leftover, triggered his gag reflexes. Swallowing his nausea, he returned the plate to the belt. What time was it? It felt like eight hours already, though it had to be more like three. He pushed down his rubber glove to peek at his wristwatch. 8:12 a.m. How was that possible? He'd barely been here an hour. He crouched down and took another swill.

If only he could come up with another way to find Dagmar. As soon as he did, he could stop drinking. Every morning, he went to work thinking today was the day he was going to figure out his next move and sober up. He would spend all morning scrubbing plates and racking his brain, and then in the late afternoon, when he still hadn't come up with a plan, he would start counting down the minutes until he could ditch work and buy a six-pack at the *kolbo*.

Yossi came around the dishwasher, looking more weary than angry. "Adam, I think this is the same plate. The same yolk on the same plate."

"What?"

"You have to scrub hard." Yossi grabbed the steel wool out of Adam's hand and demonstrated. "Scrub, scrub." Adam watched, annoyed and impatient, and fully aware he had no right to be.

"All right." He took back the clean plate. "Got it."

"What happened, Adam? You were so good. And now you don't show up half the time, and when you do, you're a mess. I'm begging you, please, please, get your act together. I can't come over here again today."

After Yossi walked away, Adam imitated him under his breath, "Scrub, scrub." Why did they have to scrub each plate clean before it went into the dishwasher? What the hell was the dishwasher for then? Adam took one last galvanizing gulp, the last one, he vowed, until quitting time. When he stood up, the room seesawed. He leaned on the conveyer belt again. When the dizziness passed, he picked up a bowl and wiped off milky porridge.

The dream hadn't started out so bad. It was nice to be back in the apartment again, surrounded by the old records and the pigeons cooing on the air conditioner. It all felt so real, realer than the kibbutz with its cabbage-patch fields and lollipop lamps. And then there came the knock on the door.

"How about Moishe's for brunch?"

Zayde stood in the fluorescent-lit hallway.

"I thought you were dead."

The old man brushed past him and into the apartment. "Just give me a minute to freshen up."

It was powerful to see his grandfather move again. His conscious memory was quickly reducing him to a few static images, but in his sleep he heard him, smelled him, saw him walk with that old-man grace of his, at once doddering and dandy. That's why it was hard to say if he was having a pleasant dream or a nightmare. Did it matter that he had been rotting in a coffin for five months? Adam followed him, looking for signs of decomposition. Leaning in the bathroom doorway, like he did when he was a boy, he watched the old man comb his thick, gray hair and splash aftershave on his neck. He looked a little pale, but nothing ten minutes of sunshine wouldn't cure.

Together they stepped onto Essex Street, Zayde in a straw Panama hat, Adam a backwards Yankees cap. It was one of the first warm Sundays of the year, the air ripe with the scent of thawed garbage. Young women, legs and shoulders bared for the first time in months, licked low-cal ice cream in front of Tasti D-Lite, and under the yellow awning of a dingier bodega, the one that sold Adam beer before noon on Sundays, Mexican men in church suits stood smoking and squinting into the sunlight.

Moishe's didn't have an electric sign, only a blue wooden shingle. Taped to the storefront window, beside a faded *cholov yisroel* certificate, was a yellowing *New York Post* article, "Best Bagels in Town," with a picture of Moishe at the counter back when his hair was still brown. Adam had avoided their old haunt since Zayde's death, and it felt great to be back.

"Hey, look who's here!" Moishe called as they pushed through the door. "Franz is back! How often do you go to a man's funeral and then he comes into your deli? How you doing, Franz?"

"*Gut, gut.* Can't complain."

Moishe followed them behind the counter. "I tell you, if anyone can rise from the dead, it's Franz."

Franz scanned the cream cheeses and salads behind the glass. "It's not the first time. I've done it before."

"I know you did," said Moishe. "You all did."

Without fail, Zayde mulled over the different salads as if he weren't going to order the same thing he always did: schnitzel with kasha varnishkes. Luckily, they didn't have to wait for a table. Laying his tray on the plastic red-and-white checkered tablecloth, Adam relished how good it

felt to be a regular guy out on a Sunday afternoon. All around them regular people enjoyed their Sunday: older couples, young families, teenagers
slurping sodas. Zayde arranged his blue Anthora coffee cup and paper
plate and napkin just so before proceeding to eat his kasha with his plastic
cutlery as if he were dining with fine silverware at a five-star restaurant.
Adam chomped on his bagel.

"You have cream cheese on your face."

Adam wiped his mouth on the back of his hand.

Zayde pointed. "The other side."

Adam tried again.

Zayde laughed and waved at him to forget it.

Adam unwrapped his black-and-white cookie. Now that they were
halfway through their meals, surely his grandfather was going to bring up
the brooch.

Instead the old man said, "Did I tell you the one about the old Jewish
woman on the train who was thirsty?'"

Adam had heard all the old man's jokes hundreds of times, and yet he
never tired of them. Not because the jokes were so great, but because of
the joy they brought the old man, his black eyes shining with amusement.
Even before Zayde died, Adam would feel preemptive grief when the old
man told his jokes.

"Of course," Adam said. "But tell me again."

It was as if the theft and betrayal had never happened. And hey, if a
man could come back from the dead, anything was possible. Maybe the
brooch was still safe in the shoebox, and everything was back to normal,
except for one thing: Adam was more appreciative, and he was going to
do everything he could to make Zayde's last years happy. He was going to
make sure the old man didn't survive everything he had survived just to die
with nothing but an empty shoebox and a thieving grandson.

"That brooch . . ." Adam couldn't wait until they got home to check
if it was in the shoebox. If he was getting a second chance, he wanted to
start now.

"Yes? What about it?"

Apparently Zayde hadn't found it missing. He had never stolen it. The
relief was overwhelming.

"Can you tell me that story about it again, the one with the rubble?"

Zayde rose to his feet. "All right. Just as soon as I get back from the bathroom."

His grandfather shuffled gracefully toward the back of the restaurant and disappeared behind a door with a handwritten sign: TOILET ONLY FOR CUSTOMER'S!!!

Adam overheard the couple next to him, a chubby thirtyish man and a bespectacled woman, debating whether to check out the MoMA that afternoon, and Adam wondered what he and Zayde should do with their day. They could just go to the park, or do something really touristy like ride to the Top of the World.

How long had the old man been in there? Adam watched the bathroom door, leg jackhammering. He sucked the last of his Coke. He hoped the old man was okay. A woman with a red purse knocked on the door, waited a second, and went inside.

Adam jumped to his feet. Zayde had forgotten to lock the door. Why didn't the woman come flying out? The door remained closed. A minute later, the woman emerged with the red purse calmly slung on her shoulder.

"Wait!" Adam charged toward the bathroom before the next person in line could go inside. All the happy Sundayers watched him bolt past their tables. "Wait!"

He was too late. An obese guy listening to a Walkman slipped in. Adam waited outside the bathroom. Come on, come on. He tried the handle, though he knew the guy was still in there. What the hell was the fat fuck doing for so long? Diarrhea? Jacking off? He jostled the handle again. His grandfather had to be inside. It made no sense. He didn't remember the bathroom having two stalls, but maybe it did. But then why would it lock?

The guy opened the door. "Asshole."

Adam pushed past him. No stalls. Just a toilet. He scanned the tiny room as if his grandfather might be hiding behind the cloudy mirror or bin of overflowing paper towels. Where was he? He hurried back to their table, where the only things on it now were his cookie wrapper and Coca-Cola cup. No blue Anthora coffee cup, no kasha, no plastic cutlery that had been used like fancy silverware.

"Hey!" Adam interrupted the MoMA couple. "Did you see what had happened to that old man I was with? You know, the guy with the Panama hat?"

The husband gave his wife a headshake and ignored Adam.

"Hey, buddy! I'm talking to you!"

The guy, still looking at his wife, ran a napkin over his mouth, and Adam turned to the other diners to confirm the MoMA jerk was crazy for ignoring him. The whole deli stared back, Moishe with a crestfallen face. One of the teenagers cackled at Adam, and an older woman muttered, "Holy moly, could this city get any worse?"

Adam turned back to the jerk. "Answer me! Answer me before I smash your fucking face in! Did you see what happened to the old man I was with?"

The guy laid down his bagel. "Listen, pal, I hate to break it to you, but you've been sitting there laughing and talking and going on like somebody was with you, but nobody was. Nobody. The whole time, you've been talking to yourself."

Adam tried to understand: Did this mean he wasn't getting a second chance?

He felt the bowl get whisked from his hands.

"Enough. It would be easier without you."

It took a second for Adam to grasp where he was and what was happening. He reached for the bowl. "Sorry, I got distracted. I'll pay better attention."

Yossi held it out of reach. "No, Adam. You have to go."

"Come on, I just said I'd pay better attention, didn't I?"

"Your breath stinks. I can smell the alcohol from here."

"Please, Yossi. Eyal'll kick me off the kibbutz. And I don't have any money. I'll have to leave here without a penny. I swear I'll do a better job. I swear on my life."

Yossi shook his head.

Adam stared at him, waiting for him to change his mind. When Yossi merely stared back, Adam lunged at the bowl. He snatched it and furiously scoured, hoping Yossi might slink away, give him another chance. Instead Yossi tried to retake the bowl. He got a hold of its rim, but Adam refused to let go. Adam jerked the bowl left and right until he'd yanked it free, and then threw it. The bowl flew over the conveyer belt, across the dishroom, and shattered against the cinder-block wall.

"Fuck you!" Adam grabbed another plate and was about to hurl it too when Yossi seized his wrist. In seconds, Adam's arm was twisted behind his back, and his chest and cheek were pressed against the hot dishwasher. He struggled to free himself, but the smallest move brought sharp pain.

"Okay." Adam squeezed his eyes to keep back the tears. "Okay. Enough with the fucking Krav Maga. I'll go."

Yossi released him, then stood, arms hanging by his sides, looking very sorry about it all. "I liked you, Adam. I really did."

Adam grabbed his water bottle and stormed out of the dining hall. He walked toward the volunteers' section, finishing it off. When he got to his room, he flung the door open so hard it smacked the wall and sent Golda fleeing into a corner.

He marched over to his chest of drawers and tried to heave them over. They were heavier than he thought. Steadying the bottom with his foot, he tried again, pulling with all his might. At last, the chest toppled over, drawers falling out and hitting the ground first, his yellow Discman snapping upon impact, the Soul Asylum CD skidding across the floor.

He slumped down next to the dresser and rested his head on its dusty back. What had he done? All he had to do was wash some dishes and he could have stayed here as long as he liked, looking for Dagmar. But he couldn't manage it. Why? His grandfather managed to keep going; so what was his problem? What did he know about suffering? His alky mom died when he was a kid. Okay. He never got to meet his dad. All right. He had a hard time resisting booze and cocaine. On a scale from one to ten—where Buchenwald was a ten and, say, being bound to a wheelchair a five—where was his lot? One? One and a half?

Adam lifted his head off the dresser. It wasn't over. He didn't have to give up. He still had the brooch. As long as he had it, he could still get it to Dagmar. And he hadn't been kicked off the kibbutz—not yet. He could go to Eyal before Yossi did and beg for one last chance.

He spotted the little dog trembling in the corner and rushed over. "Golda!"

Collecting the shaking bundle in his arms, he said, "Did I scare you? It's just a bunch of drawers!" Golda calmed, lapped his hand, and Adam pressed his face against her fur. "Don't worry, I would never hurt you."

*A*fter forty-five minutes of plodding under the beating sun, Ulya descended the potholed road into Kfar Al-Musa, the Arab village nestled in the foothills of Mount Carmel. She checked that the rosary she grabbed off her roommate's nightstand hung over her loose tank top. Walking into this ramshackle village was unpleasant enough without being mistaken for a Jew. She had heard stories of Jews in Arab souks getting knifed in the back.

A piebald mutt abandoned the trash scattered alongside the road to run up and bark at her, an earsplitting bark, but Ulya knew to never let an animal see your fear, be it a dog or human. Fear fed the thirst to attack; she never could have shoplifted for so long if she had let the dread of getting caught show on her face. She kept walking, chin up, eyes ahead, until the mongrel lost interest and trotted off.

What a lazy people, thought Ulya, as she entered the outskirts of the town. Half the houses were unfinished, their top floors roofless, just concrete pillars sprouting rusted rebar, and yet there wasn't a construction worker in sight. She was thirsty, but the cave-like shops were uninviting, their Coke bottles probably warm and covered in dust. She passed a barebones café but saw only men inside puffing on hookahs and drinking coffee, not a single woman. If these people had been living in this village for seven generations, as Farid so often pointed out, why did it look like such a shit pit? The Jews irritated people with their striving, but as far as she was concerned, it was the only good thing about them. After only fifty years, they had red Spanish roofs, satellite dishes, green lawns with yellow rosebushes. Maybe the question shouldn't be who got here first, but who was going to make the most of it.

As she approached the center of the town, the houses got older and more bunched together. One thing was certain: seeing this third-world village further convinced her, as if she weren't convinced enough, that she was right to seek an abortion. The only reason she was coming to tell him about it was to hurt him. She wanted to punish him for not fighting over her, for not running after her when she stomped off into the orchard, for being too big of a coward over the last few weeks to try to get her back.

The village's main plaza amounted to a triangle of cracked cement with two benches and an old man selling pitas from a wooden pushcart. A whiny Arab pop song wafted out of a store, its door propped open by a garbage bin holding plastic brooms. Could she and Farid have grown up in more disparate places? Mazyr's Lenin Square was an expanse of gray cobblestones surrounded by magnificent buildings: the rose-colored theater with its centuries-old chandeliers glimmering in its windows; the yellow church topped by three golden cupolas, though its doors had been boarded all her life; and the giant gray technical college gridded by hundreds of small square windows. In the middle of the plaza, a statue of Lenin raised a black fist at the overcast sky. It was under this statue that she had smoked her first cigarette. How disorienting to think her mother still crossed that square every single morning with her basket of dried perch. If her mother could see her now, pregnant and walking through this Arab town, she would die.

Ulya double-checked the rosary and walked up to the old pita peddler. "Do you know where Farid lives?"

"Farid who?"

He ogled her breasts, now too big for her bras, and she imagined him thinking, look at this promiscuous white woman about to give it to this Farid.

"I don't know his last name."

"You don't know his family name?"

The old Arab's Hebrew was worse than hers. They were both speaking a language they didn't like.

"I already told you no."

"What does he look like? How old?"

"He's tall. Twenty-five years old. Has gold eyes." As she described Farid, her skin prickled, and she blamed the harsh sun. She'd forgotten to put on sunblock, and her arms were pink. "He works at Kibbutz Sadot Hadar."

"Sahouri. Farid Sahouri." The old man pointed up a sloping street. "Gold eyes, yes. Lives with his parents. Not married. One, two, three . . . the sixth house."

Ulya slogged up the inclined road. *Sahouri.* Imagine having a child with such a name. Even worse: she would be Ulya Sahouri. Horrible!

Four girls were coming down the hill wearing jeans, long-sleeved T-shirts, and colored headscarves. All their eyes were on Ulya, making her second-guess her short jean skirt and low-cut tank top. Who were these girls to make her feel cheap? Did they enjoy being subservient to their brothers? Did they like covering every inch of their bodies? It was a hundred fucking degrees! As the girls passed her, she gave them the finger, happy she had painted her nails hot pink that morning. The girls' mouths opened as they looked from her to each other. Ulya laughed and carried on, but she was angry and remained angry as she counted five houses and walked up the cement path to the sixth one's door.

The house wasn't as miserable as she had expected. A stained-glass fanlight decorated the wooden door, and crocheted curtains shaded the window. She rang the bell. She didn't have to come and tell him. As it turned out, it was easy to get an abortion in Israel. All she needed was authorization from a "termination committee," and they always gave approval for conception out of wedlock. The doctor estimated she was eighteen weeks along, meaning she would have to do it soon or risk having a rarer, more gruesome kind of abortion where they suctioned out its brain so the head would pass more easily out her vagina. The physical risks for that kind of abortion were as low as any other, the doctor said, but some women suffered emotionally when the fetus was more developed. She wouldn't have that problem, but there was no reason to put things off.

A little boy opened the door.

"Hello," she said, smiling at him.

A stout older woman waddled up behind the boy, wiping her hands on a dishcloth.

"Yes?" she said in Hebrew.

"Shalom. I mean, salaam. Is Farid here?"

The white headscarf framed a doughier, saggier version of Farid's face. It was from his mother that he got the eyes. She ushered Ulya into the cool shade of the house and looked back curiously—accusingly?—before starting up the stairs to fetch Farid.

Alone with the little boy and the smell of fried onions, Ulya considered the inside of the home. An orange ceramic vase sat on a glass console table, and marble thresholds divided the rather spacious rooms. She had to admit it beat the cramped two-room apartment she had shared with her parents, brother, and grandmother. When they were placed in the "disposable building," it was supposed to be for a short time, just until communism alleviated the housing shortage, but fifteen years later, they were still living between its uninsulated walls, going to bed in their winter coats.

Ulya heard footfalls upstairs and fluffed her hair. Had her eyeliner melted down her face? She should have consulted her compact before ringing the bell. Aside from a few distant glimpses in the dining hall, it had been almost a month since she and Farid had seen each other. She hooked her fingers into her belt loops and straightened her back.

Farid came down the stairs behind his mother. He looked taller, but maybe that was due to the weight loss. He must have shed ten pounds.

"Ulya."

"Farid, we need to talk."

He beckoned her up the stairs, and she climbed behind him, eyes on the back of his jeans, feeling how odd it was for them not to kiss or hug hello, to be so close without touching. He led her down a hallway and into his parents' bedroom, where a busy comforter covered a double bed and a collection of unbranded perfumes sat on a dresser. He closed the door and guided her onto the balcony. With the sun coming from behind the house, the shaded balcony was like a box seat to the dazzling white village below. A slender minaret rose from the white, its crescent black against the cloudless sky. Limestone and grayish olive trees dotted the surrounding hills, brown and dry from the long summer. In the distance stood the kibbutz's water tower. In a dusty patch below the balcony, kids ran around, hosing a donkey.

Farid leaned on the iron railing. "I thought maybe I was exaggerating your eyes in my head. But no, they are so blue. Bluer than peacock feathers."

Ulya smirked at his attempt at poetry. She didn't confess her astonishment at finding his eyes as gold as she remembered, as gold as Adam's brooch.

"For twenty nights, I went to our place and waited for you."

"I'm pregnant."

"Pregnant." He parroted it back with no emotion.

She nodded and watched his face, waiting for the shock to turn to joy, fear, but it remained frozen. He said nothing.

"Hello? Are you having trouble understanding, Farid?"

Farid breathed deeply through his nose and then seemed to hold his breath.

"It's yours, if that's what you're wondering. I haven't slept with anyone else in a year."

"But I . . . I thought you said . . . Chair. . . Chairee. . ."

Ulya squeezed the railing. Why was she supposed to be on top of the whole Arab-Jew mess, but he couldn't get this one name right?

"Chernobyl. Yes, that's what I was told. I was told I was infertile. But now I'm over four months pregnant."

Farid regarded her belly, though nothing could be detected under the loose tank top. She had expected him to be unable to hide his happiness and then to be crushed when she told him about the impending abortion. Either the information was still sinking in or he was going to prove a coward again, too chicken to ask if she was going to keep it.

"Of course, I'm going to abort it."

Farid turned from her, squinted out at his village. "Can you? Is that legal?"

Ulya turned to the village too. "Yes, the baby is as good as gone."

She waited. Now would he beg her not to do it? Plead with her to keep their child? No. He dropped his head. What a fucking milksop. The kids below ran circles around the donkey, imitating its bray. Imagine if one of those boys were hers, all dirty and spraying a donkey. She gave Farid a few more seconds to reply. He didn't lift his head.

She turned away. "I guess there's nothing more to talk about."

She left the balcony and walked across the bedroom, listening for him to call out to her as she had listened in the orchard. Now, she thought, bringing her hand to her belly. He's going to cry: *Stop, Ulya!* All she heard, though, was the donkey's neigh.

She laid her hand on the door handle. Still nothing. When she turned to look at him one last time, he still stood on the balcony, back against the railing, facing her. He was just going to watch her go.

"You know why this baby is going to die, Farid? Because its father is a fucking coward."

Farid opened his hands on either side of him, as if to say *What do you want from me?* and stepped into his parents' bedroom.

"Tell me, Farid, do you want me to have your baby? Yes or no?"

Farid's lips parted, but no words came out. She could see him thinking of what to say, and for the first time it dawned on her that the answer might be no. The thought gave the bedroom's diffused light a pale, cold quality.

"Well? Do you want me to have this baby?"

"Ulya . . ." He reached his hand out, as if in apology, and then dropped it.

"Oh . . ." Ulya looked around the room in disbelief and was confronted with her reflection in the oval mirror over the dresser—fake red hair stringy with sweat, smudged eye makeup, sunburned arms, loose tank top hiding the bump of the baby he didn't want.

Her lip quivered. "You don't love me."

He had loved her once. She was sure of it. He must have fallen out of love when she didn't show up for those twenty nights. And what had she been doing instead? Sitting in her room, savoring the idea of him lying heartbroken on their blanket all night, listening for her and getting nothing but the plunk of the falling mandarins. She had enjoyed torturing him, and now she wondered why he didn't love her?

Farid walked toward her with his arms extended. Horrified at the prospect of a pity hug, she put out a hand. Maybe he had never loved her. Maybe she had been his fool and not the other way around. When he would ask her to marry him every night, he knew she'd say no. He may have never been willing to marry a non-Arab. He tried to hug her, and she smacked his arms away.

"Ulya, Ulya." He attempted to get his arms around her while she thrashed left and right.

"Fuck you!" she cried. "I hate you."

He caught her wrists and held tight. "Ulya! Please! Listen! Please!"

Tears—embarrassing tears—streamed down her face as she tried to free herself while simultaneously not wanting to lose his touch.

"Ulya! Listen! Listen! . . . Of course I want you to have our baby!"

She heard him, but had trouble calming down. She breathed hard, waiting to hear more.

"I assumed you didn't want it. I still want nothing more than for you to be my wife. Will you be my wife?"

Ulya drew a short breath, looked anywhere but at him. He wrapped one arm around her shoulders and pulled her close. She remained stiff at first, then dropped her head on his shoulder, giving into the comforting smell of him. He then wrapped his other arm around her lower back. He did love her, and yet the light in the room didn't lose its sadness.

Farid lowered his head so their cheeks brushed. "I had given up hope of ever having you in my arms again, and now I'll be able to hold you every day for the rest of our lives."

Looking at their reflection in his parents' mirror, Ulya wiped the streaks of mascara from under her eyes. The panic over Farid not loving her was swiftly being replaced by the panic that she was going to hate her life. She couldn't let that happen. She pulled back her head and fixed her eyes on him. "I'm not going to live in this run-down village and work on the kibbutz until I die."

The fear returned to Farid's eyes. She was relieved to see how quickly the tables turned back.

"I'm going to get that restaurant. Eventually."

"Eventually isn't good enough. This baby is going to be here in five months. You have to have the restaurant in five months."

"That's impossible."

"Why?"

"I don't have enough money saved."

She knew he had no money saved. Most of his earnings went to his family, and the pittance left over he had spent on the wine and chocolates he brought her every night.

"If you haven't been able to save the money until now, what makes you think you'll be able to do it after this baby is born? How much money do you need to open a restaurant?"

"A lot. At least a hundred thousand to lease a space. And maybe thirty thousand to purchase kitchen appliances, tables. I'd have to get a sign. Maybe a helper. I don't know. I guess I'd need a hundred and fifty thousand shekels. More perhaps."

The idea of stealing the brooch was already there, as if she had been looking, waiting, for an excuse. She had said she would only steal it if she needed it to survive; well, now she needed it to survive.

"I can get us twice that. Maybe more. And I can get it by tomorrow."

Farid looked at her sideways. "You're not planning to rob a bank, are you?"

For the first time in her life she would be open about being a thief, and not a petty thief, but the kind that stole the truly valuable, the irreplaceable. Something that would break the owner's heart. And all this time she had worried what people would think of her shoplifting hand cream.

"No. We're going to steal a brooch with a sapphire the size of my thumb. It's worth at least a hundred thousand dollars. That's four hundred thousand shekels, Farid!"

"Steal?" Farid released her, rubbed his forehead. "I don't know."

"You don't know? You're always going on and on about your father's father's father, how happy he was with his olive trees and blah blah blah until the Jews took over. Well, now you can take something back. Remember that old Jewish bag you tried to help down from the truck? How she shooed you away like you were a dirty fly?"

"Yes, but it isn't her brooch. Is it?"

"No, it belongs to the American who barged in on us. So we're not just talking about a Jew, but an American Jew. Believe me, he'll be fine. And we need it to survive."

Farid hooked Ulya's hair behind her ear. "Survive? Isn't that a small exaggeration?"

"No. It's not. We either get that brooch or forget it. The baby. The marriage. The whole thing. I can't risk being stuck here in this horrible village for the rest of my life."

Farid closed his eyes, as if that would make the whole proposition disappear.

"I mean it," she said.

"I could try to get a few friends . . ."

"No." She shook her head. "These friends might keep the brooch or want to split the profits, and I don't trust you to stop that from happening. I'll do it."

"How?"

"Don't worry. This is something I can do."

Ulya scrutinized her reflection in the mirror. Did showing all that leg offset the baggy T-shirt that hung off her achy breasts, hiding the repulsive bump? Her body had been hijacked. She felt bone-tired, queasy, like she constantly needed to take a dump—nothing like molten lava.

She dabbed on lip gloss. "So is this friend a man friend?"

Claudette sat on her bed, hugging her pillow. "Yes."

Ulya turned from the mirror. "Is this who you've been spending every night with?"

Claudette nodded.

"So you're not just friends, are you? You're romantic?"

Claudette didn't answer this time.

Ulya turned back to her lip gloss. "Why are you inviting me and Adam to tag along?"

"It was my friend's idea."

Ulya had been shocked when Claudette invited her to a party. Not only was it strange to see the word *party* come out of the weirdo's mouth, but she couldn't understand why she would want her to come. She'd never been nice to her. But she accepted. Gladly. Not only did she love getting dolled up, but a party provided the ideal setup for stealing the brooch. So far, despite having followed Adam around for a week, like that pathetic dog of his, she hadn't come close. When he said the brooch never left him, he hadn't been exaggerating. She even pretended to fall asleep on the empty bed in his room and then waited all night for him to either remove the brooch from his pocket or to take off his jeans; but he fell asleep in the jeans and in the morning wore them into the bathroom. She would have snuck into the bathroom while he showered if the showers here had tubs and curtains like they did in civilized countries. Even slurring drunk, Adam didn't seem to forget about his brooch. Half the time his hand was buried in that pocket. Parties, though, had distractions. Mishaps. Lights pulsed. Drinks got knocked over. Things were lost. People danced, pushed, flirted. The mere thought of all that fun blasted away her fatigue.

A knock came at the door. When Ulya opened it, she found a teenage boy.

"Hi. I'm Ofir."

"*You're* Claudette's friend?"

He nodded. "That's right."

Ulya smiled, amused. "I'm Ulya."

She had hoped to see proof on the boy's face that she looked good, but his strange eyes already stared past her at Claudette. Noting the teardrop pupil, she registered this was the seventeen-year-old Ofir from the bus bombing. He wasn't a handsome boy, but he was tall and self-possessed for his age.

She grabbed a pack of cigarettes from her dresser and told the boy, "This party better be good."

Ofir shrugged; clearly he couldn't care less if he impressed or disappointed her. "I can't make any promises. I never used to go to these parties, but . . . things change."

Ulya turned to look at her roommate, who stood, gazing at the boy, hands clasped in front of her white sundress, painted lips in a small smile. Everything about Claudette seemed different: her hair longer, cheeks pinker, eyes brighter. She was so much prettier than upon her arrival. How had she not noticed this transformation?

"Yes, things change," said Ulya, heading for the door. "I'll get Adam."

When Adam heard the knocking, he didn't budge. He remained on the bed with a beer in one hand, Dagmar's note in the other. For the hundredth time, he searched the words for a clue. It was almost two weeks since Eyal, after much begging, put him on probation, and though he'd managed since then to do a passable job in the dishroom, he'd made no progress with his search for Dagmar. Or his sobriety.

The knock came again. He stared at the door, hoping the person would just go away. The knock came a third time before Ulya poked in her head. "You ready?"

"Ready for what?"

She stepped into the room. "What do you mean 'ready for what'?"

Ulya didn't know what to make of Adam's expression. As she walked toward him, his eyes enlarged. Oh my God. She came to a stop. He could tell. "What? Why are you staring at me like that?"

"You look . . . you look . . . incredible. More stunning than ever."

Ulya breathed again. She shook her head as if she were above needing such flattery, but inside she felt the rush of his words.

"Well, I'm all dressed up for the rave, remember? Come on, we're leaving now."

"Rave?" He shook his head. "No thanks."

"But you promised you would come."

"No, I didn't. That never happened."

"Come on." She took him by the wrist and pulled. He remembered that first day when she wanted to show him the magazine, and it felt like a long time ago. "You have to come!"

"Why? Why do I have to come?"

"Because I . . . I want you there."

She hadn't had to pretend to be in love with him yet and was hoping she could get the job done under the guise of friendship. Adam, however, couldn't help but wonder if she were reconsidering him. Why else would she be hanging around all the time? She wasn't being flirty, but she watched him like she did before, when she seemed to be waiting for him to do that one thing that would settle her mind about him. He didn't know how seriously to take the renewed attention. She might just be lonely, now that she no longer sneaked off to see her Arab boyfriend. But then, maybe, just maybe, after not seeing or speaking to either of them, she had realized that it was him, Adam, that she missed. Yeah, right.

"Come on, Adam who will always be young."

He smiled, touched that she remembered him saying that.

"Come on!"

She could see him wavering, that all he needed was one more nudge. "There's going to be free alcohol."

Free alcohol? He looked down at the six-pack waiting on the floor beside the bed. He'd drunk two. If he went to this party, he could save the others for tomorrow. A week after getting his monthly stipend, he'd already blown through half of it. In another week he'd have no money for beer. Maybe that was a good thing, having no way of buying booze for two weeks.

"All right, let me get dressed."

She gave him a big smile and released his wrist. After the door closed behind her, he chugged the rest of his bottle and schlepped to the bathroom. He splashed cold water on his face and ran a hand over his stubble, assessing his reflection. He could really use a shave. He picked up the razor but then decided against shaving with that dull blade again. He'd already made that mistake three times. After much effort, he squeezed a smudge of toothpaste out of a shriveled tube and brushed his teeth for a count of ten, nowhere near Zayde's hundred. He shook the can of hair mousse but got nothing.

Everything in his closet was nasty. He hadn't had his clothes laundered in weeks, even though he just had to drop the shit off. The hangers were empty, everything heaped on the floor. He rooted through the shirts, sniffing their pits, until he found a red tee that stunk a little less than the others. He swapped his work pants for jeans, deciding no underwear was better than dirty ones, and transferred the brooch.

Heading for the door, he passed Golda's empty bowls. How long had the water bowl been dry? In a panic he looked back at Golda curled on the unused bed. Had it been days? He hurried to fill the bowl in the bathroom sink. The moment he set it on the floor, Golda flew off the bed. The chihuahua lapped at the water, the desperate little slurps killing Adam. Tomorrow he couldn't forget to bring chicken back from the dining hall.

Outside he found Ofir, Claudette, and Ulya around the picnic table. Ulya pointed into the tree, its red fruit now closer in size to softballs than baseballs. "Pomegranate."

"That's pomegranate?" Adam felt ill.

Ofir laughed. "What? All three of you have never had a pomegranate?" He rose from the table and searched the boughs, inspecting the fruit with the aura of experience. "They're probably a week away from ripe, but maybe you can try one on the outside of the tree that got a lot of sunlight." He pulled a fruit off and held it out for them. "In Hebrew it's called *rimmon*, the same word for hand grenade, because the earliest grenades looked exactly like them. Some modern ones still do."

"Ah," Claudette said. "*Pomme, grenade.*"

Ofir steadied the pomegranate against the table and pulled a Swiss Army knife out of his back pocket. "It's packed with little seeds the way a hand grenade is packed with gunpowder."

Held on its side like that, with only three of the spikes in its little Budweiser crown visible, Adam could see how it looked a little like the stylized pomegranates on the brooch, but the spikes on the brooch were much longer, almost as long as the fruits themselves, making them look more like jester hats than crowns. Maybe if the goldsmith had seen a pomegranate, he would have made something Adam might have recognized. Mr. Weisberg guessed the goldsmith had never seen the fruit, only dreamed of it the way he dreamed of seeing the Promised Land. And here Adam had been in the Promised Land for months with a pomegranate tree right outside his window. The little flowers in the brooch's other quadrants were probably the red flowers that bloomed on the tree the week he arrived.

Ofir sawed down the sides of the fruit and broke it open, revealing jellylike beads reminiscent of the red salmon roe at Russ & Daughters. Ofir handed them each a wedge. Ulya picked a seed off with her sky-blue fingernails while Adam brought the wedge to his mouth and pulled off some seeds with his teeth. Ofir shook his head. "Too sour. Try again next week."

The four of them walked to the parking lot, where many of the cars had been taken out for Friday night. While Ofir fetched a key, Ulya inhaled the warm smell of summer, a bouquet of baked asphalt, dried pine needles, and swimming pool chlorine. What did old people smell when they smelled a summer night—nostalgia? To her, this was the smell of being young and free and knowing anything could happen tonight. She loved that feeling, the feeling that it was all up in the air, nothing had landed yet. Funny, she had told Adam only a few weeks ago that she never thought about growing old.

As they walked toward their car, she watched her reflection in the windows of the other cars. Though she felt bloated and bilious, Adam was right: on the outside she looked as gorgeous as ever. And then it struck her: this was the last time she would be young and free and gorgeous at a party. Of course, she knew all that was going to come to an end with a baby, but somehow she hadn't recognized that tonight would be the last hurrah. Now she watched her image pass over the car windows as if she were watching someone she loved walking away forever.

They climbed into a compact and drove away from the kibbutz, down the hill and onto a country road flanked by fields. Ulya stared out the window, and once again Adam found he preferred to watch Ulya looking out the window than to look out it himself. Her face was pensive tonight, darker than it had been that day they went to Tel Aviv. As Ulya bloused her T-shirt away from her belly, she noticed Adam's gaze on her. She forced herself to smile at him, and he thought, yes, she was definitely being nice again.

Ofir slowed the car and turned into a field of wheat, not onto a road traversing a field, but into a wall of wheat. The car plowed through the dense straw, headlights blanching the stalks seconds before they smacked the windshield and smothered the side windows.

Adam leaned between the front seats. "Ofir, are you a serial killer?"

Ulya laughed. "Oh! It's a secret party!"

The headlights landed on the back of a jalopy covered in PEACE NOW bumper stickers. They had joined a slow-moving convoy making its way toward a concrete rotunda rising out of the wheat like an ancient temple. Ofir turned off the AC, and they rolled down their windows, letting in the wafts of pot and the muffled thumps of techno music. Ulya caught Ofir giving Claudette a covert wink.

None of them knew what to expect as they entered the silo. No disco ball hung from the towering dome, no strobe lights roamed the open space, but the darkness still flashed with color. The people jumping to the electronic bass waved orange and yellow glow sticks. Some blew on neon whistles. Many sported tank tops and pants with glow-in-the-dark designs. On their feet were sneakers, sandals, or nothing at all. Only Ulya wore high heels.

Three young men hurried up to Ofir and took turns giving him hugs. "Ofir! It's so good to see you! So, so good! How are you?" One of them pointed at the three foreigners: "And who are your friends?" When Ofir gave no special introduction to Claudette—they were all just "volunteers from his kibbutz"—Ulya put together why she and Adam had been invited: so he could bring Claudette without giving away that they were a couple. The boys insisted Ofir come say hello to others who would be relieved to see him out and about, and he allowed them to drag him off.

Adam scanned the silo for a bar. "I can't dance to this electronic crap. And where's the booze? You said there would be free booze, Ulya."

Ulya had to resist giving him a dirty look. He was right, though; she didn't see a bar. She hadn't really expected there to be free drinks, but none? How could you have a party without alcohol? This wasn't good for the plan. It was going to be harder, if not impossible, to get the brooch off Adam if he were sober and irritated the whole night. But she couldn't let this bring her down. If this was her last hurrah, she was going to enjoy it.

"This is not my fault. I was told there would be free alcohol."

Bopping her head to the music, Ulya scanned the silo for what everybody hoped to find at a party—someone hot. But how could any man look sexy in those ridiculous fisherman pants? And then her eyes landed on the eyes of a man a head taller than everyone around him and so handsome she almost stopped swaying to the beat. She gave him a slow crooked smile that said, I see you staring at me and I don't blame you. The guy broke into a grin, and the promise shot across the silo that before long he would come over to talk to her.

Oh, wow. Ulya looked away, trying not to let on how much fun she was having, more fun than she remembered this being. She rubbed her glossy lips together.

"Your boyfriend . . ." she shouted over the music at Claudette, who was nervously twisting the waist of her white sundress. "He's a child, yes?"

Claudette looked down as if she had dropped something.

"How old is he?" she asked as if she didn't know.

Claudette scrunched her face and raised her shoulders.

Ulya brought her mouth to her ear. "How old is Ofir?"

"Eighteen. Almost."

"What?" She wanted to make her say it again.

Claudette spoke a tad louder: "Eighteen. Almost."

"Almost?" She laughed. "Almost half your age, you mean."

Her teasing brought back much of Claudette's homeliness—that bloodless, straight-lipped look—but then she felt a little bad about it. Hadn't she been living in fear of people teasing her about Farid? She patted

Claudette on the shoulder. "Well, good for you!" Under her breath, she added, "*Lyubov' zla, polyubish i kozla.*" Love's evil, you'll love even a goat.

Adam had given up on the idea of a bar and now searched for someone who'd brought their own booze. Otherwise, he didn't know what he was going to do. There was no way to escape this party, to get back to the kibbutz. He was trapped, surrounded by a field of wheat, reminding him of those Vietnam movies where impassable jungle surrounded the POW camp. His forehead bristled with sweat, and the wafts of weed sickened him. That was the one drug he couldn't stand, nor the slow "everything's cool" potheads who smoked it. Wait: if this was a rave, there was ecstasy. Was that it? No alcohol because everyone was on X? He hoped not. At least when it came to drugs, he still had four months clean.

Adam observed the rapt crowd gathered around Ofir—guys nodding, girls gazing up with starstruck empathy. It was fucked up, but he couldn't help feeling a little jealous. Ofir was woven into history now, his pain a part of something bigger than himself. His wounds had gravitas, nobility; they weren't meaningless. Or shameful. Adam's own pain wouldn't be quite as shameful if he too could claim he was a victim—a victim of being born weak, or burdened with a terrible dread in his chest, a dread worse than other people's. Sometimes he allowed himself to believe that was true, but the fact remained that he still had a choice every time he brought a bottle to his mouth or snorted a line. Or maybe he didn't. No, he did. Of course. And anyway, choice or not, there was nothing noble about fingers burned on crack pipes.

A man-made thunder rumbled inside the dome, followed by a dreamful piano riff. Everyone burst into hoots and whistles. This had to be the song of the summer, because anyone who wasn't already dancing abandoned the cement walls and rushed for the dirt dance floor. Ofir came back and said: "Maybe we should dance too." Claudette followed him into the crowd, as did Ulya, who was eager to start dancing. Adam, not wanting to be left alone, tagged after them.

Beneath the pretty piano and the rumbling thunder, an electronic sequencer built up from a low bass, getting faster and faster, and higher and higher, while everyone swayed in what looked like blissful anticipation, eyes half shut, smiling. Ofir, Claudette, and Adam stepped side to side. Ulya, keeping her feet in place, gyrated her hips. Sexy dancing wasn't this party's style, but she didn't care, she liked sexy dancing. Not to mention a girl could only move her feet so much in five-inch heels. The sequencer got still faster and higher until it was a solid high-pitched whistle. A distress signal. People stopped swaying and waited, waited—

Boom! The signal exploded. *Boom boom boom boom boom.* The crowd jumped, jumped, jumped, beating the air with their fists, tweeting their whistles, whooping. Ofir started jumping and shouted at his guests as if this weren't his first rave: "Come on! *Yalla!* Jump!" The three foreigners looked around at the jumpers, mostly army-aged kids, meaning many had either just finished their service in the West Bank or Lebanon or were about to start it. They looked hell-bent on having a good time.

Claudette jumped first. Initially she barely lifted off the ground, but gradually her jumps got higher. Adam raised his eyebrows at the woman who normally moved like an automaton jumping up and down. "Jump!" Ofir shouted at him, and Adam shook his head. "Come on, jump!" He rolled his eyes and gave one jump. And then a second. Soon, like Claudette, he jumped higher. He had to laugh, because the more he jumped, the more he felt like jumping, like a little kid. He missed being a little kid.

That left only Ulya. The jumpers did not look cool to her. Were they jumping like this in Manhattan? But what could she do? This was the party she was at. Her last party. She kicked off her stilettos and, unlike the others, jumped as high as she could right away. Ofir took Claudette's and Ulya's hands and told them to take Adam's. The four held hands with the beats coming at them so fast they couldn't think, only jump, jump, grinning and laughing at one another, each with their own reason for wishing they could jump like this forever.

When the song ended, Ofir whisked Claudette away through the sweating bodies. Panting, Adam turned to Ulya, who had given herself to the next song, throwing her hips from side to side, whipping her cherry-red hair. He had her all to himself on a dance floor, what would have been a dream only a few weeks ago, but now he couldn't enjoy it, not without a drink. He wiped the sweat from his upper lip and shouted at her that he was going to be right back.

"Why?" She propped her arms on his shoulders. "Where are you going?"

Her touch surprised him. The dancing had put her in a good mood. "To look for some booze."

"Oh. Oh, yes. Go do that! But promise to come back."

Adam left the silo through a towering rectangular exit in the cement. Outside, the night was hot but the air felt fresher. Only a few people loitered on this side of the silo, smoking cigarettes, making out; most people, he supposed, were on the other side, where the cars had flattened down the wheat. Maybe one of those cars had a cooler in a popped trunk.

After taking a piss in the stalks, Adam started around the outside of the moonlit dome. Where the hell was he? The question came to him, the one he'd been pushing away: What if it were time to go home? He didn't think he could bear it. But he also couldn't bear being here anymore. The wheat was nightmarish, the army of stalks standing dead still and then, when the wind picked up, swaying so uniformly, so unfeelingly.

As he circled the dome, hunting for beer, he was reminded of that first night he snorted coke, how he walked around the outside of Bryant Park, back when it was bordered by tall hedges and half its lamps were busted, giving dark cover to streetwalkers and dealers. He must have rounded that block—the massive library and the park behind it—ten times before giving in and buying his first bump. Actually, he didn't buy it: the pusher, a skinny black kid nicknamed Haircut, gave him his first for free, so long as he promised to come back and buy from him if he liked it. Haircut had him rub the dollar bill on his gums. That was 1984, a week short of his sixteenth birthday, two months before his expulsion from Stuy. For a long time he thought if only he had circled the block an eleventh time and gone home to Zayde. But that was ridiculous. If not then, it would have been the next day or the next year. That night, it was the library's stone lions that lacked sympathy, staring out with their pupil-less eyes.

Adam neared some kids standing in a circle and had a feeling about them. Peeking out of the corner of his eye as he passed, he found he was right: a boy with brown skin and bleached yellow hair doled out pills. Adam stopped. "That X?"

"Yeah. From Tokyo."

"I've never done X." He edged toward them. "Done everything else, crack, smack, but never ecstasy. Not a huge rave scene in the States."

The teens nodded as if they met crack smokers all the time. These were the kind of kids who thought cool meant never being impressed.

"You want to try?" A girl extended an arm swathed in friendship bracelets. In her open palm was a yellow pill stamped with a blue butterfly, like something he might have found at The Sweet Life, the candy store on Hester Street, back when he used to get his fix from Nerds and gummy worms.

"Does it make you hallucinate? I never do anything that makes you hallucinate. I fucking hate hallucinations." Adam hoped the girl would say yes.

She shook her head. "No. It'll just make you feel good. Really good. You won't fucking believe how good."

How many hours were left until he was back in his room with the four beers? Five hours? Maybe more. He could crawl into the uncaring wheat and white-knuckle it. That's what he should do.

The girl retracted her hand.

"Okay! I'm in."

She dropped the yellow butterfly pill in his palm.

"Banzai!" said the platinum blond boy, and they all tossed a pill into their mouths.

Adam pulled out the remnants from his stipend, worried he might not have enough for the pill, but the boy waved him off. "Forget it. It's on us."

"Aw, man, thanks."

"Just spreading the joy."

Adam walked on, waiting for the pill to kick in. He felt bad about taking it, so he hoped it took effect soon, wiping out that guilt, too. He leaned against the silo. Still nothing. The pounding base came through the cement walls. He checked his watch. Ten minutes. He started walking again. Probably an old pill. Or fake. The stupid kid had been ripped off, believing the dealer's bullshit about Tokyo.

He rounded the silo to where the cars were parked, feeling a slight tingling at the base of his ribs. He stopped to concentrate on it. The tingling spread so fast, surging up his spine, blooming in his chest, his head. The wheat and the parked cars and the night sky, they all, just like that, lost their menace. How could he have seen wheat, which fed people—only made them happy—as anything but good? What the hell could be bad about wheat?

He reentered the silo with explosions of joy going off inside him like fireworks. Holy shit, this stuff was good. Smiling, he leaned against the concrete wall and watched the dancing people. Look at them! Human beings—how he loved them, flaws and all. The love didn't come from the

X; no, it merely allowed him to feel the love that was always inside him, buried under the dread. And didn't it feel like the crowd loved him, too? Or rather that each person in it would love him if given the chance? He even had the feeling his grandfather was looking down on him with love. Forgiveness. No. He couldn't bring Zayde into this. Leave Zayde out.

He spotted Ulya talking to an absurdly handsome guy, and he didn't hate him, wasn't jealous. Not one bit. Who cared if he was so tall Ulya had to crane her head to make eye contact? That guy had his own problems. His own heartache. We all had our stories, Adam thought, closing his eyes and concentrating on the electronic beats pulsing under his feet. The beats traveled up his legs and through his groin and out the top of his head like the mild spasms preceding an orgasm, except there was no climax. The currents just kept rolling through him.

When he reopened his eyes, Ulya was no longer talking to Mr. Handsome but dancing again, swarmed by guys trying to groove near her. He watched her dance close to this one and then that one, never giving any of them too much of her time. Her dancing nirvana was mesmerizing, hips going round, hands in the air, short skirt riding up her thighs. She burned so brightly everyone else seemed to dim and disappear. Soon only she shone in the middle of the silo.

"You guys ready to go?"

Ofir had startled him. "Go? Now?" He pulled a stalk of wheat from Claudette's hair, and she turned in embarrassment.

"It's three a.m."

"Three a.m.? You're shitting me." Adam referred to his watch. He couldn't believe it. This drug made an hour pass in a second. It made sense, he supposed, time flying being the downside to happiness. "Okay, I'll get Ulie."

As he walked toward her, he found it wasn't as if the other dancers had disappeared; they had. Ulya was one of a handful of stragglers still dancing. How long had he been watching her? She must have danced nonstop for hours. When he tapped her on the shoulder, she spun around, hair stringy with sweat, black eyeliner smudged into shiners. He pointed at the exit where Ofir and Claudette stood waiting to go, framed by the tall rectangular doorway like a painting, the wheat and starry sky behind them.

Ulya flapped her green T-shirt for air. She had enjoyed the party, done nothing about the brooch. "I loved dancing."

Adam smiled. "Yeah, I could tell."

She stood still—paralyzed, it seemed to Adam. "I loved being young and free."

"*Love*, not *loved*, my little babushka. You need to work on your verb conjugation."

Driving away from the silo, along the path of trampled wheat, no one spoke. When they turned onto the country road, Ulya snuggled up to Adam. His high was wearing off but not yet gone, and her head fell onto his chest like a pebble into a pond, setting off concentric ripples of love and horniness. He had heard ecstasy heightened your sense of touch, but hadn't experienced it, since no one had touched him the whole night. No one had touched him, really, in months.

"Can I see that brooch?" Ulya zigzagged her finger across Adam's stomach.

Adam, emboldened by her attentions and the X, said, "You know where it is."

His stomach tightened as she traced her finger down to the front pocket of his jeans. "Here?"

He nodded and sucked in his breath as she squirmed her hand inside. Her being so close was excruciating. It felt like if she didn't touch him, he would implode, and if she did, same thing. He wheezed. "To the left."

Ulya knew that wasn't the brooch on the left. Did he have a hard-on? She'd assumed he was too out of it. She bit her lips and thrust her hand deeper. Adam emitted a small groan as she whisked out the brooch.

She held it up to the window. "Wow. It really is amazing."

Ulya had a theory that sometimes it was best to make a show of having the desired object in your hand. She did it shoplifting all the time, made certain the saleslady noticed her oohing over a dress, trying on a pair of earrings, parading around from one mirror to another with the silk scarf. Sometimes she would even ask if the scarf looked good on her so the saleslady would let down her guard, thinking, well, she can't possibly be planning on stealing it.

Adam pointed. "Those little things are pomegranates."

Even in the pale light the gold gleamed like something out of a fairy tale and the gemstones were blazing pools of color. On a school trip to Moscow, she and her fellow classmates had pressed their faces against the display cases in the Kremlin, goggling the Romanov jewels—the gold crowns encrusted with diamonds, the emerald earrings a princess wore shortly before her execution. Sitting on dusty velvet, it all looked so lifeless. What a difference there was between seeing a jewel in a museum cabinet behind a thick pane of glass and holding it in your hand, out in the breathing, sweating, struggling world.

"Can I put it on?"

"Um . . ."

"Come on. For a second."

"For a second."

Adam pinched her baggy T-shirt and pierced it with the gold pin. As he pushed the stiff pin under the hook, he felt Ulya's breast against his knuckles. When he sat back, Ulya continued her show, leaning forward and tapping Claudette. "Look! Have you ever seen anything so magical?"

Claudette considered the brooch. "The blue stone is very big."

Ulya scrambled to come up with her next move. Could she open the door and roll onto the road? She could run into the fields before they had a chance to stop the car. She might be too hurt, though, to run, not to mention the damn baby. Maybe she could ask Ofir to pull over so she could pee and then make a break for it. But how could she evade all three of them? Especially barefoot or in five-inch heels? None of them were in great shape—a lush, a disabled boy, and a freak—but still, the odds were against her. What if she pretended to lose the brooch? That was an idea . . . But how? They were stuck in a car. It was a long shot, but her only option was to make Adam forget about the brooch long enough for her to say goodnight and disappear into her room.

Adam moved for the brooch. "Okay, time's up."

Ulya cupped her hand over it. "Please, Adam. Let me wear it for five more minutes. It makes me feel like a queen."

Adam sighed. He felt too good, too high, to say no. He would take it back in five minutes.

"Queen Ulya," she said, slipping her fingers into his thick hair. She scratched the back of his head. With the last vestiges of X, it felt like heaven to him.

Okay, Ulya thought. The show part was over. Time for stage two. From this point on the most important thing was to keep his attention away from the brooch. The radio clock glowed 3:54 a.m. Based on the drive to the rave, they would be back on the kibbutz in fifteen minutes. She could do this. Seeing how much Adam relished the head scratch—much more than she could have expected—she upped it. She ran her fingers right through his hair, from the base of his skull over his crown and down to his forehead and back again. Adam groaned with pleasure.

She was still fondling his hair when they drove through the front gate of the kibbutz, but Adam wasn't enjoying it anymore. The high had worn off, leaving him lower than he'd started. A lot lower. His brain cried out, starving for whatever the X used up, serotonin, dopamine, he didn't know, but he was lucky he didn't have another one of those fucking butterfly pills. He would have popped it, done anything, to put off this hell for later.

Ofir pulled up to the volunteers' section, and Adam and Ulya climbed out the back. The car drove away with Claudette still in it. Ulya couldn't believe her luck. Adam seemed to have forgotten about the brooch, and her roommate wouldn't even be around to see her fleeing with it. She folded her arms over the jewels, a bit too high on her chest to look natural, and walked ahead, taking the steppingstones as fast as she could without drawing attention.

Adam descended the steps, jerkily. He felt like a broken jug glued back together all wrong, pieces missing. In two hours he had to be in the dish-room, ready to scrub jugs and plates for eight hours. How was he going to do it? He called out to Ulya. "Wait up!"

Ulya looked over her shoulder, readying to give back the brooch.

At the bottom of the stones, Adam paused with his hands on his waist to catch his breath. "So depressing."

"What?"

"I don't know."

Ulya walked on, heart going wild. She veered toward her building. "Goodnight, Adam," she called, trying to sound natural. "See you tomorrow."

She walked the final stretch toward her door, unzipping her vinyl purse. Oh my God. She had it. She had it! She stuck a trembling key in the lock. As she turned it, she heard: "Ulie."

Again she looked over her shoulder, careful not to turn her chest to him. "Yes?"

He stood at the end of her path, shoulders hunched, looking miserable. "Can I sleep in your room? I don't mean have sex. I won't touch you. Just sleep. I don't want to be alone right now."

She tried to think fast. What would be the safer move?

"I don't know, Adam, we only have two hours before work, and Claudette might—"

He turned away, head lowered. "Yeah, I figured."

She pushed open the door to her room. One hundred thousand dollars—at least. Four hundred thousand shekels. A billion Belarusian rubles! Oh, oh. She could send her mother money, so she could fill her cupboards with tea, buy new boots. All she needed was Adam to not remember the brooch for one more minute. Just one minute. That was all she needed to change her shoes and run.

She slipped inside her room while Adam walked toward his, past the pomegranate tree.

Pomegranate.

He dug his hand into his pocket.

"Wait!"

Ulya heard him as she was closing the door. Not knowing what to do, she closed it anyway, and then listened to him marching up her walkway.

He knocked. "Hey!"

She stood on the other side of the door, breathing as quietly as she could, struggling to think of what to do next.

"Hey!" He banged hard. "You still have my brooch!"

She waited to see if, by some miracle, he would go away, decide to deal with it in the morning, but he struck the door with a flat hand. "Open up! Open up!"

Of course, he wasn't going away. She hurriedly unpinned the brooch from her T-shirt and stuffed it down her skirt, into the front of her panties.

"HEY!" He pounded on the door, likely waking up every volunteer. "Open the fuck up! If you don't open up right now, I'm going to kick the fucking thing in!"

Ulya opened the door and feigned irritation. "I was in the bathroom, Adam." She glanced down at her chest. "Oh . . . Oh, no."

"Oh, no, what? Give me the brooch."

She raised her head, tried to look as shocked as possible. "It's gone."

"Gone?"

Before she had a chance to nod, Adam shoved the door and came at her so fast she stumbled backward, heels slipping under her.

"What do you mean gone?!"

Adam no longer felt tired or depressed. He was pure panic. He clutched Ulya by the arms and drove her back until he had her pinned against the far window, its concrete sill jabbing into her back.

"What do you mean it's gone?"

The violence in Adam's black eyes startled her. She didn't think he had violence in him, not after his encounter with Farid. But she had been wrong. She could feel in an animal way that she was in danger, that if he found the brooch on her, he could kill her. She had been scared while stealing before, but not like this.

"It . . . must have fallen off . . . in Ofir's car."

"Then we'll have to go get him."

"But it's so . . . late. We'll do it tomorrow."

Adam squeezed her arms so hard, her hands numbed. She prayed that he didn't lean against her, didn't feel the brooch against her pelvic bone.

Spittle hit her face as he shouted: "It's not Ofir's car! The whole kibbutz uses that fucking car. We have to get it NOW!"

She stammered, "O-o-okay."

He let go, allowing her heels to return to the ground and the blood to rush back into her arms. She followed him toward the door. It wasn't working, pretending the brooch had fallen off. He wasn't going to let it go until he found it. And she couldn't keep it on her body any longer. It was too dangerous.

She trembled as she closed her door, not daring to take the time to lock it. Adam ran for the steppingstones. Dizzy with fear, she thrust her hand down her skirt and hurled the brooch at the grass.

"Adam!"

He turned. "What? We have to hurry."

"Maybe . . . it fell off after I got out of the car. We should keep an eye on the ground. Look here in the grass first."

"Look fast." He jogged down the stones. "Fast, fast, fast."

Adam moved the grass around with his feet while Ulya searched on her hands and knees. She figured it would be better if he found it, but it was getting harder to wait for that with him screaming ever more loudly: "Where the fuck is it? Where is it?"

"What's that?" She pointed at gold glinting in the blades behind him.

He whipped around. "Where? Where?"

She crawled over and picked it up, hoping she looked genuinely relieved, happy for him.

Adam grabbed it, clutched it to his chest. "Oh my God. I would've killed myself."

Ulya rose from the grass. Without another word, Adam turned for his room, and she watched him walk away with the brooch. She had come so close. For a minute, it had been hers.

She headed back to her room. She would have to try again, and next time not let the threat of violence deter her. She was running out of time. Adam might get kicked off the kibbutz any minute; and even if he suddenly got his act together, she had another clock to beat. Soon it would be too late to have an abortion. If she wasn't careful, in a few weeks she would be poor and pregnant and living in an Arab village with dusty Coke bottles and donkeys.

She closed her door and slipped out of her heels. The floor felt cool against her feet, sore from all that dancing. She climbed onto her bed and, sitting with her back against the wall, lit a cigarette. As she rubbed her feet, like she used to do after a night out in Mazyr, the memory of Adam's rage started to subside. Instead she pictured the tall, handsome man, the infatuation on his face when he struck a match for her cigarette. God, it was fun. Everyone's eyes had been on her tonight.

She blew smoke.

Could that part of her life really be over?

For the first time in months, Claudette rolled over to turn off the alarm and found she wasn't covered in sweat, that her T-shirt wasn't glued to her clammy chest. The breeze coming through the window was fresh, the sunlight mellow, and the oscillating fan stood still. She was supposed to stay for the summer, and the summer was coming to an end. It was the first week of September. At home she would be pulling on wool stockings. Would they let her remain here through the winter?

When she stepped outside and saw the pomegranate tree, she remembered Ofir's prediction that the fruit would be ripe by now. She picked one to bring to Ziva, though Ziva hadn't eaten in two days. As she climbed the steppingstones, schoolchildren were coming down the main road wearing colorful backpacks and spotless new sneakers.

The main square was unusually crowded. Claudette walked around the people standing in pockets, speaking loudly, hands waving in exclamation. Rounding the white golf cart that still sat in front of Ziva's place, she wondered what was going on. She knocked on Ziva's door as if the old woman could answer it, waited a courteous second, and went inside.

Quiet dominated the apartment. Ziva rarely used the television Eyal had set up for her. Claudette walked toward the bedroom, hoping she would find the old woman coherent. For the first couple of weeks Ziva was confined to the bed, she mostly knew where she was and who was visiting her, but over the last week the confusion had worsened. She increasingly called Claudette *Mutti* and asked for her cookie recipe or to see her latest painting. Claudette ignored these requests. Often she had no choice because Ziva spoke to her in German.

"Look at them!" With her adjustable bed raised to its most upright position, Ziva pointed out the window. "They've just voted! I should be standing by that door, handing out pamphlets, answering questions. Not lying in this goddamn bed!"

So that's what everyone was doing in the square. Claudette hadn't realized today was the big vote. Of all the days for Ziva to be lucid. She walked over to the window and gazed out at the scene. A circle of people burst into laugher, their laughter loud enough to reach the sad bedroom.

"I'm sure they won't vote to end the kibbutz, Ziva."

Ziva clutched the waffle blanket, held it under two tight fists. "How can I just sit here?"

Not too long ago, Claudette believed, the old woman would have rolled off the bed and dragged herself across the square to intercept the voters. But after five weeks of withering and yellowing in the bed, even Ziva's incomparable willpower could no longer overcome such a body. The doctors decided against treating the fractured hip of a dying woman, and they'd stopped pumping her stomach. All they offered now were painkillers.

Ziva tried to reach the Styrofoam cup on the nightstand. "This is the longest I've gone without working. How long have I been stuck in this bed, Claudette? Two weeks?"

Claudette hurried to get the cup for her. She couldn't lie so she said nothing. What would be the point of informing her it had been twice that?

"I told you I didn't want to die in bed. Didn't I tell you that?"

"You won't die in bed, Ziva."

"Oh no? Then what am I doing right now?"

Ziva took a shaky sip of water, holding the cup in both hands, her index finger circled by a red scar where the tip had been sewn back on.

"I don't know." Claudette sat in the visitor's chair. "You don't know. You never know what the Lord has planned."

"The Lord? Please, Claudette, you know I can't stand that nonsense."

Claudette returned Ziva's cup to the nightstand. In the past she would have come to the Lord's defense, but she was still waiting for His sign. All she had asked for was one small sign to prove that it hadn't all been lies, and, so far, nothing.

Ziva rested her hand on the mountain her stomach made under the white blanket. "You know what the doctor claims, Claudette? She claims I took a turn for the worse because I messed up my pills. Took far too many. I told her that I may have lost control of my body, but not my mind. My mind, I told her, is as sharp as ever. Only . . . I can't explain it. I have run out of all my pills ahead of schedule."

Claudette opened her mouth, but she couldn't get the words out.

"Tell me, Claudette, have I become feebleminded without realizing it?"

Claudette lowered her head, tried harder to push out the confession.

"Have I, Claudette? Have I shown signs of dementia?"

Claudette saw she wasn't going to get away without answering Ziva's question this time. She would either have to tell the truth or tell a lie. She shook her head. "No."

"Oh, I want to believe you, I really do, but I can see you won't look me in the eye, and there's no denying the pills are gone. I can't explain that away."

"I took them." She said it so quietly, she barely heard it herself.

"What's that, Claudette? Speak up."

"I took your pills, Ziva."

Ziva regarded Claudette with suspicion. "I don't understand."

Claudette pressed her clasped hands against her face. "I wanted . . ."

"Claudette, are you making this up just to make me feel better?"

Claudette shook her head.

"Then why? Why would you take my pills?"

"I wanted to kill myself."

Ziva knew the young woman suffered—she knew it ever since she saw the fear in her eyes that day in the laundry—but if people could survive Auschwitz without killing themselves, what excuse could anybody have? It demonstrated the worst weakness of character to throw away life. And yet, Ziva wasn't entirely comfortable calling Claudette weak. Every day she cleaned the feces from her bedpan without a flinch, not even in the back of her eyes. She had watched for it.

Ziva straightened the hem of her blanket. "No matter. You didn't do it in the end. Intention without action means nothing."

Claudette closed her eyes. "I should have told you sooner, Ziva. I'm sorry."

Ziva turned to the window in time to see Hanoch, the man who would sell his soul for a television, disappear through the dining hall door. His decrepit dog sat outside waiting for him.

"Never mind sorry. Like intentions, sorry is worthless. Learning, moving forward, that's what counts. To tell you the truth, I'm thrilled to find out I haven't lost my mind."

Claudette nodded, feeling at once guilty and proud of her lie, of sparing Ziva the knowledge that part of her was already gone. What was right and wrong was no longer clear to her. She said, "I hope when I'm old, Ziva, I'll be able to look back on my life, the way you can, and be happy with my choices. Of course, I could never expect to feel as proud as you do, I'll never do anything half as grand, but I'd like to have no regrets."

Yossi, the dishwasher, bicycled alongside the square, calling out to Larry the archivist and Chaim the lazy bum. Ziva couldn't be sure what any of these people had voted. She smacked her mouth, already dry again.

"No regrets? That's a bit much, Claudette. Few regrets, perhaps. But none? That's probably impossible."

Claudette was surprised to hear Ziva say such a thing. Over the last few weeks the old woman had told her so many stories from her life, full of perseverance, courage, anger, pride, but never regret. "Does that mean you have regrets, Ziva?"

Ziva turned to the younger woman. "I just told you that I think it's impossible to get through life without them, so obviously I do. But I also told you—didn't I?—that I don't see the use in dwelling on things. What's done is done."

Claudette didn't dare push it, and Ziva faced the window again. The women sat in silence. People left the dining hall; others arrived. Boisterous schoolchildren filed inside for their early lunch.

Without looking away from the square, Ziva said, "There's one moment I would like to go back and do differently. I don't want to go back and redo whole years. Just one moment. All of five or ten minutes."

Claudette leaned forward in her chair, well aware that any of these stories might be Ziva's last. "What happened?"

"I've never told anyone this. It was the day the United Nations voted on whether to partition Palestine. A very important day. The vote was broadcast live over the wireless, and all over the world Jews huddled around their radios."

As Ziva described the people crowded around the wooden radio in the dining hall, she doubted she could ever get this young Canadian, this Catholic girl, to understand what she and the others felt that night, listening to the tinny voices coming through the round speaker, no bigger than a dessert plate.

Afghanistan.

No.

Argentina.

Abstain.

To encourage communal listening, the kibbutz had only the one radio, and its reception was good on that unseasonably mild and cloudless November night, so good Ziva could close her eyes and imagine that she stood in the grand hall in Flushing Meadows, New York, that there weren't ten thousand miles between Palestine and the strangers deciding its fate.

Only the one yes from the United States and the ten noes from the Muslim nations were certainties; every other country was a question mark. They needed two-thirds to vote yes for there to be a Jewish state, and that seemed impossible to the kibbutzniks and survivors clustered around the dining hall radio. They had long ago come to expect the rest of the human race to either turn their backs on them or actively seek their destruction.

Costa Rica.

Yes.

Cuba.

No.

Could the Jews soon have a country that could vote like this? Ziva hunched, holding her ear as close to the speaker as she could without blocking it. Dov stood behind her, hand on her shoulder, grip tightening every time a country announced its decision. When a delegate said yes, they all looked to one another in excitement; when the answer was no or abstain, Ziva didn't know what the others did, because she remained still, head bowed, waiting for the next vote. It was all happening in a matter of minutes, but to Ziva it felt as if they'd had their ears pressed against that speaker for two thousand years.

France—

Only when France announced yes did a hubbub sweep through the UN assembly and the kibbutz dining hall. France had Arab colonies, and they still voted yes. Next Greece voted no, and everyone quieted down again and remained quiet until it was announced: *The resolution of the partition for Palestine is adopted by thirty-three votes, thirteen against, ten abstentions.*

The dining hall burst into chaos. People rushed into one another's arms, jumped, shouted, sobbed, climbed on top of the tables, broke into song. Some stood, too shocked to move, hands in front of their mouths or pressed against their chests. Friends clasped arms, saying, *I can't believe it! Can you believe it? If only my father were alive to see this! My wife, my sister, my little boy.*

Ziva and Dov hugged each other, tightly, as if to squeeze out the disbelief. Beside them a survivor, a former yeshiva bocher, read aloud from the Bible: *In that day . . . the LORD shall set his hand . . . recover the remnant of his people . . . the outcasts of Israel . . . from the four corners of the earth . . .*

Ziva gazed up at Dov. "God had nothing to do with this."

Dov took her face into his hands. "I know. It was all us."

Ziva smiled. "And maybe a few others."

Dov lifted her, and she laughed as he spun them around. When he returned her to the ground, they joined the others singing and marching out of the dining hall. Ziva sang as loud as she could: *Our hope is not yet lost. To be a free people in our own land.*

Ziva glanced around for Franz. American Danny grabbed her hand and pulled her into the dancing. The hora drew her along, and she sang and smiled and returned hurrahs while scanning for her secret lover of the last two years. Where could he be? The more she searched for Franz, the angrier she became, not at him so much as at herself. Here she was in the middle of a historical moment, the climax to one of humanity's most epic stories, a story of literally biblical dimensions, and what was she doing? Being distracted by her own sordid little side story.

It would be two hours before she spied Franz leaning against the new medical clinic, hands in his trouser pockets. When he caught sight of her pushing through the crowd toward him, he didn't wave, didn't move, only watched her with a despondent face.

Panting, she said, "Where have you been?"

He shrugged, still leaning on the wall, hands in his pockets.

"Franz! What's the matter with you? Where have you been?"

He smiled, sadly, then nodded his head as if agreeing with one of his own thoughts. "I've been so stupid. I actually thought maybe my yearning, my little personal yearning, could compete with this."

"Franz, I don't understand you. The world could be bursting into flames, and you sing and dance like Fred Astaire, and now here we have the first good news of the century, maybe the first good news our people have had in two thousand years, and you stand there with a long face."

"Exactly. Two thousand years of yearning. It's stupendous. Truly."

"Why are you being sarcastic?"

"Because, Dagmar, now I have no chance."

"No chance of what?"

He looked off to the side. "No chance of having you come to America with me."

Why did this have to happen now? On what should be the happiest day of her life? She had always known, of course, that their affair would have to end someday, that it couldn't go on forever, but then she had also begun to wonder why not. Everyone knew about them. It wasn't referred to aloud, but they knew. She and Franz never kissed in public, but neither did she and Dov. Dov had never mentioned Franz, never asked her to stop seeing him. And she knew that he never would, because Dov believed no one should be owned. She didn't even know if the affair hurt him; if it did, he couldn't let on, because then she would have stopped, and that would have been a form of control. She should have known from the beginning that it would be Franz who forced its end. He had never hidden his want to own things, and the healthier he got, the more he wanted—his own home, his own clothes, his own wife.

Ziva looked to the dancers, where she should be. "Can't we please talk about this tomorrow?"

"I watched you listening to the radio. I was in the room, and you didn't even notice. Your face when they announced the results . . ." He shook his head. "I've never made you that happy. And it was grandiose—ridiculous— of me to think I ever could. I've been living in a world of wishful thinking, Dagmar. I was always going to America alone."

Ziva stared at Franz leaning against the white wall, his glistening black eyes looking anywhere but at her, his face unshaven for once. She couldn't bear the idea of never seeing him again. It was wrong of him to do this to her right now. She deserved to be happy today, and he knew that. If he had been fooling himself for two years, what was one day more?

She crossed her arms. "Maybe I'm more likely to go to America with you now. Now that I've done my duty. Now that I'm not needed as much."

Franz dropped his head. "It's not like you to say things you don't mean, Dagmar. I'm in enough pain as it is."

He was in pain. She saw a glimpse of the fragility he had that day he arrived in his oversized beige suit.

"I think what I'm saying makes sense." She didn't say it was true, only that it made sense.

Franz lifted his head. "Dagmar, what exactly are you saying?"

Not the truth. Obviously she would never leave the new Jewish state. She would never go off with him to do whatever it was people without a mission did with their days. She should tell him that if she did go to America to hang off his arm and love him the way he yearned to be loved, she would cease being the Dagmar he loved. But she didn't say that. She stood, thinking, please, not tonight.

Seeming to take courage from her silence, he pushed off the wall. "I just can't be a part of all this. Singing anthems together. I can't even go to sports games; it makes me so uncomfortable to be a part of a cheering crowd. I know it's not the same for you, but I still thought . . . Well, like I said, it was stupid, but in my stupid daydreaming, I thought in America, we could just be Franz and Dagmar, whoever they are when they're allowed to just be, to just live. Aren't you curious who you would be without all these . . . distractions? It never ends. Do you really think a hundred million Arabs are going to sit back while you set up your little Jewish country? You could be fighting Arabs for the next five or ten years. Aren't you sick of it? Aren't you sick of fighting every day just to stay alive? I know I am. I'm sorry, but I can't do it anymore. I can't stay here."

Ziva didn't know where to begin, didn't see how she could respond without ending everything right here. And she had already decided that she couldn't say goodbye to him now. She couldn't ruin this night. Tomorrow, all right, but not tonight.

"Franz, I don't need to hear anymore. I told you, I want to be with you."

Ziva cringed at her voice, her words. *I want to be with you.* It was the dialogue of a silly girl in a romance novel. So cliché. Bourgeois.

"Am I hearing you right, Dagmar? Are you saying you love me, want me, more than—" He gestured at the people singing and dancing the hora, the small white houses Ziva had helped build with her own hands, the dark fields beyond the houses, the silhouette of Mount Carmel. Boys and girls lit gunpowder, filling the air with the crackle and smell of battle and celebration.

She could take it back. She could still answer his question honestly, snuff the hope in his eyes. For the first and last time in her life, Ziva lied to spare someone's feelings. And they weren't Franz's. "I'll go with you."

Franz didn't speak immediately. He allowed the words to sink in. Then, eyes brimming, he dug into his trouser pocket and pulled out the brooch.

This wasn't the first time Ziva was seeing it. He had shown it to her one Saturday afternoon while they lolled by the river under the twisted branches of an old juniper tree. When he claimed the brooch had been in his family since the Black Plague, she had teased him for proof, but she stopped teasing him when he choked up, saying his biggest regret was not listening to his mother when she told him the history, especially the story about the yellow butterflies.

"I promised my mother that I wouldn't let it end up in the wrong hands, that I would only give it to a worthy woman, someone special. And you, Dagmar, are special." The brooch sat in his hand, glinting up at her with accusation—gaudy accusation. "According to Jewish law, if a man hands an object to the woman he wants to marry, and she accepts it, that's it, they're betrothed. The truth is you and Dov were never legally married, not by a rabbi or a state. We can still be man and wife."

Ziva didn't reach for the brooch. How could she? Franz waited. She knew he must be wondering why she wasn't taking it. Did he think she was too beside herself to move? Did he fear she was changing her mind? When his hand started to tremble—she was surprised to see love make a man tremble—she grabbed it.

Now it was her turn to see him happier than she had ever seen him before. In a flurry of words, they agreed to meet the next morning by the front gate. They would catch the noon boat from Haifa to Athens. Franz insisted they get on a boat right away, because who knew what was going to happen to the ports after tonight's vote.

She put the brooch in her pocket. "Tomorrow, Franz."

"Tomorrow, Dagmar."

Not caring who saw, she pressed her lips against his, pressed with all her being. He must have thought the force of feeling came from the prospect of soon being his wife. He couldn't have known that she was trying to put a whole lifetime into that last kiss.

She returned to the hora, joining the outer circle, next to Dov, who gave her a smile too tepid for the occasion. Was that in her head, or had he seen her kissing Franz? It would be all right. Franz was going. And she and Dov still had decades to be together, years in which to mend. The hora circled around so that Ziva could see Franz walking away. His gait was jaunty, full of things to do and the joy of getting out of here. This was the last glimpse she would have of him.

Hours later, when the birds cheeped under a pale yellow sky and the last of the revelers had gone to bed, Ziva sat at her desk. She wrote her farewell note while Dov slept in the next room. Standing in her doorway, she called to a boy collecting the spoils of the celebrations, the fallen coins and cigarette butts. The boy stuffed his findings in his pockets and scampered over. Yes, he said, he would like a secret mission. No, he would not make any detours or lose the brooch. Yes, he promised to go directly to Franz, waiting by the gate. Ziva watched the boy bicycle away, thinking, so this is what it feels like to be a coward.

Claudette sat on the edge of the visitor's chair, looking pensive. Ziva wondered if her regret had disappointed her.

"I suppose it might not sound like the most monstrous mistake to you. When you're young, you fear making these big mistakes. You don't realize how many of your deepest regrets are going to come down to a few words you wished you hadn't said, small things you wished you'd done or didn't do that would have made all the difference. If I could change those ten minutes . . . All I wish is that we'd had a proper goodbye. For years, I waited for a letter from America, so I could write to him, tell him what I just told you. But I never got a letter. I don't know why. Did he forgive me, love me, and not write because he knew that was the best thing he could do for me? Leave me alone? Or did he never write because he hated me, regretted having ever loved me, believed I never really loved him? Maybe it was neither of these things. Maybe he simply forgot about me. I could have spared myself decades of wondering. I could have given the time we had together the dignity it deserved. If I had just looked him in the eye that night and said, 'Goodbye, Franz. I am going to miss you.'"

Claudette removed her hand from her mouth. "It was a brooch?"

"What? Oh, yes. A brooch."

"With a big blue stone in the middle?"

Ziva didn't remember describing the brooch to her. Had she? It was impossible to deny that once in a while, like now, she did feel a little confused. Was it possible she had heard about the brooch from Adam? Did she know the boy was Franz's grandson? Ziva spoke carefully, waiting to see what Claudette knew.

"Yes, a sapphire. It had many jewels, but the sapphire was the largest. To be honest, I thought the brooch was hideous, absolutely hideous, with all its showy gems and gold busyness. It was difficult to stomach how much time and devotion went into—what? A useless object. A glorified safety pin. Didn't even work as well as a safety pin. I would have tried to convince Franz to give it to the kibbutz, so we could sell it and do something meaningful, but it would have been a waste of time. He was enamored with the thing. Absurdly sentimental about it."

To Ziva's relief, Claudette asked no more questions. She didn't know Claudette was waiting for her to fall asleep so she could run and tell Adam that she had found his Dagmar. It had occurred to Claudette to tell Ziva that Franz's grandson was on the kibbutz, but it seemed more romantic to let him tell her. She would have to get to him soon, though, while Ziva was coherent. Who knew what she would be like tomorrow?

Claudette went to the kitchen to fill a pitcher with water, leaving Ziva alone with her thoughts. The boy likely had the answer to that question she'd been carrying all these years. Judging by the bitter way he asked for Dagmar's whereabouts, it was probably the answer she didn't want to hear, that Franz had hated her. But why would the boy need to tell her that? And was that truly the answer she had feared most? No. What she had feared most was Franz forgetting her; and his grandson's search meant at least that hadn't happened. Though wouldn't that have been the best thing for Franz? You see, love did make one selfish. It had probably been selfish of her not to give the boy his say.

Ziva didn't fall asleep after lunch as she normally did. She remained alert, staring out the window. As more and more people came to vote, the pain of the present edged out the pain of the past. She squinted against the sunlight to see who was entering the dining hall. Claudette listened to her worry aloud.

"Why would they vote to end the kibbutz? They wouldn't, would they? I've probably been nervous all these months for nothing."

It was only after the sun had gone down and Ziva had swallowed her evening painkiller that she dozed off, allowing Claudette to rise from the visitor's chair and tiptoe out of the bedroom. As soon as Claudette was out of the apartment, she broke into a run. She darted through the voters gathered in the square and across the dark lawn and down the stepping-stones toward Adam's glowing window.

Ziva sat with the back of her bed raised high, watching the late-night news in the dark. The annoying red ticker at the bottom of the screen showed 11:21 p.m. She had awoken from sleep just as the ballot box was closing, over an hour and a half ago now. Eyal had promised he would bring her the verdict as soon as he completed the tally. He understood the rest of the kibbutz could wait until morning, but not her. So where was he?

After a segment on the fat-free fad sweeping America, the handsome anchorman announced breaking news: the Nobel Peace Prize this year would be going to Yitzhak Rabin, Shimon Peres, and Yasser Arafat. Ziva hurriedly increased the volume. *Nobel committee member Kaare Kristiansen quit rather than be a part of giving a peace prize to Arafat, whom he called the "world's most prominent terrorist," but many Israelis welcome the news.*

The broadcast cut to a young crowd waving PEACE NOW flags in Tel Aviv. A reporter interrupted revelers for their thoughts. A girl with a hoop in her nose talked excitedly under the blanching camera lights. "Who do you think you make peace with? Your friends? No, you make peace with your enemy."

Ziva switched off the TV and sat in the dark. What to think? Had the Arabs really, finally, accepted the existence of Israel? Did they no longer want to get rid of the Jewish state? It was hard to believe, but she would never know. She wouldn't be here to find out. The next century, whatever it held, didn't hold it for her. She closed her eyes. She liked having her whole life contained in one century. The divisions between centuries just fell where they fell, it probably didn't mean much, but still, she liked it.

Born in 1915, during the first winter of the Great War, and dying now in the autumn of 1994, she was the twentieth century. Some people, like her mother or Claudette, straddled centuries, like immigrants, starting in one and ending in another, never fully belonging to either. The twentieth century, it seemed to her, had been the darkest and brightest in human history. Did everyone feel that way about their era? Or had hers been particularly dramatic?

"Ima."

She opened her eyes.

"How long have you been standing there?"

He held an accordion file in his thick fingers. The muted lamplight coming through the window glowed on his bald head and left the bags under his eyes in shadow. She didn't know what to make of his hangdog expression—had he won or lost? She could never tell with her son: he never made a decision and then got on with it. He always wasted energy second-guessing and grieving over what had to be compromised.

"Well?" she said. "Spare me and spit it out already."

"It was close." Eyal considered one last time lying to his mother. She was dying. He could tell everyone to keep the truth from her, and she would leave this world believing her life had been a triumph.

Ziva smacked her hand down on the bed. "*Nu?* Do you enjoy torturing me?"

It had crossed her mind that Eyal might lie, but the fear hadn't lasted a second. Her son might be a lot of things—maybe even a capitalist—but he wasn't a liar. How many times could he have saved himself in the middle of one of their long and loud arguments by fibbing to her? He never did. In almost fifty years, she never, not once, had to stop and wonder if he was being truthful. She hadn't realized this until a few days ago, and so she hadn't valued it all these years. She wished she had.

Eyal held the files against his chest, like a shield. "Differential incomes."

Differential incomes. Ziva shriveled at the antiseptic sound of it. It had all the passion found in the teeny print no one bothered to read at the foot of a legal form. She would've preferred if her victors had marched through her bedroom, brandishing signs, blowing horns in her face. To be told she had failed in such a lifeless way made the defeat all the more defeating, as if what she had fought for her whole life hadn't been worthy of a passionate enemy.

"So we're not a kibbutz anymore?"

Eyal shook his head. "Not really."

She turned away. "It was all for nothing?"

She hadn't been asking him, but Eyal said, "No, Ima! You know the kibbutzim were crucial. You know that. Communism failed, but Israel wouldn't be here if it weren't for you and the other pioneers."

Ziva gazed through the window at the empty square. "All for nothing."

Eyal sat down in the visitor's chair without turning on a light. He watched his mother's head drop. She said nothing more. It was the first time he had seen her defeated. His whole life he had wanted to make her proud of him, and now, on her deathbed, he managed to disappoint her more than he would have thought possible. Her silence was as loud as any death knell. He had prepared for hours of accusations, questions about the future, vows to keep on fighting, for a barrage of her favorite socialist zingers. Had he and his mother already had their last quarrel? He struggled to think of what it was. Oh yes, two days ago, they had been debating charging people to use the pool, which badly needed repairs. *Unthinkable*, she had said, pounding her bed with a jaundiced fist. *We can't have some children able to swim and others not.* Eyal couldn't believe their arguments were done. The chance for them to make their relationship right was over.

He picked up the pomegranate on her nightstand and turned it in his hands. What was there to say to his mother now? "Who brought you this, Ima?"

Ziva glanced at the fruit. "Claudette."

He fingered its thorny crown. "I couldn't deal with this today, but she will have to leave the kibbutz. Apparently she's been sleeping with Ofir, and his mother's going out of her mind. She wants to press charges, but he's seventeen, over the age of legal consent."

Ziva recalled that walk in the rain, when Claudette confessed to never having kissed anyone, and she had told her she must try it. So she had, and more. Over the last few months the girl had gained all the life force she had lost. She was happy for her friend. Her first friend, she thought, since Dov.

She shook her head. "People busy themselves with the stupidest things. He's seventeen. When I was his age . . . ach, forget it."

Eyal had long ago decided that he would never ask. But maybe because they had nothing else left to speak about, or perhaps because he knew he would never have another chance to ask it, he did. "Ima, I know people busy themselves with the stupidest things, talk nonsense, but over the years, with so much, you know, talk, I couldn't help but . . . but wonder if there wasn't some truth to the story about Dov not being my father."

His mother regarded him with an unreadable expression. Since he hadn't planned on asking tonight, he hadn't imagined her reaction. When he had imagined it years ago as a teenager, he had pictured her exclaiming, "What *shtuyot*!" but tonight, she looked confused, undecided.

He wiped his sweaty palms on his jeans. "Ima, I don't care. I won't be mad. After all, I never knew Dov or any dad. I'm just curious, I guess. Was he? Or was it somebody else?"

It had been so many years since Ziva had given it any real thought. When the boy was born, she figured the father's identity would become obvious as he grew to look like one or the other, but with his round face, strong nose, close-set hazel eyes, and, before the balding, thick, curly, brown hair, he looked like her. As the years passed, she came to like the uncertainty. Not knowing made either scenario equally true: Dov had a child born in the fledgling Jewish state, and there was a human being who was a mixture of her and Franz.

"Never mind." Eyal retreated from her silence. "It's not important."

Ziva closed her eyes, and Eyal assumed she was trying to escape him, but he was wrong. She was considering whether it were even possible for him to be Dov's son. Twelve years she had slept with Dov every Shabbat and never gotten pregnant, and then Franz came along, and after two years, despite being careful about timing their encounters, she was carrying a child. Often, Dov didn't even climax. He would try, because he was a trier, but eventually he would roll off, exhausted, and, with a hand on her shoulder, kiss her on the cheek, as if to say it didn't matter, that he enjoyed loving her anyway. Many many many years later, when such things were talked about, when Rock Hudson died of that new disease and the front page of the newspaper showed a picture of two men walking with their hands in each other's back pocket, she had wondered and dismissed and wondered again and decided no: it was just that they were best friends, not lovers; or maybe Dov simply wasn't a sexual person; or perhaps it was the culture of the kibbutz at fault, its belief that sex was a necessary but lowly distraction. Only then, she would catch herself wondering again and dealing with the devastating idea that all those years they'd been together,

Dov had been suffering inside, suffering alone, that she hadn't been there for her best friend. But how could she have possibly guessed? They were running away from the old, effeminate Jew; they were the strong New Jews. The outside world, Berlin, Tel Aviv, New York, had deviance, but sociologists would actually come to the kibbutz to study their impressive lack of criminals and drug addicts and homosexuals. It would have been so unthinkable that Dov, the kibbutz's strongest, bravest pioneer, was a homosexual that maybe it had been unthinkable even to him.

Ziva opened her eyes, and Eyal shifted forward in his seat.

"I guess I'll go now, Ima. I have to go to Tel Aviv tomorrow morning to meet with the banks."

"Wait. I'll answer your question."

Eyal sat back again while Ziva told herself she didn't need to think about the past, the answer sat right in front of her. She studied her son more closely than she ever had before. It was strange looking for the young father in the middle-aged son, Eyal being at least fifteen years older than either Dov or Franz the last time she saw them. She considered his eyes, bloodshot from going over the kibbutz's budget night after night; often she would get up in the wee hours to go to the bathroom and see the light still on in his office. She contemplated his creased forehead and the groove between his eyebrows, lines etched over the seventeen years he had overseen the kibbutz, a job he compared to running around desperately plugging leaks in a giant roof about to collapse on hundreds of people. Those lips, pressed together, patiently awaiting the answer, she knew that stubborn little mouth well; ever since he was a boy, she had watched it argue, argue the most vexatious things, but passionately, inexhaustibly, caring deeply. Her gaze traveled down to the uneven shoulders, thanks to a collarbone break during the Six-Day War, when his jeep came under fire and rolled down a hill outside Jerusalem. Then there were the thick hands nervously gripping his thighs, the hands that had leafed through all the votes tonight. Nobody, despite Eyal's role in the referendum, had demanded a second person double-check his tally. He had counted alone. That was how much everyone, including her, trusted him.

A choke rose in Ziva's throat. She reached out a trembling hand.

Eyal, confused, looked behind him to see what she could be reaching for. He searched for a glass of water, a remote control, but saw nothing she might want. Had she slipped again into the past? The other day she had tried to tie a tent flap that was blowing in a long-gone wind.

Then he felt it—her hand on his. He froze, facing away from her. Did she think he was somebody else? He slowly turned around and found his mother beholding him as if for the first time. Her eyes were wet, and his welled up too. To ease the strain on her arm, he moved their clasped hands onto her bed. She squeezed his hand.

"You are Dov's son."

Ziva felt as she did that night Dov had cholera, when she realized that she loved him, but thought it was too late. Except this time it really was too late.

"If you had been anyone else's son, you would have left the kibbutz a long time ago. You would have gone off with that woman, taken care of yourself. Not stuck around and tried your best to save it. All these years."

Eyal's chest expanded so fast and wide it hurt. Maybe it was pathetic at his age, a half a century old, to be so happy that his mother took pride in him, but there it was.

"Thank you, Ima."

Ziva wanted to tell her son that she loved him, but even though this could very well be the last time she would ever see him, she couldn't. She gathered the breath for the words, but she couldn't say *I love you* on the night he ended the kibbutz. The air left her mouth carrying only the sour taste of medicine and the mucus collecting in her throat.

Eyal squeezed his mother's hand again as the pleasant realization came over him that life never stopped doling out surprises. Yes, they came less often than in one's youth—longer and longer interludes of uneventful life came between the surprises—but then, when they did come, they were all the more staggering and bittersweet.

"But make no mistake, my son, you have all just evicted yourselves from the Garden of Eden."

Eyal nodded, grateful for this last ember from his mother, the extinguishing firebrand. He continued to hold her hand, the way he had wanted to hold it when he was a little boy and she was the young woman on duty in the children's house. He held it until her grasp relaxed and her head fell to the side in sleep. Then he stood, picked up the folder of votes, and walked out, quietly closing the door behind him.

Ulya laid her hand on Adam's knee. They were sitting on his bed, Adam swilling the bottle of vodka she had brought him. This was the second night she'd come over with vodka. Adam had run out of money, and she knew it wouldn't help her if he were forced to sober up. Not to mention, he had stopped opening the door for her. This changed quickly when she started showing up with a bottle.

Adam eyed the hand traveling up his thigh. "What are you doing?"

She had no choice but to stoop to this. A week had passed since the rave, and she was lucky that Adam, who had called in sick for the second time in a row today, was still on the kibbutz. Eyal was probably too busy with the referendum to kick him off, but tomorrow the referendum would be over. Last night she had summoned the courage to try to take the brooch after Adam passed out. Terrified, she slowly, slowly inched her fingers into his pocket while he seemed dead to the world—dead until he suddenly smacked her arm away. It was so shocking and painful, she barely caught her scream in time. With a welt blooming on her arm, she had backed out of the room, unsure whether he had done this in his sleep or immediately fallen back to sleep and forgotten. Tonight, she had to get the pants off him before he passed out. And for that, she had to offer more than friendship.

"What do you think I'm doing?"

"Honestly, I don't know."

He didn't. He couldn't understand why she was stroking his thigh, bringing him gifts, bottles of vodka. If she wasn't into him when he was sober and a hell of a lot more fun to be around, why would she like him now? Was it the green card? In any case, she was wasting her time. When her hand reached his crotch, he closed his eyes to concentrate, but it was no use. She might as well have been rubbing someone else's dick.

He opened his eyes to take a swig and was confronted with Ulya's frustrated, even angry, expression. She was quick to replace it with an encouraging smile, but it was too late. He brushed her hand away. "It isn't you, Ulie. You know how much I wanted you. I'm just depressed."

Golda, curled up on the other bed, looked depressed too. He wasn't playful with her anymore. Poor little thing, she had hitched herself to the wrong wagon.

Ulya sat back on her heels and started unbuttoning her work shirt. He shook his head. "Seriously, it's no use."

She ignored him, working her way down her buttons. He watched. She dropped the shirt off her shoulders and hurried to hold it in front of her small belly. Adam ogled the swollen breasts, barely contained by the overstretched bra. A tiny white bow was recessed between two swells of nylon stretched to such sheerness it looked as if the pink nipples might poke through. Ulya had to laugh at his dumbstruck expression because even she found their current fullness titillating. She arched her back to undo the clasp.

Adam smiled, sadly, one corner of his lips turned down. "You wouldn't even kiss me. I tried to kiss you . . ."

"Forget before. I'm letting you kiss me now."

She leaned forward, balancing on her arms, breasts hanging beneath her. Adam hardly seemed to be breathing, but the little air puffing out of him smelled so bad it brought her back to the filthy drunks who used to hang around the railway station, begging for *vobla*. She pushed through her nausea and planted her mouth on his. Cold. His lips were disturbingly cold. When she pulled back her face, Adam noticed for the first time a black freckle under one of her eyes.

She took his hand, the one not holding the bottle, and placed it on her breast. He appreciated the weight in his palm, the knob of nipple. Pressing his fingers into the flesh, he felt a stir in his groin. He let her take the bottle and set it on the bedside table. She kissed him again.

Ulya struggled to decide which would be less repulsive: his cock in her mouth or in her vagina. Both prospects sickened. Most tolerable would have been to lie on her stomach, bury her face in a pillow, and let him do his thing while she daydreamed that she was already hurrying down the dark country road with the brooch. But Adam was never going to wake up and take the helm. He lay like a saggy pouch of yogurt. It was a lot harder to have unwanted sex when you were the one doing all the work.

She brought her face to his fly. Adam still didn't get why she was doing this, but every button she opened made him a little hornier and more forgetful. Nothing compared to the forgetfulness of arousal, better than booze even. It wasn't always available like booze, and it didn't last long, but while it did, the amnesia was more complete.

To Ulya's revulsion, Adam wore no underwear. She freed his warm, half-flaccid cock and put it in her mouth. She sucked, thankful that at least he didn't have Farid's massive thatch of hair with its smell of dank soil. Bobbing up and down, she imagined herself out on that country road, the kibbutz gate behind her.

Adam swelled in her mouth. He groaned and clutched the hair on the back of her head. She groaned too, pretending this was a turn-on, and gripped the sides of his jeans. She tugged them down to his hips. This was working. Repulsive, but working. She pulled the jeans down to his thighs. Almost there.

A knock at the door.

She tried to ignore it. Was it Eyal come to kick him off? Now? Please no. Please let this person go away. Adam seemed to be trying to disregard it too. To help him with that, she cupped his balls in her hand, sucked more enthusiastically.

The knocks got louder and longer, causing Golda to run and bark at the door.

Adam pushed Ulya's head away. As he hiked up his jeans, she wiped the saliva from her face with the bed sheet. Her heart pounded from the humiliation, the anger. She searched for her bra, couldn't find it, and hurried to button on her shirt while the knocking intensified.

Adam called out. "All right, all right! Coming!"

He chugged vodka and staggered for the door, remembering when Bones's messengers would come knocking, how he would step into the hallway so Zayde wouldn't hear. Like Ulya, Adam figured this was Eyal, or one of his messengers, here to walk him to the gate. And so what? He didn't need to stay on the kibbutz anymore. He was never going to find Dagmar. He opened the door.

"Claudette?" This was the person pounding like that? "What's the big panic? Is Jesus back?"

Golda ceased barking and stood beside Adam, still his faithful body-guard. Ulya rose from the bed, ready to kill.

Catching her breath, Claudette said, "It's the old woman I work for! Ziva! She's Dagmar!"

Adam didn't understand. Couldn't. Maybe he was too drunk.

Claudette tried again. "She's the one your grandfather tried to give the brooch to."

Adam shook his head. "No, it's not possible. I asked her. I sat in her apartment and asked her."

"Was your grandfather's name Franz?"

Adam turned back to his room, eyes darting around, at first in shock, then increasingly as if looking for something, someone, to punch. He grabbed the bottle from the bedside table. All this time, she had been *right there*. Dagmar had sat in front of him on a bench, fucking inches from him, and asked how his search was going. What kind of psycho did that? He had known something was off about her. He fucking knew it. That fucking bitch—if she had told him the truth, he wouldn't be in this room right now chugging vodka. He would be at home, in the apartment, sober and several months into his new life. He wiped his mouth and threw the emptied bottle at the garbage, knocking the plastic bin over.

Claudette edged into the room. "You need to come see her. Now."

"Now?" Adam laughed. "Fuck you, and fuck her."

Dizzy, Adam leaned on the dresser. Ulya hurried over. She had to keep him from going to the old lady. If he left to give her the brooch now, she would never get it. She rubbed his back. "Yes, fuck her. If she needed to talk to you so bad, she wouldn't have lied to you."

Claudette clasped her hands, crept toward Adam. "You said your grand-father never stopped loving her. She should hear that. But you have to go tell her now, because she's coherent tonight. She might not be coherent tomorrow. She might . . . she might not even be . . ."

"Be what?" Ulya bore her eyes into Claudette. "Alive? Please, the woman isn't dying *tonight*. You're crazy! We all know, everybody knows, that you're crazy, Claudette."

Adam rubbed his forehead. He couldn't think. He needed to think. He didn't want to give the brooch to the lying bitch. But what else could he do? Keep it? Put it back in the Florsheim shoebox like nothing happened? Donate it to a museum as Mr. Weisberg had wanted him to, so some strangers could give it a glance and forget about it? He had set out to give it to the only person Zayde had deemed worthy, and he could still do that.

"Fine, I'll go." He had trouble moving his mouth around the words and could hear he was slurring. "Just give me a second to calm down."

"All right." Claudette sat on the unused bed. "I'll wait."

"You don't need to fucking wait!" Adam stood over her. "I know exactly where she lives."

After Claudette left, Adam stood waiting for the room to stop wheeling around him. Whenever the world spun like this, he thought of the Rotor ride on Coney Island. Once a summer Zayde would take him on the N train all the way out to the amusement park on the seashore, where he would claim to be too old for such nauseating rides and would wait, holding Adam's baseball cap, while Adam rushed up to the Rotor three or four times in a row. Round and round the rotor would go with the promise that any second the floor would drop.

He bent over, swiped his Converses off the ground.

"Wait!" Ulya grabbed the shoes from his hands.

Standing up too fast, Adam saw gray speckles, like TV static. He squeezed his eyes and opened them again. "What? What are you doing?"

She held his rancid sneakers behind her back. "It's stupid to give the old lady the brooch. You heard Claudette, she's going to die soon, maybe in a few days—and then what? Your family's brooch will go to the kibbutz. Or—oh my God—Eyal! You hate Eyal."

He didn't hate Eyal, not after he gave him a second chance. That didn't mean he loved the idea of the brooch ending up in his fat fist, but that was beyond his control. What Dagmar did with the brooch was on her conscience. "I don't care. I have to get it to her."

"Why?"

"Please . . ." Adam fumbled for his shoes. "Give those back."

"Why? Tell me why you have to give this old bitch the brooch."

"Because I promised myself, okay? After Zayde died, I fucking promised myself I would get the brooch into the right hands."

Ulya's mouth dropped. "What? You mean, you didn't promise *him*? Your grandfather? You only promised *yourself*?"

"It's still a promise. I'm tired of not keeping my promises."

Adam lunged for his sneakers, and the walls and floor lunged with him. He stumbled, then forced himself to stand straight, but this time the walls didn't follow, or followed too slowly. He was going to be sick. He staggered for the bed and sat with his head hanging between his knees.

Ulya sat beside him, resting her hand on his back. "Adam, why do you have to give the old woman the brooch?"

His voice was muffled. "Because it would make me feel better."

"Why would it make you feel better?"

He raised his head. His face was bright, his eyes glossy. He was on the verge of tears. A grown man crying, it disgusted Ulya. Why did he feel so sorry for himself? He could hardly be luckier. He was free. He was a man. He had American citizenship, an apartment in Manhattan. He didn't have to run away from his country, leave his family, not knowing whether he was ever going to see them again. He wasn't told he couldn't get pregnant and then got pregnant. He was his own biggest problem.

She wrapped her arm around his shoulders. "Just tell me, Adam. Why are you doing this? What do you want?"

Adam's face crumpled. He took the brooch out of his pocket, and Ulya's insides lurched. Gazing at it in his hands, Adam sobbed so hard he had to gasp for breath. His nose pinched and whitened while the rest of his face blotched under a film of tears. Snot poured over his lips. In a high voice, barely getting the word out between the gasps for air, he said: "L-l-l-love."

"What?"

"I w-w-want l-l-love."

Ulya tightened her arm around Adam, not only to keep him from going to the old lady, but because, to her surprise, she felt pity for him. As he gulped, chest heaving, she stared down at the brooch. Could she really take it from him? He said he would kill himself if he lost it, and now she suspected that might be true. But then, what was he going to do if he got to keep it?

And then she had a revelation. A stunning one. Not only could she take the brooch, she should. Never mind Adam's pain. Never mind her selfish wants. She should have the brooch—objectively. If she were a stranger looking at this from the outside, it would be obvious that out of all the people the brooch could go to, it should go to her. Who else? Adam would soon lose it somewhere or pawn it for booze. The old lady was days from the coffin, if not hours. Her son would give it to the kibbutz, which would divide its value amongst its hundreds of members, leaving each kibbutznik a hundred dollars or so. A hundred dollars didn't change a person's life. She was the only person whose life could be transformed by the brooch. *Her* hands were "the right hands."

She said, "I can love you."

Adam had calmed some. His chest shook, but he no longer wheezed for air. He still couldn't believe Ulya, didn't see how her loving him was possible, but it felt so good to hear those words.

"Say it again."

Ulya thumbed a tear from under his eye, telling herself that she had nothing to do with this pain of his, if anything she was alleviating it for a bit. "I can love you, Adam."

"Again." He chewed his bottom lip. "Take out the *can*."

Ulya drew a deep breath. This was worlds harder than anything she'd ever had to do in the past to steal. And that was fair, she supposed. It was worth worlds more.

"I love you, Adam."

Adam closed his eyes, while she kissed his hot, wet cheek. His temple. She could tell she wasn't going to have to go near his penis again. Sex wasn't what was keeping him here. She draped an arm around the front of his chest, and brought her mouth to his ear. "I love you."

Adam felt her pushing him back, felt his head landing on the bed. He should go to Dagmar now. He really should. Even if she was a fucking liar.

Ulya glanced at the brooch, still between his index fingers and thumbs, resting on his stomach. She lay down next to him. "I love you, Adam."

Adam couldn't believe she was saying it again and again. Like a dream. Maybe he was dreaming? Had he already fallen asleep? If not, he should get up and go. Right now.

As Ulya kept whispering "I love you," waiting for Adam to pass out, she again pictured herself hurrying down that country road—maybe in just a few minutes—and it occurred to her with a shock of excitement that she didn't know—not for sure—which direction she would walk once she got to the bottom of that road. Maybe she wouldn't walk toward the Arab village after all. Maybe she would walk in the opposite direction, toward Haifa, where she could catch a bus to the diamond district in Tel Aviv. The brooch would provide her with more than enough money for a nice hotel while she got an abortion, a flight to New York, a green-card husband. Though she wouldn't even get to say goodbye to Farid.

Adam's breathing deepened, evened. Had he fallen asleep? She was afraid to say *I love you* again and afraid not to. What was more likely to disturb him? She gently lifted her head. His hands had relaxed, palms resting down on his stomach, the fingers surrounding the brooch, but no longer touching it. It was there for the plucking. Should she go for it now? Move too soon, she might wake him up; wait too long, and he could rouse on his own, feeling better, the chance lost.

She would wait until she was ready to run out of the room before going for the brooch. The last thing she wanted was to be caught with it in her hand and face that violence in his eyes again, especially when he was so drunk. Careful not to disturb the mattress, she held her breath and curled up to a sitting position. Then, feet on the ground, she leaned forward inch by inch, imperceptibly rising off the bed. Once again, she was a performer without an audience. Controlling her body like a dancer.

She stood over Adam, lying so peacefully. She had a flash of how he would feel tomorrow morning when he woke up. She pushed the thought from her mind. She had to concentrate. She bent forward and prepared her fingers around the brooch.

One . . . two . . . three.

She closed her fingers on it. The plan had been to gently lift the brooch from his stomach, but her hand trembled too much. She jerked her hand up, and held the brooch an inch above his body, waiting, watching his face.

He didn't move.

Now she had to get out of here. Fast. Silently. She tiptoed for the door, leaving her sandals by his bed. The little dog slept on the other bed, its eyes two black slits. She softly pressed down on the door handle and slipped outside.

She bolted across the quad for her room. The Russian guys around the picnic table watched her curiously, the same guys she used to dread teasing her about Farid. Farid—she did love him, but in twenty years, when she was a middle-aged woman still living in Israel, would she regret it? The idea of never seeing him again broke her heart, but this didn't tell her what she should do. She knew she would miss her mother, but she still left Mazyr.

She flung open her door and charged for her dresser. No time to make a decision now. She had to get out of here. Hurling T-shirts out of the drawer, she fished out her Israeli passport and stuffed it with the brooch in her purse. She slipped on her work boots—she needed to be able to run—and hurried to tie the laces while glancing at the door, frightened that any second Adam would break through it.

She couldn't leave, however, without her most prized possession. She yanked the old suitcase from under the bed and rushed to unsnap it. There it was, not a golden family heirloom, but still.

As Ulya left the room, clutching her magazine, she didn't know which way she would walk when she reached the junction at the bottom of the hill. She would only know for sure when she got there.

dam woke up to Golda licking his cheek. It was early in the morning, the light soft. He lay on his back, brain thumping against his skull, stiff from sleeping with his legs hanging off the bed. He sat up, a feeling of alarm coming over him before the reason why. He felt an absence against his thigh. He jumped to his feet, dug his hand into his pocket. No. Why were Ulya's sandals on the floor? No, no. He tore the blanket from the bed, shook the sheets. Ulya's bra fell out.

He ran in his stockinged feet for her room, thinking, she better be there, she better be there. The door wasn't locked, not a good sign. He threw it open and found her dresser drawers hanging ajar, shirts flung all over the floor. The ratty blue suitcase lay open, empty. His heart pounded behind his eyes. He buckled over, leaning on his knees. The vomit came out in staggered spurts like water from a rusty pipe. The clear puke puddled on the ground, specked with dark beans of blood.

Claudette, returning from Ofir's, found Adam lying on the floor next to the vomit. She crouched beside him. "Adam? Adam, are you all right?"

He hugged his legs into his chest and buried his face into his knees as if trying to curl himself into nonexistence.

"What's wrong? Should I get a doctor?"

"It's gone."

"What's gone?"

When he didn't answer, Claudette laid her hand on his shoulder, something she never would have been able to do a few months ago. "What's gone, Adam?"

"I can't give it to Dagmar now. The cunt stole it."

Claudette took in the chaos of the room, and the understanding sank in that her roommate had taken the brooch in the same way she had stashed that bottle of shampoo into her work shirt. How could she do it? To Adam? To a dying woman? Only the brooch didn't matter to Ziva, did it? She didn't even like it.

"You don't need the brooch to go to Dagmar. She only needs to hear that your grandfather didn't hate her."

Adam pushed Claudette's hand off him. All for a drunk fuck. No, wait. Did he even fuck her? He remembered her breath in his ear, the whispered "I love you." It was so pathetic. He had traded the brooch his family had safeguarded for seven hundred years to pretend for a minute that someone loved him.

"I can't."

"Please, Adam. Go now. It can't wait until tomorrow."

Tomorrow—the idea of it made him want to throw up again. Another night followed by another morning and another night and another morning. "Leave me alone! Please!"

"I think it will—"

Claudette stopped midsentence when Adam started convulsing as if he were caught in an electrical current. The spasms intensified. He rolled onto his back and shuddered, hands opening and closing, head shaking. His eyes bulged. He sucked air through his nose in loud snores, and white spittle foamed at his mouth.

"Adam! What should I do?" Claudette wanted to run for a doctor but was afraid to leave him. "What should I do?"

Adam coughed, and the shaking calmed. He hacked, trying to clear his chest. Then he sat up. Breathing heavily, shiny with sweat, he looked around in confusion.

Claudette kneeled in front of him. "You had a fit."

"What?" His voice was small, childlike.

"You had a fit."

He squeezed his eyes, wiped his mouth. "Now?"

"Yes. Is there anything I can do?"

"Get me something to drink."

"Water?"

"No. Alcohol. Please. It'll make it stop."

"From where?"

"I don't know. But please. If you get me something, I'll go to Ziva."

Waiting for Claudette to return, Adam sat on the floor, back against the bed, eyes on the faded lilac lining of Ulya's old suitcase. How many people had owned this suitcase before her? Had it been packed for a long-ago honeymoon? An out-of-town funeral? Zayde dancing with his imaginary partner: that's what the lining looked like to him. How much time and place and loss and regret could be packed into one life? He was too weak for it. He didn't care how low he was on the suffering scale. Life came with so much fucking pain, even the bare minimum—level one and a half—was asking too much.

Claudette rushed in with a bottle of vodka. "I got this from Eugene."

Adam took the bottle—only a quarter full but better than nothing—twisted off the top, and chugged. The warmth hit his stomach, soothed his trembling. When the numbness reached his head, he used the bed to push onto his feet. "Let's go."

They stopped by his room for his shoes, and he grabbed the goodbye letter. Golda tagged along as they climbed the steppingstones. They walked alongside the dining hall's wall of windows in silence, just like they did that first morning after the interview in Eyal's office. Adam kept his head turned so he wouldn't have to see his reflection.

Claudette opened Ziva's front door and blocked Golda with her foot. She led Adam through the quiet of the apartment. Adam's hand came up to pat his hair, but then, realizing what he was doing, he stopped. Styling his hair, that was hilarious.

When they entered the bedroom, the old women didn't turn from the window to greet them. The air was stuffy with death and the talcy smell of old age. As they approached her bed, Adam waited to see the old woman's expression when she laid eyes on him. Would she still feign ignorance? He would have thought he'd feel more hate in the presence of the old liar. Last night he would've, but this morning, all his hate was consumed on himself. There wasn't much left even for Ulya.

They reached the edge of her bed without Ziva registering them. Claudette was shocked to see how much she had deteriorated overnight, more in one night than in all the weeks she'd been bedridden. Was it because of the results of the referendum? She looked dead already, staring vacantly out the window, yellowed cheeks collapsing into her half-opened mouth. Her breath rasped in her throat.

Claudette gently laid a hand on her wrist. "Ziva."

Ziva turned and glared at Claudette as if she were stranger, one who had no business laying a hand on her. Her eyes then drifted, confusedly, fearfully, until they alighted on Adam. Her face lit up.

"Franz?"

Claudette's heart sank. This wasn't a coherent day. With the way Ziva looked, she feared there would never be another one.

Adam could almost laugh. After months of denying she knew his grandfather, now she thought he was him? "I'm Adam, his grandson. Remember me? The guy you've been lying to?"

Ziva furrowed her brow and looked to Claudette for an explanation. Claudette leaned forward and enunciated each word as if that made a difference. "This is Franz's grandson. From New York."

A perplexed expression remained on Ziva's face, and Claudette turned to Adam. "I'll wait outside. Hopefully her memory will come back for a second."

As Adam listened to Claudette leave, he avoided the old woman's eyes. He wasn't sure why he had agreed to come. To confess how his grandfather had died? To explain how he lost the brooch last night? The front door closed with a thud. He wiped his brow, the sweat smelling of alcohol.

"I came here, all the way from New York . . ."

"New York." Ziva nodded with a small smile. "That's where I always pictured you. While working in the fields, I would often wonder what you were doing at that exact moment on the other side of the world, and I always pictured New York City."

"I'm not Franz. I'm his grandson," said Adam, causing Ziva to eye him as if he might be playing a trick on her. Unsure how to tell his story, he started again. "I know you know how much my grandfather's brooch meant to him. He kept it . . ."

She interrupted once more, this time as if suddenly realizing where she was. "You're Franz's grandson. The one with the little dog."

"Yes, Dagmar. Why have you been lying to me?"

Ziva closed her eyes and let the "Yes, Dagmar" echo in her head. No one had called her Dagmar in fifty years. She saw Franz in his brown fedora, the way he would wear it on Saturdays when they would walk in the hills, the iridescent green feather stuck in the black band. She wouldn't let them rest until they had reached a peak with a view of the valley, and he would tease her, saying, "Yes, Dagmar. Of course, Dagmar. Dagmar won't rest until she gets to the peak."

Ziva chuckled and opened her eyes. "Remember that time we came back too late for dinner, and you snuck into the kitchen and ate all the cherry jam? The whole jar, meant for the children! I was furious. And an hour later, while you were rolling around with a stomachache, you had the chutzpah to say that I didn't understand, because I didn't love cherries like you did. I didn't appreciate the *wonder of cherries*. Who do you think planted those cherry trees?"

Adam nodded, sadly. At last here was a memory about his grandfather. "Yes, he did love jam. Especially marmalade. Ate it every morning. Not me, my grandfather."

Ziva scowled at him. "I know that! I meant your grandfather."

Adam dug his hand into his pockets, felt the emptiness. "I wanted to give you the brooch. That's why I was trying to find you."

Ziva looked down. "Why would you give me the brooch?"

"It's a long story, which I'll tell you if you want, but, in short, it would've made me feel better."

She shook her head. "I never understood that. Why it would make you feel better. Your mother doesn't know you went back for it. She can't know. And the brooch doesn't care who pins it on. It can't tell if it's in the *wrong hands*, as you say. It's just an object."

"Just an object?"

"Yes. And not even a useful one."

This, from the woman he had desperately tried to give it to. The woman whose goodbye letter sat in a felt bag with the brooch for half a century. Not only was she rejecting it a second time, but she was professing that it should have no importance to anybody.

"You're wrong, Dagmar. And I'm not Franz."

Ziva hated the way the boy kept correcting her. "I know who you are, young man!"

"I wanted to give you the brooch because, whether you deserved it or not, you were the only person Zayde—Franz—ever wanted to have it. He died with this in his hand."

Ziva regarded the paper Adam held out to her with wariness before shakily reaching for it. She unfolded the delicate note, hands shuddering so much Adam feared she would rip it. Lean, slanted cursive. Her old handwriting—so familiar and shocking. She felt the same disorientation she did when confronted with old photographs. On the kibbutz's fiftieth anniversary, Eyal had posted pictures in the dining hall of the early years, pictures of bright-eyed, plump-faced people she had grown accustomed to seeing with deflated cheeks and sunken eyes. She held the note at arm's length.

Mein liebster Liebling Franz.

She drew a sharp breath. Adam, seeing her pain, lowered his eyes.

Her cowardly note. She had been right to fear what the boy had in store for her. *My dearest darling Franz.* She remembered writing those words, feeling like they weren't her kind of words, that they were too trite for the occasion, and yet she couldn't come up with better ones. It seemed impossible to her not to sound hackneyed when it came to love since love was something everybody did, even the laziest and most ordinary of people, probably especially them. She had loathed how conventional love was, but now, faced with the *liebster Liebling* she had penned so long ago, she knew her nostalgia was just as conventional, as commonplace as old age itself, and she didn't care. It was powerful.

Adam said, "I don't know how you can say an object's just an object when that's clearly not true. I don't know if something—an energy or whatever—sticks to a thing, if it soaks up meaning every time something happens to it, or what. But it's impossible to say that that brooch was just a brooch."

Ziva tried to clear her throat, but she couldn't swallow. The mucus clogging her chest made her breathing sound like a low roar. She knew what she was hearing: her own death rattle. She didn't want to die under this ceiling, palish gray like a cloudy morning sky. Would she ever be under the sky again? It was quiet in the room, just the uneasy presence of the young man and the breeze blowing through the window and that low roar— waves coming in and out, lapping against the shore. Seagulls circled in the cloudy sky. What had the news reported the other day about seagulls? They found a fossil that was thirty-three million years old. For thirty-three million years gulls have circled the sky. It made Jerusalem seem young. It made her feel young.

She shook her head. "Objects, personal possessions. Please, Franz, I can't have this argument again. Not now."

Adam's shoulders dropped at her calling him Franz again. She had let go of the note, and it had tumbled onto the floor. He moved to retrieve it, but then didn't bother. What for? Who would be left to care about it? And what good would it do to correct the old woman again? He could tell her for the umpteenth time that he wasn't Franz but his grandson, or he could just say, *Okay, let's not argue.*

"Okay," he said. "Let's not argue."

Ziva turned to him and looked into his eyes. Adam felt uneasy but held her gaze. He stood by a deathbed in the musty building for old people, while Ziva stood on the wooden platform of the Haifa seaport as it might have been on the morning of November 30, 1947. The Mediterranean was as gray as the sky, except where the two met in a pale yellow ribbon on the horizon. Though overcast, it wasn't cold or likely to rain. An Arab peddler pushed a barrow of lychees past British soldiers in pith helmets. The waiting ship's striped exhauster resembled a giant barber pole.

"I made it just in time," she said. "I was afraid we wouldn't get to say a proper goodbye."

Adam didn't know how to respond. The old woman wasn't here with him, clearly, but where was she? Was she saying goodbye to his grandfather?

He mumbled, "I'm glad you made it."

Time: Ziva smelled it in the salty air. She heard loss in the roar of the waves, the squawking gulls. The wind blew through her hair with the heartache of choice. It was all so keen because she was thirty-three years old, an excruciating age, when the opposite ends of life tugged equally hard, tearing a person down the middle. She was young enough to still have choices, but old enough to feel their weight. Old enough to know loss, and young enough to still have so much left to lose. Old enough for goodbyes, but not so old that they didn't matter: decades were left to miss a person. The future stretched out like the sea.

"If you don't write to me, I'll understand it's because you don't want to interfere with my work here."

Adam nodded, still feeling awkward about pretending to be his grandfather. He hoped Claudette didn't walk in now. "Okay."

The steamship honked, and Adam's headache tapped on his temples and took hold of his teeth. He would need to drink something soon.

Ziva gripped the blanket. "You know that I loved you, don't you, Franz? That I didn't take us lightly?"

Adam tried to think: What would his grandfather want him to say? The woman had broken the man's heart, but he did die half a century later clutching her note.

"I loved you, too, Dagmar. All these years, I never forgot you."

Her thin lips quivered. "Goodbye, Franz."

Adam leaned forward and planted a kiss on the old woman's forehead. "Goodbye, Dagmar."

As he walked out the room, he felt her eyes on his back, on his young grandfather's back.

Outside, once again in the bright morning sunlight, he stormed past Claudette. He didn't know what he was going to do if the *kolbo* wasn't open yet. Golda scampered after him. Claudette followed him too—"Adam!"— but then, to his relief, she stopped.

He crossed the square, not knowing what to think about his encounter with Dagmar. He didn't get to give her the brooch, but maybe Claudette was right. Maybe he gave her something more valuable: one last chance to be with his grandfather. He never got to say goodbye to Zayde. Or his mom. He would do anything for that, wouldn't he? And the brooch . . . it was just an object. Adam, hearing his thoughts, felt sick. What was he doing? Rationalizing again. After everything—Zayde, Mr. Weisberg.

He glanced down at Golda, who was working her tiny legs double time to keep up with him.

"Why are you still following me?"

Golda trotted on, tail curled over her back.

Adam stopped, repeated: "Why the fuck are you following me?"

The little dog stopped too. Sitting back, she looked up at Adam with her big round eyes. He could see his towering reflection in them.

"You're following me because you don't know me. You love me because you don't know me. Now go! Get out of here!"

The large ears crumpled back.

"Go! Go!"

The little dog kept her eyes on Adam as she lowered her trembling head. Her whole body shook.

"Yeah, that's right!" he shouted. "Now you're getting it! You see? I'm a fucking asshole! So get out of here!"

The dog would not go, and Adam, as if to solidify once and for all what kind of asshole he was, pulled back his foot and kicked. He felt his toe make contact, saw the brown fur buckle around the dirty blue sneaker.

He turned for the store. Behind him came high-pitched yelps, but he walked on. He pulled on the chiming door and strode for the fridge. He grabbed two six-packs and headed back out, ignoring the cashier's "Hey!"

He carried the beers across the kibbutz's main lawn, the grass blowing in the September wind. He was going down. He hoped he went down so fast and hard that when he hit the pavement it broke every bone in his body. Especially his skull.

*C*laudette sat in the visitor's chair, watching Ziva sleep. The old woman dozed off after Adam left and hadn't opened her eyes in two hours. Her mouth hung open, the breath fighting its way in and out. Every so often the croak was so loud Claudette jumped to her feet, thinking Ziva was choking on her last breath. When another croak followed, she would sit down again in the hard plastic stacking chair. She hadn't noticed how uncomfortable this chair was when Ziva would tell her stories, but in the silence it grew ever more unbearable. At last, Claudette decided to drag over the armchair from the family room.

Unused now for over a month, this room with its WORKERS OF THE WORLD UNITE! banner exuded death even more than the one in which Ziva lay dying. Dust floated in the air and mantled the coffee table, but that wasn't what gave it its desolation. It was the feeling that Ziva would never sit on its green couch again, never record her thoughts on that pad of paper.

Claudette opened the window and held her face against the fresh air. Did she smell autumn? Not in the way her body expected it now, the smell of burning leaves that preceded the snow. If she stayed on the kibbutz through the winter, she wouldn't see any snow. No snow . . . She felt her first twinge of homesickness. She hadn't realized how much she loved the white heaps on the windowsills, the stacks balanced on the bare branches, the thrill of walking across a fresh blanket of snow, feet sinking into the powder.

Dragging the armchair across the floor, she paused before the old portrait of Dov. Head turned to the side, it looked like his clear eyes were staring into the future. Ziva loved Adam's grandfather, but she had also loved this man. She spoke of him with such pride and affection. Claudette didn't know what to make of that. Could she feel the way she did about Ofir for someone else? If she could, did that lessen what she felt for Ofir? She wiped the dust off Dov's portrait with her shirtsleeve and then did the same for young Ziva.

For hours Claudette sat in the armchair, hoping Ziva would come to, if only for a minute. Once in a while, the old woman moved her head, but without waking up. A red mottling had spread over her warped hands. Concerned, Claudette touched Ziva's hand and found it frighteningly cold. Wrapping her young, warm hand around the cold, bony one, she remembered how Ziva hadn't wanted to die in bed, head on a pillow.

Claudette leaned forward and rested her own head on the mattress, where the smell of laundry detergent mingled with the scent of Ziva's withering body. Was Ziva really on her way to Hell? What about Ofir? Surely he didn't deserve eternal damnation. And Dr. Gadeau and Sister Marie Amable? Were they assured a home in Heaven so long as they confessed their sins in time, said a few words with genuine feeling—but who wouldn't feel something genuine when faced with eternal damnation? No, she couldn't believe God would be so unfair. That is, if He existed. She desperately wanted to believe He did, but He still hadn't given her a sign. All she needed was a nod, a small nod that said, don't worry, Claudette, here I am. Why hadn't He sent it?

Ziva still hadn't stirred when Claudette walked over to the dining hall to fetch lunch. It was after two, and the only people left in the hall were the women removing the containers from the food bar. Claudette hurried to make do with what was still out: rice and turkey for her and a cup of chicken broth for Ziva, just in case. She carried the tray across the square, but once she was back in the room she found she had no appetite.

While the walls took on the golden glow of late afternoon, Claudette kept nodding off. She was exhausted from the night with Ofir, the stressful morning with Adam, and now this unbearable waiting. When she blinked, her eyes wouldn't open again, and she would immediately drop into a dream or nightmare. She dreamed she had to count the white hairs on Ziva's head or she would die. One hair, two hairs, three hairs. She lost count and would have to start again. One hair, two hairs . . .

Every time she forced her eyes open, she would panic and hurry to check that Ziva hadn't passed away. A rasping inhale and a feeble puff of breath on the back of Claudette's hand would flood her with relief. She still had her. If only for a little longer. For months, Claudette hadn't known what to make of this affection she felt for the old woman. What a broken person she must have been to not recognize friendship. She was losing her friend. Her only friend.

The sun had set when at last Claudette succumbed to the sleepiness. She curled up on the green armchair, resting her head on its worn back. Closing her eyes, she told herself this was only a brief nap. She drifted off to Ziva's faltering breaths. Life in. Life out. Life in, life out. In. Out.

"Claudette!"

Claudette opened her eyes. The room was dark, except for the pale light pouring through the window behind Ziva, who sat on the edge of her bed, legs dangling off the side, spindly arms holding her up. Hunched over, the collar of her nightdress hung open, exposing a laddered chest and withered breasts.

Claudette sprang out of the armchair. Was she dreaming? Had the old woman died and this was her ghost? The bedside clock glowed 4:48 a.m. She had fallen into a deep sleep, as she did that night she listened to Ofir. How could she have passed out like that? And how was Ziva sitting up? She hadn't sat up in weeks.

In a faint voice, Ziva said, "I need your help."

"Of course." Claudette hurried to help her lie back down. "What can I get you? Water? There's chicken broth here. Do you need to go to the bathroom?"

Claudette bent down to lift Ziva's bony legs back onto the bed, but the old woman shook her head.

"No," she whispered. "Take me to the fields."

"The fields?"

Ziva hoped Claudette wouldn't put up too much of a fight. She didn't have the strength to beg. "Please, Claudette. I can't get there on my own."

Claudette lowered her head to think. What would people say? Who would take a dying old woman out to the fields in the middle of the night? Because that old woman, half out of her mind for a week already, had asked her to? She could get hurt, fall on her bruised hip. Everyone would blame her, and rightly so. But if she didn't take her, Ziva would never see her fields again.

"I'll get you a sweater."

Ziva closed her eyes in relief.

Claudette returned with a brown cardigan and drew Ziva's cold arms through the sleeves. She wouldn't bother with pants; the nightgown was long enough. Draping Ziva's arm over her shoulders, she lifted her off the bed, slowly, afraid of causing her pain. The old woman's legs crumpled beneath her, but she was so light, Claudette managed to hold her up.

"Are you okay, Ziva?" she asked before starting the journey across the apartment. "Are you sure you want to do this?"

Ziva's whole body cried out in agony. And she was so tired. But she had to get to the fields. "Yes."

Claudette staggered toward the bedroom door, leaning heavily to the side, resting Ziva's weight against her. They entered the unlit family room, where the wind blew through the window Claudette had left open. Ziva stared at the portraits as they passed, and Claudette was glad she had dusted them off, allowing them to stare back.

The predawn was chilly, but Claudette didn't dare go back to get herself a sweater. She lowered Ziva onto the golf cart's low seat, hoping she would be able to start this machine and get them to the fields without crashing into a streetlamp. She'd never driven anything before, not even a bicycle. When she bent down to lift the old woman's feet onto the floorboard, she found bare feet with thick curling nails, the jaundiced skin covered with the same mottling as the hands. She had forgotten about shoes.

"I'm going to get you some slippers."

"No," she wheezed. "Let's go."

Claudette preferred not to leave Ziva alone, so she hurried around to the driver's seat. Looking over all the levers, buttons, and pedals, she tried to remember Eyal's demonstration. She flipped the red switch and the cart hummed to life. Now which pedal was go, which stop? Holding her breath, she pressed her foot on one, and the cart rolled forward, toward the apartment. She slammed on the other, and it lurched to a stop. She looked over to make sure Ziva was all right and found her looking better than she had in weeks, sitting straight-backed, chin raised, hand grasping a side rail. If not for the ghastly breathing, it would have seemed the old woman had made a miraculous recovery. Returning her attention to the controls, Claudette lowered a lever from F to R and tentatively pushed on the pedal again. The cart trundled backward onto the path.

After that, driving the cart was easy. She might have even found it fun under different circumstances. They rolled across the quiet square. The round streetlamps glowed here and there, but otherwise the kibbutz was in slumber. The cool air carried the faint hum of the factory and the sweet, earthy smell of cow manure. Hopefully she could drive Ziva out to the fields and back again without anyone seeing them. A hem of lighter sky ran along the tops of the pines.

As they drove, Claudette suppressed the urge to keep asking Ziva how she was doing. She understood the old woman was taking everything in for the last time. They circled around the bomb-shelter bar and rolled along the back of the *kolbo* and the dining hall. They drove past the car lot and then the laundry house, a lace tablecloth hanging beneath its tin awning. They followed the windbreak of cedars that separated the white houses from the fields below. Ziva saw all this, but also the earlier versions of these buildings, and before that the tents, and before that the dry, rocky hill she and Dov and the others saw that first morning they arrived with their bags and one truck of supplies.

After the swimming pool, Claudette turned the cart onto the dirt road that descended into the fields. They jostled past the corroded steel sign— KIBBUTZ SADOT HADAR, 30 GOOD YEARS, 1933–1963—and through the open gates, draped with bougainvillea. Only a couple of weeks ago, there would have been workers in the fields at this hour, putting in the time before the punishing summer sun peeked over the horizon, but now they had the fields to themselves.

Claudette paused the cart. "What field do you want to go to, Ziva?"

Ziva took stock of the fields and sky. What would be ready now? She tried to smell, but she hadn't smelled anything in days, her nose having already given up. Still she could feel it in the air. After so many seasons, she felt the harvest in her marrow.

"The peanuts."

Claudette started the cart again. She knew these fields well, from her days working with Ziva and her nightly wanderings with Ofir. The cart bumped along the dirt road dividing the cabbage and carrot fields. A cool wind brought a waft of the spearmint, and then a gentle, loamier smell.

The peanuts came after the onions and before the lychee orchard, where she and Ziva had first worked together. Half of Claudette longed for this drive to be over already, for them to be safely back in Ziva's room; the other half wished it would go on and on, that the two of them would never have to stop driving together into the dawn.

By the time they arrived at the peanut field, the lighter blue had slinked up a third of the sky. When Claudette stopped the cart, Ziva surprised her by proceeding to climb out. She had assumed they were only going to look at the fields. She jumped out and hurried around the cart to help. Hands under Ziva's armpits, she eased her out of the passenger seat. When the mottled bare feet reached the dirt, Claudette held her up, as she did in the room, by draping Ziva's arm over her shoulders and cupping her around the waist.

Ziva pointed into the field. Again, it seemed crazy, dangerous. If anything happened to the old woman, thought Claudette, she would get in trouble, but what could happen that was worse than dying? So she guided Ziva down the path between the uprooted plants, pulled from the ground and lain on their sides so the pods could dry in the sun.

"Here. Sit." Ziva spoke so quietly, Claudette could barely make out her words.

"You want to sit down?"

Ziva nodded.

Claudette crouched as slowly and steadily as she could, her back aching as she gently lowered Ziva onto the dirt. Once the old woman was sitting on the narrow path, flanked by two rows of plants, Claudette pulled the nightdress down to cover her bruised, bony legs.

"Come back. In a bit."

It took Claudette a second to understand Ziva was asking her to go away. "You want to be alone?"

Ziva tried to clear her throat. "Going to pick a few peanuts."

"Pick?"

Claudette imagined someone driving by and seeing the old woman, alone in the field, in the middle of the night, working.

Working.

Now Claudette had trouble getting the words out. "All right. I'll be back in a little bit."

Claudette walked toward the cart, resisting the urge to keep looking back at Ziva. How did Ziva know she was dying right now, and not in a couple of hours, or tomorrow, or next week? Could she control it at this point? Was it merely a question of letting go? What if she didn't die? Was she going to be disappointed? Maybe Claudette had misunderstood; maybe Ziva couldn't plan it and only wanted a few minutes alone in the fields.

After Claudette settled into the driver's seat, she turned to wave to Ziva, but her white head was lowered. Claudette switched on the cart. She would drive around the lychee orchard and check on Ziva when the road circled back to the peanut field.

Ziva pinched a pod on the nearest plant. The shell was hard between her fingers. Ready. She was pleased that she had been right about the harvest. She plucked the pod and dropped it in her lap. How good it was to be out here again, and not in that damn bed.

Breathing had become such a chore; it was going to be easier to stop than keep at it. When she used to hold her breath in the fancy Hochstrasse Natatorium, trying to impress her mother, it took all her willpower not to come up for air. Under the pool's water, she would watch the wavering marble columns, the golden blur of the vaulted ceiling, her mother, standing on the deck, arms crossed, waiting for her to come up. How many times over the decades had she pictured her mother looking at her through the water? In a moment even that memory would be gone. Her mother and Dov would no longer exist, not even in someone's mind. Franz would live for a while longer in that boy's head.

The sun peeked over the hill of avocado trees, its yellow light beaming through the wispy clouds in thick bands. Ziva picked another peanut. Now that she knew the kibbutz would not last, if she could, would she do it all again? What if her son was right, and the kibbutz, though destined to disappear, had been a steppingstone to the Jewish state? Well, what if that too didn't survive? Sooner or later the United States would lose its power, and then who would raise a hand against Israel's destruction? Europe? What if the State of Israel ended up being just another tragic chapter in the book of the Jews? Would she do it all again?

The sun inched across the land, driving the shadows toward Mount Carmel. She plucked another peanut and added it to the collection in her lap, knowing, without a doubt, that yes, she would do it all again. The dignity lay in the effort, not the results. She had always known that. She had told people that her whole life. Why had she questioned it for even a second? Foolish.

She lowered onto her side, until she lay on the ground, cheek against the soil, eye to eye with the peanut plants. She was exhausted. As she should be.

Claudette drove along the far side of the lychee orchard, unable to see the peanut field. She paid attention to the morning air on her face, wondering if she might sense something if Ziva died, her soul rushing past. That day they worked in the cemetery, Ziva had grumbled that only when it came to death did the kibbutz have trouble keeping out religion. Claudette could see why. If Ziva had the timing right, instead of finding her friend in the peanut field, there would be a dead body, one that she would have to lift into the back of the golf cart as if it were a sack of potatoes. It didn't befit the life.

Claudette drove around the corner of the lychee orchard. Up ahead lay the peanut field, basking in the early morning light. When she reached its edge, she turned and drove alongside the field, searching for Ziva. Where was she? She stopped the cart and scanned the sea of uprooted plants. And then she spotted her, lying in the middle of the brown field, her white hair looking like dandelion snow.

Claudette climbed out of the cart. She didn't hurry. She understood Ziva was gone. She walked into the field, the wind rustling through the low-lying plants. It felt as if the ground were whispering, whispering something older than words.

She stopped. Ziva lay just ahead, so peaceful against the soil.

For we are God's fellow workers. You are God's field, God's building.

Claudette's chest rose sharply as she drew in the morning air.

God had made her fall into that deep sleep. So she could be there to help her friend. He couldn't take Ziva to the fields on His own, but neither could she.

He had sent His sign.

And she could not have asked for a better one.

*C*laudette pulled the white waffle blanket over Ziva's body, leaving her face exposed. Beyond the bedroom window, people crossed the square, headed for breakfast. As Claudette picked a leaf out of the white hair, she felt none of the indignity she had feared. She didn't even feel it when she was lifting the body into the back of the cart, and the blue nightdress caught on a metal corner, exposing a withered backside. The body was just another thing Ziva had left behind, no different than the green sofa or the clothes in her closet. She tried to pull down the wrinkled eyelids, but they kept popping back up like faulty nightshades, revealing a thin ring of hazel around yawning black pupils.

Claudette rang the Tel Aviv number Eyal had scrawled next to the phone. The hotel clerk informed her that Eyal had checked out very early, which meant he could be back on the kibbutz. She dialed his home and the office, but all she got were the answering machines. She went to look for him in the dining hall.

The hall was noisy with breakfasters: factory workers in green jumpsuits stood in the food line, women chatted by the coffee urns, children raced to their chairs. Claudette walked down the centermost aisle, scanning the long tables for Eyal. All the faces were familiar to her now. She raised her hand at Dana from the laundry house, but she didn't wave back, even though her gaze followed her.

More and more eyes seemed to fix on her, tables hushing as she passed. Was that in her head? It had to be. A layover from years of believing people should regard her with revulsion. But why get that sensation now, so powerfully? Was it from sneaking Ziva's dead body across the kibbutz? No one was staring, she told herself. *It isn't true. It isn't true.*

After a few more steps, she had to acknowledge that it was true. The dining hall had silenced, and everyone's focus was on her. Claudette stopped and turned around in confusion.

"You pervert! You sick piece of shit!"

An obese woman marched toward her, the silver roots of her long, thin hair gradating to dark brown tips.

"He's just a boy!" She stood before Claudette, lips quivering, eyes glossy. "Who cannot see. Or hear. And you . . . you come from wherever it is you come from and take advantage of him? A boy wounded in a terrorist attack!"

Claudette understood this was Ofir's mother. And she felt sorry for her. The woman had so many reasons to be angry at the world, but Claudette didn't believe she should be one of them.

"I didn't take advantage of your son. We love each other."

"*Love* each other?" The woman raised her hands as if to strangle Claudette and held them there, face turning an alarming red. "You're a thirty-something-year-old woman! He's a seventeen-year-old boy!"

The diners gawked, forks hovering over their oatmeal and eggs. Were any of them watching in terror, knowing it could be them standing where she was, being publicly shamed for something in their private lives? It didn't matter. Even if everybody were gaping at her with pure disgust, she no longer believed she was a monster.

"Yes, love."

Ofir's mother pointed at the back door, where Claudette had stood listening to Ofir playing the piano. "Go! Go pack your bags. Before I kill you!"

No one rose to object, not Dana or the ponytailed cook or the cashier from the store. With everyone's eyes on her, Claudette walked toward the door. As she pulled it open, the dining hall filled again with chatter and the clinking of utensils against plates.

Back in her room, Claudette stepped over Ulya's T-shirts to reach her bed, where she pulled out her backpack. Unzipping the bag, she worried that she wasn't going to get to say goodbye to Ofir. Could she go to his room? She had almost no possessions to pack, just some clothes and the white sundress. Before packing Tropical Sunrise, she considered the tube in her hand, thinking how strange it would be the next time she saw it, in Montreal. After zipping the bag closed, she began taking off the kibbutz work clothes.

Dressed again in the knee-length brown skirt and white button-down she wore the day she arrived on the kibbutz, she lifted Christina the Astonishing off the dresser. What should she do with the necklace? She wasn't angry with the patron saint of the mentally ill; she just didn't think she was her saint. She stowed the necklace in her skirt pocket.

"I'm coming with you."

She turned and saw Ofir in the factory worker's green jumpsuit. She had forgotten that he was starting work today. He followed her eyes and looked down at his overalls. "Exactly! I don't want to work in the fucking factory. I'm going to leave the kibbutz some day, so it might as well be now. With you."

Having only met at night, they'd never seen each other in bright daylight, at least not alone and not this close. At most they had glimpsed one another across the lawn or dining hall. The daylight brightened Ofir's gray eyes, accentuating the misshapen pupil, and highlighted the red shave bumps riddling his boyish skin. Did she appear as old in the sunshine as he did young?

"How can you come with me? I don't even know where I'm going."

"I'll go to Tel Aviv right now and get a visa to Canada."

"Do you have money for a plane ticket?"

He didn't. And Ofir knew he had no way of getting it today. He couldn't ask his mother or the kibbutz. In a year, when they divided up the kibbutz's assets, he would have some private money, enough to get by for a while in Montreal. He strode forward and grabbed Claudette's hands. "Maybe I can't go with you today, but I'll come as soon as I can. Will you wait for me?"

Claudette lowered her head, stared down at his work boots.

He squeezed her hands. "One year. I know it sounds like a long time, but will you?"

A year didn't sound like a long time to her. She could easily wait. But in a year, Ofir would be almost nineteen years old and wouldn't—shouldn't— want to move into a small apartment with a woman entering her middle years. For him, a year was a long time, long enough to fall in love with someone else. Or maybe find a passion to replace music. By the spring he could be dreaming again of great universities in London and New York. She wanted that for him.

"Please. Say you'll wait."

Claudette raised her head and met his pleading eyes. "I don't think you're going to come in a year. And I don't want to pretend that I do. We need to say a proper goodbye."

"Why? What's so crazy about me coming in a year?"

"Please, Ofir, I need you to hear me. I need you to know this time with you . . . it will stay with me for the rest of my life. I've never been happier. I may never be that happy again."

Ofir blinked back the tears. He didn't want to accept that they would never be together again. Even though he knew that she was right, had always known, on some level, that they couldn't be together for long.

He took a deep breath and nodded, reluctantly. "I don't know what would have happened to me after the bombing if you hadn't been here."

Claudette picked up the backpack, and Ofir, wiping the tears from his cheeks, took it from her. They walked outside, where the dawn had fulfilled its promise to turn into a pretty autumn day. Under the ripe red fruits of the pomegranate tree, Golda lay in the grass, licking her paws. Claudette wondered where Adam was and hoped he was all right. She took Ofir's hand, and they walked in silence up the steppingstones onto the main road.

When they reached the gate, she said, "Let's separate here."

The guard on duty, a young woman somewhere between their two ages, held up the hardcover she was reading as if to give them privacy.

Ofir leaned in and kissed Claudette for the last time. It wasn't a peck, nor a drawn-out kiss. Their lips already felt unfamiliar to one another, as if they both knew this wasn't their real last kiss, that their real last kiss had been the one they didn't know was their last.

Claudette pulled away and, taking in Ofir's young, serious face for the last time, fought a powerful urge to do something to keep him safe: kiss him three more times to make it an even number, walk to the bus stop without stepping on a crack, say "Ofir" ten times. *It isn't true, it isn't true.* She couldn't do anything about the rest of his life. She could only hope that God would watch over him.

Claudette started down the road. After a few steps, she looked back. Ofir still stood under the rusted wrought-iron sign that arched over the entrance. Fields of Splendor. He raised a hand. She did the same and continued on.

Four and half months ago, when she made her way from the bus stop to the kibbutz gate, she saw nothing. She had walked up the hill with her head down, making sure not to step on the cracks in the asphalt, going over and over why she had awoken on the plane with her thigh pressed against the man beside her. Now she noticed the horses swishing their majestic tails, heard the shouts of children in a nearby schoolyard, smelled the resinous eucalyptuses lining the side of the road. A motorcycle zipped past, sun glinting on its handlebars.

She remembered how she had panicked in the Sea of Galilee while Ofir's "You Are Here" cigarette tip glowed on the dark shore, how much she dreaded the moment passing. Now she saw God's hand more clearly. Impermanence was painful, almost unbearable, but that was how He made everything precious.

She glanced behind her once more and found Ofir still standing by the gate in his factory overalls, only she was too far away to make out his face anymore. Beside him the sun shone through the banner flapping against the chain-wire fence: A STRONG PEOPLE MAKES PEACE.

As she neared the end of the road, she spotted legs sticking out of the willow herbs. Recognizing the blue high-top sneakers, she jogged to where Adam lay on the ground, cheek pressed against the yellow grass, eyes slits in a swollen face, hand clutching the neck of a beer bottle.

She shook his shoulder. "Adam, Adam."

Adam half opened his eyes and saw Claudette's face looking down at him, her oak-brown eyes, the willow herbs blurry behind her. He was disappointed to still be able to see. He hadn't drunk enough.

He slurred, "Leave me on the tracks."

Claudette felt a swell of sadness for Adam. She feared he would never find the peace she had found this summer. She pulled the necklace from her pocket and draped it over his head.

At the bus stop, Claudette sat inside the cement shelter, surrounded by graffiti—declarations of undying love, lewd sketches, anarchy signs, peace signs, four-letter words, racist slurs, and the simple pronouncements that so-and-so was here in such-and-such a year. She looked up the hill, but she could no longer see the kibbutz gate.

New York City, 2014

*M*etal scaffolding shaded the engagement rings in the window of Weisberg's Gold and Diamonds. Inside the store, Isaac scrolled through Facebook on his iPad, though he knew he should be avoiding his newsfeed now more than ever with the war in Gaza. And yet, whenever he was about to polish the watches or revisit the Q2 spreadsheet, there he'd be again, scouring his newsfeed the way the OTB shickers would scan their inky booklets for that lucky horse. Only what did he have to win?

He paused on an Instagram of blueberry pancakes dusted with confectioner's sugar, a yellowing filter meant to give the still unconsumed pancakes the magic of nostalgia. The photo was posted by a woman he went on one date with three years ago when he was still dating, a recent divorcée, a failed actress of about forty, who cracked him up with her impersonation of her squeaky-voiced therapist. When he sent her an e-mail the following day, inviting her to see an off-Broadway play, she had said no, thank you, she didn't think they had that je ne sais quoi, and then immediately sent him a Facebook friend request. Why he had paid witness to everything this woman had eaten for the last three years was a mystery. She had stopped posting pictures of herself, and he wondered if she no longer believed she was much to look at. Above the pancakes was written: *Best. Dinner. Ever. Life is good!*

The door chimed, and Isaac shut off his iPad and jumped to his feet, but it was only the owner of the store next door.

"Oh, hi, Patni."

"You look sad to see me, Weisberg." Patni smiled, well aware no one was ever sad to see him. He had that bonhomie that made people want to be around him, even when he was driving a hard bargain, which he always did.

"I thought you were my first customer of the day."

Patni, the first Indian to open a store on the block, was now one of a handful. No doubt they were going the way of Antwerp. When Isaac took over the store after his father's "accident," as his mother and sisters called it (though what was accidental about getting pistol-whipped in the head, he didn't know), the gemstone industry was run by Jews, as it had been for a millennium. But in the twenty years since, that reign had come to an end. Seventy-five percent of the diamond traders in Antwerp's Square Mile, the diamond capital of the world, were now Indian. Cafeterias served kosher curries, and Indians sealed deals with the traditional handshake and Yiddish benediction *mazel und broche*—luck and blessing. His father wouldn't have believed it.

Patni rested his hand on the glass counter, a thick gold ring on his pinky finger.

"Our Internet is down. I was hoping we could jump on your Wi-Fi. Only for an hour or so. Just until those Verizon bastards get here."

"Of course. No problem."

Isaac jotted the password—*iwouldprefernotto*—onto a scrap of paper, one of the scraps kept on the counter for writing out calculations for the customer: the price if he knocked off fifteen percent, what would happen if they bought two, this was his final offer. He handed it to Patni.

"This is a strange password, Weisberg. But very good. Thank you."

Patni headed out, a bloom of sweat on the back of his white shirt. He paused at the door. "You are coming to my daughter's wedding?"

"Of course."

"You need to remarry, Weisberg. You are not too old. Find a young pretty thing; that will wake you up."

Thing, Isaac thought as Patni walked into the sunshine. Calling a woman a "thing" was so far from what he would have heard from his colleagues at the community college. How he missed that tatty office and the conversations they would have in it, the heated debates about Tolstoy's moralism while eating Thai delivery, though in the end he had found intellectual coercion there too. Sure, it was nowhere near as restrictive as what he'd grown up with, but there were still party lines to walk or risk being ostracized, a conformity that was surprisingly scary to buck. At least his yeshiva had never claimed to be a bastion of free thought.

He returned to Facebook. Someone he hadn't seen in thirty years wanted to play FarmVille. *ISIS takes over Christian village in Iraq. This cute dog has a chicken for a best friend.* His father never sat around reading a newspaper. He couldn't; someone was constantly coming through the door. Who would have thought people would ever buy engagement rings on the Internet? Everything happened out of sight now, the trading, the cutting. Instead of old Jews he'd known his whole life cutting the gems right here on the block, demanding up to $300 a carat for their artistry, now most stones were cut for five bucks a carat in Gujarat. Patni had offered to find him a good factory there, but Isaac couldn't do it. How could he trust rubies and diamonds to people he'd never met on the other side of the world? *In this business, it's trust, trust, trust*: that was his father's mantra. *No deals with anyone you don't know and can't trust.* Ironic, considering how well he knew that junkie. "A drug addict you could smell a mile away," was how his mother described him.

His pocket buzzed. He pulled out the phone and saw a blue text bubble from his daughter Sam: *R u coming this wknd.*

Yes, he typed, worried that she secretly hoped he wasn't coming. She was twelve, budding breasts, teeth no longer too big for her face, maybe she didn't want her old man taking up her free time. What could he add that was playful? *Prepare for some fun.*

Wow, that was lame. He watched the ellipsis, the promise that she was writing back.

Ok but I'm going to the mall and a bday party on Sat.

So he'd been right. She wasn't looking forward to seeing him. Now what? Should he take a three-hour train out to western New Jersey and sleep in a hotel all for a breakfast on Sunday at the Country Griddle? His older daughter, Clara, now in college, must have withdrawn at this age, but he never noticed, probably because he still lived with them and was too busy fighting with their mother. And because he still had baby Sam, who seemed so far away from growing up.

All right, but Dave Sunday . . . Oh, *farkakte* spell-check! He hurried to erase *Dave.* Now his response was taking too long, making his words seem less casual and cool with it all. *All right, but save Sunday for me, ok?* Seeing how that could sound a little angry, he tacked on a smiley face.

When no ellipsis appeared, he looked from the iPhone to the shop, where he had been forced at Sam's age to spend the little free time he had between studying and more studying helping his father. The shop looked much the same then, only instead of a mirror covering the opposite wall, there had been fake wood paneling. His sisters never had to help out, never had to learn the ropes; the store obviously wasn't going to them one day. While he would arrange the rings in the window display, on the other side of the glass, boys no older than him would walk by in bell-bottoms and trucker hats, chewing gum and laughing, heading off to who knew what adventure. Maybe the Ziegfeld. That became his dream, to visit the palatial cinema only a few blocks away. He could still picture all the movie posters from those days pasted on the subway station walls: *Mean Streets*, *The Exorcist*, *American Graffiti*. It would be years before he dared to sneak into a movie, but he soon started checking out books from the library and hiding them behind his bedroom dresser. After that first book—*Lord of the Flies*, recommended by an amused librarian—he knew he could never live without *trayf* books again.

"Binghamton? What is this Binghamton?" his father said when he finally told him he was leaving it all. He was sitting at the kitchen table with his evening snack, always one poppy-seed rugelach and a cup of decaf. He had to have been fifty-three years old at the time, exactly the age Isaac was today, the short *payess* tucked behind his ears more salt than pepper.

"It's a college upstate, Papa. Not far from the city."

"What do you want to go upstate for?"

"To study . . . literature."

"Literature? What are you talking about? If you want to go to college, all right, go. Take some business classes at Yeshiva, like the Habermans' boy, so when you take over the business you can run it even better than me."

"I'm not going to take over the business, Papa."

"What?"

"You heard me. I'm not taking over the business."

His father fell silent, stared at him in shock. Perhaps he had done too good a job hiding the books and movie tickets. How had his father not seen this coming? When he did speak again, his father wasn't angry, not yet—the shouting until his voice was hoarse would come over the following days. For now there was only confusion.

"Our family, Yitzchak, we've had this business since 1656. In five different countries, we've had this business. It has seen us through . . . everything. Without it, I wouldn't exist. You wouldn't exist. If you don't take over the business, a family tradition hundreds of years old comes to an end."

And he said: "I don't care."

Isaac had no regrets about leaving, but was the "I don't care" necessary? Though if he really put himself back in that kitchen, really remembered being eighteen years old, his anger was understandable, given that's precisely what his father had to say about his dreams: "I don't care." Though now he understood it wasn't that his father didn't care, exactly; he just believed he knew better what would make his son happy, keep him safe. Isaac checked to see if Sam had written back. She hadn't. He returned to Facebook.

Hubbie just brought me coffee in bed. Feeling blessed.

When his father called to tell him about the brooch, he had been a free man for fourteen years. He was alone in that office at LaGuardia Community College, working late on a paper about social class in Fielding's early poems and plays. He answered the phone hoping it was his wife. They were happy then, married only two years. If he'd known it was his father, he probably wouldn't have picked up.

"Yitzi, it's the most incredible thing I've ever held in my hand. Like holding history. Our history."

As his father waxed on about this brooch, Isaac stared out the window at western Queens, a bleak, wintery scene as different from a leafy green college campus as possible. Students walked along a cement overpass, traversing a vast rail yard. Above the sea of tracks was a tangle of black telephone and electrical wires. In the distance the gray buildings of Manhattan looked like a jumble of giant gravestones. After his father described every detail of the brooch three times, he said, "Will you come and see it, Yitzi?"

"Uh, sure. When?"

"Why not this Thursday? You can come for dinner, and I'll bring it home from the shop."

"Hmm. This Thursday? . . . I don't think so, Papa."

He had to get this paper written and accepted before the end of the school year. The clock was ticking. His wife, herself a lowly adjunct in art history, was pregnant, putting the pressure on him to find a better teaching gig, one with a livable wage, health insurance, some security. That was the excuse; truthfully he had little hope of securing a tenure-track position, even if he got this paper out. The fact was he had been avoiding his family for years: at first, when he was in his early twenties, he was unable to pull himself away from his newfound freedoms for even an evening; later, when he was older, he just didn't like being around them, their boring conversations, their ignorance. Their world was too small. Too depressing.

"I can't even entice you to visit me with a seven-hundred-year-old treasure?"

Give me a break, thought Isaac, it's just a fucking brooch. Once again, his father couldn't step out of his own interests.

"Sorry, Papa. I'll come as soon as I send out this paper I'm working on, okay? It's really important."

"Really important," his father muttered.

And that was the last time he heard his voice. Two weeks later, while Isaac was working on the Fielding paper that would only be rejected by every journal anyway, that drug addict came into the store to get his grandmother's brooch back. At first it looked like Papa was going to pull through. Though the skull had a dent, the doctor explained, pointing at a CT scan, the pressure on his brain was minimal. "We'll get a titanium plate in there, and chances are he'll make a full recovery." But late that night, before the old man ever woke up, he had a brain hemorrhage and died.

While they were still in the hospital, his mother asked, "So, will you take over the business now?"

ISRAEL IS COMMITTING GENOCIDE!!!

Another article posted by Sandra, one of the adjuncts from LaGuardia, now a tenured professor somewhere in the Midwest. Every few weeks she sent around another petition to boycott Israeli academics. It was hard to understand her obsession with Israel, given how little she cared about anything else going on in the Middle East. She had never once mentioned the plight of women in Islamic countries, and she was a feminist literary critic. As usual, he opened the article and went straight to the comments.

Isra'ILL' - disgusting parasites . . . since forever #adolph_hitler

zion is zion, since moses their trade is blood of innocent children but i give you happy message muslims are coming to wipe this cancer from middle east

Wake up, America! Your gov, newspapers, schools, businesses, all controlled by Jews.

Who was leaving these comments? Were they psycho outliers, or did they represent how most of the world felt about Jews? He didn't know. He really wished he knew. When his father used to claim the Jews would always be targets, that was just the way it was and would always be, he thought the old man was being paranoid, that Jews in general were a paranoid bunch, understandably so, but he believed they could calm down now. Only this summer, for the first time, his certainty had been shaken. Yes, the thousands chanting "Gas to the Jews!" in Berlin were Muslim immigrants this time, not white Europeans, but what difference did that make?

After reading the infuriating article, he went back to Sandra's Facebook page and put his cursor in the comment box. All their old colleagues were going to see this, and other professors too, people of influence; he should try to shape the conversation, right? But he couldn't think of a single thing to say without hearing their dismissals: not the Holocaust card again, you're trying to silence people by equating anti-Israel with anti-Semitism, you're an Islamophobe, a warmongering racist right-wing nut job, a Zionist, as if that in itself were a bad thing. He typed in anger, *If the Israelis wanted to commit genocide they could be done in an hour.* And then erased it. The cursor blinked.

Without writing anything, he moved on, scrolled down the newsfeed—*Long Island Grandmother Does What?* His heart beat madly, as if he'd been running from an assailant, not sitting with an iPad and some faceless comments. You're not a coward, he assured himself. He didn't write anything because he didn't want to be forced into a public, time-consuming debate, and an accusation of genocide shouldn't be dignified with a rebuttal anyway—and maybe that was all true, but he still hated himself. And Sandra. And the commenters. And the rioting Muslims in Europe. He was afraid he was starting to hate humanity. And it was lonely. He scrolled, barely seeing what was passing under his eyes.

Until the brooch.

Looking at the photo, he could hear his father describing it over the phone, a conversation he had played over in his mind countless times.

It was attached to a *New York Times* article: "Black Death Treasure at the Cloisters." He pounced on the link, like if he didn't tap on it fast enough it might disappear.

Up came an enlarged picture, and it was definitely his father's brooch. It was all there, the details he had described three times, which his mother had later relayed to the police—the large sapphire in the center, the stylized pomegranates, the florets, the pins through the pearls. He read the article.

....

BLACK DEATH TREASURE AT THE CLOISTERS

Today "Gems of the Plague" opens at the Cloisters, the Metropolitan Museum of Art's medieval branch in Fort Tryon Park. The exhibition, which originated at the Musée National du Moyen Âge in Paris, showcases a 700-year-old hoard discovered in 2004 during the construction of a large apartment complex in Terfur, Germany.

Before construction on the apartments began, archeological excavations of the area were conducted, since it was known to have been the site of a Jewish quarter that was razed in a pogrom in 1347. The pogrom was one of a wave that swept through the Holy Roman Empire in response to the Black Death, which was regularly blamed on the Jews. Although records show that the plague would not reach Terfur for another year, it was not uncommon for Jews to be massacred in an attempt to stave off the epidemic.

During the excavations, the sole finding was the stone foundation of a synagogue, dating to the first half of the twelfth century. It was only after the excavations were complete and the apartment developers were digging the underground parking garage two feet deeper than initially planned that the treasure was found. If the original blueprint for the building had been followed, the treasure might have remained underground forever.

Though the digging equipment did damage some of the artifacts, it is still an impressive collection. Not only do the intimate, well-crafted objects give insight into medieval life, they bear a terrible pathos. The Jews likely hid these objects, their most valued possessions, with the intention of returning for them, but in one night the entire Jewish population of Terfur, approximately 1,500, was slaughtered and burned by the town's residents. The *Judengasse* became a feeding ground for livestock and years later was overbuilt with row houses.

The treasure includes belt buckles, cloak buttons, drinking vessels, a silver hairbrush, a cosmetic set, a magnificent brooch (seen right), and one of only two surviving examples of a medieval Jewish wedding ring.

Share on: Facebook
Twitter Google+
Pin Tumblr
LinkedIn Reddit
Permalink Email

How could that brooch have been a part of this treasure trove? He had to go to the museum straight away. Unfortunately a jewelry store took time to close. Moving as fast as he could, Isaac pulled the rings and bracelets and watches from the display counters and carried them down the stairs to the vaults under the back office. Then he did the same for the wall displays and the window. His whole body buzzed with impatience as he activated the alarms, checked the cameras, and locked the register. At last, he was rolling down the store's steel grate.

Patni was outside, having a smoke. "Cutting out early, Weisberg? Is everything okay?"

"Yes. There's something . . . someone I have to meet. I'll see you tomorrow."

"Oh." Patni gave a mischievous smile. "Very well, then."

To avoid having to take two trains, Isaac walked at a clip for Eighth Avenue, where he could ride the A train all the way up to 190th. Twenty years ago his father had asked him to come see this brooch, and now, at last, he was on his way. Summer tourists clogged the sidewalks. He weaved through people snapping photos of Radio City Music Hall and pausing in front of store windows. As he crossed the pedestrian plaza in Times Square, skirting the tables where hungry sightseers ate pizza slices and ice cream, he glimpsed the new World Trade Center rising in the gap of sky at the far end of Seventh Avenue, the cranes finally removed from the top. Thirteen years. Hard to believe. Sam was three months from being born. As he was about to descend the stairs into the subway, an unshaven, middle-aged man in a sandwich board—MANI/PEDI $40— shoved a flyer at him, and Isaac thought: Could this drunkard be him?

Every day, he looked at someone and wondered if this could be the low-life who killed Papa.

He paced back and forth on the sweltering platform, sweat trickling down his face. When his father used to grumble about the heat down here, he would want to answer back, well, why the hell are we wearing long black coats in the middle of July? His father disliked so much about the trains: the black goo oozing down the station walls, the smell of urine, the indignity of being crowded against strange women. And yet, he had lived his whole life without ever getting a driver's license and almost never allowing himself a cab. The ambulance ride from the store to Mount Sinai was one of the few times he didn't take the subway.

The woman next to him on the train was playing Candy Crush with the sound on. The boy on his other side listened to hip-hop, a tinny bass escaping his giant headphones. Normally he too would have been looking down at his phone or listening to an NPR podcast, but for once he had no desire. For once he felt present, not happy necessarily, but here in the moment. At the museum he hoped there would be a way to know for sure that this was his father's brooch. The picture fit his description exactly, but he would like to have no doubt about it. The truth was it couldn't have been in the hoard and be his father's brooch.

After a long half hour, he emerged from the subway. He walked through Fort Tryon Park toward the hill-perched Cloisters, its rufous tower and terracotta roof peeking over the trees. On the other side of the Hudson River were the bosky banks of the New Jersey Palisades, barely a building in sight. A bird cawed over the drone of the West Side Highway, but he couldn't see the highway or anything that let on he was still in Manhattan and not in Europe. As he climbed the cobblestone drive to the medieval building, a conglomeration of five abbeys dismantled stone by stone and shipped across the Atlantic, he had a strong memory of being young and walking up some cobblestones to yet another old cathedral or museum on his backpacking trip through Europe. It was the summer after college, and he had had a wonderful time, sightseeing during the day and getting drunk on cheap beers at night in the hostels. He had cherished the freedom more than the other backpackers because of how far it was from the life he was meant to have at twenty-three years old—married, the father of at least two children, five years into a lifetime sentence at the jewelry store—and yet, for all the fun, an eerie feeling hung over that journey across Europe, the feeling of walking through a beautiful, sunlit cemetery.

He waited inside the rib-vaulted stone foyer for the woman behind the ticket counter to finish straightening out the brochures. She had gestured at him to hold on a moment, and instead of feeling impatient, he found he was glad to wait. Now that he was here, he didn't want this experience to pass too quickly. Out of the gift shop floated Gregorian chants, as if a choir of forty men sang among the souvenir spoons and art books. The choral music filled the airy hall, giving it both a sincere and Disneyish quality. As Isaac paid for his ticket, his phone buzzed. A text message from his father's longtime partner in Antwerp: *Poddar will start buying tomorrow. Get long positions in place.*

Isaac followed the map in the brochure through an ogival doorway and down a long ambulatory lined with iron-latticed windows. At the end of the hall stood an enormous wooden crucifix. He was relieved to be here on a Wednesday morning and not a Saturday. Only a few tourists milled about. He descended a circular stone stairwell and emerged in a chapel where towering stained-glass windows blued the air. He asked a guard wedged between two sarcophagi to point him toward the treasury, and was sent down a hall of Virgin Marys. He passed stone Marys, wooden Marys, painted Marys, all holding their son, either the manlike baby with the two raised fingers or the dead adult son splayed across their knees.

The phone buzzed again.

Reply with "YES" to confirm your appt. at 2:15PM on 09/27/14 (Mon). Thanks! Your friends at Midtown Optical.

He held down the power button, watched the phone shut down.

Next to the treasury's glass and brass doors a sign read, GEMS OF THE PLAGUE. NO PHOTOS PLEASE. He pulled open the door and stepped inside. Unlike the rest of the Cloisters, this room resembled a typical museum: low ceiling, humble drywall, the relics displayed in simple wood showcases. He walked along one wall, searching the displays for the brooch, the anticipation shortening his breath. His eyes passed over a gold wedding ring, a porcelain hair barrette, a handheld vanity mirror with a cracked glass.

When he arrived at the end of the wall display, he looked up, and there it was, just a few feet away, propped in its own freestanding case, gleaming under four small spotlights.

He walked toward it. Slowly. When he reached the case, he avoided looking at the brooch and read the placard.

Brooch

Gold, sapphire, rubies, imitation ruby, amethysts, garnets, pearls

•

GERMANY (MIDDLE RHINE) 1300–47
ON LOAN FROM THE ISRAEL MUSEUM, JERUSALEM, ISRAEL

•

This superb and well-preserved example of fourteenth-century jewelry was not found in the Terfur hoard, but it bears the same inscription to "my Anna" as two of the jewels in the treasure and displays a similar artistry to several of the relics, suggesting they were made by the same goldsmith. As with a number of the pieces, one of the recurring details is nonuniform, which may have been the goldsmith's trademark. In this case a floret in the bottom left-hand quadrant is short one petal.

Isaac reread the first sentence two more times—"was not found in the Terfur hoard."

The brooch seemed to glow, a mystical glow, but, of course, Isaac thought, that was only because of his personal history with it. Knowing his father, he could see why he loved it so much. The outdated goldwork, thin gold belts across the uncut gems. The exquisite, handmade filigree. The tiny pomegranates, that allusion to the Promised Land.

If only it weren't behind glass, he could hold it in his hand, the thing his father last held, the thing Isaac might have held in a much younger hand had he gone over that Thursday night. Now it was right there, only several inches away. Imagine if he punched through the glass. His hand throbbing, bloodied. He would only get to hold the brooch for a matter of seconds before the police descended on him, carried him away. But it would be so satisfying. He would feel so alive.

He reached out and laid his fingertips on the glass.

"Sir, you can't touch the displays." A security guard waved him back. "You have to stand behind that line, sir."

Isaac stepped back. If he wasn't going to punch through the glass, he wasn't sure what more there was to do. He had seen it now. He could go. But he didn't want to, because as soon as he turned to leave, it would be over, this story between him and his father. He stared at the brooch, feeling as if he too were in a box, the air growing stale, every day a little less satisfying to breathe. He knew his father had wanted the brooch in a museum, but he had never seen it here, plucked out of the chaos of life.

It had been decades since Isaac believed in the power of prayers and wishes, but he made a wish anyway. He wished that one day the brooch—whether it was in a hundred years or four hundred years or a thousand—would find itself outside a museum case again, set free by an earthquake perhaps, or a looting, or a mismanaged shipment between exhibitions. He wished it for the brooch's sake and for his and his father's, because then a part of them would be out there again in the world.